OMNIHUMANS: WITHIN A CONCRETE LABYRINTH

Tom Leveen

ISBN: 978-1-7347777-0-3 (Hardcover)

Library of Congress Control Number: 2020905225

Any references to historical events, real people, or real places are used fictitiously. Names, characters, and places are products of the author's imagination.

Front cover image by Book Cover Zone
Author photo by Yvonne Wan

First printing edition 2020.

FTJ Creative LLC

OMNIHUMANS: WITHIN A CONCRETE LABYRINTH

Tom Leveen

FTJ Creative LLC

Vigilance.

Diligence.

Humanity.

Motto taken from the
National Normative Policy Division Officer Handbook,
Third Edition, Washington D.C.,
Office of the President

ONE

Manic grinned at his wagon mates in the warm confines of the forest-green six-wheeled APC. One of the men, Chandler Krakowski, was a new kid, fresh from NPD selection. He met Manic's eyes unswervingly through the clear blast-shield on his helmet.

"You ready?" Manic said through his smile. At work, his smiles were always genuine, if not necessarily mirthful.

"Yes, Sergeant!" Krakowski said.

"'Cause you look a little nervous. He look nervous to you, J.T.?"

Manic's best friend, Jamal Theodore Jackson, a giant of a man twice even Manic's bulky size, nodded sagely. He wriggled his broad shoulders under his body army and cleared his throat. "He does, bro. Big time."

The other officers in the wagon laughed the easy laugh of veterans.

"Don't mind Sgt. Cruce," said Chief Miller, boss of the wagon and elder statesman of the team at age 40. He kicked Manic's shin guard. "He likes to eat 'em young."

All the sixcops laughed, including Manic. Beneath the red operating lights inside the vehicle, Krakowski appeared to relax a bit.

The light spasmed to green as the wagon jerked to a halt. The men reacted automatically, jumping out as the tailgate fell to the ground with a clang. Above them, secure in her revolving turret, Sgt. Jane Bennett opened up with the .50 cal, placing five precise laser-sighted shots that rattled Manic's helmet, comforting and invigorating.

The officers fell into formation against the heavily armored wagon for cover.

"Yep, deev at high noon," said Dumb Tony—Officer Anthony DeAngelo—over the officers' headsets from his position behind the wheel. "Come on in, boys."

The officers left the safety of the APC, weapons held tight to their bodies. Dumb Tony clicked on the PA system and ran through the standard announcement: "Threat, threat, threat. Attention citizens. This is the National Normative Policy Division. Please evacuate immediately. Threat, threat, threat. Evacuate immediately. Threat, threat, threat."

Almost since its inception, the agency had earned the incorrect abbreviation "NPD." Some joked that it stood for Normative Police Department. The joke was not a stretch, although Manic and his cadre were not sworn law enforcement officers.

Not for normal people, anyway. Not for real humans.

Civilians were already on the move. Per usual, the announcement functioned as an afterthought—no norms stuck around when an NPD wagon rolled up, green beacons flashing bright in the Los Angeles night.

Even amidst the panicked populace sprinting away from the NPD vehicle, there was no mistaking the Level Six deviant running away from them in the city park. The thing, apparently male, stood well over three meters tall. Manic guessed it was a psychotic to risk coming out of whatever cesspool it called home. The Level Six boasted a third, muscular arm jutting from the center of his torso. A third, limp leg dangled from his hip, giving his attempted run a gangly gait. The "six" wore no shirt, revealing lean muscles. Its jeans had an oval cut out of them to make room for its extra appendage.

The six seemed to be screaming something, but Manic didn't care what. He would have spit if not for his face shield. Damn things disgusted him endlessly. Five years on the job and still they made his soul queasy, no matter what perverse shape they came in. But at least this deev could be readily identified. The ones who couldn't, the ones who blended in . . . they were the real threat.

"On it!" Manic said gleefully into his mic, plucking a cylindrical grenade from his tactical vest. He threw the canister expertly toward the six while his buddies took up flanking positions and moved in, ready to unload a variety of incendiary and armor-piercing rounds into the six if the grenade failed to do the job.

Among his many martial talents, Manic had a hell of an arm, and the entanglement grenade landed perfectly, just beneath the fleeing monstrosity. It exploded instantly, sending electric, crimson tendrils up and around the extra-limbed deviant like a cocoon, wrapping him tightly and bringing the deev to the ground. Often called net bombs by civilians, the small canisters were designed to burst and fling a double-dozen sticky, stretchy strands of fibrous material based on the molecular structure of spiderweb onto a target. A neat little toy, one that hadn't yet failed to give NPD cops at least a second or two of time to further restrain a deev.

"Quarterback goes deep and nabs a score," Dumb Tony joked from the wagon cockpit.

The other officers slowed their approach, keeping their weapons trained on the twitching deviant. Manic got there first, as he usually did, the only one on the team not actively slinging his weapon.

"All right, Crackhead," he called to Krakowski after ascertaining the deev was contained. "Welcome to the team. Tag him and load him up."

Krakowski's eyes widened briefly. "By myself?"

"What's the matter?" asked J.T., putting a calloused palm on Krakowski's shoulder. "Didn't you do any deadlifts during selection?"

"I know I did," Manic said theatrically. "Lots of 'em. Like, *dozens.*"

"Squats, too," J.T. agreed. "You gotta lift with your legs, you know. Some of those sixes get pretty big."

Everyone but Krakowski laughed and moved back toward the wagon, leaving the junior member to figure out if his new teammates were joking or not. Manic cast a glance behind him as he walked with his team, and caught the multi-limbed man in the net glaring hatefully from between two of the net's tendrils.

"Ew doan unnerstan!" the six said, his mouth muffled by the netting. "Mmm naw uh siss!"

"The hell you looking at?" Manic snarled, and raced back to give the detained six a kick in the flank.

"Manic, whoa, hey," J.T. called easily. "C'mon, you're scaring the locals."

The normal humans who had run scared from the six drifted back toward the scene now that NPD had things well in hand. It happened like that every time. Not a brave nor daring soul among them until the deev was packed up nice and tight in NPD netting. Or dead. Manic didn't blame them; they were the reason why NPD existed, just like they were the reason local cops existed or any other federal agency existed. Most men and women were sheep, and needed sheepdogs to keep them safe. He treasured and savored that reality.

"Did you get him?" J.T. said to Sgt. Bennett.

Bennett leaned back in the turret, keeping the barrel in the direction of the deev but tilted up, providing cover for Krakowski as he struggled with the six's weight. "Damn skippy," she said. "Bounced five rounds right off his ass. Didn't make a dent."

"Man," J.T. said as the men gathered around the wagon to watch Krakowski curse and drop the six. "Is it just me or are they getting tougher?"

"Fifty cal to the butt cheek," Manic said, not quite with respect. "That ain't nothing."

J.T. coughed, hacked, and spit into the grass as the other team members muttered their agreement. "What if they're all evolving, man, you ever think about that?"

"Nope," Manic said. "I gotta be able to sleep, bro."

J.T. laughed, which triggered another cough. Manic started to ask what he was coming down with, but two norms cut him off.

"What was all that about?" said a young man, who wore a logo T-shirt that made Manic ball his hands into fists: a black numeral six with a red line and circle over it. A protest symbol sweeping the country. What would have otherwise been an insignia meaning "No More Six," the nation understood to mean "No More Classifying People As Sixes." The logo essentially demanded Manic no longer have his job. Classifying, apprehending, and icing sixes like the one just a few yards away was his day-to-day routine.

A young woman sporting white-girl dreds and a face full of righteous indignation stood beside the young man. They were both Manic's daughter's age. Hell, maybe they even went to her university. It wouldn't have surprised Manic in the least; they were in the neighborhood.

Manic raised his hands. "Hey, easy there, pal. You're safe now."

"That's not what I asked, officer. Why did you open fire on that man?"

"Here we go," J.T. muttered as the rest of the team turned their attention to Manic. They knew where this was headed.

"Okay, sir?" Manic said with faux patience honed during his years with LAPD. "I'm gonna need you to just step back."

"I will not step back, officer. I want to know why that man was fired upon."

Manic pointed his index finger, weapon-like, at the young man's chest. One of his sixcop buddies sucked in a soft breath between his teeth, probably calculating the kid's odds of going home with his lips intact.

"Number one, he ain't no man," Manic said with a savage smile that made the hippie girl take a half-step back. "And B, you were just given an order by a federal officer, you might want to obey it before things go badly for you."

The kid crossed his arms, lifting his chin. "He was looking for help. I heard him."

"Is that right," J.T. said, as Manic's smile twitched. "Now what kind of help might that be?"

At this, the kid's face clouded a bit. "I'm not sure. But when people saw him and called you guys, he just started screaming. Kept saying he was a four."

"Oh yeah?" Manic said. "Lotta fours running around with six freakin' limbs, meatpole?"

"Possibly! Physical birth defects do still happen sometimes, officer!"

"All right, you little—!"

Chief Miller stepped into the fray. "Sgt. Cruce, stand down. That's an order. Young man, it's time for you to clear out."

"Aren't you going to write any of this down?" the kid asked, looking at Miller.

"I know I got a good memory," Manic said, well past the point of knowing what was good for him. "How about you, Chief? You got a good memory?"

"Manic . . ." Miller warned.

"It's just, he wouldn't stop screaming," the kid said. "Instead of running, he kept screaming. 'I'm a Four, I'm a Four,' over and over. He said, 'It's not my fault.'"

"Uh-huh," Manic said, with as much boredom as he could fake. "Well, why don't you put all of that into an e-mail to me, and be sure to CC *I Don't Give A Shit*. A six will say anything when he knows a deev wagon's on the way."

"Don't call them that," the girl said, piping up for the first time. Manic traded glances with his teammates, who then stared impassively at the witnesses, the stony glare of warfighters that made lesser folks crumble.

"We're done here," Manic said. "Thanks for the info."

He and his team turned to go, but the kid wasn't finished.

"Hey!" he barked. "They're people, you know!"

Manic froze.

"Manic—" Chief Miller said, *again*, but by then it was too late.

The big sixcop spun and grabbed the kid by the front of his shirt, slamming him into the side of the armored vehicle. The team jumped to pull him off . . . but not very quickly. The girl whined at Manic to let him go, her words flailing uselessly in the warm air.

"Listen, meatpole," Manic snarled into the kid's shocked face. "That three-armed motherfucker took five rounds of fifty-caliber rifle shot and they bounced off his hide like a racquetball. That sound about right, Sergeant?"

"That's affirmative," Bennett called lazily from the turret. She'd kept her gaze trained on Krakowski and his struggles with the netted six.

"So when he decides to come after you and your little girlfriend there, who's gonna bail you out, huh?" Manic went on, nose-to-nose with the young man. "You think about that."

Several hands were on his shoulders and arms now, not restraining so much as cautioning. NPD got away with a lot while on a call, but even a doomed lawsuit wouldn't reflect well on Miller's squad.

"Drop it, Manic," J.T. said amiably. "Come on, you don't want the paperwork."

Manic gave the kid a none-too-gentle shove into the steel plate of the wagon before letting go and stepping back. His teammates welcomed him in, keeping hands on his armor in case he decided to jump again.

"Just remember that!" Manic snapped at the kid. He turned on one Lalo boot and let his comrades lead him away, pretending to say to them, "Ungrateful Level Three tango." He made sure the words landed on the kid behind him, who now—wisely—decided to keep his own counsel, and who likely had no idea that *tango* stood for *target* in NPD parlance.

Once the kid and the girl had been escorted away from the wagon, Manic's team burst into laughter. Manic, still genuinely outraged at the kid's attitude, took an extra minute before he could join in. When they heard Krakowski—now and forever known as Crackhead thanks to Manic—hit his knee on the deev wagon's tailgate while he struggled to load the six inside, it brought out another round of laughter from the vets.

Manic sucked it all in, loving his place in the world. He went on laughing long after the others had stopped, because he knew it wouldn't last forever.

Hell. It wouldn't last the night. He still had an appointment to keep.

TWO

It took Malikai all night to find his first victim. That was unusual. Typically he found them within minutes of starting his patrol.

Summer nights in Phoenix reminded him of the recently dead: it seemed as if there was still life in them somewhere. Night after night, Malikai could feel the city wanting to revive and breathe again. But dead was dead. No one came back from it.

Most of the time. He was an exception—a word that suited him in more ways than one.

He realized the assailant he raced toward on silent feet was not male as he'd expected. From her hunched posture at the end of an alley, hidden in three-quarter darkness, driving punch after punch into a helpless boy at her feet, the assailant had all the hallmarks of a flesh-peddling pimp, extracting money or loyalty out of a prostitute. The vast majority of such peddlers were men, Malikai had learned over the past year. But as he got within striking distance, he heard that the peddler's caustic curses had a feminine pitch, and her chest belonged to no man. She wore tight-fitting clothes twenty years too young for her body, with shoulder-length dark hair in need of shears and pride.

Malikai rammed the peddler with his shoulder, sending her flying into the opposite cinder block wall, her body crashing against decades' worth of gang graffiti. She recovered quickly, spinning and dropping into a low, combat-ready crouch, teeth bared, fingers splayed as if they were switchblades.

"Enough," Malikai stated, standing straight, his body turned at an angle to present a more slender target.

"Mind your business," the peddler growled. "This ain't your prob'."

Malikai glanced at the boy still lumped on the ground. He seemed to sense Malikai's gaze, and looked up. No more than sixteen, yet older than that by far in body and soul. The boy used the back of one hand to wipe blood from his lips. Their eyes met, and Malikai saw his expression change from one of defiance to one of terror. Malikai's crimson sclera and mercury-colored irises told the boy all he wanted to know.

This savior with the red and silver eyes was a six. A Level Six Normative Deviation, to use the legal term. A mutant, a freak, an aberration. Or simply a "deev," the kind of slang never heard on television. There were other terms, none of them gentle. The list grew each day and each new insult served but one purpose: to dehumanize the deviants just a little bit more than the day before. Many politicians had been elected to office on anti-deviant platforms in the last election cycle. One state senator very nearly campaigned with the slogan "Kick A Six," only to pull it at the last minute, and let his social media trolls do the dirty work for him. He was elected in a landslide.

Polite company referred to Malikai's kind as omnihumans. Malikai rarely found polite company in the spiritual wasteland of Phoenix after dark.

Malikai knew from experience the boy was more afraid of him than of his assailant. Nevertheless, the vigilante faced the flesh-peddler.

"How much does the boy owe you."

"Sixty bucks!" The peddler wiggled her fingers like an Old West gunslinger about to draw. Malikai perceived no weapons on the woman; certainly she was ready to fight and didn't fear his inhuman features the way the teenager did. Perhaps the peddler was more than she appeared? Malikai reminded himself to use caution. There was no such thing as a routine rescue, not in this forsaken city.

He moved his hands deliberately so the peddler could see him do it. His right hand arched backward to grip the hilt of a Tang dao sword slung over his shoulder, while his left hand swayed to the hip pocket of his simple gray cotton pants.

The peddler watched each movement, awaiting his attack or plotting her own. The boy, still languishing on the piss-soaked alley dirt between them, made no movement other than to spit blood and raise himself up on one arm.

Malikai pulled a wad of cash from his pocket. The bills were folded once, allowing him to easily count them with his thumb. He didn't take his eyes off the peddler, whose gaze darted between the hilt of his sword and the money.

"There's double." Malikai let six twenties flutter to the ground and shoved the remainder back into his pocket. "He walks home now."

The peddler laughed, a grinding, cynical sound that made Malikai's lip curl.

"I have a better idea," she said, and struck.

Malikai slid backward, drawing the sword as he moved. Something thin and serpentine whipped past his face like electric eels. He heard and disregarded the sudden scream from the teen—it was a cry of shock, not pain. He was no less safe now than he had been a moment ago. The peddler was focused on Malikai.

Although the woman stood ten feet away, arms raised toward him, her fingers stretched from her palms the entire distance, wriggling and snapping like bullwhips, seeking his limbs. Having dodged her first attack, Malikai watched as her fingers whisked back to their normal proportions, sucking into her hands like an unlocked tape measure.

"Give it to me!" she shouted. "Kick in that cash before I kick in your face!"

Malikai pointed the tip of the sword at her eye level and took a defensive stance. He spoke plainly. "No. He goes home. You go home. Take what I've given you."

With a screech, the deviant woman let loose the long fingers again. She swept her hands toward one another as if in the start of a clap. The impossibly long fingers of her left hand sailed toward Malikai's head, while the right-hand fingers sought out his feet. Duck or jump—either way, she'd grab him.

He bounded forward. She was, in essence, using a distance weapon, no different than a pole-arm or flail, so the best way to neutralize it was to move in close. He did not know *how* he knew such a thing, only that his body responded instinctively, as it did every night he patrolled this crumbling, scorching city.

Malikai covered the distance between them in one burst of speed that ended with the sword tip an inch from the woman's left eye.

"End this," he said.

She smiled at him with teeth the color of pus as the eight extended digits of both her hands swirled around his body and the sword, pinning his arms to his torso. The blade pointed straight up and pressed against his chest.

The flesh peddler cackled, her breath fouling the air. "Whaddya think now, you smart-ass son of a baaaaaaargh!"

Malikai's dao glowed white-hot and readily split through the woman's fingers like an arc welder pressed against butter. Elongated segments of her mutant fingers fell to the ground and lay still. The woman howled and lurched backward away from Malikai, who countered her movement forward.

"You son of a bitch!" she cried, stuffing the stumps of her fingers under her armpits. Blood seeped down her shirt.

She backed into a wall and Malikai sprang, holding the blade crosswise to her throat. The sword warmed again under his direction—neither spoken nor thought, but merely willed—lighting his face with dire shadows. He leaned closer to the deviant he now had pinned against the alley wall. On the other side of that wall, he knew, a strip club did moderate business for a Monday night; lonely men with money to burn watched lonely women dance naked and coo at them. Malikai didn't care about the sins of the dancers or their patrons, though. They were acting of their own free will. Forcing a teenager into selling his body, that was another crime entirely.

The peddler's expression changed as the blade heated enough to singe the tips of her hair. Clearly she hadn't expected to end her night at the mercy of another Level Six deviant wielding what appeared to be a fire-hot sword.

"H-h-hey," the peddler gasped. "We're all on the same side, asshole. You're a deev, right? How you doin' that shit with the sword, huh? You magic?"

Something inside Malikai winced at the word. *Magic* . . . it was spoken in hushed tones by normal human beings, he'd discovered, as if speaking it aloud would bring about some type of curse. He knew nothing of magic; whether it existed or not, whether his sword or his own self possessed some of it, whether it was part of this world or not. He knew only what he'd been taught—helping the least of these would someday return to him his forgotten past.

The peddler tried to distract him. "That's some crazy shit you—"

"Quiet," Malikai stated, making the sword burn white.

She obeyed.

He turned his head a fraction, but kept his eyes on the peddler. Addressing the boy on the ground, he said, "What's your name."

"Kelly," the teen said, climbing slowly to his feet.

Malikai took the remaining money from his pocket and held it out. "Take this and go. Get off the streets before it kills you. Get a room. Clean up. Eat. Go to the library in the morning and ask for help."

He risked looking away from the peddler to give Kelly a stern glare.

"Before you end up where *she* is."

Kelly licked his bloody lips and spat again, eyes bouncing from the money to the pale face of the vigilante with the long, silver hair the color of new steel; the six who was a hair's breadth away from murdering his employer, who was *also* a six. Kelly didn't appear shocked at the revelation of the peddler's true nature.

"I'll fuckin' find you, Kelly," the peddler snarled. "You know I—"

She sucked a breath in between her teeth as Malikai's sword grew even hotter beneath her chin.

"Kelly," he said. "Go."

The teen grabbed the folded bills—Malikai knew they totaled nearly a grand—and ran fast down the alley. He should have escaped as quickly as possible, but as a human, a probable Level Four, he of course had to stop and make his distaste of them known loud and clear.

"You fucking deevs!" Kelly screamed, and only then did he dodge around a corner and disappear into the oppressive Phoenix heat.

The insult came as no surprise to Malikai. He was used to it. He turned back to the peddler.

"You hear that?" the peddler wheezed. "He hates you, too, dumbass. They hate all of us. Why not make 'em pay a little for the privilege, huh?"

"You have double what you came for. Leave the boy alone. Forever. Leave them all alone. Find new work."

He angled his head. "What do I say next?"

The peddler snarled. "Or you'll find me."

"Correct."

"I got no fingers," the peddler growled.

Malikai leaned closer, close enough for a kiss.

"Be grateful that is all you have lost this night, pimp."

He slammed a knee into her sternum and stepped back, leaving the six room to keel over. Malikai walked silently to the sill of a recently boarded-up window—there were many in downtown Phoenix these days. His hair draped between his shoulders and waved like a curtain as he used the sill as a boost to leap easily to the edge of the roof, which he caught with his fingers. With a quick tug, he launched himself up and onto the flat roof, a feat of acrobatics the most skilled parkour practitioner would have applauded. No human could have done it.

"I'll see you around!" the woman deviant shouted from below as Malikai walked across the roof.

The vigilante neither responded nor cared. The population of Phoenix had dwindled over the last several years, and the only people moving in were criminals and deviants like the peddler.

Yes. Eventually, they would again cross paths.

THREE

Manic's shift ended at 5 a.m. He hung back with the team as usual, waiting to go last for the showers back at base because there was zero reason for him to rush home. Miller gave him a cursory warning about jacking around with norms while on a call, which Manic dutifully took without complaint. Miller slapped his shoulder and headed out for an after-shift beer.

J.T. hung back too, as he frequently did. The two men sat on a lacquered wooden bench in the locker room, finishing getting dressed in their civvies. By then the rest of the team had taken off.

J.T. cleared his throat and spit a wad of phlegm perfectly into a trash can five feet away. "I tell you what. That kid tonight. He bothered me, bro."

"Yeah, me too," Manic growled, pulling on a sock with a mighty hole in the big toe. "What're schools teaching them these days, right?"

"No, man. Not that snowflake pro-six stuff, I mean what he said."

"What's up, whaddya mean?"

J.T. scowled. "Probably nothing, but . . . that's the second time someone's said it wasn't their fault."

"That deev?"

"Yeah. About six months ago we dropped a guy with some kind of horns sticking out of every joint in his body. Like out of the cartilage. Crazy-looking. On the drive back to base he kept saying he was a Four, that somebody did this to him."

Manic gave a dismissive hiss. "Dude, come on. Lookit, you were a big bad Green Beret, but that ain't the same as what I was doing at LAPD. Those monsters will say anything, trust me. *Anything*, bro. They're just born liars, all of them, norms and deevs both. They can't help it. Guy was trying to get something out of you, that's it."

J.T. was nodding before Manic finished. "No, I know, they're all full of shit, but. The exact same lie?"

"They probably all come up with new ones together wherever they sharpen their claws."

J.T. grinned. "Yeah. I'll buy that."

They finished dressing and walked out of the locker room. Manic asked, "How's the baby?"

J.T. smiled so big, it could have powered their entire base for the day. "She's good, man, she's good. Tough, you know? So strong. Eleven months old, and I think she'd beat me at arm wrestling."

"I remember. Lilly was a runt when she came out but she had a grip on her."

His buddy laughed. "How *is* Lilly?"

"Ah, she still wants to save the world from us insensitive sixcops, you know how it is."

J.T. snorted his sympathy. "So easy when you're twenty."

"You know it."

The two men processed out, passing through a secure airlock before reaching the clear California morning air. J.T. veered for the walled car lot. "Want a ride?"

"Nah, gonna walk it off, go catch breakfast with Lil. Been a while since I seen her."

"Right on, m'man. Take it easy."

"You too, bro."

J.T. swung himself into a decade-old black Jeep as Manic shoved his hands into his bomber jacket pockets and shuffled his shoulders around in the coat against a vague morning chill, replaying the night's encounter. The six-limbed deviant had been their only call.

Not a four? Manic thought. *What kinda lie was that?*

While the world still chased its own tail trying to determine for sure where exactly the deevs had first come from, they sure as hell were born, not made. Both his training and common sense told Manic that most if not all deevs were psycho in one manner or another. Whatever jacked-up genes had mutated and empowered deevs . . . often, they also scrambled their minds. That, or the sheer fact of their power went to their heads. It happened to norms with intangible power all the time, how much more so to a bullet-proof six?

He didn't blame the deevs for their psychopathy, necessarily. The six they'd dropped tonight had shrugged off fifty-cal rounds. That would definitely make a man cocky.

Except that by all accounts, from the 911 call to what that little college asshole had said afterward, this six hadn't been cocky.

Manic sniffed the thought away. Whatever. Dumbass six never shoulda stuck his head out in public.

"Hey," a voice said.

Manic pulled up short and shot a look to his right. He'd been way too lost in his thoughts. Should have kept himself at yellow alert, watching the environment.

But the voice belonged to a skinny white guy, youngish, who had the eyes of a junkie. Manic knew the look. Why the hell was he lingering in an alley instead at one of the free clinics getting his dose?

"Spare?" the kid asked, sticking to the shadow of the alley.

"Go to a clinic, jackhole," Manic said, and tried to take a step.

~~~*Oh, now that's no way to talk to a friend.*~~~

Manic blinked. It was the doper's voice, but it hadn't come from the alley. It had echoed inside his own head.

He tried to cuss his surprise, but couldn't.

~~~*We are friends, right?*~~~

the voice went on. Manic watched helplessly as the doper slid closer to him from out of the shadows. Manic saw now that what he had assessed as Caucasian ancestry was actually milk-white skin, fish-belly pale.

The doper reached out a narrow hand.

~~~*Oh, I hear you don't like guys like me. That's okay, friend.*~~~

~~~*We are ancestors of the stars.*~~~

~~~*Everything we have ever known is made of the same basic elements.*~~~

~~~*Humans share half their DNA with the banana you ate for breakfast.*~~~

~~~*Humans are ninety-five percent identical to chimpanzees.*~~~

The doper reached Manic's coat and began sliding his fingers inside, searching.

~~~*So then, are we so truly different, you and I?*~~~

~~~*If beneath our skins we are nearly the same as the common white laboratory mouse, how much closer must you and I be, friend?*~~~

~~~*Now . . . relax . . . relax . . .*~~~

Manic resisted internally, fought back psychically. NPD had recently completed training on just this sort of thing, and that training came through for him.

He forced the voice out of his head with a sort of psychic aikido, blending with the thoughts at first, which caused the doper's power to slip forward and become "off balance." In that moment, Manic's mind struck back and broke the hold.

"*Fuck you!*" Manic roared.

The white-skinned deev jerked back, but too slowly. Manic seized his wrist and twisted. The deev went down with a squeal.

"You fucking mentalist piece of shit deev!"

Manic stomped one workboot against the six, right where his shoulder met the outstretched arm that Manic still held in a joint lock.

The deev screamed piteously as Manic's blow ripped the joint from the deviant's socket. Manic released his hand. The deev's arm flopped uselessly against the concrete as if boneless.

Manic fell upon the deviant. The sixcop's fists, sheathed in leather sap gloves filled with shot at the knuckles, crashed into the six's face. Manic fired blow after blow against the six, crushing bone and spraying pinkish blood. The thought of what a creature like this "man" could do to his daughter snapped all sense of self-control. So what if he'd only been going for a pickpocket? That didn't mean he wouldn't stoop to worse.

It occurred to Manic that he could have drawn his personal pistol, a nine millimeter, from his concealed holster and kept the deev pinned with the threat of a gunshot, assuming the six wasn't bulletproof. But that wasn't what he wanted. What he needed. What he needed to was feel this perverse monster crunch apart beneath his hands.

The sixcop punched the deev again, smashing the man's nasal cavity to pulp. The deviant went limp, his head thunking solidly on the concrete sidewalk.

Manic climbed off the unconscious form, shaking the deviant's blood from his hand as much as he tried to shake the fear of what deevs like this were capable of doing to Lilly, never mind to the rest of the world. He had to fight an urge to spit on the six's face for daring to invade his brain, his mind. Tentacled carjackers and teleporting bank robbers were bad enough. He could nominally respect their physical abilities. These mentalists bothered the veteran officer on a deeper, almost spiritual level.

Manic pulled a small satellite phone from the pocket of his jacket and raised it to his mouth. His five-day scrub of beard scraped against the microphone as he spoke. "Able Delta four-four-two, got a deev down on—"

He glanced for the nearest street sign and squinted at it.

"—Dixon and Butterfield. Level Six, probable Class M. Over."

The radio hissed. "Manic? Hey, what're you doing out so early in the morning?"

"Shut up, Toole. Just got off work. You gonna send a wagon out here or do I gotta carry this sack of shit back to the office?"

"Calm down, bucko," said Sgt. Toole, who had been transferred to dispatch after an encounter with a six cost him both legs below the knee. "A wagon's en route. Should be there in three. What's he look like?"

"Human," Manic said, and this time did spit, but against the sidewalk. "Worst kind."

"Copy that. I'll make an appointment for you with the shrink."

"I'm fine, Toole."

"Rules and regulations, Manic. If the deev's an M, you gotta go in. First thing tomorrow, all right?"

The deviant stirred and moaned. Manic sneered and stomped on his face with one booted foot, disfiguring his jaw and sending him to unconsciousness again.

"Yeah, sure," he said. "Rules and regs, bite me. Manic out."

He shoved the sat-phone back into his pocket. A group of joggers headed his way down Dixon Street, saw the broad-shouldered man with a flat military hair cut standing over an apparently weaker unconscious man, and crossed the street.

Manic flashed his irridescent green NPD badge. The folks seemed to acknowledge it, but continued moving away. No one wanted to get too close to a sixcop and a deviant, even if the deviant was out cold. The damn thing could be hibernating, waiting to strike. It could be doing *anything*, who knew?

Manic enjoyed their fear. Not only was it good for them, likely to keep them living another day in a world filled with Level Six deviants, but it also—and he had no problem admitting this to himself—made him feel strong. Not just strong; *mighty*. It took a hell of a human to suit up and go after sixes. The National Normative Policy Division attracted a lot of former spec-ops types. Guys like J.T., guys who'd seen the worst humanity had to dish out, who'd seen what a round from a fifty-cal could do to a normal human torso. Even some of those men and women washed out after a couple of months dealing with the sixes.

The horror of battle was one thing. Level Six deviants were another. These beings—not human, but merely playing at being human in Manic's opinion—could pull off the worst that every old comic book had to offer.

None of them were superheroes. Not to Manic's reckoning. Every so often some deev would pop up wearing tights or a Halloween mask and try to enforce his own brand of justice. They all ended up dead or worse.

Manic sat on the curb, resting his arms on his upraised knees. Distantly, he heard the piercing cry of the deev wagon coming nearer. He wasn't far from a station. In a city as big as Los Angeles, with an estimated ratio of one deviant per thousand citizens, it behooved the city to have sixcop stations dotting as much of the landscape as possible.

He'd come to NPD from LAPD, and suddenly that felt like a long time ago. He should have been up for a promotion to detective, but an LAPD record of reprimands and internal investigations prevented it. Other than the small bump in pay that he'd missed, Manic didn't care about the loss. Every cop knew upholding the law was one thing and keeping streets safe was another. That's what he did and did it well—kept people safe. People who couldn't take care of themselves.

He didn't mind being a hero, no sir, not one bit. Sheepdog strong. And if that put him crosswise with more than one board of inquiry, so be it. Another kid might sleep tight that night.

Another kid like Lilly. No matter how old she might be, she'd always be his *kid*.

Manic watched the exercisers scurry by on the opposite side of the street. One of them shouted a quick, "Thanks, officer!"

Manic tipped a salute back. He didn't mind the praise.

Malikai slid across the roof of the strip club. He hopped down on the other side of the building, his bare feet soundless. He landed on a broken beer bottle, but hardly registered it; the jagged edge dented his skin, not drawing even a bead of blood.

He'd learned over the course of many nights that this odd departure—climbing onto a roof only to come back down the other side—helped him gain valuable insights: Thinking he'd disappeared, victims or assailants would often make phone calls or mutter to themselves over their harrowing experience of either being soundly beaten or having their lives saved. He could listen to the immediate aftermath of one of his little interruptions and hear names, locations, habits, penchants . . . and on occasion, learn who the real bad guys were. Lately the real bad guys were a west coast gang horning in on Phoenix territory.

He slid into a shadow opposite the strip club, listening to the female flesh peddler talking to herself in the alley around the corner. He risked a look at her, and saw her wounds had stopped bleeding. Perhaps her deviation allowed her to heal more quickly, like he himself did. Many Level Sixes possessed just such a gift. She scooped his twenties into the palms of her hands one a time and shoved them into her pocket.

The peddler swore eternal pain on Kelly as she stuffed the last bill away. Malikai wondered if the teen would heed his advice or not; take the money and use it to start a better life somewhere else, somewhere like Los Angeles perhaps, which he'd heard was quite near to becoming the world's first utopia. As for the peddler, he knew she'd soon find another runaway to put to work—she'd praise and cajole and hand out money and food and attention at first. Then when the time was right, the beatings and threats would begin, and another child would be condemned to the short, violent life of a prostitute in one of the most dangerous cities in the country.

The cycle never ended. Malikai knew he could spend his entire existence out here on the dismal city streets and never make a lasting difference.

"Never quit," his mentor, Xavian, had said. Sometimes daily. "Never, ever quit, Malikai. Do justly, love mercy, walk humbly."

Malikai listened to the peddler go on for another minute or so, her profanities and expletives turning the air blue before she hurried away into what remained of the Phoenix night. Having heard nothing of value, Malikai crept silently from shadow to shadow, working his way toward his motorcycle.

The Harley got him from home to the city and back again, a prize he'd obtained from a gangster biker a year ago when he began his crusade in the gutters of Phoenix. He never used it to patrol the alleys and dark corners of the city, preferring to go on foot where his gift of silent footfalls could be utilized. The bike would be too loud, attract too much attention. Malikai would ride the motorcycle to downtown after sunset, park the bike somewhere out of the way, and spend the rest of the night doing those things he'd been taught to do.

Justice and mercy for the defenseless. Humility for their oppressors.

Malikai stopped. The Harley, parked behind a convenience store, had attracted the attention of three men of probable Ice Dragon gang affiliation—boys, really, not quite men, with pure white handkerchiefs showing on different parts of their bodies. One had his folded neatly in his back pocket; another had his wrapped around one ankle; the third, tied around his wrist. All three bore ornamental scars on their shaved heads. In addition to the usual initiation rites, the Ice Dragons were known for their permanent skin etchings. Tattoos alone were not enough for their brand of loyalty.

Malikai stayed still in the shadows, blending in, watching them, waiting to decide whether to attack or not.

The three Ice Dragon teens—surely low-level enforcers based on their ages—circled the Harley with a mix of appreciation and desire. Malikai had learned that except for biker gangs, most gangsters didn't bother riding motorcycles, but they could spot a quick black market sale. His fingers tensed, wanting to reach for the sword over his back, but he didn't move. His was a Spartan existence. Theft of this nature, against himself, did not necessarily require interdiction. It wasn't local law he enforced—any American laws he happened to abide by came about from happenstance, not intent.

What would Xavian have him do?

Fifteen months ago, he'd awakened in the desert outside of Tucson, Arizona, with no memory of anything other than his name, and even that felt like a piece of borrowed clothing. He'd been naked and without supplies. Only the Tang dao was there, laying beside him in its ornate red scabbard. He had as many questions about the weapon as he did his own past, but one thing was clear: he *owned* the sword as far more than a belonging. Possessed it in some mystical way he could not define. It obeyed him, more companion than mere weapon.

One of the Ice Dragons climbed onto the Harley.

Malikai wanted to cut off a limb or two, but remained motionless. Dismembering teens for sitting on his motorcycle didn't trip the moral compass Xavian had instilled in him.

Silently, Malikai drifted away from the bike. Either they'd take it or they wouldn't, and he'd replace it some other time. He could find a junker car owned by some street-level criminal to steal if necessary—another bit of crime his teacher didn't object to—or else find a rooftop high from prying eyes where he could spend the day, rather than trying to walk home in the sunlight. Dawn was yet an hour away, but his current home was an hour's drive from downtown.

He swept shadowlike through the urine-stained alleys and

exhaust-choked back streets of Phoenix, senses attuned for anything that might signal a cry for assistance. In most cases, he'd learned, people didn't actually call for help. Few would come to their aid in this part of town even if they did. Mostly he just listened for screams. Or gunshots.

A shout did waft past his ears just then and he paused to assess its quality. Male. Outraged.

A sure sign of trouble.

Malikai turned right, following an alley behind an abandoned strip mall. Pot and crack smoke teased his nose, emanating from squatters in the old building, but he dismissed them. Laughter bounced jaggedly through a broken window, coming from inside one of the old shops. A junkie enjoying his fix. Not the source of the shouting.

He continued on, hearing another shout. Words, clear and distinct now.

"I'm not gonna ask you again!"

Malikai darted left to an opposite building, drawing his sword. He paused at the corner of the building and peered around it.

Two men. One, hands up, stood backed against a windowless brown van. He wore faded jeans and a white T-shirt, his black hair thin and hanging past his shoulders, his mustache thicker and more meticulously kept than the rest of him.

The other man also wore jeans, but they were clearly boutique and expensive. His short brown hair had been trimmed recently, and while his dark button-up was untucked and buttoned only halfway, the material gleamed expensively in the light of a lone white street lamp planted in the sidewalk on the other side of the building.

This second man, perhaps in his forties, stood with his right hand extended, pointing a pistol at the long-haired man. A revolver. Malikai knew instantly that the man holding it was untrained and inexperienced, as if he'd purchased the weapon not long ago and probably never so much as taken it to a range.

The long-haired man being threatened spoke in Spanish as he rattled out what Malikai took to be a frightened denial. The armed man took a menacing step forward, shortening the distance between them to about five yards. Any second now, the gun would fire and a man would die.

Malikai could not let that happen. He leapt.

FOUR

Manic checked the mentalist deev. Still out cold. He wondered, not for the first time, where these inhuman things had come from. If not for Devon Boone, the former Hollywood star, would the world have ever known about the deevs? Boone had begun his career seventy years prior, as a young man of twenty. And he stayed twenty. For a long time, the tabloids talked about surgery, then about computer animation being used in his films to cover his age. Eventually the façade gave way, and one of Boone's assistants came bursting into the offices of the *Times,* telling a Hollywood-worthy story of a man who could take his skin off and put it back on at will.

That broke the door open, Manic remembered. He'd been seven or eight years old at the time, just a scrawny kid in the city of Shitstain, state of Who Gives A Rat's Ass, making a living running errands for the two-bit criminals who kept his neighborhood in bread, milk, and opioids. First tabloids and the web, then legit papers picked up Boone's story. Suddenly a hundred and then a thousand stories not unlike it began showing up all over the place. Seemingly overnight, Olympic-level record holders were having the screws put to them; never mind doping, what about a Kenyan who could run a marathon in under an hour, and was believed to be faster? A pole vaulter who, when pressured, could vault without the damn pole? Gymnasts balancing vertically on the floor on a pinky finger?

They're everywhere, Manic thought. Sliding around in sewers with gills instead of lungs or flying up in the air like Superman but without the morality. All of them were bad, as far as he was concerned. And the citizenry tended to agree—anyone with abilities beyond a certain threshold, beyond a Level Five, needed constant surveillance.

Freedom? You had to be human for that. Science could prove a person's humanity, and the duly elected government decided if a deev's abilities were a threat. After all, civilized society had done the same with crazy people for centuries. Deevs deserved nothing less.

Enter Officer Frederick Thomas Cruce, one of the best sixcops the feds had ever recruited and trained.

A forest-green deev wagon roared up to Manic. He didn't bother to stand. A team of sixcops leaped from the back and took up defensive positions with their rifles at the ready. Loops of galvanized steel cable gleamed on their belts, ready to be cinched tight around the limbs of any deviant under apprehension.

The chief of the wagon came over to Manic while three sixcops bound the deviant. "Morning, Officer Cruce."

"Larry."

"Want to tell me what happened out here?"

Manic didn't care for this particular chief. Each wagon, a heavily armored and well-equipped combat vehicle based on U.S. Army APCs came with a seven-man team: chief, pilot, gunner, and four officers. Chief Larry Garza didn't impress Manic, having been promoted up through the ranks based more on his ability to kiss ass than to take down a deev. He got his job done, but at work Manic preferred the company of folks who'd bled. Off-hours, of course, he tended to prefer no company at all, excepting J.T. from time to time.

"Just walking home, Larry," Manic said, while the team worked with trained efficiency beside him. They fit the deev with a sensory deprivation helmet and hogtied his limbs with high-tensile aircraft cable. Traffic coming down Butterfield Street, seeing an NPD take-down, either detoured or sped past quickly. It paid to stay out of NPD's way.

"Yeah?" the chief said. "Most people drive or take a bus."

"That's what I hear."

"Sir," the chief suggested.

Manic stood. "Uh-huh."

Chief Garza let it slide. Nobody wanted Manic mad at him.

"The report is, this lump of shit blew some mental smoke and tried for my wallet," Manic said. "So I kindly invited him to stop. That's it. I'll sign off on it when I come in tomorrow."

"You'll need to see the—"

"Toole set it up, I'll see the psych doc in the morning. Have a nice day, now."

Manic shoved his hands into his jacket pockets and went on walking down Baker. Several of the sixcops bade him their own gruff farewells as he went past.

By the time they got the deev loaded into the wagon, Manic was a block away, shaking internally and needing a fix.

He'd prepared for it. Everything was waiting for him at home. But he'd have to wait. He had his appointment to keep, and no deev was going to keep him from it.

Manic quickened his pace until he reached Buzz Café, a coffee shop nestled in a cozy collegiate enclave of Los Angeles proper. He wanted to get there before Lilly.

Assessing the cafe to be secure at a glance, Manic rushed to the restroom and took off his blood-soaked gloves, shoving them into his coat pockets. He washed his hands vigorously and made sure there was nothing too incriminating on his clothes before he went back out to the seating area. A few wisps of pot smoke wafted from a cluster of students in a corner booth, making Manic's nose itch, but potentially unlicensed marijuana consumption wasn't under his jurisdiction.

Lilly had arrived while he washed up. Twenty-one and with a college kid's hungry frame, she sat at a small square table by the windows. Manic slunk into an upcycled leather chair opposite his winsome daughter, his jacket crunching aggressively at the shoulders. He tried heroically to offer her a natural smile. The effort resulted in a cramped expression that immediately put Lilly off her ice water.

She pushed the frosted mug toward him. "Geez, Dad. Brush your teeth, huh?"

Manic gladly crushed the smile. "Ah, at least twice a week. Leave me alone. How you doin'?"

Lilly blew a strand of her henna-colored bangs from her eyelashes, a habit she'd had since being a little one. Manic would have grinned if the nostalgia of the gesture hadn't stabbed his heart.

"Honestly," Lilly sighed, "not all that great."

Manic squinted his tiny, copper-colored eyes. "No? How come? Is it a guy? I gotta pay someone a visit, sort 'em out for ya?"

Whether he'd said "got to pay someone a visit" or "get to pay someone a visit," Manic wasn't sure, and didn't bother to clarify. He loved saying stuff like that.

"Dad, stop. It's not that. It's more . . . financial."

"No joke?"

"None whatsoever. I can handle the rest of the semester, but after that, I don't—"

"What the hell is that?"

Lilly blinked. "What."

Manic pointed at her chest. "*That*. That thing you're wearing."

Lilly glanced down at herself. Over a long-sleeved black thermal, she wore a fitted white T-shirt that looked good on her. What drew her father's attention wasn't the fit, it was the logo on the T-shirt: the same one as the young guy had worn earlier at the city park, a black numeral six with a red line and circle over it.

"What I'm wearing is clothes," Lilly said. "That's still legal, isn't it, Officer Cruce?"

"Would you cover that up?" Manic glanced around as if a hippy coffee shop in a college town could be filled with conservative senators who might end his career at NPD.

Lilly smirked. "What, I'm decent."

"I swear to God, Lil, put something on over that or I'll take it offa you."

She folded her arms and sat back in her chair, raising an eyebrow. Her plum-painted lips pursed. "No."

Manic scooted his chair back.

"I'll scream," Lilly added.

Manic hesitated. "You'd really do it, wouldn't you."

"Yes, I would. Or should I say, 'Your flippin' A.' Does that help make it more clear for you?"

Manic sat back down, giving his head one severe shake. "It's embarrassing."

"For you, maybe."

"Yeah, for me! What if my boss came in here and saw that?"

An event they both knew would never happen. In his off hours, Chief Miller wouldn't be caught dead in a place not serving an IPA.

Lilly grabbed the canvas strap of her bag. "Okay, we're done. I'm declaring an end to this lovely early morning snack. Peace, Pops."

"No no," Manic said, more quickly than he wished. He leaned back in his seat, subconsciously mimicking his daughter's pose. He tapped a finger on the table top. "I mean, if you got somewhere to be, then. Whatever."

Lilly barked a laugh. "Listen to you. You sound like a kid. When are you going to grow up? God, why do I even do this? Why'd you have to stay here while Mom left the freaking state? You know what, no, forget it."

She stood for real now, slinging her pack over one narrow shoulder and stepping toward the exit.

Manic tried to let her go. Couldn't.

"Lil!"

She did not turn or slow. She got a hand on the door handle and pushed.

"Please!"

The word ripped him in two inside, making him feel weak and stupid. *Please? Pretty please with sugar on top? Nice work, tough guy. Very nice.*

Even as he thought it, he also reminded himself: *She's your kid. Shut up and do whatever it takes. She agreed to see you. Don't waste it.*

Lilly stopped at the word, door half open as the coffee slingers professionally pretended to not see the great drama unfolding. Or maybe they weren't pretending. They probably saw break-ups and fights and maybe even the odd proposal or two. They were paid, in part, to show some decorum and grace, two things Manic had never had an abundance.

Lilly hesitated before coming back to the table. She sat down silently, but did not unshoulder her bag. "Are you going to talk to me like a human being?"

The remark brought a broken smile—a real one—to the former cop's face, creasing his unshaven mug like a cut. She knew how to phrase an insult. Manic fought his first impulse to reply, *Are you going to keep defending baby-killer sixes?*

Instead he replied, "Yeah."

Lilly set her bag down.

Manic exhaled his relief, quietly. "How's your mum?"

"Small talk? That's new."

"Dammit, Lilly, whaddya want? I'm trying, huh?"

Lilly rolled her eyes slightly, but allowed a nod of understanding. "Sorry. She's good, she's okay. Seeing someone."

If she meant it to sting, it didn't. Marisol Hernandez—she'd kept her maiden name when they married—could go on to fame and fortune and true love. It wouldn't bother him a bit.

"Good," Manic said, not enthusiastically but not apathetic.

Perfectly neutral. Marisol's love life hadn't interested him when they were together and it didn't interest him now. He'd never been a ladies' man. Old friends in the neighborhood back east used to say he had to find the Right Woman. So far, it hadn't happened.

Lonely? Sure, whatever. But safer for everyone.

"He an okay guy?"

"Seems like it."

"What's he do?"

"Lawyer."

"Ha! Great."

He saw Lilly try to resist a smile before giving up and letting it show. The expression made Manic feel as if his lungs had expanded to twice their capacity—pure pride and deep joy. Not for the first time, he wondered how any piece of him could have made so beautiful a girl—woman—as Lilly. And she was his; Marisol had done a paternity test to prove it to Manic, even though she and he both knew at the time of her conception that Marisol was not the type of woman to sleep around. She could have; it wouldn't have upset Manic in the least. Once she'd realized Manic wouldn't mind is when she left, and he'd made no effort to stop her. He'd loved her just enough to let her go.

Manic took Lilly's water glass and slurped from the rim. "What's this about school? Money?"

A dark expression shadowed Lilly's face. "Yeah, well, Makura Bio went belly-up—"

"Who now?"

"Makura Biolabs. It's the company my scholarship grant's from. They went belly up, or at least that's what they say. They're very sorry, there's a lawsuit . . . I don't know. All I know is that when the semester ends, so ends my tuition."

Manic shifted in the leather chair, disliking the direction of this conversation even more than the previous one. Two things the veteran sixcop did not know about were women and money.

An almost frightened sort of anger burned between his shoulder blades. "They can't do that. You worked too hard for this, Lil! What the hell're you supposed to do? They can't just take it away."

"Well, Dad, they can, and they have. It's not my fault."

"I know it's not your fault, you're a freakin' genius, they're the jackholes!" He fumed for another moment while Lilly's face showed a trace level of gratitude for his paternal protectiveness. "So what're you gonna do?"

"Thought I'd become a cop."

It took an extra second for her dry humor to sink in, but when it did, Manic laughed. It was a foreign sound and hurt his chest.

Lilly sipped her water, clearly savoring the reaction.

But the laugh cooled his outrage only briefly. "I don't have the money to cover this, kid."

"I know. Don't worry about it." Her tone held a note of finality to it; Lilly didn't rattle easily. She changed the subject, and Manic groaned before she'd finished the sentence:

"You know they aren't being freed."

He'd rather talk about women or money than wander into politics. Rubbing his forehead, Manic said, "Dammit, Lilly. Sure they are. The safe ones are."

"Yeah? And who determines which ones are safe?"

"People a whole lot smarter 'n you or me, princess."

"Oh, I don't know, Dad, I'm going to be a nuclear biologist, I'm pretty smart."

"You know what I mean."

"They're vivisected," Lilly stressed. "You have to know that, you can't spend every day at NPD and not know that."

He studied an artsy-fartsy print on the far wall. "I only know what they tell me."

What he didn't add, because he didn't need to, was that he did know. Or suspected. No one knew, not for sure. But yes, he'd heard the rumors. Cops of all kinds passed rumors around; they were worse than a knitting circle stitch-and-bitch in Manic's opinion. LAPD and NPD both. So yeah, he'd heard what might happen to some sixes. The ones who required it. How else could the public be protected? How else could *Lilly* be protected? She had the blood and vinegar of a typical collegian, but lacked any practical understanding of what slithered beneath the city streets.

Manic did his job well. He kept her safe. And he knew that when Lil was out and about in the fairly secure Los Angeles streets, she had the instincts of a cop's kid . . . but she lived in a fantasy land when it came to deviants.

Those monsters like the one who'd just tried to mug him? They threatened the entire human race as far as Officer Frederick Thomas Cruce was concerned. And he wasn't alone. The federal government understood the threat these things posed and so formed his unit and thousands like it to keep the deev population under control. It wasn't a job, it was a vocation. It was a calling.

Lilly looked as if she wanted to spit on him. "So that's how you sleep at night, huh? You just do your job, consequences be damned."

Manic rubbed his finger joints under the table. They ached. "Pretty much, yeah."

Lilly leaned forward. "What if you found out a five-year-old boy was being systematically autopsied while still alive to find out why he seems to be bullet-proof? What would you do if you saw that happening in some alley, Dad? Tell me."

Manic crackled his knuckles. Thick scar tissue stretched white across them as they bent and flexed. "I don't buy the premise."

"It's happening."

"Tell you what. You find me proof, bring back some pictures, I'll go in myself and make sure that that bullet-proof five-year-old gets a nice cozy cell the rest of his life. Everyone wins."

"Imprisoning an innocent child. How is that winning?"

They'd crossed back to his turf now. He met her eyes. "'Cause one day that five-year-old's gonna be twenty-five. And bullets won't be able to stop him. What do you think he might do with that kinda power? I got a pretty good idea. I seen it before. I seen it *last night*. This thing running around a city park, bouncin' fifty-cal off his ass. How about a little gratitude for the men and women out there making sure that thing's not a threat, huh?"

Stymied—for the moment—Lilly twirled the water mug. "I don't suppose you have any spare cash lying around."

"So we're changing the subject again? Just trying to keep up."

Lilly sighed theatrically, like when she was ten. Manic could have wept at the memory. "Whatever," she said. "I should go. I need to look for a job."

Instinctively, he reached out for her hand, his big mitt covering her thin fingers. "Lil, anything I got is yours. But what I got is jack."

"I'm not asking you for money, Dad. I was kidding."

"I know. But I'm telling you, if I had it—"

"Yeah," Lilly said. "I know. I have to go."

She stood, sliding her hands out from under his. Then, to Manic's surprise, she came around the table and kissed the brown-gray stubble on his cheek.

"I'll tell Mom you asked about her. Unless you don't want me to."

He waved it off, uncaring, then regretted the gesture immediately. "Sure," he said quickly. "Tell her I'm glad she's happy."

"Oh, I didn't say *that*." She gave him a wink. "You working again tonight?"

"Yeah."

"Okay. Well, be safe regardless."

"You too."

"Dad."

Lilly paused until he looked up at her.

"Show a little mercy, huh? Tonight, if you go on a call."

"I'll do my job." It was the best he could come up with. Sixes often didn't leave a lot of room for mercy.

She patted one shoulder of his leather jacket. "Yeah. That I know. See ya."

Lilly swished out of the café, leaving the ice water behind. Manic grabbed it and chugged the rest as one of the young coffee slingers wandered up to his table.

"Evening," she said brightly. "Can I get you something to drink, or?"

Not looking at her, he yanked out his iridescent green badge and showed it for half a second. "Coffee."

The server gasped at the sight of the badge. "Oh! Well how about I bring you a, uh . . . a vanilla mint mocha? It's one of my favorites, and I can put some—"

Manic waved dismissively, feeling like a colossal jackass yet unable to stop himself. The server scurried off to fix his freebie. He wasn't supposed to accept free food back at LAPD, but everyone did it. Once in awhile the normcops got busted on it, but after a month or so they'd start right back up, accepting free coffee and crullers at any number of joints around town.

Sixcops, on the other hand, had no such prohibition, and Manic appreciated that; most of his meals, while not chock full of nutrients, kept him fed and watered well enough. If he spread out the freebies in his beat, he could get three meals a day without visiting the same place twice in a week. Being in NPD paid crap, but all medical and dental was taken care of in-house, and he'd have a nice retirement if he lived long enough to cash it out. Most NPD didn't, yet there was never a shortage of men and women vying for a slot on a deev wagon like his.

Deviants simply pissed off normal people enough that plenty of fours and fives happily joined the ranks of NPD to bring them down. Those that didn't were happy to hand out coffee and donuts to say Thanks.

Feeling antsy, Manic left the café before the server could bring the coffee to him. He hoped she'd give it to the stoner college kids in the booth instead and not waste it.

His department was a solid ten miles from Buzz Café. Manic checked his watch—the most expensive item in his wardrobe—and broke into an easy jog, enjoying the summer air and pretending he could smell the ocean.

He also hoped for a good bust on his next shift. He needed to release everything that his visit with Lilly had built up inside him. Fortunately, he could take care of that part at home.

Malikai darted into the alley, sword brandished and gleaming. Before either of the two men could have sensed his presence, Malikai appeared beside them, sword flashing, slicing a deep wound across the back of the hand of the man holding the revolver. The man squealed and fell back as the pistol dropped.

"Leave him alone," Malikai ordered.

The long-haired man took the opportunity to bolt, his work boots scrabbling against the gravel as he ran toward the street.

Malikai extended his sword, the angled tip aimed at the wounded man's face as he wailed. But after only a moment it became clear the cut on his hand wasn't what elicited his cries.

"*No!*" the man screamed, raising his hands to his hair and pulling. "No, no, no goddammit, *why?*"

He faced Malikai. Something deeper than rage ran across his face and Malikai felt the first stirrings of doubt.

"What did you do?" the man shouted, his expression crossed with rage and disbelief. "I had him! It took me a month to find him and now you just—you just—God, *why?*"

Almost but not quite involuntarily, the tip of Malikai's sword lowered.

The man gestured with his wounded hand. Blood splattered across the dirt. "They took her! Don't you get it, you bastard? They took my girl!"

Took—?

Malikai sprinted for the corner where the long-haired man had disappeared. The vigilante pulled up short; the street beyond was brightly lit by streetlights, and early morning traffic cruised steadily, white-collars on their way through the blue-collar downtown. Too much noise and activity to get a good fix on where the man may have run to. He'd disappeared completely, either due to his street skills and knowledge of the area, or else he was a Level Six with some kind of invisibility or superhuman movement. Malikai guessed the former, because if the man had deviant abilities, he likely wouldn't have ended up on the wrong end of a revolver.

Malikai returned to the alley, considering his options. Had this really been an error on his part? As with the flesh peddler and the boy Kelly, those people doing wrong were always easy to pick out. So it was here: a man with a gun threatening another man. It had seemed so obvious . . .

His victim in the well-to-do clothes crumpled to the ground on his knees, now holding his wounded hand tightly. Blood seeped between his fingers. He wept openly. The pistol lay not far, yet the man made no attempt to retrieve it.

The fact that he did not go for the gun convinced Malikai that he had made a grievous mistake. What he wanted to do then was go back to his Harley—if it hadn't been stolen by the Ice Dragon kids—and go home to nurse his shame.

Do justly. Love mercy.

He hunkered in front of the wounded man.

"Who was he?" Malikai said.

"Hell do you care?" the man spat. "I had that son of a bitch and you just came and screwed it all up!"

"Tell me who. I will help."

"*Help?* Go to hell, 'hero.' You did enough already."

The man stood quickly and marched toward the sidewalk where the long-haired man had vanished. Malikai watched him, knowing the inevitable result: the man looked one way, then another, cursed, and groaned loudly to the unforgiving night sky.

Unable to stop himself, Malikai came near, standing behind the man.

"Please. Tell me what happened so I may help you."

The man turned and stared at him, nearly delirious. "Are you kidding me? Are you *kidding* me?"

"I must help."

That much certainly felt true. Malikai knew in his bones that helping this man was now his life's mission. Xavian would have had it no other way.

"Some gang," the man said, shaking his head in disbelief while choking on tears. "Human traffickers."

Malikai gently pulled him back toward the alley, away from the streetlights where a normal human might catch a look at the omnihuman with the metallic hair and silver-red eyes. Humans didn't care for his kind. Teams of trained, human killers were patched into the 911 system. One quick call to report a "six sighting," and he'd be on the run.

"They took my daughter," the man went on, speaking mostly to the ground. "The police haven't been able to do anything, but I found a guy who . . . who could track down people like *that* . . . and I got a license plate and I found him, I found him *here*, and you just . . . *Julia* . . ."

The man—the father—wept anew. Watching him, Malikai's realization deepened. This guy was no street slug. While Malikai had guessed as much before striking, instinct demanded he go after the person holding the gun. This man might be an investment banker or something similar, something safe and mundane that came with health benefits, someone who should be driving in the morning traffic instead of standing in an alley, bleeding. This was not his neighborhood, possibly not even his city. He was lucky to be alive.

Malikai sheathed his weapon. He walked to the gun, picked it up, and held it toward the man, who, shocked, reached out and took it back.

"I will find your daughter. You are not safe here. Is this your van?"

"Find her? *Find her?* You're crazy! I spent weeks tracking this bastard down, and two days following him, waiting, and I haven't slept and—"

"*Is* this your van."

". . . No," the man said, in clear awe of Malikai's words and, perhaps, finally taking in the inhuman crimson of his eyes. "No, I parked over at—"

"I will find your daughter. Drive to the urgent care clinic just past Interstate Seventeen and Pioneer Road. Be there by dawn. I will help you there."

Malikai walked to the van's rear doors. They were unlocked and he flung them open. The back smelled of sweat and something fruity, but a false fruit, a flavor, not the real thing. Lengths of rebar had been welded to either side of the cargo area. From one of them, a pair of handcuffs swayed gently.

He reached inside and pulled out the only other object. A small pink quilt, loved to tatters. That's when he guessed the source of the faint fruit smell: flavored lip gloss, of the sort enjoyed by young girls.

The realization incensed him. He'd encountered abused children before, but infrequently. Youngest victims tended to be abused behind closed doors. Older young people like Kelly, those in their teens, roamed the street, or were *made* to roam the street by evil men and women exploiting their fear and powerlessness. But this van wasn't about runaways or drug addicts. It was about little children. Taken.

Malikai dropped the blanket inside and carefully shut the doors, as if not wanting to hurt the ghosts of any lingering young spirits. Rescuing adults and teens who had chosen, in one manner or another, to take their chances on the street was one thing. This—this was something else. Something wicked.

"You're a deviant!" the wounded man said, as if only now summoning the strength to say the words out loud.

"Meet me, or not," Malikai said, not looking at him. "The choice is yours."

He climbed into the van's driver's seat and found the keys still in the ignition. A pristine white handkerchief hung from the gearshift, expertly knotted and folded. Malikai rubbed the cotton between his fingers for a moment, considering what the symbol meant. Then he turned the engine and drove out of the alley, into traffic on the street beyond.

The vigilante drove straight for the urgent care, having chosen the location both for its placement halfway to his base of operations and for the fact that it had little in the way of overhead light at night. The clinic didn't open until nine a.m., so he knew there would be no activity there this early. He considered driving past the motorcycle to see if it had been stolen, then decided it meant nothing to him now. The Ice Dragons could have it if they wanted it. His business with the gang now eclipsed such petty offenses as theft. The man who had driven this van, the man who'd been connected to the abduction—either he claimed Ice Dragon affiliation, or the owner of the van did. Either way, attacking street-level teen gangsters over a motorcycle wouldn't aid Malikai's newfound quest.

Would the man—the father—come to meet him? Impossible to know. From what Malikai had learned about humanity since he arrived in this city, there was a good chance the human would simply call the authorities, the NPD they were called, who were tasked with apprehending people—beings—like himself. Doing so would get the father no closer to finding his daughter, but he could hardly know that. He had no reason trust a deviant, particularly one who had just interrupted what he no doubt thought was his best chance at recovering his child.

The compulsion to help the man swelled strongly in Malikai, that was all he knew; a deep desire, like an ache, to gather information and determine some way to make amends to the grieving father. He could do so without the man's help, but it might take months, even years. If the man would talk, give him intelligence to operate from, that time might be reduced to days.

He considered this evening's encounters. Apparently, Malikai thought with bright malice, Xavian's brief education hadn't been enough to help him distinguish the good guys from the bad. He might have been able to locate the man's daughter before dawn if his training hadn't driven him to attack a man holding a weapon. Malikai was used to leaping into action without worrying about who was right and who was wrong—the situation had always been quite clear up until now. Finding this daughter would go a long way toward assuaging his confusion and guilt.

The urgent care clinic sat empty as he'd figured. Malikai drove the van around the back, parked, and got out. It took only a few moments to render the security system useless, and he mused briefly how long it might take Highway Patrol to get here in the event of a break-in anyway, considering its location next door to the middle of nowhere. Like the rest of his unknown history, Malikai had no inkling how he knew what sorts of supplies to get to treat a sword wound. Anyone could figure out a bandage of some kind; even a child would know enough to at least wrap a shirt around the father's hand. Malikai moved silently through the clinic, finding specific items in proper quantities: gauze, tape, sutures, antibacterial ointments. Plainly he had experience in treating sword wounds.

Headlights flashed across the glass-walled front of the clinic. It must be the father, pulling into the parking lot. Malikai took his supplies out the back door as the father drove around to the rear. He stopped his car, a white Lexus two-door, and climbed out. He had indeed wrapped a shirt around his hand.

"All right. I'm here. Now tell me where—"

"Lay your hand on the back," Malikai said.

The father eyed him skeptically.

"I'm going to treat your wound."

The man hesitated, glancing at the hilt of the Tang dao protruding over Malikai's shoulder. Then, shaking his head, he followed the order.

Such was the love of a father, Malikai thought. He would risk listening to a man he no doubt thought should be locked up or worse.

Malikai met him at the back of the Lexus. The man unwrapped his hand and laid it palm-down while Malikai arranged his pilfered supplies.

"You a doctor?"

"No."

"I don't even know what I'm doing here. You're the one who cut me."

Malikai didn't answer.

The man grunted, as if in disgust of his own gullibility. Then he asked, "Got a name?"

"No."

"Aw, for God's sake!" The father pulled away from Malikai as he dabbed the wound with cleanser. "This is ridiculous. I don't know what the hell I'm doing here. What *are* you?"

Patiently, Malikai poured more disinfectant on a sterile pad. "Do you want her back?"

"*Where is she?*"

"I don't know. You are going to tell me."

Unsurprisingly, the father reached into his waistband and withdrew the pistol. He leveled it at Malikai. His hand shook, but he was close enough that he wouldn't miss.

"Why aren't you afraid of this gun?"

"I've been shot before."

"Yeah, you're a deev, you're a *six*."

"I don't know what I am. It is what I can do that should interest you right now."

Malikai watched the father struggle with that concept. The gun wavered, and the man's eyes slid from side to side, wrestling with the position he'd put himself in.

Malikai made the choice for him. He set the medical supplies down and walked toward the van. "You are wasting her time."

"Wait!"

Malikai paused. The father lowered the gun.

"Come back. All right? I'm sorry. Please just . . . I've tried everything else, no one has been able to do anything . . . how can you help?"

Malikai strode to the Lexus and picked up the gauze once more. The father put his gun away and joined him, setting his bleeding hand on the trunk.

Malikai cleaned the wound again.

"Tell me everything."

The jog home took Manic less time than usual. He kept his fists jammed into the pockets of his jacket, shoulders hunched as if it were chillier than the actual temperature would suggest. His build and scowl kept the earlier risers out of his way, and he liked that just fine.

His apartment building had been built in the 1970s, and it showed not only in the architecture but the maintenance. Much of L.A. had been cleaned up nicely since the current governor took office—Manic had seen it for himself in what had once been the seedier parts of town. A raft of social reforms had given the notorious city a good makeover. Homelessness almost didn't exist, because small Asian-style apartments were made available for free. Mental health and drug addiction clinics sprouted up almost as quickly as sixcop stations did, alleviating an enormous amount of both petty and felonious crime almost overnight. Jobs weren't quite plentiful yet, but the government had begun a number of well-paid infrastructure improvement programs that were reducing gang activity across the board as bangers got jobs that tripled their life expectancy. A standard minimum income law was expected to pass the state legislature soon. Pot was legal and taxed, while alcohol taxes had doubled, and were rumored to eventually triple. It was a liberal's wet dream as far as Manic was concerned, but it made for cleaner streets.

Things might be close to perfect if it wasn't for the deviants. He hoped the mentalist was waking up to a big headache, and ignored the memory of Lilly asking him what happened to deevs after NPD grabbed them.

He didn't care. He just hoped it hurt.

Manic unlocked the plaque-yellow main security gate that opened into the apartment courtyard. A green pool sat in the middle, surrounded by cheap plastic beach furniture. The poolside was empty this time of morning, not that anyone would want to swim in anything the color of pickle juice. Someone's baby cried on the first floor, and old Rico on the third floor was berating his wife again. Nothing new.

Manic hopped up the stairs to the second floor and went to his apartment. Flicking on the light, he let his shoulders slump at last.

Home. It wasn't much, but it was his.

He tossed his jacket onto the kitchen table, which he'd picked up years before from an alley trash bin and polished up. He moped into the living room, though "living room" was a generous term. The whole studio was comprised of the kitchen nook, a long open space for his couch and TV, and then a small bedroom and bathroom. It wasn't much larger than those homeless apartments, Manic reckoned. And that suited him fine. He didn't own much.

He tore his shot gloves off and dropped them on a couch cushion that had molded itself to the shape of his ass. Against the far wall, across from the door, three full-length mirrors stood sentry on a blue tarp laid out on the floor, covering his balding low-pile carpet. Manic stared at the mirrors, making sure to stand at such an angle that he could not see himself reflected. He'd set them up before his shift started, knowing he'd need them when he got home after his coffee talk with Lilly.

Manic swung.

His bare fist crashed into the first mirror, splintering it to shards on the tarp and opening fresh, deep wounds on his knuckles. Before the pain could hit, he was on to the second mirror using his opposite fist. This one fell in two larger pieces and assorted glass dust. Good. The third mirror disintegrated in his right fist, smashing to the floor with a bone-chilling timpani.

Roaring, Manic fell on his knees, barely missing jagged pieces of glass. He smashed his fists down on every piece of mirror his enraged eyes could find. Blood sprayed across the wall, crimson dotting the pale tan paint. Jagged slivers drove into his knuckles, ripping open old scars.

Five minutes later, the veteran sixcop sat back on his heels, breathing heavily, blood pooling on the tarp beneath him.

Then someone knocked on his thin wooden door.

"Everything's fine, Paula," he called, trying to keep his voice even. Paula, eighty-two, half blind, and the building's requisite busybody, never failed to check up on him after one of these episodes.

The knock sounded again.

Manic tilted his head, then rolled to the side, expertly plucking his gun from his shoulder holster. The knock had been too strong and too high up on the door to be little ancient Paula. No; this was a man. One, or maybe more, standing outside against the walls, ready to cut his apartment into wedge-shaped areas to cover every angle, every possible hiding place. Vets called it "slicing the pie." Manic berated himself for not having heard the knock correctly the first time. It was the kind of mistake that got a guy killed.

"Who is it?" he shouted from behind the meager refuge of his couch. Blood cascaded down his hands, making his grip on the pistol slippery. Damn.

No answer. Just another knock.

No way was this going to end well.

FIVE

Manic slid along one wall toward the door, keeping the pistol trained there. Waiting for a hail of bullets to mow him down through the flimsy wood, he reached the door and peeked into the spy hole.

Outside his door, an impeccably dressed middle-aged man stood, hands folded primly in front of him. If armed, he'd concealed the weapon well; he didn't show the usual tells of someone carrying. Manic didn't recognize him, but he knew trouble when he saw it. No one came to this door. No one. Not even Lilly and certainly not Marisol. J.T. and his other buds in the department never stopped by. Neither he nor they ever asked to.

And if anyone *were* ever to pop over for a spot of tea and crumpets, they sure as hell wouldn't be wearing a suit like that. It cost more than Manic made in a month; his red silk tie cost at least half that. Sixcops didn't make a killing; the feds knew they could attract men and women who met a certain psychological profile, and who would gladly do a tough job without thinking twice about their take-home. Did a man become a Navy SEAL for the high pay and a generous pension? No. He became a SEAL because he could do things others couldn't. And gladly. So too the men and women of the NPD.

Manic pulled the door open and stepped back, aiming the pistol center mass.

"Mr. Cruce," the man said with a thin, humorless smile. He showed no fear of the gun.

"Keep talking," Manic said.

"I'm here about a job offer."

"I'm not hiring."

The smile widened by a fraction. "It's an offer for you. May I come in?"

"Nope."

"Your reputation precedes you. Please, I'd like to—"

Manic surged forward, digging the gun barrel into the man's gut and quickly assessing the walkway. The sidewalk was clear. The muffled shouts of Rico bawling at his wife thumped through the walls, but that was all. The complex looked dead. Still too early for the usual activity.

Partly satisfied that at least an attack wasn't imminent, Manic pulled back from the suited man but did not put his weapon away. "How about we lounge poolside, be like a little beach party."

The man cast a mild sneer over the railing of the walkway at the motionless, decaying swimming pool. Having a pistol jammed between his ribs didn't seem to have bothered him. That reality raised Manic's red flag even higher.

"Not very private," said the suit.

"Sure it is. Bein' in public is the most private. Move."

Shrugging with easy disinterest in Manic's paranoia, the man turned and walked to the stairwell. His black leather shoes were the finest style, the cuffs of his trousers perfectly hemmed. Either he had money, or his bosses did.

And he did have a boss or two. Manic could smell it on him. He carried himself with the air of a servant, not a master.

Manic studied the man's gait. This guy wasn't law enforcement, not even at the upper echelon. Not military, either; he didn't have the bearing. No, this guy was a bureaucrat from the inside out. The only question was whether his particular bureaucracy was legal.

The suited man walked easily into the gated area of the pool, where he paused and looked for the least-dirty seat. Not an easy task. He ended up choosing a chair beneath a torn sun umbrella. It surprised Manic that the guy didn't set down a silk handkerchief first to protect his precious ass.

Manic sat across from him after taking another survey of the apartment complex. A woman who lived on the first floor came in through the gate, wrangling two toddlers and three shopping bags. He recognized her, but didn't know her name. Other than that, true to his word, Manic and the suited man had privacy.

He kept his gun out, but not pointed. Blood from the wounds on his knuckles dripped down the barrel. He'd have to clean that later.

"All right," Manic said. "Dazzle me. Make it fast, 'cause I gotta catch up on my soaps."

"I'm Donald Weber. I represent a member of your state government." Weber crossed his legs at the knee, making Manic wince internally. How the hell dudes could sit like that, he'd never know.

Weber plucked at his slacks to keep them from wrinkling, and went on as Manic gazed at him with a mix of suspicion and distaste.

"He's putting together a cohort of sorts. The kind of thing you might be interested in."

"I'm listening. I don't *care*, but I'm listening."

Weber smiled patiently. Manic wanted to punch the expression off his face.

"What I am about to tell you I relay in the strictest confidence.

If I am ever questioned about it, I will deny it, and both you and any people you chose to speak with about it will find yourselves in very uncomfortable legal positions."

"Oh no. Not lawyers. Please, stop, I'm scared to death."

Weber's face darkened. "We want you to kill deviants."

Another smart-ass response came to mind, but died before it could escape Manic's mouth.

Weber wasn't kidding. The jokes were over. Manic felt it in his gut.

"Come again?" he said, leaning in a little and adjusting the grip on his pistol. Thick drops of blood pooled on the concrete under his feet. If Weber noticed, he didn't indicate it.

Weber, too, leaned forward. He laced his fingers on top of the metal table. All semblance of his pretentious attitude disappeared. Now he looked to Manic like a shark circling a wounded seal.

Manic did not like the shift. It had come on too quickly, with too much confidence.

"Officer Cruce, your record speaks for itself."

"I've seen this movie," Manic interrupted. "You know all my dirty little secrets and you're gonna hold them over my head unless I do what you say, right? Man, we really are living in Hollywood, huh?"

"I do know your dirty little secrets," Weber said with an unshaken clarity that further unnerved Manic. "But so do many people. I'm not here to make threats. If you'd like to cut the tough guy act now and listen to the proposal, I'd like to share it with you. May I?"

Manic believed him.

If Weber was up to something other than exactly what he said, he was a master liar. Manic had two decades of LAPD and NPD behind him, and could spot a liar with the shocking speed and accuracy of most veteran cops.

Weber was not lying.

Manic nodded slowly, considering his options. He holstered his weapon. "What happens if I tell you to piss off while I just toddle on back up to my apartment?"

"Absolutely nothing. You'll never see me again, and that will be that. This is a one-time, take it or leave it offer. But you are under no obligation. As I said, this is not a threat. It is an offer. Nothing more."

Manic took off his unironed blue button-up shirt. He began sopping up the blood on his hands with it, spherical biceps flexing. He used the moment to stall, to think through Weber's claim. The worst of the bleeding had stopped when he reached his decision.

"Okay. Go ahead, let's hear it."

Weber gave him a shallow nod and sat back in his chair.

"You and I both know that the deviant population is dangerous to this nation," Weber said, steepling his fingers. "Their abilities cannot easily be contained. Everything about them threatens our way of life. They threaten our freedoms and our rights. Would you agree?"

"Wouldn't put it like that, but yeah. I smell what you're shovelin'."

"Those of you apprehending deviants, the so-called 'sixcops,' have seen the tip of the iceberg. But there is more, Manic. Much more. Creatures using their godforsaken abilities to cause immeasurable harm. Not long ago there was a deviant incarcerated in Oklahoma who could only survive by consuming the pituitary glands of infants. *Infants.*"

Manic nodded. He'd heard that rumor. Nor did he miss that Weber had used his nickname with easy familiarity. It was not the kind of tidbit one found in a mere records search. Weber really had done his homework, talked to people, gotten a sense of the sixcop before approaching him. Spook stuff.

"I'm sure you'll agree," Weber said, as if barely restraining his outrage, "that such a being, one that must essentially eat children to survive, can hardly be classified as human."

"Now wait a sec," Manic said, squeezing his shirt tight over his left fist. "You're really talkin' about assassination here, yeah? Tell me I'm wrong."

"You're not wrong."

Weber's expression seemed chiseled from solid ice. Manic

reevaluated the man; not that he'd been wrong about Weber's background as a bureaucrat, that part he still felt confident about. But he'd underestimated the depth of the man's hate, his capacity to accept violence. All people were capable of it; the vast majority did not prefer it, much less pursue it.

Weber was not one of them.

"Pretty sure killing sixes outright is still illegal," Manic said, a little more carefully than he usually chose his words.

"Would you like to hear the statistics on how many deviants die while under the watchful eye of the NPD?"

"Nope." Manic didn't know the exact figures, but he knew what Weber was getting at. Sixes did tend to go missing after being apprehended by NPD. Lilly had been right about that, all right, fine.

"You accepted a position with the NPD for a reason, Manic. You *hate* sixes. You want them off the streets. Correct?"

Manic shrugged. There were some things that he knew not to say out loud, even with friends, and Weber was no friend.

"Well then understand the request. These aren't garden-variety sixes. These are creatures, animals . . . *beasts* that want to destroy this world. They won't show up on a routine NPD sweep. They're wild and dangerous, and in most cases, quite canny. Getting rid of them requires a certain style that can't be exercised within even the relatively loose red tape of the NPD."

Weber picked a bit of fluff from his slacks, a nancy kind of gesture in Manic's opinion.

"New Bibles are being written right now that will be holy scripture in a decade or two. Religions are forming around these creatures. Cults are starting up. I'm sure you've heard of them."

Manic snorted. He had.

"They'll start to think they're gods," Weber said, flicking the piece of lint away. "Then they'll start acting like it. Do you know what our human holy texts have to say about the behavior of angry gods?"

Little Freddie Cruce spent three years with Sister Shannon in preschool and kindergarten. He had a pretty good idea.

"Sixes," Weber said through a dour expression. "Our new lords and masters. Nothing makes me more sick to my stomach than that very thought. Wouldn't you agree?"

Manic did, but didn't want to say so. "How about you just send a couple wagons after these guys?"

Weber was shaking his head before Manic finished the question. "The NPD is still very much a police force, and a young force at that. Apprehensions come with online videos and the press corps, which means NPD cannot screw up. Do you have many screw ups, Manic? Do your friends on the team? No. NPD is only sent on busts they are almost sure to win."

Fury burned in Manic's chest. "Wait, *what?* Say that again?"

"NPD cannot have failures, not now. The public must trust you implicitly. Your people never *answer* the 911 calls, you just go where you're told. You're sent after low- and mid-level sixes, that's all. The real bad ones must be dealt with in an entirely different manner."

Betrayal wormed through Manic's veins. He and his buddies were being spoon-fed?

The sense of betrayal cooled, however, as he tried to imagine the sort of sixes they *weren't* seeing in their typical workday. Good God, what else was out there?

Weber went on. "To make matters worse, the more liberal elements of our culture would do away with NPD outright. If they have their way, and they just might someday, then these sick monsters would roam the streets with impunity. The man I represent can't have that happen. *You and I* can't have that happen. The time to strike is now, before the law gets any more involved and we suddenly have a million drooling deviants asking for drivers' licenses and the right to vote. Next thing you know, we'll have one for president. Let that image sink in. 'Put your hand on the Bible, sir. Oh, certainly—your tail or horn or tentacle will be just fine.'"

Manic nodded on autopilot. There was a certain wisdom and truth to Weber's words. He didn't for a moment believe a six could rise to the presidency of the local chess club, let alone the United States. Still. Weber's hypothetical landed in his guts and twisted them. People like his own daughter or the college kids last night . . . yeah, they had a misguided way of looking at the world of norms and deevs. Dangerously misguided.

"How about drones?" Manic said. "Swarm drones, or tactical snipers?"

Weber waved and came perilously close to rolling his eyes. "Robots and drones have their place in any police or military force. You of all people should know some jobs require a personal touch."

Manic snorted an agreement, but wasn't satisfied. Not quite. "What you're talking about is against the law. I mean, *technically*."

"Technically, yes. But you would be protected."

"Oh, yeah? How do you reckon?"

"You'll remain on the NPD payroll," Weber said diplomatically. "Every so often, you'll receive a packet of information on a certain target. When the target is eliminated, you'll leave behind a small transmitter that will notify other members of your cohort of your location. They will dispose of the remains. Your fee—"

"Bounty."

"Your *fee* will be wired into a separate bank account that is immune from taxation. That's it."

"I still punch the clock?"

"No. You'll be on the books as a consultant, working your own hours, receiving pay and benefits in addition to the fee for completing the job. But you will not gear up with any team, and you will carry no identification. And, of course, you will tell no one."

"Identification can be a handy thing."

Weber shrugged. "Very well. That's up to your discretion. Understand that you are, of course, expendable."

"Of course."

Even as he said it, possibilities began to blossom in Manic's mind. Real, life-changing possibilities. A way to make the world a better place. A way to make sure Lilly could finish school, and be safe from the worst of the deevs crawling the city streets.

He wondered suddenly how the mentalist he'd beat up was doing. Then gleefully decided he did not care. Had that been any different than what Weber was proposing? Not by much, if at all.

"And if I bend a couple rules?"

Weber chuckled. The sound made Manic scratch the back of his neck as if an insect had landed there and begun to feed.

"There are no rules. Obviously, or perhaps not so obviously, we expect a certain amount of decorum. Innocent lives must be protected, and we can't very well cover up an explosive car chase in the middle of downtown L.A. We expect you to work quietly and efficiently, not take down a skyscraper. Can you do that, Manic?"

"I can do that."

He'd done it before. Maybe he knew a thing or two about the death rates of deviants under NPD care than he wanted to admit, to himself or anyone else.

"Each job pays ten thousand dollars," Weber said.

Manic couldn't help his eyes widening for a moment.

"Once a job is completed, you'll receive another assignment, depending on what intelligence your cohort is able to obtain."

"This cohort you keep talking about. Who are they?"

"No one you know, and no one you will ever meet. You work alone. Your cohort works behind the scenes. You will never cross paths. If for any reason you do, do not expect to exchange pleasantries. You do your job, they will do theirs."

"If they come to pick up the trash, won't we see each other?"

"When a job is complete, you'll activate the transmitter and walk away. They'll handle the rest."

"What if I got a question? Who do I ask, you?"

"Everything will be handled through a drop box nearby. All communication will go through it."

"And if there's an emergency? Don't I get a secret phone number or nothin'?"

"We are paying you to ensure there are no emergencies."

Manic finished dabbing at his knuckles. He'd have to bandage them tonight. Again. "And I suppose if anything happens to me, you deny all involvement."

"Naturally."

"'Cause I'm expendable."

"An asset, yes. You're free to say no if these terms are not agreeable."

"I want twenty."

Weber cocked his head, like a hawk. "I'm sorry?"

"Twenty thousand each. That's the deal. This little adventure's gonna cost."

"I'm not prepared to—"

"Don't BS me. I'm the first guy you asked. Or, maybe the only one, yeah? Yeah. That sounds right. I'm the guy with the record. All those inquiries? Somethin' goes wrong, the story's baked in: I went crazy, went off the rez. Perfect fall guy. There can't be too many like me, I'm all you got right now. And you all haven't actually tried this yet. I'm the test balloon. You need to do some, uh . . . beta testing before a wide release. Am I right?"

Weber smirked. "You are more insightful than you look."

"I know, right? It really bugs people. So here's the thing. There's gonna be factors and flubs and FUBARs. Those things cost money, hate to break it to ya. I'm happy to be the test pilot, but you're gonna have to kick in a bit more. Twenty thousand each." He smiled humorlessly. "You're free to say no if these terms are not agreeable."

Surprisingly, Weber grinned, but showed no teeth. "I think my supervisor has chosen the right man. Twenty it is. Is there anything else?"

"Yeah," Manic said. "One last thing."

He lifted a fist. The blue shirt had turned mostly purple with his blood.

"You didn't ask me about my hands."

Weber stood up and straightened his tie, which did not need straightening. "We know about your hands. We don't care. But a good therapist might do you some good. For twenty thousand, you could even get a nice one in Beverly Hills."

Manic snorted a laugh.

"There's a mailbox store three blocks north of here. Ask for the key to box twenty-two. You'll find everything you need."

"And you're sure there's no other way to get in touch with you?"

"The box will be sufficient. Manic, you should give yourself more credit—neither of us can imagine a situation in which you'd need to speak to me immediately. You'll either be successful or dead."

"True."

"You'll do your due diligence," Weber went on. "Looking me up, trying to figure out what it is you're getting into. I wish you luck in that endeavor, but you might want to save your time. I don't exist."

Manic stood. Weber was taller, but not by much. He looked the bureaucrat up and down. "We'll see."

"Of course. In any event, I've left you a good set of fingerprints on the table top."

Cocky bitch, Manic thought. "Yep. I know."

"Excellent. Good day, Officer."

Weber pivoted on one shiny leather shoe and escorted himself out of the pool area, heels clacking like a woman's stilettos. Manic watched him go, then took one last double-check look around the complex before going up to his apartment.

Manic tried hard to keep up his natural police officer's paranoia, but found it more difficult than he would've expected. Mostly he felt excited. The money was a windfall, the job a good fit. He knew there were a double-dozen ways for things to go wrong, but he couldn't focus on them.

Instead he focused on how soon his first assignment might happen; how soon he could get Lilly *twenty thousand* dollars.

That's what a dad does, he told himself. *Hell yeah it is.*

After bandaging his hands, he went back downstairs to collect Weber's prints.

The man Malikai had wrongfully attacked introduced himself as Nicholas Lawson, a senior financial analyst for a capital market company. Malikai understood but did not comprehend any of those words except his name. The vigilante's line of work, so to speak, didn't bring him into contact with many financial analysts for capital market companies.

"Julia's been missing for a week," Nicholas said while Malikai finished suturing his wound. "The police say she was targeted. She fit a certain profile. Caucasian, blonde hair, nine to eleven years old. She just turned twelve last month. The cops wouldn't say it, but a friend of mine who's in security, ex-special ops? He told me they'll . . ."

Nicholas clenched his teeth, his hands, his eyes. Malikai expected the word *rape.*

". . . Groom her."

Malikai tensed. Somehow those words were worse.

"They'll do things to her, he wouldn't tell me what, but he didn't have to." Nicholas stared at nothing on the blacktop, eyes unblinking. "They'll break her. Brainwash her."

He paused.

"Then sell her."

Malikai had eaten nothing in the past year; hadn't so much as taken a tiny piss, either. Like everything else in his odd life, he didn't know why; he knew only that he needed no food and no sleep. As Lawson spoke, for the first time since he'd awoken in the desert, he felt something new: sickness. A sort of nausea that momentarily weakened his legs. He wanted to draw his sword. Attack, maim, kill. Not Nicholas Lawson; just *something.* Anything. The kind of animal who would treat a child the way Nicholas described deserved nothing less than extremely swift punishment.

Malikai methodically screwed the cap back onto the cleanser. "Who are they."

Nicholas breathed out a sigh, as if trying to refocus his thoughts. "Just a bunch of bastards. Kidnappers. Kind of organized, I guess. I mean, I'd heard a couple stories before . . . people stop at intersections, and these guys'll just try opening a passenger door and grabbing a kid right out. You don't think it really happens, and wouldn't ever happen to you."

"They took her from your car?"

"No. Not Julia. They, uh—they followed her. They knew our routine. Cops said they'd probably been watching about a week. Probably watching a dozen kids or more, like some kind of spy network."

"You have names? Locations?"

Nicholas shook his head. "This friend of mine, the special ops guy, he did some looking around for me. Posed as a broker. Not like the financial kind, but like a middle-man, you know? He pretended to represent me as a client who was looking for a certain . . . type of . . . sweet *Jesus*. These people really are out there."

Malikai knew they were. "Who was the man in the alley? The driver of the van?"

"His name's Angelo Wilkins. At least, that's what I knew him as. He was one of *their* middle men. I got too scared, too excited, you know, I just pulled the gun and—"

Nicholas cut himself off, tilting his head back and staring helplessly at the stars cautiously disappearing overhead. It would be dawn soon.

"Is this his van?"

"I assume. It's what he showed up driving, if that's what you mean." Nicholas dropped his gaze back to Malikai. "Why should I trust you, man? Look at you. You look like a goddamn vampire."

Malikai knew well enough what he looked like. From what cultural literacy he'd obtained the past year in Phoenix and from Xavian, he figured Nicholas's description was more or less accurate. While his teeth were no different than any other man's, certainly the pallor in his face, his impossibly colored hair, and red eyes with irises like molten silver would leave a dramatic impression on a normal human.

"I have made you a promise, and I will keep it."

"Where are you from?" Nicholas asked. "You're Chinese?"

Malikai cocked his head, perplexed.

"I do a lot of business in China," Nicholas said. "You sound Mandarin. Slight, but it's there, I think. Is that where you're from?"

Something in his words caught Malikai's psyche like a fish hook and tugged. He tried in vain to follow it, to discern its source, but came to no conclusion. Perhaps he *was* from China. Perhaps he was from Mars, or Kapteyn-b, or *Hell* for all it mattered.

"I do not know," Malikai said, characteristically emotionless.

Nicholas rolled his eyes. "Figures. So what now?"

"I will look for her. When I find her, I will return her to you. That is all."

Nicholas flexed his wounded hand, as if testing to see whether Malikai had done a suitable job of patching him up. "This is crazy. I don't know what the hell I'm doing out here."

Malikai said nothing.

"You know deviants aren't allowed to carry weapons, right? Or be out at night. Do you even have your D-card?"

Malikai said nothing.

"Cripes, you're probably worse than the guys who took Julia. Right? I mean, you're all violent, crazy animals, aren't you?"

Malikai said nothing.

"Say something, dammit!"

"I will look for her. When I find her, I will return her to you. That is all."

"But you've got some *powers* of some kind, right? Magic, or whatever the hell. I don't know why else I'd be standing here having this conversation."

"You have tried the human way. Even had I not interceded in the alley, you would have failed in finding your daughter."

"You don't know that!"

"I do know that. I live it. Every night. I find those who do wrong, and I try to prevent them from doing more. That is why you are here *having this conversation.*"

The men locked eyes and held them—Malikai, brow furrowed and sincere; Nicholas, eyes wide and desperate and paternal.

Malikai stepped back and forced his expression to ease. "Do you have a photograph of her?"

Nicholas held his gaze a moment longer. Malikai watched him struggle in silence, debating, no doubt, the merits of entrusting his little girl's safety to a six.

Then, grumbling quietly, Nicholas handed over an iPhone. "Here. The password's 0102. Everyone I know is in there, pictures of Julia—everything. You find her, you can find me with that. And hey . . . if you do find her, I'll pay you anything you want. If that helps."

"It doesn't."

"I'm only doing this because I'm out of options, you know."

"Yes."

Malikai appreciated two things about Nicholas Lawson as he studied the cell phone: most normal humans carried their lives in their phones, so this would be a good source of intelligence. He was smart to hand it over for that reason. And, unless he took the battery out, Malikai had also just accepted what amounted to a tracking device. He could tell Lawson knew what he was doing. The man was not without some sense of tactics. Doubtless he would cancel any credit cards and other critical information within the hour so Malikai would not have access to that, not that the deviant cared.

Without another word, Malikai walked to the van and got in.

He pulled out from behind the urgent care clinic and headed to the freeway. Already the sky turned faint pink in the east. He didn't want to be out in the sun.

He considered Nicholas Lawson's words as he drove the speed limit toward the abandoned farmhouse that he'd made his home base. *A goddamn vampire.* The phrase echoed in his head. He was no vampire, he knew that much. Vampires drank blood to survive. Malikai neither ate nor drank, nor did he need to breathe except to speak. It was possible, he thought, that he very well may have been damned by God to live forever.

No, he was no vampire. Sunlight did not burn his flesh, holy relics did him no harm. He avoided going out during the day for the mere fact that humans got trigger-happy around omnihumans, and he didn't want to bother with the inevitable chase and potential harm that would happen if a normal human saw his features under the light of the sun. Those who looked as different from the norm as Malikai were frequently convicted of imaginary crimes and punished immediately on the street.

Looking different was not against any written law. The law of the land was another story.

Arriving at the weed-choked property, Malikai drove the van into the empty barn, parked, and climbed out. He closed the swinging barn doors and walked through the dawn sunlight toward the old house, a tiny place of two bedrooms, one bathroom, and a large country-style kitchen. Each room sat uselessly collecting dust since he, its sole occupant, had no reason to avail himself of its amenities. It wouldn't have mattered anyway, as the house had no power or other utilities turned on. Whoever owned the property either was having a difficult time selling, or perhaps had already forgotten about it, or was using it as a dead loss to balance taxes . . . something like that. In any event, no one yet in the past year had come bothering him.

Malikai sat in the middle of the floor of the empty master bedroom and set his sword down beside him. Since he had no need for sleep, he would spend the day in meditation, searching his mind, or heart, or soul—if such things existed—for hints of his past, for the faintest aroma of his former life.

Perhaps he'd misplaced it somewhere in China.

Malikai let his eyes close as he sought the stillness of deep meditation. Had he been born this way? This was just one of a million questions he had not been able to answer. Certainly he seemed to have been dropped into this world, fully formed and prepared for combat and vengeance. He felt no particular yearning for a place or a thing, nothing apart from his sword, anyway. The dao was as much a mystery as the rest of his life, his *past*. Was the weapon magical? Technological?

Or even something utterly beyond either designation? Swords did not glow white-hot, and certainly not at the whim of their bearers. Yet his did.

If either Malikai himself or the sword were some angel or demon, the deity that birthed them remained strangely silent. Sometimes, in the depths of his meditation, he thought he could feel another presence, a memory; sensations of warmth, care, and pain. But not his own pain. Some other's. But all beings were born, in some fashion—he must have had a childhood, someone must have raised him.

Beings. The word swirled and mutated behind his eyes. He was in fact a being; four limbs protruding from a central trunk, possession of language and other signs of intelligence, of instinct and . . .

Malikai grimaced.

Ability. Abilities unlike other "beings."

It mattered little. This world had concrete ideas of what constituted *human* beings and Malikai did not conform; one of the small percentile whose skills exceeded those of the greatest humans. Einstein, it was said, was a five; a human who fell within the realm of "normal" but who possessed the type of ability that helped humanity move forward. Olympic athletes were fives, as were any number of oddly-gifted individuals.

Not needing to eat, sleep, breathe, or excrete; not causing any sound with one's bare footfalls; turning a sword blade into a weapon of pure heat at will . . . these things put Malikai deep into Level Six territory.

Omnihuman.

All human.

More than.

Why, he wondered, would any populace spend resources like money, time, and the inevitable body count chasing down beings whose only crime was being born different? Somewhere out there, a little girl named Julia lay in the clutches of actual evil men, and what were the authorities doing about it? Investigating. They let themselves be bound by laws and strictures when it came to the life of an innocent child, but neatly skirted or outright ignored other laws pertaining to the treatment of "inhuman deevs."

These thoughts disturbed Malikai's pseudo-slumber, making it difficult to focus on his meditation. Injustice and corruption rose like a stench from the streets on up, all the way to the world's halls of power. Yet instead of fighting those men, he was bound to the street, to the blood and dirt and blacktop. He sensed honor in the type of work he did; surely freeing young Kelly had been a genuinely good act. But he was only one. How many more were victims that night? How many more children taken and abused?

For all his power, at moments like these with no other way to kill time, Malikai felt utterly impotent. He knew then that he would stop at nothing to find Julia Lawson. However long it took, whatever pains he must endure, she became a totem, a symbol of his ability to do right in a world gone bad.

Malikai tried again to recenter himself and meditate. To prepare.

Hours later, the sun went down.

SIX

Manic's first assignment showed up Wednesday morning.

The sixcop, who had never owned a car in his life, woke up earlier than he needed to and took a detour on his way to work. The detour happened to take him right past the mailbox shop Weber had directed him to.

It wasn't without some skepticism that he approached the counter and asked the zitty young man there for a key to box twenty-two. His skepticism dimmed when the kid handed over a pair of small silver keys without so much as a blink.

"You don't wanna see some ID, nothing?" Manic said, tossing the keys from hand to hand. Both were bandaged thickly with white gauze and tape like a boxer but with more dexterity in the fingers and palm.

The kid shrugged. "Just do what they tell me."

"Yeah? Who's 'they?'"

"I dunno. *They.*"

So the kid was on the take somehow. Had to be. Weber, or whoever it was Weber worked for, wouldn't just call up the mailbox place and tell whatever teen happened to answer that these were his instructions.

Manic gave the kid a nod which the kid didn't seem to notice. He took his time meandering to the bank of aluminum mailboxes, berating himself for not having asked Weber point-blank for the name of Weber's boss.

Except Weber wouldn't have told him. He knew that. But why open this mysterious mailbox without any more information? Manic planned on working up a dossier on Weber as soon as he got to work, since he had no computer at home. The thing that had sealed the deal in his mind, and it wasn't exactly crackerjack police work on Manic's part, was Weber's presentation. If he was anything other than what he purported to be, Manic felt sure he would have known it. Sensed it. Not in a deev way, but in a vet cop way.

Manic pulled a plain manila envelope from the box, then shut and locked the door. He stuffed the envelope into his half-zipped coat and left, headed toward his station. The envelope didn't feel heavy; he guessed he'd find only papers inside, and not many at that. He found himself grinning somewhat stupidly as he walked, feeling a lot younger than he had in some time.

Damn it if this wasn't *fun*.

Busting deevs was good for a laugh and gave him a sense of purpose, but this cloak and dagger game with Weber reminded him of the good old days as a kid, when playing cops and robbers blended seamlessly with running brown paper packages from Tony's Deli to Vito's Restaurant and back while avoiding anyone even remotely smelling like a cop.

Good times, good times.

He checked his watch as the NPD station came into view down the street. Real men wore watches, his inherited father taught him back in the day, and Manic sprung for good ones, saving up the money each year for a new model. He had fifteen minutes before he needed to clock in, so he veered to the right and sat down at a concrete table in a small park that once had been the domain exclusively of the homeless, prostitutes, and gangsters. This morning, the park was populated by families and joggers, with no less than four strollers parked or being walked, and a handful of toddlers racing around a sandy playground while moms and dads watched, looking thin but fed.

Manic had one hand on the envelope in his coat, but didn't pull it out just then. Instead, he watched the families for a moment, thinking that not many years ago, he'd be busting half of them for possession, solicitation, vagrancy, congregating without a permit— anything he could come up with. These days, LAPD spent more time walking their neighborhoods and helping old ladies cross streets than prowling in their cruisers to shake down dealers and pimps. Manic guessed that some of the people at the park today probably did, in fact, have criminal records of some kind. But while the strollers weren't brand new, they weren't shopping carts, either. These folks had money, real money, money for food and kid clothes and strollers. Things were different now in the City of Angels.

And Manic loved it.

Loved it like he loved his own daughter. The rest of the nation was turning to Los Angeles for *guidance*, for ideas on how to transform their own metropolises, and the only thing disrupting the good news here in town were all the damn deevs.

That's when he pulled out the envelope. He'd still run a background on Weber, but now his thoughts had whetted his appetite for Weber's offer. The least he could do was take a look in the envelope.

Manic shook papers out onto the table. Other than them, he found only a small square device about the size and weight of a quarter. Sticky tape coated one side, with a thin strip extending off the edge, obviously designed to be pulled off and discarded, like the strip on a new ink cartridge. Manic figured it must be the transmitter he was supposed to leave behind after a job. He set it aside and ignored a few printed pages, choosing instead to look at a handful of 8x10 color glossies.

"Yeah," Manic muttered with a grin. "You're a cute one."

The first photo showed a vaguely humanoid shape clad in blue jeans and nothing more. The reason for going shirtless was clear: the deev had an upper body size and muscle tone Hollywood would worship. He seemed to have muscles where no muscle could actually exist, like abdominals which started almost as high up as his ribs and appeared to reach down to his groin and wrap around his flank. Unfortunately for the deviant, this musculature included his face as well: the tiny muscles that on a Level Four or Five would allow for humanity's wide array of expressions were, on this creature, exaggerated to a painful degree. If he smiled, he'd look like a jack-o-lantern. If he frowned, he'd look like a fist. In this photo, the deev was screaming. How a photographer got close enough, even with a telephoto, to take the shot, Manic could only guess. Maybe it had been taken by an intel drone.

The other photos were more relaxed, even casual. Manic understood without yet reading the doss why this deviant needed to be taken out. The photos showed the deviant to be in the employ or at least company of the 56 Tigers gang, notorious for enforcing their drugs and guns territory with brutal violence. Their numbers had dwindled the past six years or so as the governor embarked on his Clean The Streets campaign. At first, many of the Tigers went to prison, then not long after, many simply stopped banging as regular jobs began to open up, jobs that didn't cut their lifespan to an average of twenty-two years. The guys in these photos were older, guys who had lifestyles to maintain and reputations to protect. Deevs could be hired cheap. Muscle Boy here was probably on their payroll as a scare tactician or debt collector.

Smiling, Manic turned to the deev's dossier. According to the printed report—it was not on any official form or letterhead, Manic noted—the deev went by the street name Fracture, so earned by his propensity for popping people's bones out of their arms or legs as ordered by his 56 Tiger bosses.

"Good to know, good to know," Manic said, nodding, and enjoying the squirt of adrenalin surging through his blood.

Fracture, the report went on, was believed to be nearly impervious to blades of any sort, and blunt-force trauma likewise seemed to have no affect on him. There was no record of whether or not he'd ever been shot, but researchers believed him likely to dismiss low caliber shots at anything less than point-blank range. One unnamed source recommended NPD start with a .50 caliber and work up from there if deadly force was needed.

Manic took the source at its word. One didn't join the 56 Tigers without getting shot at a couple times per week by the likes of rival gangs such as the Ice Dragons. Manic's usual sidearm wasn't going to be enough for this gig. A .50 started sounding like a good idea.

He finished reading the report and the request:

Civilian casualties unacceptable. Tiger casualties regrettable but not forbidden. As Manic had guessed by the photos, the only 56 Tigers remaining these days were the older guys who'd stayed alive and very young guys who were either enamored with the lifestyle or else threatened and pressed into servitude by the older gangsters. Manic decided he'd make sure the youngsters wouldn't get hurt. Not *too* bad. About the old guys he couldn't care less. With Governor Savage's sweeping social reforms, they'd had their shot to go legit and passed. So be it.

"Down to business," Manic said, shuffling everything back into the envelope. He tucked the package into his jacket and stood, pausing a moment to once more take in the scene at the park.

Children slid down slides, swung on swings, dug in sand. Parents smiled, many as if in disbelief that this was their lot now. Yet all it would take is one deviant like Fracture to cut them down in a matter of seconds and run away before the NPD could even mount a counter-attack.

Manic wouldn't stand around and let that happen. He headed for the sidewalk and continued his walk to work, reminding himself that Weber's cash would mostly go straight to Lilly, who deserved to finish her education.

Even if she was a deev lover.

Manic figured she'd grow out of it. It was easy to take umbrage at some perceived social injustice when the real world hadn't yet kicked in your door and opened fire. If going after these deevs would help prevent Lilly being exposed to that real world, then Manic was happy to do so.

He entered the NPD building at the rear. Access through the reinforced vault door required both a retinal scan and a palm print, which he provided with casual familiarity. He punched in his PIN and waited for the guard inside to take a good look at him through the lens of a high-def camera and run him through a facial-rec program before opening the door.

"Morning, Manic," the guard said.

"Howdy, Hank."

Manic accepted a small plastic cup from Hank and spit into it. He handed it back across the solid concrete outer layer of Hank's security desk, and Hank tapped the saliva into a DNA reader bolted to the counter-top.

"Got a note here says you got to see Dr. Ong first thing, buddy."

Manic growled as the DNA reader indicator lights turned from blue to green. "I really don't have time for that shit today, Hank. I truly don't."

"Not my call, brother," Hank said with a sympathetic smile. "Just doing my job."

"Lotta that goin' around. J.T. pop in yet?"

"Naw, out sick."

"Damn."

"Yeah, send him some flowers or something, would you?"

"Yeah, yeah, up yours, snowflake."

Hank laughed and used his own thumb print to buzz Manic through the small room's only other door. Manic went through and followed the short hallway—a designated choke point on the off chance any deevs got this far—to a third reinforced door. Stenciled above it were the words *Diligence. Vigilance. Humanity.*

As was his habit, Manic tipped the words a casual salute. He believed in them.

After clearing another set of security measures, Manic gained access to the guts of the NPD station. For all that NPD was tasked to do, these unmarked branch offices were fairly Spartan in their appointments. Here in the circular field team communications room, men and women manned banks of computers, communicating and coordinating field units while supervisors wandered around with tablet computers and made minor adjustments as needed. The routers, as the communications people were called within the unit, rarely need much correction. The NPD didn't take just anyone into their ranks.

Manic greeted no one on his way to the locker room and prep area. Small talk and chitchat wasn't allowed here in the comm. No distractions. Distractions got sixcops and civilians killed.

He found Dr. Ong waiting for him in the locker room. Steam clogged the air, and an odor of sweat and oil mingled in it as men and women showered off their shift's accumulated grime in private shower stalls.

"Ah, *hell*," Manic griped when he saw Dr. Ong.

"Officer Cruce," Ong said, rising from where he'd been lounging in a folding metal chair. The tall, narrow physician smiled warmly but not without a bit of exasperation. "I know you must have been on your way to the psych lab, but I thought I'd pop in here to make sure you didn't get lost."

"You're a ballbuster, doc, you know that?"

"By profession, yes. It's a learned skill. Top of my class, you know. Come on, Manic. Let's just get it over with." Ong gestured to the door Manic still held open with one hand.

Some of the other guys getting geared up for the day both jeered and cheered Manic as Ong escorted him from the locker room. Manic flipped them friendly birds, eliciting laughs from the others.

Encounters with mental-powered deviants such as the one Manic had floored last night required a thorough exam by physicians trained in deviant physiology, as well as a team of doctors from other disciplines, particularly neurology and psychology and their various specialties. The NPD branches all came equipped with medical labs costing millions, which were used not only to treat their officers' wounds as necessary, but to run batteries of tests on officers after encounters with deviants.

And, sometimes, on deviants themselves. This fact did not get broadcast to the public.

"I'm fine," Manic groused as he followed Ong. "I think I'd know if some mentalist got in my skull and scrambled my gray matter."

"We all have our orders," Ong said, showing Manic a sympathetic smile.

But when Ong made a right turn instead of going straight on down the hall to the lab, Manic stopped. "What's up?"

"Oh, we need to swing by my office first. No big deal."

The shift confused Manic, who'd only been in Ong's office once, during his final interviews for the job. He shrugged off the change and fell into step behind the doctor.

Ong's office sat between and among several other bureaucratic offices—supervisors and assorted pencil pushers. Manic didn't think less of most of them; the NPD promoted from within, and every boss who worked directly with the street teams had to have street experience themselves. Ong and the scientists like him were an exception, but like all docs in militaries the world over, were held in esteem by the soldiers they patched up.

"Come on in." Ong opened the door for Manic using a hand print and retinal scan. Manic took a seat in one of two upholstered chairs in front of Ong's desk. Like the rest of the NPD innards, the office wasn't anything to get excited about—a couple of bookshelves, mid-sized wood desk, and two large monitors. Ong's chair, which he sat in as soon as Manic entered, looked like a middle-of-the-line self-assembled job found at any office supply store.

Manic glanced around the office, noting nothing had fundamentally changed since he was last here. "What's with the pit stop?"

Dr. Ong cleared his throat and maneuvered the office chair closer to the desk. He picked up a mechanical pencil and toyed with it, not meeting Manic's eyes. "Have you been to the box yet?"

"The what?"

"The mail box. Box twenty-two."

Manic, being in a place he most closely associated with home, didn't hide his shock. "You know about that?"

Now Ong looked up. "Absolutely. I recommended you."

Manic sat back in his chair and slapped his thighs. "Get the hell out."

Ong grinned. "It's true. You were always someone I kept a close eye on ever since you came in. The time felt right to bring you to their attention."

Now Manic leaned forward. "Okay, who, dammit? Let's start with Weber, who the hell is he?"

"Weber's a prick." Ong's grin turned wry. "No one likes him much. But he's good at his job."

"What exactly is his job?"

Ong eyed Manic carefully. "There are still some things you can't know, Manic. It's a matter of safety and protection. Hell, there are a lot of things *I* don't know. That's just how it goes. You know what it's like working for the government. Need-to-know basis only."

"So Weber's a fed."

"He might be. He might *not* be. I don't know exactly who he works for, but I know he gets the job done. Did you accept the offer?"

Manic pulled out the manila envelope and brandished it as proof. "What more can you tell me about this guy Frac—"

"Stop," Ong said, holding up a thin hand. "Don't talk to me about anything in that envelope. That's none of my business. It's between you and your handler."

"I got a handler?"

"Someone who gets the dossier to the mail box, yes. That's all. You'll never see him or her, and that's another precaution for everybody."

"I could stake it out."

"Manic, don't take offense to this, but there's you, the guys who get the job done. Then there's the guys who facilitate the *getting done* of said job. You'll never see them, trust me."

Manic accepted that. He was no spook.

"Doc, we go back a few years now. I gotta tell ya, I don't know if this makes me trust Weber 'cause you're signing off on him, or if it makes me not trust you at all anymore."

Ong nodded and offered a shrug. "I understand. If you don't want the job, put the envelope back in the box and walk away. You'll still have your job here."

"Is this an NPD gig?"

"No. That much I can tell you. Of course, I could be lying, I suppose. But for what it's worth, no. This has nothing to do with NPD. They're just another part of your support system now."

Manic turned the envelope over a couple of times in his hands. The paper scraped against his bandages. "You know I'm gonna do a workup on Weber, right?"

"You won't find him."

"I dunno, doc, I'm a pretty talented guy with some pretty impressive computers out there."

"You *won't* find him."

"Because you've already looked."

"That's affirmative. There is no Donald Weber."

Manic put his elbows on his knees and leaned even closer to the doctor. "Okay, you see how this all sounds, right? Guy shows up outta nowhere to my apartment, offers me this gig, and now I find out you're in on it, but that any research I do on my own won't mean shit . . . the whole thing sounds bad."

"Are you refusing the job, then?"

"You sayin' I should?"

Ong folded his hands. "I believe I'm now going to sit here quietly while you wrestle with your decision."

Manic tapped the envelope against one bandaged hand, and realized Ong hadn't asked him about the wounds. Maybe he already knew.

"What happens if I say no?"

"Nothing. You suit up, go back to work. And don't tell anyone, naturally."

"Sure." Manic kept up his tapping, letting the sound get louder in the small office, waiting to see if it would unnerve Ong. It didn't.

"All right, screw it," Manic said. "If you're on board, I'm on board."

"Excellent," Ong said. "Go get your psych workup done. That'll be your last official duty as NPD. Then meet Weber at the L.A. public library."

"Why."

"I have no idea. Those were my instructions to pass along. He'll tell you everything you need to know."

"You people are spooky, you know that?"

Ong smiled. "Yes." He stood and extended a hand. "This will likely be the last time we speak. It's been an honor serving with you, Officer Cruce."

"Don't I get to clean out my locker?"

"All your belongings will be waiting for you at home. There will also be some . . . let's say, *cash and prizes* I think you'll enjoy."

"All right. Sounds good. But what if I talk to Weber this morning and change my mind?"

"You'll be transferred to another NPD branch of your choosing."

"Anywhere?"

"Almost anywhere. I hear France is nice this time of year. Greece. Japan, the U.K. . . ."

"Yeah, yeah, I get it. All right." The NPD model had been widely adopted in the western world, and while the United States did not have oversight of any international force, much like in the United Nations, its influence rang strongly.

At last Manic shook Ong's hand. Unceremoniously, he turned and walked out of the office, tempted to try and skip the psych eval, but following orders instead.

"Your life is different from other people's, pal," he muttered. to himself. He paused in the empty hallway and pulled out his phone, tapping to Lilly's number and checking his watch. Normally, she'd be about twenty minutes away from starting class.

She answered. "Hey, what's up, Pops?"

"Hey, kid. Question for ya . . . how much tuition you need?"

"Uh . . . what?"

"We both got places to be, Lil, just give me a ballpark, how much tuition you need to cover whatever this, this grant thing used to cover?"

He heard water running in the background. It stopped before she answered. "You mean like, to finish my undergrad? I don't know . . . thirty thousand."

"For everything? Room and board and books and all that?"

"Okay, maybe a little more. Forty, forty-five. Why?"

Manic nodded to himself. "All right, lookit. When would that need to be paid?"

"Dad, what're you—"

"Lil!"

She huffed. "I mean, I have some time. I'm funded to the end of the semester, so . . . I don't know, next month maybe?"

"Next month. Got it. Listen, don't drop out, don't fill out any paperwork or quit the apartment or anything, okay? You talk to me first. Gimme a couple days to work some stuff out and I'll take care of it."

On her end of the line, a door opened and closed. Manic imagined her leaving the tiny studio apartment.

And imagined Fracture watching from a parked car or hidden in some bush. His heart rate doubled.

"Dad, what're you doing, what's going on?"

"Nothing, don't worry about it. New job. Everything's gonna be fine."

"New job doing *what?*"

"Love ya, kid. Talk to you soon. And you wait for me. Don't quit *anything*. See ya."

Manic ended the call even as she tried to interrupt him, and stuffed the phone into his pocket. He headed for the psych lab flexing his hands under the bandages. Forty thousand? That's *two* deevs. No problem at all. Pop two deevs and call it quits with Weber, get his old job back, here or someplace else. That was a pretty sweet deal.

That he might not survive two deevs never crossed his mind.

But he did wonder what Fracture was up to right then. And if it was hurting anyone.

SEVEN

Manic found Weber sitting casually on a bench outside the north entrance to the Los Angeles Public Library. The spook—that was the best job title Manic thought fit the man—was dressed as well as he had been yesterday, and came off looking like one of those *Shark Tank* guys, master of his universe. Manic felt an urge to go buy a chocolate milkshake and dump it in Weber's lap.

"Officer Cruce," Weber said as he approached. "Have a seat."

Manic sat beside Weber, but left as much room between them as possible. He scanned the area instinctively, looking for threats, surveillance, or anything else that might trip his instincts. He came up empty.

"What's up."

"The man in the red shirt," Weber said, keeping his eyes focused forward. "Behind you on the left. He's wearing latex gloves."

Manic leaned back on the bench and flung his left arm over the backrest. He waited a few moments, then casually turned his head, not focusing on any one particular thing, but instantly noting the man in the red button-up shirt. Upon closer inspection—an inspection lasting less than a second as he continued to swivel his head—Manic saw Weber was right. The guy had gloves on. He'd missed it during his initial scan of the area because the gloves were translucent, nearly matching the guy's pale skin. Other than that, there was nothing suspicious about the guy. He sat reading a book with LAPL markers on it, and if he was keeping anyone under surveillance, he was either doing a shitty or incredible job of it.

Manic let his head swing back to center. He did not look at Weber. "Got him. So?"

"That's Joseph Lexington. He holds a Ph.D. in electrical engineering from Stanford. Brilliant man, by all accounts. And, also, if he removes those gloves and touches a live circuit, such as an outlet or an empty light socket, his body will take the form of pure electricity, and he can travel along electrical lines, popping out at any other outlet he chooses."

Manic chuckled. "Okay."

"You don't believe it?"

"Oh, I believe it. I just never seen anything like it. So, what, you want me to whack him?"

"No. He's on our radar and we keep close tabs on him. To date, he has not posed a specific threat. We are currently relying on this man's good nature, if it in fact exists. But imagine for a moment what a creature like that could do to our local, national, or global infrastructure."

The chuckle Manic had let out suddenly felt a thousand years old. A guy who could do that, really and truly do what Weber was saying . . . he could tear apart the entire country and be done long before anyone knew what was happening or what could be done about it.

"How do you stop something like that?" Manic said.

"Water. Anything from a squirt gun to a fire hose negates his power, at least temporarily. As I said, he's on our radar. We don't need you to do anything about him. He can be taken at any time."

Manic spat to one side. "Who the hell are you, Weber?"

Weber turned to face him at last. "We both know the danger people like that man pose. People like whoever is in the envelope you picked up this morning."

"You don't know what's in it?"

"No. I only know that you indeed picked it up."

"You and your buddies all need to communicate a little more."

"Be that as it may. The politics of your new job are well beyond your grasp, or mine. We both have our orders, and we follow them. Correct?"

Manic nodded despite himself. And also despite himself, he glanced back toward the man in the red shirt. Other than turning a page, the deev didn't move.

"So I hear you're a fed," Manic said, studying the red-shirted guy just to see if he would pick up on Manic's scrutiny.

"You did not hear that, I'm quite sure, but the answer is no." Weber did his leg-crossing routine like he'd done at the pool. "I work for the state. More or less."

"Now, see, you're doing that spook stuff again," Manic said. "That makes me nervous."

"I understand. What *you* should understand are the stakes involved. Finding the right person to do this job is a long and laborious process, Manic. And every moment you hesitate, another six like that man is out on the streets, hurting innocent normal people."

"Does guilt usually work? I'm just curious. You sound like my grandma."

"You want to know who I answer to. I will not tell you. You want to know more details about the structures and policies in place for this job. I will not tell you. I have given you everything you need to know, officer. An offer has been extended. If you wish to accept, then do so. If you do not, then please let me know now and *stop wasting our time.*"

Frederick Thomas Cruce once slammed a guy's arm in a car door. Multiple times. He'd felt nothing as he did it, nothing except exhilaration. But the thrill came not from the violence itself. The thrill had come from following the orders to do it. Tony and Vic in the old neighborhood trusted him to get things done, and he'd done them. Being a guy the other guys could count on mattered intensely to him. All said and done, he did well taking orders. He might've ended up in the military if LAPD hadn't happened. And he knew he would have done well there. He'd be a grunt on the ground, doing whatever it took to get done whatever job in front of him needed getting done.

It wasn't a comforting realization to come to, and it had only come within the last few years working for NPD. Once the truth of it had settled in, Manic accepted it. There didn't seem much point in *not*.

So as Weber, a suit's suit if ever there was one, talked down to him like he just had, one part of Manic felt compelled to repeat his arm-in-the-car-door bit on every single one of Weber's limbs.

The other part of him felt like saluting.

"One more question," Manic said.

Weber sighed. Manic ignored it.

"Do you know how it happened?"

He didn't need to expound. The question had become a global standard over the years, the topic of debates and blogs and arguments the world over, almost as common as "Hello." It was shorthand, understood by any person who spoke the language of the questioner.

It meant, *Do you know how and why the deviants are here?*

Weber relaxed, and nearly smiled. "At the risk of sounding . . . *spooky* . . . that's classified."

"So you do know?"

"That too is classified."

"Off the record, what do you think?"

Weber's near-smile disappeared. He uncrossed his legs and leaned closer.

"I think if you survive this job long enough, you'll find out for yourself the answer to how the deviants happened."

Manic nodded a bit. He reckoned Weber was right. Dig into the cesspool, you'll find the shit.

Weber stood, straightening his coat. "Are you in?"

"I'm in." The response came more quickly than Manic liked. He would have enjoyed keeping Weber on the hook just a few minutes— *seconds*—longer.

"Good. You'll get your second assignment after the first is complete, and so on. You may leave questions in the box. That will be our only form of communication from now on. In the event of an emergency, I recommend you call 911."

Manic smirked. "Will do."

"I'm sure Dr. Ong has explained that your belongings have been removed from your NPD station. You'll find everything in crates inside your apartment."

"Inside? So someone broke—"

"We're very efficient."

Manic stood also. "What if I get a boo-boo?"

"Report to the nearest NPD station. Their medics will aid you as usual."

"Any other bennies?"

"You'll be taken care of."

"And when I want to quit?" Manic asked, thinking of Lilly's tuition. *Just two deevs.*

"Leave a note in the box. The job ends immediately."

Manic crossed his arms, making the brown coat flex over his biceps. "You guys arrange a little accident for me, is that it?"

A mild look of offense crossed Weber's face. "Never. You're human. We're better than that."

Manic snorted, not believing Weber but not caring to fight about it. When the day came to retire, he could handle the precautions. "All right. Have a good one, Webs."

To Manic's delight, Weber tensed at the nickname. Nice to finally rattle the suit's veneer for just a second.

Weber gave him a tight nod, and walked like a priss to a white luxury sedan parked by the sidewalk. Manic watched him go, then looked for the deev in the red shirt. He'd gone.

Shrugging internally, Manic walked home. He found himself checking people's hands for latex gloves.

He reached the apartment eighty minutes later. The instant he opened his door, his eyes widened and an involuntary *Whoa!* blurted out of him.

Weber and Ong understated their description of what would be waiting for him. Manic's paltry furniture had been moved aside to make room for a dozen metallic security boxes stacked neatly in the living area.

Manic recognized the crate technology—NPD had engineered the sec-boxes to be similar to the "black boxes" on airplanes, able to withstand a tremendous variety of types of damage without harming the contents. Whatever they'd sent him, it was secure. Larger versions were often used to transport deviants, though they were far too expensive to be widely available.

Each crate came with its own palm and retinal scans. Manic closed the door and chucked his coat onto the kitchen table, approaching the silver crates with growing anticipation. It felt like Christmas, or what he assumed Christmas was supposed to feel like. Holidays hadn't been important growing up, and he'd only offered token support for Marisol's wishes when it came to family traditions.

Manic unloaded the sec-boxes, studying each item in turn before laying it out on the floor with careful precision. When he'd emptied the last of the crates, he stood over his new arsenal, hands on his hips, smiling.

Mr. Fracture was going to have a tough time very soon.

*

Tuesday night, Malikai parked the van at a public library garage where the lights had been destroyed by vandals and not yet repaired. The garage smelled of piss and booze and spray paint, intermingling in a way that advertised the depths into which the city was crumbling. Malikai wondered, not for the first time, if this was his home town. It didn't feel like it; he'd explored most of the city's dark corners, ascended its tallest buildings and surveyed the entire valley a hundred times. None of it struck emotional or familiar chords.

He remembered every square foot of dirt, concrete, and glass he'd come across the past year, so in that way, Phoenix did feel like a sort of home. He'd come to learn who hung out where. The biker bars, the gangster parks, the tong gambling dens and yakuza basements. He'd also learned which illicit activities each was most known for, though crossover was widespread—bad guys dealt in whatever made the most money the fastest, that was the plain economics of it. There was no honor among thieves, and no crime not worth committing if money or sex was involved.

The criminals did have a roughshod code of sorts, both on the street and the overcrowded prisons where so many of them lived their lives. First among them: don't hurt a child. Malikai knew sexual predators had to be isolated in prisons for their own safety, though he had trouble understanding why a person of such proclivities should be afforded any amount of safety when their victims had none.

Keeping silently to the shadows, Malikai made his way, slowly and carefully, with the patience of a sniper, to the roof of Almeida's, a bar featuring pool tables, naked women, and cheap beer favored by the Wild Coyotes, a motorcycle club who tended to take orders from anyone stronger than its own clique; a band of guns and muscle for hire, not much more.

Malikai perched on the roof unobserved while AC/DC played seemingly on repeat, thundering the roof beneath him. Once in a while, glass would shatter and laughter would erupt. Malikai wondered idly how the bar covered its glassware costs.

Four hours later, his target came into view, roaring up on a custom-built bike with ape hanger handlebars. Its rider parked at the edge of the dirt lot and hauled his prodigious body off the motorcycle with some effort. Malikai waited until he was twenty feet from the door.

"Meet me in the back," Malikai said—softly, yet his voice carried with pinpoint accuracy into the obese man's ears.

The biker shuddered and froze in place with a small gasp, looking up at the roof where the vigilante sat staring down at him.

Malikai's sword glowed blue. "Or I'll *bring* you to the back."

The biker grimaced and spat. Grumbling and reaching into his leather jacket to pull out cigarettes and a Zippo, he waddled around the corner of the building while Malikai stalked him from the roof, checking for observers.

Malikai didn't know the biker's real name and guessed not many others did, either. He'd earned the unfortunate but apt nickname "Thud" early in his criminal career, a title bestowed upon him by friends—half of whom were already dead now—based on the sound his skull made when it hit the blacktop during a street race crash. Thud never sought emergency help, preferring to have his friends treat the wound. How much permanent damage his brain had sustained, Malikai could only guess.

Thud went to the rear of the bar, loitering near the industrial garbage bins and smoking nervously. He eyed Malikai with distaste, distrust, and any other *dis-* the eighth-grade dropout might have been able to muster. The two were not friends, nor so much as occasional allies. Even low-level thugs like Thud did not ally themselves with deviants. Not unless that deviant had something of value.

Malikai dropped to the blacktop without a sound, a point even Thud's slow mind could interpret and react against. It was like watching a cat leap, and seeing a humanoid figure do so clearly unsettled the biker.

"What now?" Thud grunted, drawing deeply on his cigarette.

Having dealt with Thud in the past, Malikai knew to speak slowly and to not mince words. Thud posed no threat physically or intellectually, but he could surely raise an alarm before Malikai could stop him. That would bring the entire gang out into the alley, and while Malikai didn't fear such a confrontation, it served no useful purpose this night.

He'd decided to start with the obvious, just in case. He held up Nicholas Lawson's phone.

"Have you seen this girl."

Thud blew smoke at the screen, squinting. "Naw."

Malikai knew Thud to be a poor liar—good liars tended to ascend to higher ranks among the Wild Coyotes, not unlike legitimate gangs such as those found in politics and business. When he denied having seen Julia Lawson, Malikai could see he was telling the truth.

"Do you know Angelo Wilkins." Though phrased as questions, Malikai's voice was devoid of an uptick—many of his inquiries came out as statements.

"Naw, I don't think so. Why, what'd he do?"

"He is the middleman for a person or group who kidnapped this girl. I need to find her. Who can tell me where she is?"

What Thud lacked in common intelligence, he made up for in street wisdom. Something passing for understanding crossed his greasy features. "She got picked?"

"Picked?" Malikai had not heard the expression previously.

"Yeah, like, targeted. Yeah. Somebody picked her up, like. Grabbed her. For like a P.O.?"

"What is a P.O.?"

"Purchase order. Somebody put in an order for her. Her age, her hair, her—"

Malikai resisted an urge to smack the man, just to release some of the disgust he felt at his words. "Yes."

Thud nodded slowly. "All right. Here's what I got to tell you."

Malikai's grip tightened on the dao, half-hoping Thud would try to attack him.

"Whatever six hole you crawl into every night, go back to it. 'Cause you don't want none of that."

"None of what."

"None of what'll be comin' for you if you go stickin' your silver-ass nose inna this."

Malikai lit his sword with white heat. Thud reacted immediately, raising his hands and taking a step back.

"Hey, don't cut the messenger! I'm tryin' to help you, deev. You go down that road, you ain't comin' back. Period, thu' end."

"Pretend I am unimpressed."

Thud snorted. "All right, then. Your funeral. Thank fuck. When they take her?"

"One week ago."

Thud blew smoke. "She's prolly in L.A. still. They got to, uh, *process* her. But maybe she already been moved."

"Where in L.A."

"Dude, I don't live there, I'm telling you everything I got, don't cut another fuckin' finger off."

Thud absently rubbed what remained of his left middle finger. He and Malikai had initially met under different circumstances, circumstances in which the penalty was one lost finger. Thud was easily manipulated, easily frightened. Since that night when Malikai had prevented him from looting a liquor store, he'd returned from time to time to squeeze information from the biker. Thud's fear made him a particularly easy rat.

"Who can tell me?"

Thud blew out another breath, but this was a practiced sigh, an act, and Malikai saw through it immediately. He let the thug talk, though.

"Dunno, man. Hard to say."

Malikai's blade grew hotter.

"But you could start at Sal's," Thud recalled suddenly. "And I mean, *you*. No norms go in there, man. But you'll fit right in."

"Sal's."

"Just ask around L.A., you'll find it, sure as shit."

Malikai doused the heat in his sword with a mere thought; not even a thought so much as a reflex. He turned to leave.

"Better watch out for the seven," Thud called.

Malikai paused, waiting for Thud to continue.

"You're a six, right?" Thud said. "That don't make you king of the hill. S'all I'm sayin'. Freakshow silver-ass bitch."

A seven. Malikai considered the possibilities, but dismissed them. Humans ranked and rated omnihumans according to some scientific scale about which he knew nothing. What he did know was a Level Seven deviant was nothing to shrug off.

He shrugged it off anyway. There was no point in worrying about it now.

Finished with the biker, Malikai thumbed some twenty dollar bills to the ground and walked into darkness while Thud muttered and lit another cigarette. Malikai decided to leave immediately for L.A. He had no preparations to make; no reason to stick around here tonight. He'd need the darkness to get into Los Angeles.

The van sat unmolested where Malikai had left it. Perhaps, he thought, it was too early for anyone to have really noticed it or tried to steal it. He climbed inside and headed straight for Interstate 10, which would put him on the long drive to California. He listened to no music, sitting and staring grimly ahead and keeping an eye on the gas gauge.

He made it as far as Palm Springs, about 300 miles west of Phoenix, before deciding he'd better fuel up. It wouldn't help matters if he ran out of gas in the middle of a Los Angeles freeway.

Malikai followed signs to a well-lit Chevron in Indio surrounded by similarly well-lit restaurants and small shops. He'd hoped for an out-of-the-way truck stop, where people were less likely to ask questions about his appearance. He hated gas stations as a matter of course. Too many people, too many cameras. In Phoenix, he knew which ones to use to fill up the Harley. Those stations cost more, but had less security and fewer people likely to phone in a deviant sighting. Such calls were typical all across the country, he'd overheard. In the darker, smellier parts of town, the calls were less frequent.

Nobody liked calling the cops in those parts, not even on a deev.

Malikai pulled up alongside a pump and prepared his "human" costume: dark hooded sweatshirt, black-lens sunglasses, thin leather driving gloves, a pair of cruddy sneakers. He'd procured each item over time in the alleys and dumpsters of Phoenix. While the outfit concealed most of his skin, hair, and eyes, it also made him look like a man trying to conceal his skin, hair, and eyes. Hoodies had fallen out of favor with many Level Fours and Fives—normal humans— as deviants began wearing them with regularity out on the streets. Most humans didn't want to be mistaken for a six. Those humans who lived on the streets, however, didn't care much what the rest of society thought, so hoodies could still be found in pockets of urban decay. Wearing this disguise every time he purchased gas, Malikai could generally count on being avoided entirely.

But that was at gas stations where other deviants and street people did business. Out here at an unfamiliar place near Palm Springs, even at this late hour, he couldn't predict what, or who, might be waiting.

Malikai scanned the concrete lot for signs of impending conflict, but found none. The only other car at the gas station was a VW Bug, being attended to by a teenage girl who looked half-asleep.

Good. Malikai sifted through a worn wallet filled with an assortment of credit cards. These he'd taken from his various victims as he'd come to realize that even he would need money from time to time, primarily for moments such as these when his current vehicle needed gas. He kept as much cash as he found on his victims, but the wad he'd given to the teen, Kelly, and then the twenties to Thud had been the last of it, and he avoided taking cash indoors to cashiers who might get a good look at him and give the NPD a call just for spite. Malikai knew these credit cards had been stolen from innocents and hacked; previously taken by the people he tended to run across in his nightly vigils. Using them did not bother his conscience. Perhaps in the service to greater good, such relatively mild trespasses could be overlooked by whatever god had put him here with no memory of his life before.

Checking one last time for trouble and reluctantly leaving his sword behind, Malikai climbed out of the van and moved efficiently but not hurriedly to remove the gas cap. He'd only rung up a dollar's worth of gas when a raised truck thundered to the other side of his pump and a white middle-aged male hopped out, belching and swearing.

Malikai tensed. He kept his back to the driver of the truck, who hawked and spat against the concrete before starting to fill his own vehicle. Malikai watched him carefully in the reflection of the van's blacked-out window.

"Fuggin' hot out, huh?" the driver said. "Fuggin' summer time, I swear. Hate it."

Malikai said nothing. He wished he could play-act as well as some of his criminal victims; they were virtuoso performers, some of them, born into a world in which he with the best sob story often made the most money. They were all bilingual, with lies being their native language.

When the silence stretched, the driver snorted and said, "Nice gloves, queer."

If he'd had to breathe, Malikai would have sighed. Somehow the man reminded him of Nicholas Lawson. So thoroughly ... *human*.

The pump rang up to ten dollars.

Like Lawson, this driver had a child. The truck's passenger door opened and Malikai saw a young boy poking his head out.

"What's wrong with his skin, Dad?" the boy asked.

The question would have been rude under any circumstance, but his voice was curious, not unkind. This child hadn't yet fully adopted his father's likely worldview.

And of course he'd noticed the silver sheen of Malikai's face. Children were far too perceptive for their own good—or, Malikai corrected himself, maybe that perception is what kept most of them alive. Had he himself ever *been* a child? He felt sure he must have. Perhaps he'd once been possessed of the same sort of curiosity and perception as this boy here.

Naturally, the driver of the truck made it his business to step over the concrete island between them and get a closer look at Malikai. The vigilante turned his head slightly to the side, trying to buy himself time.

The pump rang up to fifteen dollars.

"Hey," the driver said. "My boy asked you a question. Why you wearin' sunglasses at night?" The man laughed suddenly, as if surprised at a joke only he could understand.

"He did not ask me anything," Malikai said, cursing himself for not simply staying silent. "He asked you."

The driver gave Malikai a thump on the shoulder. Now that he stood closer, Malikai could smell beer on his clothes. The man wasn't fall-down drunk, but he might have been not too long ago.

The pump rang to sixteen dollars.

Malikai took off his sunglasses and turned to the man. "End this," he said softly. "Walk away."

The man's reaction was instantaneous. Disgust crossed his face as if he'd just stepped in dog crap.

"Deev," he said immediately.

The pump rang to seventeen dollars.

"Yes. Now go."

The driver's eyes veered quickly toward the truck and back, and Malikai knew what the look meant: he had a gun. Men like this always had a gun. He was calculating how long it would take to get the weapon from the truck and come back firing. While the world hadn't quite turned into an all-out shooting gallery with deviants as the targets, nor did Malikai know of any human who had killed a deviant and served prison time for the killing. It was as if some things were simply "understood." That more humans hadn't killed more deviants could likely be explained by humanity's fear of them—no one wanted to get close enough to a Level Six to attack. They'd rather run.

Rightly so, in Malikai's opinion. But humans also loved their alcohol. And men driving lifted pickup trucks tended to like alcohol a lot, about as much as they hated the entire notion of deviants existing in their country.

"Dad?" The boy stepped out of the truck.

"Back in the car," the driver said. "There's a deev out here."

The pump rang to eighteen dollars.

The driver's warning acted only as an enticement. Rather than obey, the youngster rushed to his father's side to get a look at the mutant freak putting gas into a nondescript brown van—which had recently been driven by an *actual* monster, Malikai thought darkly, but didn't bother to point out. Neither of these humans had the maturity to grasp the differences between monsters. The boy could be forgiven, though. He was motivated by curiosity. A natural impulse. The man's motivation came from something else entirely.

The driver didn't bother reprimanding the boy, choosing instead to have some kind of twisted teaching moment.

"See this?" the driver said, his lips curled. "This is what a deev looks like, Kyle. They should all be killed."

The pump rang to nineteen dollars.

Kyle, to his credit, asked the natural question. "How come?"

"Yes," Malikai said, staring unblinking at the driver, letting the full crimson of his eyes dig deep into the other man's irises. "How come."

"They're animals," the driver said, shifting as if he wanted to get in Malikai's face but not quite having the guts to do it. "Buncha fuggin' animals. Not good for nothin'."

Twenty dollars. The tank was nearly full.

Malikai turned his gaze to the boy. Kyle, perhaps ten years old, did not shrink away.

"Kyle," Malikai said gently. "Do not let him do this to you."

"Do what?"

"Yeah," the driver snarled. "Do what, ya fuggin' six?"

"Do not let him teach you that this is the right way to live. It will only bring you pain."

The pump rang to twenty-one. Then twenty-two.

And the driver swung at him with a grunt.

Malikai twisted his shoulder to one side, only by an inch or two. It was enough to let the driver's swing go wild and land against the van with a sick crunch.

Kyle blinked and stepped away from his father as the man howled in pain and fell away from the van. The gas pump handle clicked off, the tank full. Malikai, again operating efficiently but not quickly, hung up the handle and climbed into the van. Careful to maneuver around the wounded man, he drove out of the gas station and toward the highway. Once on the pavement, he accelerated, pushing the old van to its limit.

Malikai knew what was coming. If he still wanted to get to L.A., he'd need to get as deep into the desert as possible, as far from the gas station as the van could take him. Right now, the driver of the truck was on the phone to the police. It's just what humans did. But maybe, *maybe* if he could take the van far enough away—

No luck. It took the police only fifteen minutes to catch up with him. As the red and blue lights of the highway patrol lit up in his review mirrors, Malikai felt Xavian's voice surging inside him.

Never quit. Find the girl.

No matter the cost? Malikai asked, silently.

Do justly. Find the girl.

The police car grew closer.

Malikai slowed.

EIGHT

What Manic wanted to do was set up the fifty-cal sniper rifle he'd received courtesy of his new employers and pop a couple rounds into Fracture's skull, give the deev a taste of what his nickname really felt like. If it took more than a couple of rounds, well, that would be just peachy.

The problem was that all intel pointed to Fracture spending most of his time within a small radius of single-family homes in a still-dicey part of town. The area didn't frighten Manic in the least, but finding a place to set up and camp out to wait for a clean shot seemed unlikely. Luring the deev out of hiding didn't seem probable, either, so going into the hood remained his only option.

His doss indicated Fracture could typically be found at one of the 56 Tigers' drug dens, likely collecting money and booting people out as needed. Sometimes the Tigers brought him along on a collection or to push out anyone infringing on their turf. The deev seemed fearless; he kept to the nighttime hours like most deviants, but had no apparent issue showing off his particular skill set in public. NPD had responded to calls about him, but the deev had evaded each time, doubtless aided by the Tigers and their familiarity with the neighborhood.

Wednesday morning, Manic took a city bus to a street near the Tiger den where Fracture was believed to live more often than not. Already the sixcop's heart pounded merrily, the green backpack over his shoulder comfortably heavy with gear. Fracture had a weakness, Manic guessed; not one listed on his doss, but rather one based on what was *not* in the report.

After getting off the bus several blocks away, Manic walked the rest of the distance. He reached the street where the Tiger den was located and grinned with excitement. The October sun had only barely crested over the horizon, and the area was dead. Good. Manic walked confidently down the sidewalk on the opposite side of the Tiger house. Dropping to one knee beside a rusting parked car, he removed a compact shotgun-like weapon from the bag, set it down, then pulled out a slender, clear facemask as well. Manic fitted the mask over his face and activated the tiny air tank hanging below the chin of the mask.

Now the clock was ticking. Ten minutes of oxygen, not a second more.

Manic double-checked the load in the gun: tear gas, a smoker, and Cl-2. Perfect.

"Game on!"

He fired the first round into the Tigers' den.

The tear gas load pierced a front window and exploded. Yellow smoke billowed inside. Manic took deep, regular breaths to stay calm and focused as seconds later, shouts emanated from the house.

The front door crashed open. Three men dumped onto the lawn, frantically wiping their faces and gasping for air. A fourth figure nearly tore the door frame apart as he stumbled through it.

The man of the hour, Manic thought. Fracture.

Manic launched the next load, which exploded in the middle of the group. Thick gray smoke concealed them. Manic rushed across the street with the third round chambered.

One of the humans held a revolver, but was too choked to aim it. Manic casually broke the gangster's wrist, disarming him.

The sixcop came upon Fracture rubbing his eyes vigorously with his palms and roaring in pain. While the deviant was not actually larger than Manic had expected, the reality of his size still impressed him. Fracture stood six or more inches above the veteran sixcop, with several inches of breadth to his shoulders as well. He was shirtless, and the deev's musculature looked like polished stone.

As he screamed and tried to find his way through the choking gas and blinding smoke, Manic reached him. He jammed the barrel of the weapon into Fracture's mouth and fired.

The shell crashed into Fracture's mouth but yielded little blood; the deviant took what would have otherwise been a disfiguring or even lethal shot with little more than a grunt of surprise. Manic backed off and pulled a diamond-core knife from its sheath on his hip, preparing for a toe-to-toe if need be.

He didn't have to worry. The chlorine shell did its work quickly. Gas rocketed out of Fracture's mouth and, Manic knew, jettisoned into his lungs as well. In two seconds, Fracture fell to the ground, gargling on a scream as the poison suffused his airways. Manic stood and checked for the other Tigers, all of whom had cleared out of the area. He knew they'd be back eventually, but not soon—they couldn't see and would have a hard time breathing for several minutes. They'd be in no rush to leap into the concealing gray smoke dispersing over their front yard.

Fracture rolled on the ground and scratched at his throat, issuing inhuman cries of agony. While not enjoying the spectacle in and of itself, Manic felt no pity for the deviant; this was the type of beast who had already hurt and killed, and one day, maybe Lilly would be in his line of fire.

Manic would never torture a dog for kicks, either, but he'd have no compunction putting one down that bit his child.

Fracture's cries ended in skin-crawling silence. His lungs could no longer take in clean air as the chlorine did its work. Manic waited still until the Level Six stopped moving entirely, then dropped one of the coin-sized trackers on the dead man. The dead deviant.

Quickly Manic went back across the street, leaving the clear mask on until well clear of the gas and smoke. He heard a helicopter in the distance, closing fast, and wondered if it was his clean-up crew.

Stop and watch? He decided against it, the adrenalin in his system needing to get worked out before it manifested as puke, though that hadn't happened since his first year with LAPD. So he kept up his jog out of the neighborhood, eventually removing the mask and putting it back into his pack with the compact shotgun.

Twenty thousand, he thought. *I just made twenty thousand bucks for making the world a safer place.*

Laughing out loud, he jogged for ten miles before stopping for breakfast and paying for his first meal in years with his own money.

After an enormous, heart-stopping soggy breakfast at a dive several blocks from his place, he walked back to his apartment, showered, and called Lilly. No answer. He didn't leave a message, and suddenly his enjoyment of the morning's job drained out of him. He considered shopping for more mirrors, but discarded the idea; the wounds from his last bout were still healing. Standing in the middle of the apartment, his sec-boxes now stacked neatly along one wall, Manic's hands fell to his hips and he said aloud, "Son of a bitch."

Because, now what?

Weber hadn't prepared him for this part of the job. With NPD, he was surrounded by fellow officers, fellow soldiers. Men and women who were prepared to die in service to their city and families. Virtually all of them were divorced once, like him. Second marriages seemed to last, for reasons Manic could only guess. This new gig for the state left him with a sensation he could only relate to how it felt when Lilly went off to college—pride and emptiness all rolled into one vague ball of discomfort in his gut.

"Maybe it's just the bacon," he said, and gave himself a laugh.

At a loss, he dressed and left the apartment, squinting a little in the L.A. sunlight. He'd always been a night type of guy, and not until he reached the street did it dawn on him that he should probably get some sleep. He didn't turn back, though; he thought maybe the sunlight would improve his mood, or that seeing more people out and about would remind him that he wasn't as alone as he felt. It was Los Angeles, for crying out loud—the place reeked of people.

Manic blinked several times and laughed again once he realized where his feet had taken him. He even took a few steps back to let other customers in while he considered whether there was anything to gain by going inside, then went ahead and opened the door.

No one in the mailbox shop paid any attention to him as he meandered to his box and opened it up, fully anticipating it to be empty.

Instead, he found another envelope exactly like the one that had contained the doss on Fracture. Nothing else; no bundles of cash, no chip cards. Manic shrugged and stuffed the envelope into his coat before locking the mailbox door and heading outside, saying nothing to the same zitty kid behind the counter.

He ambled toward downtown for lack of any other pressing place to be, his fingers twitching to tear into the envelope and discover his next assignment. He chose an outdoor food court surrounded by lunch trucks and jammed with corporate types in their Monday best, downing fresh vegetable burritos and fried doughs of various shapes. He slid onto an unoccupied chair at a two-person table and scanned the area for surveillance. Finding none, he opened the envelope and shook out the contents.

Same as before, the envelope contained a few unmarked printed sheets and still photos. Attached to one photo, a yellow sticky note read in jagged script *1ˢᵗ payment posts tomorrow.*

Good enough for him. Manic crumpled the sticky note and shoved it in his pocket, then turned to the first photo.

"Meow," he said, peering at the deviant in the photograph. The photographer had gotten a clean photo, practically an actor's headshot, of Manic's next target.

He was, simply, a lion man.

The deev had long black hair that grew straight up off his head for a few inches before falling back down, reminding Manic of old pretty-boy glam-rock bands, the kind whose asses he always wanted to kick. The mouth was swollen and jutted out like a cat's, with obvious black whiskers springing from below his split nose. Manic could even see that the deev's eyes were yellow and slitted, and that buried beneath the thick hair, triangular ears perched on top of its head rather than on the sides where a normal human's would be.

"Okay," Manic said out loud. "Kitty kitty, I got it. No problem."

He went to the next photo.

"Oh," he said, not meaning to.

This photo showed the cat-man in action. His fingers were thick and padded, twice as big around as any normal person, and the reason was clear in the photo: the deev had retractable claws. Long ones. They spilled out of his fingers at least half the length of the fingers themselves. In the photo, the cat-man had downed two men and was in process of disemboweling two more. The photographer must have stayed put and out of the action, Manic reasoned. He didn't blame whoever the photographer was; Kitty Kitty would've made him a chew toy probably, had he been seen.

Manic put the photos aside and went for the printed pages.

The first offered a short history of the cat-man. Street name—Izanagi—his estimated age, last known location, previous locations, known and suspected omnihuman abilities. The cat-man wasn't overly tall, standing just under six-foot. Estimated striking force, 2,354 peak pounds—impressive. He'd been reported to be able to leap significant distances from a standstill, and was allegedly quite acrobatic. He was not known to carry weapons, which didn't surprise Manic; the deev had ten switchblades buried in his hands.

"Sounds good," Manic muttered, and replaced the doss in the envelope which he then returned to his jacket. He walked away from the food court and continued wandering the streets, already formulating a take-down plan for the cat.

A child's scream made him stop in his tracks, triangulate, then break into a run to his right. When he reached the source of the cry, his heart-rate slowed, and he grinned: a playground. The shriek had come from a toddler whose toy truck had been appropriated by another child. Two moms were already getting involved. Manic watched, waiting to see how they'd resolve it; attack each other, or correct their own children?

The moms opted for the latter, and peace was restored. The two toddlers played together then apart, together then apart, while the moms chatted each other up on the sidelines, casting frequent glances at the children.

Manic backed up and leaned against a wall, hands in his coat pockets, watching the scene. Such a normal, everyday routine playing out. The small playground had attracted moms and dads alike, many decked in athletic gear. The state government's sweeping social changes had allowed families that wanted to have just one working parent have a much easier time in doing so, and the parks reflected it.

Manic then imagined Izanagi crashing the party. Bounding into the sand from some distant rooftop and shredding through the families with those razor claws. It was, he realized suddenly, almost the same vision he'd had of Fracture at the park closer to his NPD station—as if the universe was reminding him of the stakes of failure.

"I'll get him," Manic whispered to the children across the street. "I'll get him for you."

The kids played and yelped and fought and cried and played again. Manic turned and went back the way he had come, aiming now for his apartment.

He had preparations to make.

*

By the time he took his foot off the gas pedal of the old van, Malikai had made it twenty miles from the gas station. At this time of night, traffic was not just sparse, it was all but nonexistent. The desert and hills around the highway were dark. No moon hung in the sky.

Red and blue lights flashed in the side mirrors. Malikai made his preparations as the van slowed. He slid the Tang dao out of its scabbard and placed it between the door and his left leg. He put on his sunglasses again and rolled down his window, scanning the landscape through the passenger window to the right. It seemed flat and empty.

Perfect. He did not relish what he had to do next, but recovering Julia Lawson took priority.

He eased the van onto the dirt shoulder and stopped, putting the vehicle in park. Gloves still on, he rested his hands out the open window.

A white spotlight blared painfully into the mirrors. The highway patrolman climbed out of his vehicle and approached, keeping his hand near his pistol.

"Evening," the cop said, switching on a thick black flashlight and shining it into Malikai's face.

"Good evening."

"You want to take your glasses off for me, sir?"

Sir. This one had been trained better than some.

Malikai had assumed the driver of the lifted pickup would call 911 after their encounter. The system was patched directly into the NPD lines. Anyone could report a suspected "D-free" deviant at any time: since all omnihumans were required by law to be registered and cataloged for their D-card, the mere appearance of deviance was reason enough to bring out the NPD for a quick scan of the suspect to make sure he or she had the chip implant. Humans abusing the 911 system received steep penalties, though; while a "sighting" *could* be called in, law enforcement preferred that the suspected deviant was also committing a crime, or at least seemed about to. There generally had to be some kind of threat perceived. Malikai could only guess what the driver had reported as soon as Malikai had left the gas station, but also trusted the man didn't embellish over-much; to do so and be caught at it would bring swift retribution from authorities for wasting their time and resources. Yes, this world hated deviants, but it at least had the good sense to focus most of its official energies on those who presented an immediate or deadly threat.

Malikai pulled his sunglasses off and met the officer's eyes.

"Is there a problem?"

The cop seemed to sigh. He lifted his other hand to the radio attached to his shoulder lapel, preparing to radio in. "You got your card, sir?"

Sir again. Malikai was impressed. And quite nearly regretful for what needed to happen here.

"I do," Malikai said.

"So you won't mind if I scan you real quick?"

"Of course not."

The cop gave him a professional nod. Strange, Malikai thought as he coiled his muscles, that this officer was treating him as almost human. He'd watched many at work in Phoenix, and few if any had shown such respect to deviants.

Perhaps this officer, like many humans, was related to an omnihuman himself. Such relatives sometimes held milder views on deviants. Other relatives of deviants went the opposite direction and became militant six-haters.

The officer's finger twitched toward the button on his radio.

Malikai sprang.

Reaching out the window, he grabbed the cop's shirt in two fists, and brought the human crashing face-first into the frame of the van door. The cop uttered a shocked growl, slumping momentarily in the vigilante's hands.

Malikai shoved the door open, into the cop, who was already reaching for his pistol. Before he could grab the weapon, Malikai swung behind him and locked the cop in a chokehold. He easily carried the cop to the other side of the van, applying pressure to the officer's windpipe and carotid artery. It took about a minute, but the cop soon slept, all fight leaving his body.

Malikai put the officer into the van and used his own handcuffs to shackle him to the welded rebar. He stripped the cop of all his gear—gun, Taser, radio, everything. Quickly, he ran to the patrol car and shut off all its lights before driving it off-road into the desert. He parked it behind a low mesquite tree where it would be difficult to see, then ran full speed back for the van as he saw headlights approaching. Malikai was back in the driver's seat and onto the road by the time the car passed.

The entire operation had cost him less than five minutes.

Malikai drove on, keeping to the speed limit—easy enough in the old van which could hardly get to sixty without rattling.

The cop woke up two minutes later. Malikai heard him scrambling for his gear, and coming up empty.

"Okay," he called through the partition. "Looks like you got me. What's up, man? What's next?"

"You'll live," Malikai said.

"Yeah? Hope you'll understand if I don't believe you."

"I do. But not all deviants lie. I give you my word, I will not harm you."

"All right. Where we headed?"

"I am trying to save a girl's life. You are an impediment. I must keep you out of my way long enough to achieve this goal. That is all."

"Maybe I could help. I *am* a cop, you know."

"No. I have broken your laws. Your people will come for me. I must get to my destination before they find us."

"You're making a big mistake, man," the cop said. "You know what the chances are of getting away with this?"

"Yes. They are better than you think. Please save your energy. I will not be persuaded."

"Okay. Sure thing." The cop went silent, but only for a moment. "I got two kids. You got kids?"

"No." Of course, that may or may not be true, Malikai thought. Perhaps he had several. Perhaps he had several *thousand*. Perhaps time would tell. He didn't dwell on it.

"Does it matter that I do?" the cop asked.

"No. As I said, you will live, whether you have children or not."

"Well, it's a crazy job." Malikai heard him shifting, as if trying to find a more comfortable position. "Those kids'll run you ragged, you know? Sometimes you want to slap them silly, and other times you just want to hug them so hard they break. Sometimes you want to do both at once, you know?"

"I do not."

"Never thought I'd love anything the way I love them," the officer went on as if he hadn't heard. "There's nothing I wouldn't do for them. Not one thing."

"And if they were deviants?"

The cop didn't answer. Not at first.

"Wouldn't change anything," he said after a lengthy pause, as if he had never considered the possibility. "Why? What did your family think of you?"

Something like pain wove through Malikai's dead organs. Yet it was not pain, not necessarily; or perhaps not physical.

What did his family think of him? He couldn't know—he had no more memory of a family than he did of a home or of children. And yet the cop's question triggered something, some unknown wound, maybe. Malikai seized on the sensation psychically, trying to trace its source.

Then, without warning, another sensation enveloped him: grief.

It came as an almost tangible thing, curling around his lifeless heart like a snake. If he'd needed to breathe, he would have gasped for air. Malikai fought hard against a desperate need to pull the van over and meditate, organize and then clear his thoughts, for this— this was a *memory*.

Unsolid and phantasmic, with no real sensory value—he could neither see nor otherwise sense a fact of the memory, but it was there, somewhere, creeping through his mind like an assassin, unseen but detected, and possibly deadly.

The grief mutated into something else. It took him several moments of focusing on the sensation to finally identify it, and even then, it was only a guess.

Guilt.

"Sorry," the cop said, and Malikai blinked. "I'm a nervous talker. I might not be able to stop. Hope you don't mind."

Malikai forced these newfound feelings aside with great effort. He wanted them, needed them badly, but could not afford to let his mind wander. There was a task at hand; a promise to keep.

"You are attempting to cover the sound of your efforts to free yourself from the handcuffs," Malikai said. "You may even succeed. But please believe me when I tell you that I will prevent you from leaving this vehicle before I am ready to release you. I am much faster and much stronger. You will not succeed. So please, try to relax and trust my word."

The cop sighed audibly, even through the partition. "I stood too close to your door, that's what happened."

"No. I am simply too fast. You did all you could be expected to do."

The cop barked a laugh. "Ha! Thanks. I'll put that in my report."

He fell silent, and Malikai took himself into a half-meditative state, unsure if he was trying to grasp the memory again or keep it at bay. Perhaps both.

The City of Angels beckoned. Malikai drove on in the night, and reached the heart of the city before dawn.

NINE

The latest crosstown bus Manic could take left the stop at 11:34 p.m. "They only come out at night," was a popular joke among normals, and Manic knew it wasn't true at all—deevs came out at all hours. During the day, those who looked like humans blended in. They were harder to spot. Like the brain-scrambler he'd run into the other morning or the red-shirted guy at the library, there were, unfortunately, plenty of deevs who could pass themselves off as normals, as Level Fours through Fives.

Happily, Izanagi did not fit that category. He'd be a night crawler, surely.

Manic mused as the bus thumped merrily along that there had to be some kind of stop-gap in place to prevent him from accidentally killing a normal. That whoever Weber worked for knew exactly what they were doing and could prevent civilian accidents. The reasoning was simple: NPD had to be above reproach. The kind of firepower they possessed and the operational latitude they were given required it.

Sure, the populace loved them—thanked them like soldiers returning home from war. But one wrong move, one accidental death of a normal, and things would get hairy for the NPD.

Not that it hadn't happened. Manic knew of at least three incidents in L.A. alone where norms had been killed during an apprehension. In two of them, the norms were criminals working with the deviant being sought after. The third had been a paparazzi photographer who got too close to a dude who could turn his entire body into a sort of living jackhammer, and the photographer had been swallowed in a sinkhole created by the deev.

But no deaths of normals could be blamed on the NPD directly. Nothing on record. Weber's people couldn't afford a misstep, Manic figured. He was using NPD gear, he had access to NPD medics, no one had asked him to return his NPD badge. They could call him an "independent contractor" or the laundry man for all it mattered— end of the day, this was an NPD sanctioned operation, or so it would appear to the public if they ever caught up with him.

Manic climbed off the bus near an industrial park at the far east end of the city after midnight. The landscape, just a mile or so shy of beginning to swoop upward into the foothills, stretched in a seemingly endless field of warehouses and semi-tractor trailers.

He waited for the bus to pull away, then scanned his surroundings. Nothing unusual that he could see. Half-moonlight and the white glow of parking lot lamps in the distance were his only source of light. Behind him, to the south, a dirt lot lay vacant, waiting for the right developer to turn it into something profitable. Ahead, to the north, a shipping company called Dockman Transportation seemed fairly quiet—he could pick out a few drivers smokin' and jokin' while younger guys loaded pallets into trailers.

Manic pulled out a collapsible night vision monocular and raised it. A neat little gadget, lighter and more compact than the combat models used by NPD. But the night vision yielded no new information, and after two minutes of searching, he shoved it back into a thigh pocket on his dark blue cargo pants.

"Here kitty kitty," Manic whispered, then snickered. "*God*, you're dumb, dude. Way to go for the obvious joke, dumbass."

He walked across the empty street to a chain link fence topped with razor wire delineating Dockman's property. Not bothering to try and conceal himself, Manic snapped open a titanium multitool and neatly snipped a slit in the fence, slipping through it unimpeded. Security at Dockman Transportation clearly wasn't going to be his biggest problem tonight.

According to the report in the envelope, Izanagi was believed to keep a nest on the roof of one of Dockman's warehouses, the kind of out-of-the-way corner where security might be lax but the theft of any needed food and water from the warehouses was unlikely to be missed—much of Dockman's trade came from grocers and farms.

The first fifty yards of property beyond the fence was nothing but scrub brush and weeds on a bed of hard packed dirt. Manic crossed it at a trot to get to the blacktop of the company's parking lot and driveways. Not much further, trailers not in use stood parked with their forward legs cranked down. Manic went to them for concealment, then peered around one corner. From this vantage, he could see the back of three warehouses. Activity was slow, guys loading or unloading pallets into or out of loading docks with forklifts of varying sizes. Much further out, he could see a smaller building with lights on in the windows, probably the main office.

Nothing moved on the roofs that he could see. Not surprising. Izanagi likely wouldn't be active until even later, when the fewest number of men would be at work.

Manic walked casually away from the rows of trailers, trusting the darkness to do most of his work for him. People zipping from shadow to shadow tended to attract attention from a man's peripheral vision. A guy strolling along at a leisurely pace did not. Manic never ceased to be amazed at how the mind—the human mind—worked when it came to stealth and evasion. During his stint with LAPD, he'd once had a buddy walk past a suspect five or six times. The suspect had crouched down in the middle of a white-gray driveway, curled up into a ball, and stayed still. Somehow, the cop—a respected vet— didn't notice him for several minutes. He was unable to explain it later, and the suspect hadn't turned out to be a deev, either. Laughing about it, the cop said he guessed it was just *so* ridiculously obvious that it never triggered the cop's brain.

So Manic didn't rush across the parking lot, nor did he do any *sweet ninja moves*, as Lilly liked to tease. He merely walked until he reached the dark side of one wall of the nearest warehouse. Grinning, he assessed the wall. No convenient ladder, but a rain drainage pipe and a few nooks and crannies would suffice. He ascended the wall carefully, now cautious about the amount of noise he was making. The eyes could be fooled, but the ears tended to pick up on oddities.

Reaching the edge of the roof, Manic peered carefully over the lip. A short wall, about a foot high, surrounded the perimeter, so there wouldn't be much cover close to the edge. On the roof, he spotted nothing unusual—air conditioning units and other standard rooftop machinery about which he knew little.

"I don't want to hurt you," a voice said.

Manic cursed and sank below the edge of the roof. Where had the voice come from? The roof, surely, but where? Dammit, the deev knew he was coming already.

Well, nothing to be done about it now. He vaulted onto the roof and pulled his gun, scanning the immediate area. "That's good," he answered as his heart began to dance with the excitement of battle. "So just stand still and let me do my business and go home, whaddya say?"

"You don't know what you're getting into."

Manic slowly twisted his body to one side, pivoting on the tips of his Lalo boots. He lifted the pistol with both hands. There. The voice had come from his right, probably behind one of the air conditioning units.

"Come on out, kitty. Don't make it hard."

"Whoever you are," the voice came back, "you are in over your head. Go. Now."

Manic took a cramped duck-walking step closer. Izanagi's voice had a deep timbre that surprised him, as if the six had studied Shakespeare or something. At the same time, the words came out slightly muted, as if he had a mouthful of cotton. Manic figured the deev's disfigured, leonine face was too blame.

Not that he cared.

"Look, man," Manic said to cover the sound of taking another step forward. "I got a thing to do here tonight. Come on out and save us both a lotta trouble, huh?"

"I said I don't want to hurt you," Izanagi said from his hiding place.

Manic twisted slightly to the right again, from where the voice had come from. "Why don't you come show me how you can hurt me, huh?"

"I most certainly can, but do not wish to. Please don't make me do this."

"You're all heart, buddy. I have been so advised. Now how about y—"

Izanagi flew at him from the darkness . . . on Manic's *left*.

Shit, Manic thought, just as the full weight of the deviant crashed into him. It was like the cat-man had thrown his voice in another direction like a ventriloquist.

Manic's pistol clattered away, sliding along the rooftop well out of reach. Izanagi came at him like a possessed thing, clawed hands raking and tearing at Manic's body.

Manic managed to kick one boot into what he sincerely hoped were the deviant's genitals. One never could tell with deevs.

The kick hit home, and Izanagi roared. In the brief opening, Manic scrambled backward on his hands, his shirt hanging in tatters off his chest. Beneath it, the woven Kevlar vest supplied by Weber's people showed scratches, but no deep damage. If the deviant had gone for his face—

He had no time to lunge for his gun. Izanagi quickly recovered from Manic's blow and sprang toward the sixcop, arms outstretched. Manic evaded to the side and reached for the diamond-core knife under his armpit, opposite his empty pistol holster. The knife cost close to a cool million, Manic knew, because on the street, they fetched two million or more. They weren't standard issue even for NPD because of the expense. How Weber's people came across them, Manic couldn't guess, but he was damn happy to have it. The blades cut through nearly anything.

The weapon's grip fit snugly in his fist, with a studded guard covering his knuckles over the bandages. Izanagi either had never seen a diamond-core or didn't care, as he spun toward Manic and attacked again.

Trying to block and close with the deviant wouldn't be possible, Manic sensed that immediately. The cat-man looked like an old cartoon character Manic couldn't quite remember, a blur of arms and claws so fast he may as well have been holding a solid shield. The deviant moved too quickly for Manic to find an opening, so he was forced to backpedal, keeping a boxing guard up to cover his head and body as best he could. Any second now, Izanagi would get close enough to put Manic's lights out for good and for proper.

And Manic loved it.

Though he didn't notice in the heat of the moment, he was smiling . . . possibly even *cheering* the deviant on. This, *this* was better than real life, better than a backward-thinking daughter and office politics and women. At any moment, the deviant might land the one blow that would tear his head from his body, and Manic savored each passing second in which he remained alive. The moments stretched out for him despite the speed of the battle. He breathed in, he breathed out, and right now, this moment, he *lived*. Then the next, and the next, with each possibly being his last. He even thought, remotely, that he could have taken more time with Fracture, drawn out the fight, enjoyed it more . . .

Manic's heel touched the short wall surrounding the roof. When Izanagi's next swing came, either it would connect with Manic's face, or Manic would have to dodge two stories to the pavement below.

He chose the drop.

Izanagi swung madly for him. Manic twisted to the side. The motion carried him over the roof, plummeting twenty feet to the ground.

Manic relaxed his muscles as best he could and aimed his feet down, keeping his knees bent. He hit hard on the balls of his feet, then let himself collapse to the side. This technique had taken a long time to master, and it didn't guarantee a lack of injury by any stretch, but it might keep him alive.

Manic's left shoulder crunched against the blacktop and he felt his left knee and ankle give way. He bellowed uncontrollably as pain snapped loose in his joints. If nothing was broken in half, it would be a miracle. Still—he knew instinctively that he'd fared better than most people without his training would have.

Miracles were in short supply. Izanagi landed effortlessly at his feet, having leaped from the roof, claws extended and curled, anxious for Manic's throat to hang from them.

"Crap," Manic groaned.

Izanagi hesitated, breathing hard, glaring at his prey. "I warned you," the deev said through sharp teeth. "I told you to go."

Manic tried to pull himself away from the creature. "Yep, roger that. Good call."

Two men appeared from around the nearest corner of the building. The larger of the two, wearing a puffy green vest over a plaid overshirt, called out, "Hey, what's going on out here?"

"NPD!" Manic shouted without thinking. "Get back!"

Izanagi didn't even glance at the men, who stopped in their tracks and traded glances. The deviant only continued to stare at him. Something like a sneer or smirk crossed his feline features.

"NPD," he said. "I thought you people stuck together."

"Guess I'm a rogue cop." Manic shuffled backward, trying to reach a silent forklift. Not much cover, but the cage-style cockpit was better than lying on the blacktop.

"NPD does not *go* rogue," Izanagi said, matching each of Manic's shuffles with a graceful step forward. He still ignored the two warehouse workers, who hadn't moved—paralyzed, it seemed, by the presence of a real live deviant on the property, one whose hands looked like they'd sprouted buck knives.

"First time for everything." Manic reached the front tire of the forklift. Summoning the will to resist the pain of the action, he leaped as fast as he could and flung himself into the single seat.

Izanagi followed him, gripping the protective bars surrounding Manic and leaning close. "What exactly do you think you're doing, cop?"

His breath smelled of fish. Manic winced. He leaned back against the seat, breathing hard.

"What am I doing?"

"Yes. What are you doing."

Manic faced the cat-man. It truly felt like he was looking into the face of a lion. Manic took another breath.

"Distracting you."

His left hand shot out, aimed for the deviant's throat. The blade struck the deviant just below the Adam's apple. If he'd been human, the tip of the blade would have come out the other side of his neck, severing his spinal cord. But Izanagi was no human, and the blade did only slightly more than infuriate him.

The cat-man roared and knocked Manic's hand aside, though the sixcop managed to hold onto the knife as it ripped from the deviant's throat. Izanagi crouched down, disappearing from Manic's line of sight. Manic dared to think for a moment that he'd scared the deviant off.

Then the forklift lifted off the blacktop.

"Holy *shit!*" Manic shouted.

The forklift went airborne.

Izanagi's accompanying roar Doppler-shifted as the machine flew away from him, Manic still in the seat. The forklift hit the asphalt forty yards from where it had stood, crashing to the ground with a metallic crunch unlike anything Manic had ever heard. He barely managed to keep his limbs from being pinned beneath the iron cage.

"So *that* really just happened," Manic muttered, pulling himself upward out the left-hand side of the driver's seat. The forklift had landed on its right side, and it would take another forklift to get the machine righted again. Manic wondered for the first time if maybe this gig wasn't all he thought it would be.

He spotted Izanagi walking toward him, taking his time, shoulders pulled back in a menacing strut. Manic understood then that the deviant was a cat in more ways than one—Izanagi was toying with him now, batting him around like a mouse.

And NPD would be coming soon. Not the cleanup crew that Weber had promised when he activated his transmitter, but the regular guys. His teammates. The two warehouse workers had vanished. Manic knew they'd be calling 911 right now. In just a few minutes, NPD Airborne would be en route. He couldn't let that happen. Not only would it possibly negate payment for the job . . . man, it would make him *look* bad in front of the guys.

Death first.

"That all ya got?" Manic called, laughing. It wasn't false. He really felt the entire scenario needed a good laugh, just to break the tension if nothing else. If it had the added effect of pissing off the six, so much the better.

It did. Izanagi broke into a short sprint, then leaped. He covered twenty yards in one bound as Manic snaked his right hand behind his back.

The instant—perhaps even the instant before—the deviant's feet touched the ground, Manic dropped an entanglement grenade at his feet.

Even as Izanagi was pulling back one hand to swing at Manic's head, the net bomb went off and spread its tendrils up. Nanosensors embedded in the gummy substance sought the deviant's body rather than Manic's, whose tactical vest contained repulsors to aim the net at the nearest warm body other than his own. The net spread fast, fast enough that Izanagi's eyes widened when found himself tottering in place, then falling to the ground with a strangled roar.

Manic sat back against the wrecked forklift, catching his breath. Izanagi struggled against the netting, which only made matters worse for him. The strands thickened and twisted like a child's paper finger trap, making his entrapment worse with each twitch of his muscles.

Gritting his teeth against the pain in his leg and shoulder, Manic pulled a cartridge the size of a cell phone from one of his cargo pockets and pressed a button. Short, jagged spikes popped out from one side. He leaned down and pressed the device into the webbing.

"Nothing personal," he said.

Izanagi stared at him through the mess of cords partially obscuring his face. Manic pressed a second button on the device and stepped away. Izanagi screamed—or tried to through the webbing— as bursts of lethal electricity shot through the web and into his body. Manic watched him impassively, fingering the transmitter in his pocket, waiting.

A minute later, the deviant died. Manic peeled back the protective cover on the transmitter and tapped it before dropping it on top of the body.

Time to go. He looked around the property, orienting himself, and limped quickly toward the slit he'd made in the fence. Glancing behind him as he went, he saw more warehouse workers starting to peer around corners and peek from behind trailers. Many had phones to their ears, or else pointed his direction, recording.

Well, not his problem. Their phones wouldn't catch much at this distance and in the dark, anyway. He'd followed orders. Now it was up to Weber's people to—

A helicopter zoomed by fast overhead. It looked Army green, though it was hard for Manic to be sure in the darkness. The copter flew so low he could practically see the team crouching within. Manic reached the fence, but paused to watch the helicopter land near the overturned forklift. An NPD team scattered from out of its cabin, ordering the onlookers away. One team member tossed a grappling hook on to the roof where Manic had fallen, and ascended with crisp efficiency. A moment later, he shimmied down the rope and expertly unhooked the grapple with technique Manic did not recognize.

The pistol, Manic realized. He'd gone up to retrieve the pistol. Somehow they'd known it was there.

Despite himself, Manic tilted his head back. Drones, of course. Someone with an eye in the sky keeping track of him. But for how long? All day, every day? That seemed unlikely. Satellite? Too expensive.

The team loaded Izanagi onto the helicopter. It was already lifting off as the last team member hopped on board. The helicopter zipped away into the night. The entire operation had gone down in less than a minute.

Nice, Manic thought. That wasn't any old NPD team, he knew. He and his buddies were good—really good. But they weren't some cleanup crew. These guys had clearly trained specifically for these missions: secure a zone, clear the evidence, and get out.

It made him wonder, briefly, what crimes a team like that could scrub away in short order.

Weber's people certainly had a budget to work with. Odd, though, that the team couldn't help him take down the deviant. Why not just hire an NPD team to do the dirty work in the first place?

Any number of reasons, Manic thought as he limped across the street. NPD wasn't trained to be covert, for starters. They were front-line cops, guys who got called when a crime was already in progress. Stealth and assassination weren't in their playbook any more than they were in LAPD's.

That made sense enough. Still . . . anyone with the power to get an NPD team to clean up after a night like this surely had the power to marshal more resources than an old cop with a history of insubordination.

Unless they weren't NPD at all. Just dressed like them to provide cover?

The angles dizzied him, and Manic put the thoughts away. He'd followed orders. That was that.

Manic walked alongside the road toward the city, debating whether or not to stick a thumb out to catch a ride. He didn't bother. No traffic here this time of night anyway, and Manic knew he didn't look like the kind of guy who people would pick up. Los Angeles might be safer than ten years ago, but that didn't make people stupid enough to pick up a scruffy mess like him.

He used his phone to call for a cab to meet him some miles away. The cab pulled up just as he made it to his destination, a convenience store and gas station on the outskirts of town he'd marked during his earlier bus ride. He gave the cabbie a fifty and told him to wait for a second, which the cabbie happily did. Manic grabbed a few beers and a few sodas from the store, unsure which he felt like having, and finally got into the cab. He gave an address down the street from his apartment.

His ankle and knee burned with fracture wounds—the irony of the word eluded him—his shoulder ached like it had a migraine, and his entire body felt pummeled into one enormous bruise after his landing in the forklift.

In short, he felt great.

It took him twice if not three times as long to climb the stairs to his second-floor apartment, but he smiled the entire way.

*

Los Angeles was different than Phoenix, Malikai had heard. Cleaner, more sanitized and crime-free. It had been a marked turnaround from years past; violent crime plummeted, deviant sightings went down, once squalid areas now thrived or were on the verge of thriving. If true, it certainly would be a change from Phoenix, which despite attempts to follow suit, had only fallen deeper into financial and emotional depression.

But he had never heard of "Sal's." Who was he? A deviant? Perhaps a Level Seven, of the type Thud joyfully warned him about?

Malikai cruised past the Los Angeles city limits proper an hour before sunrise. He thought he could smell the sunlight approaching, then decided it must be whatever distant ocean air wafted into the van, though he doubted it was possible to smell the ocean from here. Mildly fascinated by his first new surroundings in several years, he scanned the city streets, taking the first opportunity he could to exit the freeway and examine the neighborhoods. Indeed, the bits he'd overheard about L.A. being on the upswing seemed true, even in the darkest part of the night.

He found what he was looking for not three minutes into his patrol, which pleased him; he'd thought it would take longer, perhaps even into the following night. A hooded person rushed down a neighborhood street, arms closed tightly around his or her chest. From one sleeve, only for a moment, something like a red tentacle peeked out, and quickly got withdrawn. The figure glanced in every direction, noted Malikai in the brown van, and tried to go faster.

Malikai sped up, passing the hooded person. A half-block ahead, he pulled up to the sidewalk and parked.

"I am getting out for a moment," Malikai told the officer in back. "You do not know where we are. You could call for help, but you may not like who answers the call. Again, let me assure you, your life is no danger."

"*Yours* will be if you don't let me out of here, sir."

"I understand."

Malikai got out of the van and moved swiftly and silently to the sidewalk. The hooded figure stopped short several yards away as Malikai crossed his line of sight. In the van, the cop didn't make a sound.

The vigilante raised his empty palms and softly announced, "Six."

The figure, already turning to go another direction, stopped when Malikai spoke. Malikai didn't move; he knew not everyone announcing themselves as a fellow deviant was actually so. The hooded being had to assume Malikai could just as likely be a trap.

But Malikai was alone and that helped. The hooded figure appraised him. Malikai could barely make out a blood-red visage inside the hood.

"Shix," the figure said—*six*, or something like it. Malikai decided it was male, or something approximating male; the voice sounded like it had come through a wet sponge, dank and moist.

"Sal's," Malikai said. "Where is it?"

The deviant nodded slightly and issued what Malikai took to be a sigh of understanding. He jerked his head to one side, gesturing away from the street. Malikai followed him between houses, down an alley he would have otherwise expected to be full of debris, but instead had been swept clean. Whoever ran Los Angeles these days, he or she was doing quite the job.

Out of the glare of an orange streetlight, hidden in shadows, the hooded deviant spoke.

"What do you need?" the deviant asked.

It sounded to Malikai as if he was gargling milk as he spoke, the words more a collection of slurred noises: *whaaa ewww ewww eeee?*

"Information," Malikai said. "I'm looking for a girl who was kidnapped in Phoenix. I was told she might be here now, in this city."

Some sound that might have been anger rose from the deviant's mouth. Even standing so close together, Malikai could only make out vague inferences of features on the deviant's red face.

The deviant replied, but Malikai couldn't quite make the words out: *huh jehhellmeh cluhhh.*

Malikai didn't push the poor creature. "This Sal. Is he the one responsible?"

A damp perversion of a laugh issued from the deviant. From between whatever mucosal substance coated the deviant's throat, Malikai thought he could interpret the words, "Sal is an angel. Follow Broadway west. Find the—"

And then a sound like *kaa-hey*. Malikai repeated it. The six sighed at itself and tried the word again, slower. Malikai spoke it back.

"Cat . . . cat hay . . . cat . . . caff. Café?"

The six nodded.

"Sal's Café," Malikai said, frowning. It didn't sound like an impregnable omnihuman fortress.

The deviant nodded again, and Malikai returned the gesture. "Thank you. Get home now. Stay safe."

A thin tentacle slipped from the deviant's sleeve and lightly touched the back of Malikai's hand. The squirming appendage was warm, but not wet. The deviant curled the tentacle gently around Malikai's palm, where it pulsed twice.

A handshake. Malikai wondered how often the deviant experienced human touch.

"Shix," the deviant said.

"Six," Malikai said.

They parted, Malikai to the van and the deviant down the alley. Malikai suddenly and sincerely hoped the creature would get home safely, wherever that home might be—a culvert somewhere, or a dry drainage pipe if he was lucky. As Malikai started the van, it occurred to him that he did not remember hoping for the well-being of other omnihumans previously during his tenure as a vigilante in Phoenix.

He had met deviants, he had fought deviants, and he had aided deviants; never before now could he remember caring about them. Perhaps it had been the six's handshake; he, too, had not experienced nonviolent touch in a very long time.

"Thank you," Malikai said to the cop through the partition as he got the engine going.

"No problem," the cop said sarcastically.

"We could have been outside a police station."

"Ha. That seemed unlikely, sir."

Malikai nearly smiled. On a whim, he opened Nicholas Lawson's home phone screen and stared at the app icons. Surely there was something here that could help. The vigilante knew of technology like the internet, given its ubiquity, but he never had cause to learn how to use it. He'd been able to figure out the swipe-and-tap system as readily as any toddler, to be able to bring up pictures of young Julia, but beyond that, his skills were lacking.

Malikai tapped a map icon and managed, after several frustrating minutes, to locate Broadway and its approximate direction from where he sat in the van. He dropped the phone into the seat beside him and drove toward the multi-laned Broadway Road before heading west toward the coast. Traffic had picked up, and he blended almost seamlessly into it, searching for—for what? Whatever secret deviant lair "Sal's Café" referred to? How would he know it when he saw it?

"You are different than the others," Malikai said as he drove as slowly as seemed reasonable. "Why did you treat me with such respect?"

"It keeps everyone cool," the cop said. "Most of the time. I got no problem with deevs, not unless they're threatening someone else."

Yet you still call them *deevs*, Malikai noted, but didn't bother to point it out. Such casual prejudice was the norm.

"There are not many like you," Malikai said.

"No. I guess not. But most people would say there aren't many like you, either, so."

"What do you mean."

The cop hesitated before speaking. "I don't think you're going to kill me. I believe you. I'm still pretty pissed, and I'm going to do my best to arrest you the first chance I get. But I trust you."

That may or may not be true, Malikai supposed. The cop sounded unafraid, for sure; but whether he truly believed Malikai's word or was merely trying to keep the vigilante calm while he plotted his escape, Malikai couldn't tell. It didn't matter, ultimately—he'd been compliant.

"You would otherwise believe I would harm you because we do not look alike."

"Well, when you put it like that it sounds pretty bad," the cop said. "But c'mon, you got to be fair, here. Guys like you, you're loaded weapons. I don't know what *you* personally can do, but I've seen things out there that make me afraid for the human race. And I read somewhere that deevs are more prone to mental problems. Big ones. Like being sociopaths or developing god complexes. And, sir, no offense, but that jives with everything I've ever seen on the job. The fact that I'm being held against my will by a deviant isn't helping me consider another side to the story, if you don't my saying."

"I see."

"Do you? Because it's nothing personal. As long as you're not going to go breathing fire on my kid's school or releasing some kind of sarin gas out of your asshole, we'll get along just fine. But you can't fault people for being scared. We don't know how powerful you can be."

Malikai said nothing, but inwardly agreed. What *were* the limits of a six's power?

"But whatever you are, whatever you can do," the cop went on, "you're wrongfully imprisoning a sworn law enforcement officer. So you'll have to forgive me if I'm not feeling real charitable towards deevs right now."

"You will be released soon," Malikai said. "I give you my word."

"Splendid."

Malikai almost smiled at the sarcasm. He was starting to appreciate its rough charms. Maybe one day he'd learn to use it himself.

A few minutes later, he found the deviant's lair he'd been looking for. It turned out to be an easy process, primarily because there was a sign on the building announcing it.

In a building conveniently labeled, located on the northwest corner of an otherwise unremarkable line of shops, sat Sal's Café.

Malikai took the next left turn available to him, convinced there must be a mistake. A mistake, or worse—some kind of trap?

Turning the big van around in a parking lot, he reversed course and headed east until he came upon the little café again, earning horns from behind as he slowed.

"Sounds like you're pissing people off," the officer said.

"Indeed. That appears to be my special deviant power."

The cop laughed, sounding surprised at himself for doing so.

Malikai maneuvered the van into a small parking lot and sat in silence, staring at the café. The façade was traditional for southern California: white stucco, a little dingy and dusty, but otherwise unmarred. It may have been repainted not many years ago, for there were no mismatched patches of white to cover up graffiti. A yellow canvas awning of serviceable repair shaded the breadth of the red brick sidewalk, hanging above windows with standard-issue blinds tilted half-open. The neon sign above the awning announced this was, in fact, Sal's Café.

But this couldn't be it. *Could not.*

Sal had to be a deviant of some power to be known so readily on the street. And for that same reason, he couldn't be some small-time restaurateur.

Then, as Malikai silently watched the café, he realized little foot traffic passed directly in front of the coffee shop. People at the intersection west of the café all crossed the street first if they were headed east, bypassing the café all together. No one seemed overt about it; Malikai noted a few curious glances from pedestrians from the other side of the street, but even that might have been happenstance. He didn't believe that, though.

People—normal fours and fives—were avoiding walking in front of the café.

"What's up, what's going on?" the officer said. "What're you doing up there?"

Malikai peered up at the now-blue sky. It appeared to be the start of a perfect southern California day. Joyful sunlight beamed into the van's windshield. The scent of the ocean—if possible, Malikai still wasn't sure—came in slightly stronger now than before. Businesspeople strode quickly with their briefcases, a handful of teenagers shouldered packs on their way to classes, and city custodians swept sidewalks. They all looked perfectly normal, by their definition.

He drove away, searching for a place to ditch the van.

"I'm going to leave you soon," Malikai said as he drove. "I will park the van and go. I strongly recommend you wait quite some time before calling for help. I know you will have to search for me, but such a search will be futile. Do you understand?"

"Sure thing."

"I also apologize for how I have treated you. But my mission is more important. A girl's life is at stake."

"You could have called the cops, remember?"

"The authorities had already been called."

Malikai spotted what he needed: a shopping mall. He pulled into its parking garage and followed a corkscrew driveway to the rooftop.

"Unfortunately," he continued, "they were unable to help. I have sworn to find her."

He put the van into park and shut off the engine.

"Maybe *I* can help," the officer said. He may have even been sincere.

"Thank you," Malikai said. "But no."

He scanned the rooftop parking, planning his route away from the van.

"I do not see anyone nearby," he reported to the cop. "But the area will be busy within the hour. I suggest calling for help in approximately that time."

"So we're somewhere commercial. Strip mall or something."

Malikai made no comment. He double-checked his disguise and grabbed the Tang dao. He put a gloved hand on the door handle, but paused.

"Officer. I appreciate the work you do. You have volunteered to protect the innocent. That is honorable. Sometimes, however, the innocent look nothing like you."

"Hey—!"

Malikai climbed out of the van as the cop called for him to wait. Quickly, with his hood up and sunglasses on, he tucked the scabbard down one leg of his pants and hurried to get away from the van before the cop started making enough noise to attract attention. But he didn't hear anything as he left. The cop would be safe soon enough; right now, putting distance between himself and the van mattered most.

He thought he could feel Julia Lawson calling for him.

TEN

The smile Manic had worn the night before disappeared the next morning.

He woke up on his couch, groaning. His fight with Izanagi had taken a bigger toll on his body than the beers and soda could numb the night before. It took him ten minutes to gather enough steam to swing his feet onto the floor. He sat there for a number of additional minutes, ignoring his bladder, trying to rub the ache in his body out through his eyes. It didn't work. He'd been awake for far too long yesterday.

Muttering, he finally made himself stand and take care of his usual routine. This didn't amount to much—take a leak, splash some water on his face, and brush his teeth with a brush that might've been older than his daughter. Done and done.

Having showered again when he got home last night, Manic stood in the middle of the apartment, glaring at the empty NPD security boxes, unsure what to do next. Just like yesterday. He was used to walking to work, but that was the one place he wasn't supposed to go anymore. So now what?

He thought of the mailbox place. What were the chances a third assignment was already there? Unlikely . . . but then Weber had proven himself to be nothing if not efficient. It had taken Weber, what, two or three hours to go from the death of Fracture to putting the order in for the Izanagi hit. Manic was twelve hours removed from Izanagi's death; maybe Weber had sent the next gig.

"Nah," he said out loud, thinking of his payment. Forty grand already he'd made, and that was enough. He wasn't a kid anymore. Executing an apprehension with his wagon team was one thing, but this lone wolf routine . . . it was a lot tougher on the ol' bod than he'd assumed.

Manic shuffled out of the apartment, trying to stretch out his sore muscles as he went. The walk, though stiff at first, limbered him up some, and he felt in better spirits as he moved.

Doesn't forty-K cover it? he wondered. That was enough to get Lilly taken care of. Sure, more hits and more money would be nice, but in just a day or so's worth of work, he'd done what he needed to do for her. What any dad would do. This could be the end of it right here. Hell, he could probably even get his job back right where left it the other day, surely Weber could handle that.

Manic blinked in surprise as he realized he'd entered the mail shop. This morning, there was a girl working behind the counter, maybe Lilly's age. Or the age of his toothbrush. The shop was empty otherwise.

"Morning," he said.

The girl smiled dumbly and went on swiping on her phone. Manic shrugged as he walked to his box. He wasn't a morning person either.

Despite his considerations to quit while he was ahead, it felt like Christmas again—or what he presumed Christmas must feel like—as he opened the box and pulled out two envelopes. One was the same type as that which had held Izanagi's dossier, and a quick thrill zapped through Manic's body. He tucked the envelope into his half-zipped coat, then felt the contents of the second envelope, a simple #10 size with no markings. He felt something like a credit card in that one, perhaps shrouded in a sheet of paper or two.

Intrigued, he locked the box and headed out of the shop without a glance at the clerk, who repaid the favor. He went to the back side of a nearby Walgreens, sat—slowly—on a parking berm, and opened the #10.

It was a credit card, all right. His full name glared right up at him in raised letters, which he ran a thumb over. Brand new. So this was how his payment would work; no mob-like drops in the middle of the night, no clandestine paper bag hand-offs to Vic's. Just a straight up legit credit card.

Debit card, Manic corrected, as he flipped through the paperwork in the envelope. It would work as either one. He could withdraw cash—$1,000 a day—from any ATM worldwide; and up to the account's then-current value from a teller if he wished. His first and second payments were in the account, free and clear: forty grand for less than two days' work. The paperwork, which was not official in any way and had clearly come from a run-of-the-mill office printer, instructed him that if he lost the card, he needed to put a note in the box ASAP, and a new one would be issued.

"Nice," Manic mumbled, and put the card into his wallet, the paperwork and envelope into his coat.

Manic withdrew his limit from the next ATM he came to as he walked toward his apartment; no problems there, the PIN worked just as it was supposed to, and Manic found himself accepting—or, perhaps, *believing*—that this new job was the real thing.

Flush with holding a grand in cash in one hand, Manic pulled out his phone and called Lilly. She didn't answer.

"Hey Lil, it's your dad. I wanna take you out for breakfast this morning, okay? Meet me at Dale's. It's, uh . . . ten o'clock now, I'll be there at 10:30. Okay? See ya."

Smiling, Manic walked the few blocks to Dale's, a sticky, overcrowded 24-hour diner where for most people the service was terrible but the food worth waiting for. Manic was not "most people." Less than three seconds after walking in, one of the cooks called from his window, "Hey, Manic's here! Somebody clean a table, hustle hustle, oo rah!"

Manic tipped the cook a nod and shuffled to an empty booth that hadn't yet been cleared. A few people waiting in line to be seated scowled. Manic passed them by without a look. They could wait. They could wait until one of them damn near got his legs blown off by a high-powered six while saving the life of the owner-chef of a crummy diner like Dale's. He sat down at the booth, which was currently adorned with crumpled napkins and two plates of crumbs. Manic kept his hands in his coat pockets and rested his head back on the tall booth seat, eyes closed.

"You look like hell," a sassy voice interrupted his rest.

Manic grinned and sat up. "Mornin', Annie."

Annie the server wasn't much older than Lilly in age. In life experience, however, she might've been older than Manic, and it showed on her face. Manic didn't know a lot about Annie, but knew enough that he'd do whatever it took to ensure Lilly never ended up like her. Annie's black hair showed strands of gray already, and lines spidered out from the corners of her eyes. She'd been pretty, Manic could see. Whatever had happened between here and pretty, he could only guess. Drugs, probably. And a slow recovery. She looked clean now, very much like a young woman trying hard to get her shit together.

Manic knew the feeling. He decided to leave her one hell of a tip.

"What'll it be, big guy?" Annie asked, giving him a smile that showed a tooth missing far back on the right side.

"One metric ton of eggs and three and half pigs of bacon."

"Coffee with that?"

"You know how to take care of me."

"Coming up, big guy."

For no good reason, it delighted him that she called him that. Annie bawled at a busser to clean Manic's table, which happened with all haste. Manic checked his phone. Ten-thirty-three. No Lilly.

Maybe she wouldn't come. She rarely felt the need to jump when summoned. Then again, it was only 10:33 . . . 10:34 now. Not late. Maybe she had a class, or was sleeping off an all-nighter, or—

Manic leaped for the coffee as soon as Annie set it down. It burned his mouth and felt perfect. He hoped it would scald the taste of frustration out of him.

The eggs and bacon, along with four slices of toast, showed up much sooner than it should have, and the other diners knew it. They also knew better than to bring it up.

"You getting old, big guy?" Annie asked as she set the meal in front of him.

"Sure feels like it," Manic agreed, and barely remembered to use a fork for his first bite of the eggs which sat steaming under his nose.

Annie cocked out a hip. "Rough night at the office?"

"You could say that, but probably shouldn't."

"Righty-right." Annie thumped his shoulder. "Enjoy your eats."

"Hey, if you see Lilly coming in . . ."

Annie smiled. The gesture was warm, but on her haggard face it came off awkward and tired. "I'll send her right over, big guy."

She left Manic to his food and thoughts. The breakfast landed perfectly in his gut. Manic devoured every bite in under fifteen minutes, washing it down with two glasses of water and three cups of Dale's hottest black coffee.

Then it sat in his stomach and hardened as he checked his phone again and realized Lilly wasn't coming. All semblance of his good mood gone, Manic pulled out his wallet and dropped a fifty on the table for Annie before standing.

He crashed into Lilly.

"Whoa!" she cried as Manic's hand flew reflexively to his holstered 9 millimeter.

Manic relaxed and said her name. Lilly eyed him.

"Easy does it, copper," she said. "I got your message on the bus and got here as soon as I could. You leaving?"

"No no no!" Manic dropped to the springy bench seat and gestured to the opposite side of the table. "I got time. All kindsa time. Sit down."

Lilly slid into the seat and arranged her backpack, a red leather job sprouting sprigs of thread. Annie came over with fresh coffee and a dish of creamers. She and Lilly said hi to each other as Manic considered Lilly's mode of transportation. When Annie had gone, he said, "You said you were on the bus?"

"Sure."

"Where's the Honda?"

"Sorry baby, I had to crash that Honda."

Lilly grinned at him. Manic chuckled back. It was a line from *Pulp Fiction*, one of his favorite movies from when he was a kid, still learning how to be a collector like Vince and Jules.

"No, but really," he said.

Lilly shrugged. "Sold it."

"Sold? Lil!"

"Hey, I'm not turning tricks yet, that should make you happy."

His fist slammed down on the table before he could think to stop it. The dishes rattled—and so did Lilly.

"That ain't funny."

"Sorry," Lilly said through a frown. "Jesus."

Manic collected himself. "Look . . . just—here."

He took out his wallet again, and shoved the entire rest of his cash toward her. $950.00. Lilly looked at it like it was a dead animal.

"What's this?"

"Money. Take it."

"Where'd you get cash like that?"

"New job," Manic said without thinking.

"What kind of job? *You* turning tricks now?"

"Lilly, dammit. Just take the money. I'll be getting more, I've *got* more, let me take care of this school thing for you. I got enough to cover the whole thing, or pretty damn close, okay?"

"Okay!" Lilly said brightly, shocking Manic. His shock pivoted to understanding when she added, "Just tell me what the new job is."

"Can't do that."

"Ooo, top secret, huh?" Lilly pushed the money back toward him. "Then I don't need this."

"You gotta finish school."

"I will."

"I don't mean when you're sixty."

"Nothing wrong with sixty."

"Lil—"

"Dad, there are bigger things going on," Lilly said. "Did you hear about the guy who got killed last night?"

Manic groaned and sat back in the seat. "You'd have to be more specific."

"He was an omnihuman who—"

"You mean a deev."

"Omnihuman."

"A six."

"Whatever," Lilly said, her expression darkening. "You know what he used to do? You would have liked him, Dad. You know what he'd do? He went after pedophiles and kidnappers. He'd hunt them down, Dad. He went after real criminals. *Real* monsters. What'd you do last night? Beat up some kids with too many toes for your liking?"

"Matter of fact, *I* was out protecting the world, too! Fancy that."

Lilly leaned over the table, coffee forgotten. "Dad, this guy . . . he lived on the street, he lived on a rooftop somewhere, and he survived by eating the scraps other people threw away. When he wasn't trying to keep food in his stomach, he was hunting down a gang of human slavers. Now he's gone and those pieces of shit get to keep doing their thing. So go ahead and tell me about—"

Manic grabbed her wrist. "Where're you hearing about this stuff?"

Lilly winced and pulled her hand away. Barely. "Places."

"I'm not fuckin' around, Lil. Where!"

She didn't answer right away, but the look on his face must have convinced her she ought to. "It's a website. It's called Dialtone. There's a lot of people who are tired of the NPD, I'm sure you know that. So people get together and share info, get petitions started, that kind of—"

"What else do you know about this guy? This guy you're talkin' about."

"Not much."

"Got a name? Anything?"

"Why do you care who—"

"Just tell me!"

Lilly frowned again. "I don't remember. Something far East, maybe Japanese."

Manic's chin dropped. He stared at the empty plate in front of him as if finding constellations in the crumbs of his toast.

"Dad?"

"Yeah."

". . . What *did* you do last night?"

Manic said nothing for a few minutes, during which Lilly said his name once, then gave up and waited for him. The old cop's gaze darted back and forth across the tabletop, seeing nothing.

You would have liked him, Dad.

Manic raised his head and looked into his daughter's eyes. "I'm gonna pay for school. I've, uh . . . got some money saved up, I been saving up just in case. So you're going back to your classes, and I'm going down there to clear up any misunderstandings about you and your finances. All right?"

"I can handle—"

"I'm doin' it, Lil. Shut up and take it. Then in a couple weeks or so I'm getting you a car. Don't argue, you gotta have a car."

Lilly fumed for a few moments, but he could see her considering. At last she rolled her eyes like the teenager she'd so recently been and said, "Fine. Long as it's not blood money."

Manic's eggs jolted in his stomach. He fought to ignore it. "And I want you off that website."

"No."

"Lil—"

"Dad, no. I believe in it. I believe in the work. Omnihumans *are* humans."

"Yeah, except when they're not. They are genetically *not* human, that's the whole point." He hated that some deev had years ago appropriated the prefix omni-, as if they were God: omniscient, omnipresent.

Of course, maybe some of them were. Who knew?

"If that's the extent of your belief in what makes us human, I'm sorry for you," Lilly said.

Manic slid out of the booth, straightening his jacket. "That's nothing new. And get off that website. Promise."

"Fine, I promise. You know you can't stop me if I decide not to."

"But you just said you would and you're a woman of your word."

Lilly smirked at the comment, because they both knew he was right. Manic kissed the top of her head and said, "Let's meet up next week, okay? Anywhere you want. Call me. Promise?"

"Okay."

"Thanks. Do your homework. Love ya."

"Love you too."

Manic left in a hurry, but tried to conceal it. He had homework of his own. And he had to see a guy about a thing, because thinking things through was not his expertise.

*

Malikai climbed swiftly down to the street from the parking garage, inserting himself into morning pedestrian traffic without attracting attention.

On alert, Malikai walked the two miles to Sal's Café. He trained his eyes on the windows as he walked past them, trying to get an idea of what he would be facing. When he opened the café's single door, he saw only more of what he'd gleaned from the sidewalk: a coffee shop.

The interior seemed dated, like something pulled from an earlier decade. Malikai counted only six patrons and three wait staff. Elvis Presley's *Hound Dog* played over a sound system. All nine occupants noted his appearance, but did not stare. They took note and turned back to what they were doing: reading papers and sipping coffee at a counter, or conversing quietly in booths.

"Hey, there, love," one of the wait staff called from behind the counter, giving Malikai a matronly smile. She was a buxom woman, of indeterminate age or ethnicity, dressed in a short yellow and white gingham skirt and white top. Absurdly red hair piled high on her head.

Her eyes were solid green. Not her irises, for she had none. No iris, no pupil; just a jade green sclera not unlike the crimson of Malikai's own. But even he had silver irises and black pupils; her eyes were blank marbles the shade of pine needles.

He wanted to reach for his sword, but didn't. Somehow, it didn't seem right. "This place . . . this is Sal's?"

"That's right, honey-love. Why don't you take a seat anywhere and I'll bring you some coffee."

She had a voice from some other place in the nation; southern U.S., for sure, but that was as far as Malikai could guess, and that much based only on overheard conversations and televisions turned up too loud during his patrols. Even then, her accent seemed like a put-on; an act, or some bit of social camouflage.

Frowning, Malikai obeyed her. He carefully eased the dao and scabbard from his pants, not trying to hide that he had it, curious what reaction the weapon would garner. The wait staff noted it, nodded, and continued about their work. Malikai set the sword on the bench seat and slid into the booth. The single most remarkable thing about the booth was that it was singularly unremarkable. A dab of smeared syrup dotted one corner of the table, and the booth bench had two small tears smoothed over with black electrical tape. The syrup stain notwithstanding, he could smell that the table and seats had been recently wiped with a bleach mixture. Everything about the booth seemed exactly the kind of thing one might expect of an independent coffee shop and diner.

The green-eyed waitress reappeared beside him with an empty cup and pot of coffee. She set the cup down and filled it. "How you doing today, love?"

Malikai watched her work. Her eyes were as vacant as a doll's, yet otherwise her face was fully animated. She poured the coffee, not spilling a drop, without those jade eyes ever looking at what she was doing.

"You can't see," Malikai said.

The waitress smiled again. A white tag on her blouse read *Betsy*. "If you mean my eyes, why then, no, I can't. But I see plenty."

She lifted the pot of coffee, having filled his cup to the very rim. "Now what can I do for you?"

Malikai again scanned the occupants of the café. The sound system moved on to *Don't Be Cruel*. Two men sat at the counter, both nursing cups of coffee; the nearest to Malikai showed long, startlingly white hair, and small stegosaur-like plates running down his shirtless back, his hands covered in thick brown scales. A black fedora rested casually beside his left arm. The other man sat with a tan duster draped over his shoulders, fair-skinned with closely cropped blond hair—and a second set of arms which shuffled a deck of cards while his uppermost limbs turned pages in the local paper.

Yes, this was the right place.

"I need to speak with Sal," Malikai said carefully, uncertain if there were some formality he needed to recognize.

This was often the case on the street. Different gangs and cliques had different greetings and ways to approach a boss in order to gain admittance. His greeting to the tentacled deviant on the street this morning had been one such instance—announcing "six" to a fellow deviant was considered a courtesy and a show of friendliness, even though the same word was used as an insult by fours and fives. This greeting was also, of course, used by deviants of less than exemplary moral character, out to disarm a fellow deviant. But like most human gangs, deviants often policed their own. In Malikai's experience it was rare for a deviant to use the "six" greeting as a ruse. He'd only heard of it being done, never encountered it himself.

"And what do you need to talk to old Sal about, hon?"

"I am looking for someone. I was told he might help."

Betsy stared at him, smiling her easy smile. Of course, whether she was actually seeing him or not, Malikai couldn't say. For all the monstrous and wondrous beings he'd come across on the street, Betsy's blank green eyes unnerved him. Still—he did not feel threatened, either.

Instead of replying to his query, Betsy said, "Ooo, honey-lovins. You fell in with some bad men, didn't you?"

"What do you—"

"Oh, son, you have *no* idea who you are."

He almost grabbed for his sword, but fought the impulse. "Do you know who I am?"

"Well I can't say for certain. You go by Malikai, but that's not your name, is it, hon? No, whoever took your memories did a right fine job of it. There's nothing but a shred of you left in there."

If he'd needed to breathe, Malikai was sure he would have stopped doing so right then. Betsy knew far, far too much.

Yet he did not move. *Intrigued* was not strong enough a word for how he felt in that moment.

"Well, don't you worry," Betsy said. "We'll find you in there. Now, about this little girl you're looking for. Julia, is it?"

Malikai almost gaped. "How do you do this?"

"Oh, honey, you're in Sal's Café, the only place that's fit for our kind. How do you *think* I'm doing it? Not every six has a horn stickin' straight out of his head. Like I told you—I see plenty."

Malikai tried not to show surprise. For an essentially stoic being, his few minutes here had already taken him through a vortex of emotions.

"Now let me see here . . . oh, the little girl. Mmm, mmm. And you're on the hunt. Well, that's mighty right of you, son. Good for you. And you hope Sal can help? Well, he probably can. I'll make the call, he'll send a car around. And sweetheart, when it gets here, don't you mind the Brute Squad, they're just doing their job, all right? Can I get you anything? I can see you're not one for eating, but I figured I oughta ask."

Malikai gazed into her face for a long moment before answering. "No. Thank you."

"All right. Be back in a flash."

Betsy waggled to the checkout counter and picked up an ancient black rotary phone. Malikai sat back in the booth and turned his attention to the sunlit world outside. Still people avoided the sidewalk here by the café. He thought he understood why: norms wouldn't want to get any closer to this place than absolutely necessary. What he couldn't grasp was how a group of obvious deviants could come into this place unmolested, or how humans could know to take the long way around it.

Unless, he thought suddenly, they were being *guided* around it. Wasn't it possible that some deviant power kept fours and fives at bay, without their knowledge? After this encounter with Betsy, Malikai realized virtually anything was possible.

Who on earth was this Sal, and how had he accomplished all this? What sort of power must he wield to protect these occupants of the café?

The waitress returned moments later. "When you see the fancy schmancy car pull up, hop on in. They'll take you to Sal. All right, hon?"

Malikai nodded.

"Then whenever you feel like it, you come on back sometime, and we'll do a little snooping around in here." She touched the side of his head with one soft fingertip. "I think you're still in there somewhere, and there's nobody better to find you if you are. But hon, let me ask you something."

Malikai nodded again, curious.

"Are you so sure you want to know? I can tell that you *think* you do, but I'm asking you—are you one hundred percent positive you want to know who you were? Maybe you lost all that stuff for a reason."

He studied her intently, trying hard to read behind her featureless eyes. He saw nothing useful. Clearly, Betsy the waitress had some sort of telepathic abilities, but he could glean nothing else from her expression or questions.

"Perhaps," he said noncommittally.

Betsy reached over and squeezed the vigilante's shoulder.

She touched him.

Warmth flushed through his long-cold internal organs, shocking him into a sort of paralysis. He'd come into contact with people, of course, but always in the context of combat, of violence. Never, that he could recall, had a being touched him with any sort of concern, not even Xavian, who had been kind and brutal and effective, but not intimate. Malikai wondered if what he was feeling was some kind of deviant power the waitress possessed, but he dismissed the idea quickly. He simply couldn't remember what it was like to be touched by a caring hand rather than a violent one. He was reminded again of his handshake—so to speak—with the tentacled deviant, and how what should have been a repulsive touch was in fact genuinely reassuring.

"Wait," he said.

"Yes, hon?"

"What can you . . . can you tell me something? Anything? About who I am?"

Betsy smiled at him and sat down in the opposite bench. She took his hands in hers. "You sure, hon? I don't know what's in there, and I won't be able to hide what I find real well."

"Please. Anything at all."

She squeezed his hands. Hers were warm and calloused. "I won't go too deep. Might hurt us both. I'll just skim off the top, all right, hon?"

Malikai nodded. "Must I prepare?"

"Just relax. I'll do the heavy lifting."

He expected her to close her eyes, but she didn't. Though he couldn't have said for sure, it seemed as though she stared off into middle space as if going into a trance.

As for himself, Malikai felt nothing. He experienced no dizziness, no sudden jolts. He merely sat, watching the deviant's green eyes gazing emptily toward the tabletop.

"Oh, hon," Betsy whispered after a moment. "You really are on a mission, aren't you."

Malikai remained silent, waiting for more.

After another few minutes, Betsy smiled sadly at him and rested his hands on the table. "Son, you're a good man, now. You do right. But it wasn't always that way. Somebody's trying to help you. Might be your daddy, I couldn't say for sure."

"My father?" Malikai said, not intending to. "I have a father?"

"Yes, you surely do. I think he's been gone a long time, though. A long time. Don't bother trying to find him. You won't."

"But how—"

"You keep doing what you're doing," Betsy said with a firmer tone. "You'll get what you need. Now, that's not mind-reading, that's just common sense. You stay on your path, son. You find that little girl. Everything else will be as it should."

With that, Betsy bustled away to refill the cup of the white-haired deviant. Malikai caught himself looking at his hands where she'd held them, studying them as if for medical reasons. Could she be right? He'd experienced no flashes of intuition—not since early this morning in the van while on the freeway, at any rate—so she could just as easily be making up a story.

Only she had no reason to do that as far as he could tell. And he didn't believe she was that good of an actor. No . . . she'd given him something true. Fragments, maybe, but truth all the same. If nothing else, he knew now he'd had a father. Somehow, that was enough for the time being.

In any case, she was right about the girl. Julia Lawson must be his priority.

As he sat sorting through these odd feelings, a black limousine pulled up in front of the café. A man got out, although to call him a man strained the limits of language as much as this beast of a guy strained the shoulders of his suit coat.

"There's the Brute Squad," Betsy called. "Hop on in, hon. We'll see you shortly."

Malikai stood, his coffee untouched, and let himself out of the café.

The man standing by the passenger side of the car had a chest measuring four feet across. His black suit and tie and white collar shirt were impeccable, and as he reached to open the rear passenger door, Malikai noted the brute's hand was larger than both of his own held side by side. Behind the man's ape-like visage that made him look like a prehistoric human, Malikai saw intelligence in his eyes.

Malikai hesitated at the open door. "Where."

The brute said nothing. He only stared at Malikai with the practiced disinterest of a trained bodyguard. Malikai had encountered one or two such men in his time on the streets, though tangled with none; the paid, trained guards didn't occupy positions beneath the sort of people he routinely punished. Malikai was sure, though, that this was a man—or deviant—who would quickly die in the place of his boss if circumstances demanded it. Though how anyone or anything could kill him, Malikai couldn't guess. He also realized the brute hadn't asked for nor made a motion toward his weapon, which Malikai dangled readily in his left hand. Only supreme confidence or supreme stupidity would dictate such inaction.

Malikai felt sure it was the former.

He accepted the brute's silence with a nod, confident that if he didn't like where they headed, he could certainly escape, even if he was unable to hurt the brute. Once the door shut, he could not hear anything outside, and Malikai wondered exactly how protected this car might be. As impenetrable as a presidential limousine? As the car rolled forward, a motion Malikai only barely perceived, he thought the comparison probably came very close.

Through the heavily tinted windows, Malikai watched Los Angeles scrolling past. Now that he could pay more attention to his surroundings than when he was driving, he discovered everything he'd heard about Los Angeles was true. Like the neighborhood he'd driven through before dawn, the streets here were swept clean and the buildings maintained. They were not in downtown among the skyscrapers, and nothing gleamed like a new construction, but he got the impression this had once been a difficult area now rehabilitated. He wondered idly if his skills would be of any value here, then almost laughed at the idea of "retiring to sunny California," a phrase he'd heard more than once from the thugs he eavesdropped upon.

The limo took him to the outskirts of downtown, and down a ramp leading to the parking garage of a six-story office tower. The building struck him as being self-consciously nondescript; pale adobe colored walls dotted with mirrored windows, and no appreciable architecture to set it apart. The first floor seemed devoted to retail and restaurant space, which was doing brisk business on this workday morning, but parking for the businesses was in an above-ground garage opposite where the limo now headed.

They passed a guard booth with a black-and-white single-bar gate, which lifted as they approached. Fluorescents ensconced in wire cages lit the underground garage with bright, practical light. The circular concrete driveway went around an elevator bank. On its opposite side, a row of expensive cars that looked to have been recently polished sat in a neat row between yellow lines painted on the concrete.

The driver—Malikai couldn't get a good look at him through the privacy glass—stopped the limo outside the elevators. He barely heard the big brute in the passenger seat get out and open the door for him.

Malikai began to ask where he should go, but the brute took over, tapping the elevator button and then standing still, hands clasped professionally in front of him as the limo drove away. Almost immediately the doors opened up. The brute gestured for Malikai to step in. He followed the direction.

The brute thumbed the doors shut, then pressed an index finger over a small window beside the number 5, one floor beneath the top. Something beeped after a moment, and the elevator rose swiftly. Malikai realized then that the tiny glass panel concealed a fingerprint scanner.

Impressive security, he thought.

The doors opened on a featureless hallway appearing to extend to the opposite end of the building. The brute stepped out and marched down the flat, industrial gray carpet, and Malikai fell in behind him. Doors punctuated the walls every so often, each unmarked and windowless. Somewhere near the middle of the hall, the brute stopped and knocked on a door. He waited, and Malikai expected to hear a voice, but heard nothing; then the brute opened the door. He stepped aside, staying in the hall, hands again clasped, waiting for Malikai to enter.

Malikai stepped into an office that might have belonged to a middle-manager at a bank. The carpet here was nicer than the hallway, plush and wine-colored. Long and rectangular, the office smelled vaguely of cigar smoke, but not cheap cigarillos; Malikai felt sure this was the aroma of what his usual criminal victims might call "good shit."

Behind a large desk which nearly spanned the distance from wall to wall, a plump man in a silver-colored pinstripe suit coat sat, hands folded on a blotter. Black hair peppered gray swept back off his head in a professional style. A gold ring glittered on one pinky.

"Malikai," the man said with a hoarse and worldly voice. "Come on in, have a seat. I'm Sal."

ELEVEN

J.T. lived in what had once been a middling neighborhood, but now was on the upswing like most of the city. Yards were neatly trimmed, graffiti a thing of the past, and newer model cars sat parked where no cars had been parked before.

Manic felt something akin to pride as he walked up to the front stoop of J.T.'s typical southern California two-story, and knocked on the door. His buddy had done everything right: wife, house, kid, in that order. He supposed the pride came with some semblance of jealousy, but not much. J.T. was the closest thing he had to family after Lilly, so joy at his friend's success felt genuine, like how he imagined he'd feel when Lilly got her bio-whatever degree.

Which she could *do* now, he reminded himself.

J.T.'s wife Teri opened the door, smiling instantly upon seeing Manic. A tall, slender woman whose face made Manic think of royalty, Teri Jackson understood the bond between combat vets and respected it. Any of "the boys" were always welcome.

"Manic," she said with comfortable familiarity. "How are you?"

"Hanging in there, T," Manic said, his hands stuffed into his bomber pockets. "How's he doin'?"

Teri didn't have to answer. A baritone cough echoed from the front room, followed by a hawk and spit and J.T. grumbling something.

"You might not want to come in," Teri said. "He's got one hell of a chest cold going on."

"Nah, I don't mind, I'm, uh . . . off work for a while anyway. Can I?"

Teri stood aside. "It's your funeral, Officer."

Manic came in, and the two traded a brief hug. Teri closed the door while Manic moved to stand in front of a blank flatscreen hanging over the mantle. Then he almost swore.

Medically speaking, J.T. looked like shit. The black man's skin had a yellow cast to it that curdled Manic's stomach. J.T. sat sprawled on the couch with a knitted comforter pulled over his big body, and to Manic, it seemed like his friend had lost weight. J.T. breathed through his mouth in the way common to anyone with a hopelessly stuffed-up nose.

"Hey, man," J.T. croaked. He hawked and spit into a plastic bucket on the floor. Without looking, Manic sensed the pail held half an inch or more of spittle and phlegm.

"Hey," Manic said, starting to doubt his coming here.

"Hear you got a new gig," J.T. said.

The comment refocused Manic's attention. "That didn't take long."

"You know, us girls like to cluck in the henhouse," J.T. said, earning a light smack on the shoulder from Teri as she passed by on her way to the side room that she kept as an office. J.T. chuckled but the laugh brought up a new round of horrific, wet coughs.

As if summoned by the sound, J.T.'s little girl poked her head in through the kitchen doorway. Jessica Jasmine was six and the perfect blend of her parents, and glowing with life and potential.

"Hey there JJ, how you doing?" Manic said.

The little girl squealed and ran full tilt toward Manic, arms wide. He hunkered down, suppressing a groan at the tightness in his quads, and met her happily, one of his rare smiles distorting his face as JJ ran into his arms. They hugged tightly. Manic marveled at the strange blend of frailty and strength in the six-year-old's limbs. Such a bundle of contradictions, these little ones. Even as she squeezed him, though, he realized he felt that same dichotomy even now when he hugged Lilly.

"You bein' good?" Manic teased as JJ pulled away. "You doin' your chores?"

"Yeeeeees," JJ sang, rolling her eyes. J.T. looked on, beaming at her, and Teri reappeared, leaning against the doorway to her office.

"All right, you better," Manic said, tugging on one braid. "Can you give me and your dad a couple minutes?"

"Okay!" JJ shouted in his face. She ran off full-tilt to the sliding door in the kitchen and bounded into the Jackson's small backyard.

Teri shook her head and rolled her own eyes. Manic laughed gently at how similar the gesture was to JJ's. "That girl's going to put me in traction," she said. "Manic, is there anything I can get you? Coffee? *Beer?*"

Manic half-stood and pushed himself into a recliner near his buddy. "No, thanks, T. Just gotta talk some business real quick."

Teri tilted her head. "Everything okay?"

"Sure, sure. Just got tapped for a promotion, not sure it's what I want, you know?"

She grinned. "Oh, that old story. You damn warhorses, terrified of polishing seats with your asses. All right, you boys have your talk. J.T., holler if you need something, I'll keep JJ out back."

J.T. tried to answer, but could only cough and hack for about twenty seconds. Teri put a hand on his forehead, frowning. She seemed about to say something, but instead followed JJ outside without another word.

"Promotion, huh?" J.T. said.

"Yeah, maybe not quite." Manic brushed at his nose to stall. "Listen, bud, if I tell you something—"

"You don't tell me anything you're not supposed to, Manic. C'mon, man. Play by the rules."

Manic nodded. "All right. Well, let's say this. Let's say Lilly ran into some money trouble at school, but I got it worked out."

"Because this promotion pays well."

"Right. So I'm good, I did what I set out to do. I could pick up right where I left off last week if I wanted."

J.T. coughed, hacked, spit. "But?"

Manic hesitated. He wasn't exactly the kind of man to rehearse, and now didn't know how to proceed. He shifted around in the recliner, his muscles moaning under his coat.

"But there's . . . a coupla things."

J.T. wiped his mouth with a Kleenex, grimaced at what he saw in it, and tossed the tissue into the bucket. He said nothing.

"I really liked the gig," Manic said carefully. "Felt right, you know? But then I heard something yesterday, and it . . . well goddamn, it's naggin' at me. I don't know what to do, bud."

J.T. rearranged himself on the couch to sit up more squarely. The effort clearly hurt him. "I tell you something, Manic. If I was feeling a hundred percent I'd tell you to come back to the team, keep your head down till retirement. I see how you're moving, bud. You got your ass handed to you."

Manic snorted a laugh. Of course J.T. could read him.

"But I feel like knocking on death's door right now," J.T. went on. "Stuck here on this couch for all these days. I been thinking, what if this wasn't just a bad-ass chest cold?"

"*Is* it more than that?"

"Naw, man, I'll be all right, you know. But I've had way too much time in my head the last few days, just sitting here thinking. And you know what, brother? We're different. All the boys and girls at NPD. We're special. Sheep dog strong. And if this cough wasn't some passing thing, if I really was dying here, I'd have way too many regrets about the stuff I didn't do."

Another round of hacking brought up phlegm far too green to be natural, in Manic's opinion. He couldn't resist his lip curling a little as J.T. spat it into the bucket.

J.T. leaned forward a little, but winced as if the movement hurt him.

"Teri's right. We're warhorses. Thoroughbreds. And we don't live forever. Hell, dyin's half our job. If you still got it in you to make a difference out there with this 'promotion,' then you do it. That's what I'd do. There's not enough of us out there as it is. If you got the gas to make the world safer for my little girl and yours? Shit, man. You already know what to do."

Manic did. But it felt good to hear.

Make the world safer? Yeah. He could do that.

In that instant, he knew his next move. He'd follow up on Lilly's comments about Izanagi—and hell, maybe it wasn't even him!—just to clear his conscience. Then he'd give himself a few days to heal up and head right to that mailbox and get back to work.

That's what he *did*. Who he *was*. Do for others what they couldn't do for themselves. Maybe he'd even live long enough to give himself some kind of nice retirement, give Lilly a nest egg to start with, send her off to grad school the way he knew she wanted.

Or just keep going hard and fast till some six got the better of him. He knew the odds weighed heavily that direction. It didn't bother him a bit. He'd go down shooting.

Manic stood up, slowly. "Thanks, bud."

"You look like a man with a plan," J.T. said, grinning sickly.

"You could say that. You heal up, all right? Gimme a call when you feel better, we'll head out."

"My brother." J.T. held out a hand.

Manic slapped it and shook it. J.T.'s palm was cold and damp.

"See ya," Manic said, and let himself out. He waited until he was away from the house to wipe his hand on his pants.

"Sheep-dog strong," he said aloud as he walked to a bus stop. "Yeah. All right. Let's go to work."

He skipped the bus stop after all, deciding to work out his muscles with a long walk around the City of Angels, grinning as he contemplated his next unknown assignment.

Vigilance.

Diligence.

Humanity.

Hell yeah.

Sal sat on a large black leather chair behind the massive desk. A clear glass ashtray rested to one side on the blotter, and Sal put it to use by opening a drawer in his desk and producing a cigar as big around as his thumb. Malikai stepped to one of two smaller leather chairs in front of the desk and sat.

The door closed. Malikai turned to look. They were alone; the brute had stayed in the hall. He faced Sal again, who lit his cigar and eyed the vigilante with ease, confidence, and perhaps some degree of skepticism.

"Sword, eh?" Sal said. "Bit old fashioned, but I trust it'll do in a pinch. I've seen stranger."

"What is this place."

Sal's eyes widened, as did a grin. "Right to the point. We're going to get along fine. 'This place' is my office. I own the building. And a few other buildings here and there, if you need to know, which you don't, but I'm feeling accommodating this morning, so I'll give you that much."

"The café?"

"Yep, that's mine, too. Has my name on it and everything." Sal blew a smoke ring. Not perfect, but somehow impressive.

"It was full of deviants."

"Omnihumans. As in, *all* human, *more* human. But yes, my little restaurant is usually full of them." Sal's blue eyes glinted behind his cigar smoke. Malikai got the impression Sal, too, could read his mind, but not in any deviant way like Betsy—Sal was just that good at figuring people out.

"How is it possible? Such a place in the open."

"Certain arrangements with local government. Plus, let's say, a psychic understanding by the public. The café was built with certain security features in mind. It's a safe place for everyone inside and outside its walls."

"Betsy."

"What about her? She's a peach, right?"

"She read my mind."

Sal shrugged a bit. "If you let her, sure. She's part of our security system, yes. Does what she read have something to do with why you're here?"

Malikai's head dipped, feeling oddly penitent. "Perhaps."

"Why don't you tell me what can I do for you? Let's just start there."

Not quite ready to give up everything to this clearly powerful man just yet, Malikai asked, "Who are you, exactly?"

"How about we just agree that I'm no one to have angry at you. Now, stop right there. Before you ask any more questions, let me make a few things clear. Here's how it works with your old Uncle Sal. You tell me what you want. I'll tell you if I can help. If I can, then you owe me a favor. No ifs, ands, or buts. You owe me whatever I ask, as soon as I ask it. Failure to repay that favor will result in your hasty and ignoble death. Those are the rules. Simple."

He puffed his cigar, then gestured with it magnanimously.

"You can ask questions now."

Still trying to get a better read on the man, Malikai said, "You could help me, then I could never bother to repay the favor. I could disapp—"

"No you couldn't." Sal smiled patiently. "I've never lost anybody, not one. Now, granted, not many people have failed to repay my favors, either. I'm not an honest man, but I'm not a liar. I'm sincere and I'm pragmatic. My favors are not always an eye for an eye. I may ask you to deliver an unmarked package, or hold a bake sale for a youth group, or assassinate a foreign head of state. It all depends on what you're good at and what I need done."

"I do not understand what this place is."

Sal gave him a sigh. Smoke bellowed out with it.

"Pal, I'm on a tight schedule, so I'll give you the short version. Plus the girl you're looking for is running out of time."

Malikai shifted in his chair. "How did you—"

"I don't let people into my office without knowing their story. But I wanted to give you a chance to talk first. You blew that shot, so now quiet up and listen. I'm a good family man, so when my only son popped out looking a little different than everybody else, you want to know how much of a shit I gave? None. Zero. He was my son. Well, that wasn't enough for some people, who killed him one night when he was ten years old. *Ten.* For looking different. For appearing *less than.* I gave up my day job and set up shop out here, and I'll help out everybody and anybody who asks, who's willing to repay my favors. That's it."

"Your day job—"

"Time's up," Sal said, his voice deepening. "You're looking for a girl. Julia Lawson."

Malikai chose not to bother asking how he knew that detail already, assuming it had something to do with Betsy's mental abilities. What Sal said made sense: a man in his strange business wouldn't get far without having safeguards in place to protect himself. He might very well know more about the vigilante than Malikai knew about himself.

"Yes. Where is she?"

"I can't say for sure, but I know where you can start." Sal crushed out his cigar in the ashtray, and gave Malikai a backward nod. "You're pretty good with that sword, yeah?"

"Yes."

"You better be. Because I don't think it's going to be enough for what you're getting yourself into. You got an army handy?"

"No."

"Shame." Sal opened his desk once again, producing a single sheet of white paper and an elegant fountain pen. He wrote as he spoke.

"The people you're about to cross are known as The Gentleman's Club. I shouldn't have to tell you they are anything but gentlemen. They sprang up a few decades back, mostly smuggling folks over from different countries in Asia. They have a habit of charging money out the ass to bring a husband or father over to the States, then hanging on to any kids or wives to extort extra payment. Well, they've expanded since then. They run a pretty brisk business with human beings. That's not all they do, but it's their bread and butter. Bring native people over here, ship our Americans back over there. They pocket cash both ways."

He slid the paper over to Malikai, who took it.

"I did some looking, and this girl fits their bill for custom orders. Someone had a particular fancy and ordered it up, then The Gentlemen's Club went and found her. Depending on how closely she fit the customer's order, they just cleared half a million or more."

"Why Phoenix? Why not find a local victim?"

"Cheaper labor, believe it or not. They can put in an order from Phoenix for half what they'd have to pay here nowadays. L.A.'s gone straight and narrow . . . so they say. It's tougher on them, so they outsource. Plus Phoenix has been a smuggling and immigration hub for a long time now. They have the machinery and infrastructure already in place."

The factual nature of his words and tone irritated Malikai, and Sal seemed to know it. The bigger man leaned forward in his chair.

"I'm using those words deliberately. This is business, and *big* business. They're not going to hand her over to you just because you got a fancy sword. You're gonna get messy, and you'll likely get dead."

"I'm already dead." Malikai studied Sal's handwriting. He'd written an address and a name.

Sal shrugged off the comment. "Be that as it may. I'm telling you right now your chances are not good. Now I'll help you however I can, but I do not expect to see either you or little Julia Lawson alive after this."

Malikai looked up. "How many men are there at this location?"

"Twenty to fifty at any given time. In the whole club, a couple hundred if you count the spear carriers. The whole gang? Well, not to sound too cliché, but fuggetaboutit."

Malikai got the message. He stood up, folding the paper into the hip pocket. "Is there anything else I should know?"

Sal sat back, rocking a little in his chair, folding his hands together on his belly and appraising—or re-appraising—the vigilante.

"You're not afraid," Sal said. "And that might be helpful. But Betsy says you're looking for something else, too. Want to share that with me?"

"No."

"We might be able to help you find it. Betsy can be awfully good at that."

"Perhaps if I survive."

Sal grinned, the sarcasm bouncing off him. "Sure thing, pal."

"It occurs to me that a man with your power and resources could shut down this 'Gentleman's Club.'"

"Maybe. But another would spring up. Don't play to my guilt, pal. That angle's worn to the bone."

"For all the good you do, you are not a good man."

"Never claimed to be. So I tell you what. I'll save my lives my way, and you save your lives yours."

Malikai gave him a polite nod and turned to go.

"You know that's a Tang dao, right?"

Malikai stopped and faced the man again.

"Tang Dynasty, China, early 600s to early 900s. A *yan mao*, if Betsy pronounced it correctly to me. That little knife of yours is probably worth a few grand at worst, unless it's replica, which I doubt. Betsy said it was giving off some pretty powerful mojo."

Malikai stood still, blinking, feeling serpentine creatures squeeze his organs again.

"I poked around a little," Sal went on, quite possibly enjoying the expression on Malikai's face. "Seems the yan mao was a pretty technical weapon. Required a lot of training and expertise. Matter of fact, they stopped being made after awhile because the training was just too intense. Too impractical for your everyday Chinese grunt."

He reached for another cigar.

"Not for nothing, but those might be clues. Just putting it out there. Friendly gift. No charge."

Malikai nodded again, with slightly more deference this time, and paced silently to the door. It opened as if by magic, but revealed the brute standing outside, holding the knob.

"Good luck," Sal called, and the brute shut the door.

Malikai followed the brute to the elevator and down to the garage. Rather than lead him to the limousine, which Malikai did not see anywhere, the brute walked to a new model year gray Mustang. He paused by the trunk, holding out a key.

Intrigued, Malikai took it. Without a word—though that was unsurprising by now—the brute walked to the elevators, got into one, and disappeared from sight, leaving Malikai alone with the keys to a new car.

He didn't know much about cars beyond how to drive one, but he reckoned this vehicle might have a thing or two to show off. It was a worthy replacement, however temporary, for his motorcycle.

And driving it would be better than dwelling on everything Sal and Betsy had revealed so far. If he let himself, he'd fall down a rabbit-hole of questions and doubt. If that happened, Julia Lawson was good as dead. No. There would be time to plumb the past when she was safe.

He got into the car and revved the engine. Yes—this was much better than the Ice Dragon van.

Using the map on Nicholas Lawson's phone, Malikai navigated the city streets toward the address Sal had given him. Traffic had increased exponentially over the course of their short visit. Malikai eased the Mustang into it, grateful for the heavily tinted windows and Los Angelinos' natural tendency to be self-focused, both of which kept his peculiar features hidden. He wondered why, in a town revolving around the making of films, deviants couldn't merely walk the street in broad daylight and claim they were in costume if anyone pressed them.

Perhaps the risk was too great. A costume could be removed at gunpoint.

He passed a comic book shop called The Comic Zone. In the windows, life-sized posters of superheroes hung straight, beckoning new readers. Squinting at the artwork as the Mustang crawled along, Malikai found himself again perplexed by normal humans. There must be hundreds if not thousands of deviants who could become "superheroes" with their particular powers and abilities, yet this society shunned them in real life while paying money to see similar characters pretend to use those same powers on film or in the pages of comic books. The logic escaped Malikai completely. He wondered if maybe his old self understood this odd contradiction.

What if, perhaps, he'd been a hero in whatever his past life had been?

Tentatively allowing his mind to wander down that path while he kept an eye out for the address on Sal's paper, Malikai considered Betsy and Sal's offer to plumb his memories more deeply. Since the waitress—although the term didn't seem quite in keeping with her power—had the ability to read minds, was it really possible for her to dive into his gray matter, root around, unpack *all* the mysteries of who he was? Come up with concrete specifics? Not just the vague enigmas Sal mentioned, but hard facts?

And if she truly could do that . . . did he want her to?

Perhaps some secrets were better left secret. Perhaps she could in fact uncover his past, only for him to discover he did not very much like it. How could he be certain that he himself hadn't in some way wiped his own memory clean, for reasons that were best left dead and buried?

With his amnesia came a certain freedom.

A freedom of unconcern, of not being responsible for much of anything. In his present circumstances, he could not help but inhabit each moment; he had no family, no fealty. Yes, Xavian had instilled in him the compulsion to seek out injustice and bring about retribution; but he required little more than enough money to fuel the vehicles he stole from criminals. Only in combat and stalking did he feel as alive as any being with no heartbeat could feel.

Was that so bad? Was that the worst life to live, considering the nightly degradation and suffering he encountered?

So taking up Sal and Betsy on their collective offer to peek into his past may not be such a great idea after all, Malikai concluded. Perhaps the past should be kept there.

These thoughts circled for nearly an hour. This powerful car moseyed along at a mere twenty miles per hour. Sad, for such a nice machine. Maybe, after he got Julia Lawson back, he'd open up the Mustang on the highway. Unless of course Sal wanted it back first, in which case . . .

In which case, Sal could go ahead and send the brute squad after him. A car like this was not meant to troll city streets. It wanted to race. Malikai would return the vehicle when there was time to return to the vehicle. He felt sure Sal would understand that, else he wouldn't be handing out muscle cars to random omnihumans.

Malikai rolled to a stop at a red light and sat up in the seat.

There, out the passenger window, he saw the address he was looking for. Only it *couldn't* be; couldn't *possibly* be right.

A video arcade.

While only cognizant of his life for the past year or so, even Malikai knew this storefront business was an anachronism. The shop, open to the sidewalk, showed no overhead light, only the blue glow of stand-up video game screens. And the place was packed.

Odd.

When the light turned green, Malikai took the Mustang further down the street and began searching for an out-of-the-way place to park. He chose a Denny's restaurant not far away, and slid into a parking spot. He couldn't leave the car there forever, he knew. Sooner or later, a tow truck would come, according to nearby signs.

He'd have to risk it. Right now he needed reconnaissance. Moving about in the daytime would be much trickier than his usual nightly stalking, but waiting until nightfall did not appeal to him. Whatever The Gentleman's Club was doing to Julia Lawson, the sooner he stopped it, the better.

Malikai tugged his hood low over his forehead, scooping up his metallic hair and shoving it down his back. He put on his sunglasses before getting out of the Mustang. Upon standing, he quickly slid his sheathed sword under his hoodie and partway down his leg. At about thirty-seven inches, the scabbard was not comfortable, but this concealment would suffice for the moment. He double-checked the dao to ensure it was relatively hidden before heading to the sidewalk.

Malikai noticed no particular glances beyond what was to be expected on a city sidewalk as he walked east toward the video arcade. He wondered if he'd been right after all: that modern life so close to Hollywood led to fewer confrontations between deviants and norms.

The arcade jangled as he approached, electronic tweets and bloops and whistles piercing through the noise of traffic on the street beyond. He walked past the storefront, only glancing inside. Dozens of young men but also a young woman or two stood at the consoles, jamming buttons with fingers and palms or yanking at joysticks. A counter stood at the back of the small shop, and he thought he saw someone making change there.

Then he was past the arcade and walking toward a skate and surfboard shop. Malikai paused, and stepped out of the foot traffic to assess his surroundings.

Several things occurred to him as he let his gaze wander. First, this was a tourist spot. He overheard several different languages and a multitude of accents from the people walking by, most of whom paid him little attention. That conclusion helped make sense of the arcade; the stand-up games could only compete with home systems by virtue of novelty, tourists attracted to the sounds of their youth perhaps. They'd spend a dollar, maybe twenty at most, but that would be all. Even so, Malikai doubted quarters alone could account for what must be an enormous amount of rent for its location.

A front, then, he decided. Since he was searching for a young girl sold to a cartel of human traffickers, and this was the address Sal had given him, it only made sense that dealing in digital spaceships and yellow happy-faces eating dots in a maze would not be this place's only means of turning a profit.

Now: how to gain access?

The dao scabbard seemed to warm against his skin as Malikai considered his next move. Either the Tang dao wanted out, or he wanted to *let* it out; secrecy and subterfuge were not his strongest skills. If he could have the entire gang out in the street for a robust hand-to-hand encounter, he would have been fine with that. But such a spectacle would get him no closer to Julia Lawson.

That left two options. Wait, and attempt to sneak in; or try a more direct approach.

He double-checked the name on Sal's sheet of paper, then refolded it into his pocket and walked back to the arcade.

The video game noise assaulted him, making him wince behind the sunglasses. Somewhere inside, someone smoked an illicit cigarette, a habit banned long ago inside any public place. Whoever ran the arcade didn't seem to care. Sticky with spilled soda, the concrete floor sucked at the soles of Malikai's cruddy sneakers. He itched to take them off.

Malikai edged between the tightly packed games and gamers. Around him, excited men shouted and cursed as electronic avatars either blew things up or died in showers of sparks. Most of the people playing wore casual clothes, but two near the back playing a race car game wore suits and ties, briefcases set nearby. Something pricked at Malikai's instincts as he studied these two, and it took several moments to sink in: they weren't casting regular glances at their briefcases to make sure they were unmolested. It was as if they had no fear of anyone making off with them. In Phoenix, men like this set their cases between their feet at coffee shops, and continually glanced down to ensure their safety.

Interesting. L.A. truly had gone "straight and narrow."

Malikai approached the back counter. A single door stood behind it, plain and drab. The young man behind the counter, of Chinese descent, wore a distressed T-shirt advertising Dr Pepper.

"How much?" he asked Malikai, taking in the vigilante's hood and sunglasses without much concern.

"Jiang Kien," Malikai said, voice low, reciting the name Sal had written.

The cashier opened his cash register with bored eyes, but Malikai saw behind the expression—the cashier also scanned the immediate customers as if checking to see if anyone had overheard Malikai.

The cashier pulled a key from the register and gave Malikai a jerk of the head. Malikai walked around the counter and joined the cashier at the door. The cashier unlocked a bolt and pulled the door open, muttering something in a foreign language.

Malikai nodded as if he understood. Something in the words teased his subconscious, but he couldn't grasp it. Behind the door lay a concrete platform, perhaps five feet square. Beyond that, a staircase led down into darkness.

He stepped onto the concrete, and the door closed behind him. A solitary bulb in the low ceiling lit his way to the staircase.

Malikai paused at the top of the stairwell. The stair treads were sheeted with iron. Narrow railings were bolted into the concrete walls on either side of the staircase. While he'd never been inside a prison, he easily imagined one would look eerily similar.

Malikai stepped cautiously into the darkness. The light from the single bulb cast a pitch-black shadow before him, masking the stairs. He found his way stopped by another door at the bottom of the stairwell, twenty-odd yards from the top. He twisted the doorknob; nothing. Locked.

Not good. A trap? Certainly the cashier upstairs had called his bosses below to announce the six's approach. Malikai wondered if his own arrogance honed on the streets of Phoenix was now going to cost him.

The door opened. Malikai instantly recognized not the exact facial features but the certain type of expression worn by the man who opened the door: he was a thug, no different than Thud if Thud had been intelligent enough to serve as a foot soldier for another, more powerful gang.

The enforcer wore an AK-47 around his shoulder by one strap and kept it leveled at Malikai. Wordlessly, he gestured with the barrel for Malikai to come forward.

"*Teeg-ow needah shou,*" the man said—or something like it.

Malikai scanned the room he'd entered. Concrete walls, floor, and ceiling; industrial style lights with enormous bulbs above. He guessed they were below whatever business lay behind the arcade upstairs. An iron door lay twenty feet ahead. Three additional guards with assault rifles stood in no particular pattern around the room, each with the same thuggish face as the man speaking to him.

That guard raised his voice and his gun at the same time, repeating the same foreign yet somehow familiar language. He jerked the barrel of the weapon up.

Malikai slowly raised his hands, examining each man in turn. Yes, he was definitely in the right place; each man bore the shorn heads and scars of the Ice Dragons.

The first guard reached out to pat Malikai down. In seconds he would find the dao. He would take it away, surely, and Malikai could not let that happen. So when the hand came near enough, he attacked.

Malikai intercepted the thug's hand with both of his own, spinning to face the door he'd entered from. With a shout, the thug came along for the ride. Malikai locked the thug's arm beneath his own and bent the thug's fingers backward almost to the point of breaking while he scrambled for the Tang dao with his free hand. The other three men shouted, barking commands Malikai did not comprehend but could very well guess at.

The three men slid to new positions, trying to ensnare him in a crossfire position. Malikai crouched low as he pulled the dao from beneath his clothes. The men didn't shoot yet, concerned for their writhing colleague who squealed in pain as Malikai continued to bend his fingers away from his palm.

With the sword free, Malikai instinctively instructed it to burst to life with an intense blue flame, like the hottest part of a gas jet. The transformation made the other three guards blink back, the only moment he needed to spin away from the thug he held prisoner. Malikai turned, maintaining his low crouch, and swung the dao at the thug's calf. The limb severed bloodlessly, cauterized by the heat of the blade. The thug dropped, screaming.

Malikai rolled forward, toward the iron door and past the remaining three men. He snapped silently to his feet, sword extended.

He'd give them one chance.

"Jiang Kien. Take me to him now."

The three guards traded glances. He could see them trying to give each other silent instructions on whether to shoot or not shoot. All three ignored the screams of the amputated thug between them.

"Jiang Kien," he said again, and took one practiced step toward the nearest guard.

The door behind him opened—the door leading deeper into whatever hell lay beyond. Malikai sprang forward through the middle of the guards, grabbing one by the collar as he leapt. He pulled the terrified man in front of him as a shield, keeping his sword pointed at the figure who now approached.

If his heart functioned, it would have dropped.

TWELVE

Manic punched three tall mirrors in succession. The glass shot his knuckles with sharp slices, tearing open recently healed wounds.

It felt great and horrific at once, a dichotomy that seemed to summarize his entire existence.

The mirror shards dropped noisily on top of blue plastic tarps he'd laid out in advance to catch the broken pieces. Later, after dark, he'd dump them into his apartment building's trash. If any of his neighbors had any idea what was causing the noise, they never said. But then most people didn't tend to trade pleasantries with guys who'd earned nicknames like "Manic."

Manic knelt among the scraps of mirror. Blood rushed from his hands and spilled onto the tarp. His breathing came out short and harsh.

"You really need to get a hold of this," he said aloud to the empty apartment.

After cleaning up and piling the tarps near the door, he treated the wounds. Then he tossed himself into a kitchen chair and blew out a breath. Now what?

He leaned forward and emptied the contents of his Izanagi dossier. "Look at those claws," he mumbled. "Yeah, tell me about what a big hero he—"

Manic paused, squinting at the photo of Izanagi in combat. "What the . . ."

He leaned back in his chair and rooted in a junk drawer, fishing out a plastic magnifying glass. He poised over the photo, using this relic from bygone ages that he'd found could still be useful from time to time. A time exactly like this, in fact.

"Goddammit," he said, half in admiration and half in shame.

Goddammit, he should have seen it before. Manic tried hard to give himself a pass because the items he was looking at wouldn't pop out at anyone, not even a seasoned cop—the photos were too blurry for that.

Still. He should have paid more attention. Asked more questions.

In the photo of Izanagi tearing up four humans, Manic now saw that one of the men had a white handkerchief tied around one ankle. Another, one around his wrist. Because of the quality of the shot, he couldn't see the hairstyles of all three men, but one of them, upon closer inspection with the magnifying glass, was definitely bald and scarred.

Ice Dragon gangsters.

Manic knew of them, but had never crossed paths with any in his time with LAPD. Most of the gang consisted of teenagers, like all the street gangs in Los Angeles, with a few older guys running the younger ones in various illegal activities. The Ice Dragons had a curious way of avoiding prosecution, Manic knew. They were legendary in the cop community for their slipperiness in the courtroom. Since cops gossip—or *exchange intelligence*, as the bosses preferred to call it— Manic knew the Ice Dragon affiliate gangs also avoided trouble with other gangs. They didn't necessarily operate with impunity, but they'd oddly never been involved in a turf war that Manic had ever heard.

For a scummy street gang, they had a number of curious traits.

And if the deev Lilly had described at breakfast was in fact Izanagi, and if what she said about him going after slavers was true . . . then it was at least possible the Ice Dragons might be connected to that same slavery.

Izanagi, in this photo, might have been trying to stop slavers. Even if that wasn't true, if Lilly had her wires crossed, the four men being ripped apart in this photo weren't exactly nuns and orphans.

Manic tossed the magnifying glass aside and sat back in his chair, thumping a finger on the ancient Formica tabletop.

Izanagi—yeah, that had to be who Lilly was talking about. Had to be. Somebody last night, maybe one of the warehouse workers, had seen the fight and had a soft spot or a hard-on for deevs, and reported it to this "Dialtone" website Lilly mentioned. That made the only sense.

That, or he'd just misinterpreted her scanty information.

His next simplest move would be to head to one of the NPD stations, grab a terminal, and do some research. Yes, that would be simple, but NPD resources weren't always of the depth and breadth and reality that he needed. He'd learned from LAPD, and quickly, that records and reports had their place, but the real intel was on the street. Which hookers would talk, which dealers might squeal, which grandmas and pastors could curb violence or know where a certain mid-level banger might be hiding out that week. The street nearly cried with information, if the right guy knew the right rocks to lift and peer under.

In this particular case, Manic knew the exact place that would have the answers he wanted, and the thought made his lip curl. He'd used this place only twice before, while NPD was on the hunt for a specific deev who needed apprehension. Both times, he'd gone with Officer Toole, and Toole conducted himself with cool efficiency, getting the intel he needed and getting right the hell back out. Manic had admired that. But he'd never admire the cesspool he'd had to enter in order to get it.

"Goddammit," Manic said again, and left the apartment.

He took a bus across town, hopping off a few blocks from his destination. He walked past the place twice: once across the street and once on the same side, letting his instincts guide him and his experience protect him. Everything seemed normal in this business district. Small restaurants and shops lined the road, with taller office buildings looming behind like protective siblings.

There seemed to be nothing out of the ordinary despite the fact that in one of the nearby cafés, at any given time, at least half a dozen obvious deevs could be found.

Sal's Café was well-known by NPD. *And* LAPD, *and* probably by every alphabet agency at the local, state, and federal levels. For whatever reason, Sal's and the immediate area surrounding it was sacred ground for deviants. Manic grudgingly admitted that the folks running it—or the folks working there, at any rate—cooperated with law enforcement for the most part. Technically, being a deviant wasn't against the law, only unregistered and undocumented deevs were illegal. Sal's might not turn over a unchipped deev to the NPD, but nor would they harbor a dangerous felon. Both the deviant and law enforcement communities knew this, and left Sal's unmolested for the most part.

Furthermore—it went without saying—Sal's Café could bring its own force to bear if it became necessary, and no one wanted it to become necessary. Deevs policed their own a lot of the time, just not enough for Manic's liking.

Manic never dreamed he'd find himself walking into the place on his own, without a partner or backup. Yet that's what he did after deciding the café looked secure. He pulled his shoulders back—wincing a little at the ache in his back from last night—and tried to pull open the door.

His hand froze around the handle.

"Ah, hell." Manic took a deep breath and dove deep into his own mind, fighting against the most intangible of defenses some mindfucker at Sal's erected. Manic knew, cognitively, that the place was protected by a mid-level psychic barrier designed not to hurt a normal human, but to gently dissuade them from entering or even noticing the café.

"I hate this mental shit," Manic warned no one, grimacing.

The defense broke suddenly. Manic practically fell inside the shop. He straightened his jacket, still pissy.

The café hummed a little softer than diners like Buzz or Dale's. The clientele, about ten obvious and unobvious deviants, sat at the lunch counter or in booths lining the windows, generally by themselves or with only one other. To Manic, the place looked like a perverted version of the *Boulevard of Broken Dreams*, replacing those iconic Hollywood legends with tentacles, iridescent hair, and—yep. Some guy with fucking *gargoyle wings*.

He fought to keep the sneer off his lips as he approached the cashier's counter. Did these sixes even use cash? He didn't know and didn't care.

The waitress who came to intercept him at the register wasn't smiling. "Easy, officer," she said, and her confidence unnerved the NPD vet.

Manic shoved his hands into his coat pockets. "You threatenin' me, love?"

"Just a reminder. We can all be friends here."

He almost said *We ain't friends*, but bit it back. That sort of attitude wouldn't get him he wanted.

"Need to see someone about a six," Manic said. "People call him Izanagi."

He couldn't be sure, but thought the woman's eyes twitched. "What about him."

"So you know him."

"Knew. He's dead."

Manic nodded slightly and let his periphery scan the occupants of the café. Several were listening closely, he was sure, but he didn't sense any kind of impending attack—not until the dude with the gargoyle wings turned on his barstool to face Manic.

The deviant seemed to have been carved out of rock, and, for all Manic knew, was a real live honest-to-God gargoyle. That's sure as hell what he looked like.

What kind of genetics would let a child grow up to look like that? he wondered. *Goddamn!*

"They don't serve your kind here," this rock-faced creature said, his voice sounding like gravel crunching under truck tires.

"Slow down, Goll," the waitress said, raising a hand but not looking at the deviant. "Officer Cruce is just making inquiries. Isn't that right, Officer?"

She knew his name? So either she'd been here when he came with Toole, or she'd read his mind. He chose not to ask which. "Just Manic. I quit NPD. Call it a personal matter."

"If that's supposed to make me feel better, it doesn't," the waitress said.

Manic shrugged. "Just being friendly. Putting all my cards out there."

The waitress studied him. Manic wondered if she was a mentalist, scanning his brain for a lie. But he felt no intrusion like he had outside the café, or the other night with the Class-M pickpocket. Was she even a deev? She had to be, to work here, he assumed. What kind of human would imperil themselves day in and day out surrounded by creatures like "Goll" who looked as if he could fly right through the roof if he had a mind to?

What kind of human would deal with that? The kind like Lilly.

The thought tensed his muscles, which ached in response.

"All right," the waitress said finally. She gestured casually to an empty booth. "Have a seat. I'll make some calls. Want some coffee?"

From here? Are you kidding me? Manic managed to simply shake his head. He sat at the booth, which was the closest one to the door, where he could observe the rest of the occupants. All of them, by that point, had either noted him and turned away, or else kept a wary eye on him. But no one made a move, not even Goll, who'd faced forward again, his five-foot-tall clawed wings nearly scraping the tile floor. How the hell did that guy walk around during the day?

Manic waited patiently for an hour, saying nothing, ordering nothing. No new "patrons" came in, though five left, leaving only five behind, including Goll the Gargoyle. No one raised any fuss. Manic was half grateful, half disappointed. Any deev picking a fight with an NPD vet would bring the entire shock and awe of the Los Angeles NPD down on this place with the fury of God's wrath. That would be one way to close the place down.

It didn't happen. Just as he was feeling the first hunger pangs for lunch, a woman walked in and slid into the bench seat across from him.

And oh *shit* was she something to see.

The deviant who came into the square concrete room had to bend at the waist to accommodate his full height as he passed over the threshold. Once inside, he straightened up, not quite twice as tall as Malikai. His face was pig-like, his nose flat and squashed inward, with close-set piercing black eyes and walrus tusks jutting down over his lower lip. The tusks extended well past his chin. Malikai wondered vaguely how he ate—then figured he might well find out if things went badly in the next few seconds.

He tried a polite approach. "I only wish to speak to—"

The tusk-man roared, shaking the concrete walls and sending tremors up Malikai's legs. His breath gusted out in a miasma of rotted fruit. The two able-bodied guards sprang for the open door and took off through it, leaving their captured mate and their recently amputated comrade behind.

"I see," Malikai said.

He shoved the guard he'd been using as a shield toward the tall deviant. Clearly the deviant was unleashed for one purpose only, and it had nothing to do with the other enforcers: he caught the foot soldier in both enormous hands and threw the man aside like a sack of trash. The thug's full body slammed into the concrete wall and crunched. He was dead before he'd slid to the floor.

Malikai wasted no time; this needed to be fast and efficient. Brandishing the blade, he leaped toward the deviant.

With shocking dexterity and speed, the tusk-man batted Malikai to one side. The vigilante flew across the room, bashing into the wall just like the thug had. Malikai knew if he were slightly more human, the blow may well have killed him as surely as it did the thug.

Shaking himself, Malikai turned and assumed a defensive posture. He'd only just achieved the proper state of equilibrium when the deviant was on him again, grasping Malikai by the throat and hoisting him bodily into the air.

Thud's gravelly voice whispered in Malikai's mind: *Look out for the seven.* As the huge deviant snarled and squeezed Malikai's throat shut, he understood this man to be a Level Seven deviation.

Sixes on the NPD's human-deviant scale were rare enough; perhaps one tenth of one percent of the global population. Maybe less. Malikai knew, in an abstract faction, that he squarely fit into the Level Six category, as did most deviants he encountered. More rare were sevens—beings with extraordinary strength or power that eclipsed even the rarity of sixes. When Thud advised him to look out for the seven, Malikai guessed this enormous beast with the tusks was what he meant.

The deviant continued snarling as Malikai's windpipe sealed shut beneath one hairy fist. It hurt, to be sure, but this seven didn't know all of Malikai's secrets.

Malikai forced a smile so his opponent could see it. Not needing to breathe had many advantages and this scenario happened to be one of them. He twirled the sword so its tip reversed, pointing down now like a stabbing dagger. He raised it high and aimed it at the deviant's face, who looked comically shocked that his victim hadn't passed out or died in his hand.

The vigilante slammed the blue blade into the seven's left eye, where it smoked and seared. The seven screeched and dropped Malikai, closing his enormous hands over the blade; thus his hands, too, burned viciously. As Malikai fell to the floor and crouched for another attack, the tusk-man fell backward, yanking the sword from his eye socket with a roar.

It should have been a crippling attack. Instead, the seven swung immediately toward Malikai, who now found himself weaponless. The seven still held the dao, which had dimmed to its usual silver sheen; whatever magic or mutation gave Malikai the ability to endow the sword with additional power, it didn't work unless it was in his hand.

He braced for another attack, muscles coiling to spring away from the seven and toward the open door where the thugs had slipped away. But the deviant's next attack didn't come from his fists or feet.

It came from his mouth.

A blast of putrid air shot from his gaping maw. For a moment, Malikai would have sworn the breath had color to it—a purple-green mass of particles that smelled as horrific as it looked.

The breath caught him full in the face. Malikai assumed whatever deviant power this was, he could shrug it off as easily as the chokehold. If the seven's breath was poisonous, it wouldn't have any effect on a man who need not breathe.

He miscalculated.

As he started to dive for the door, Malikai felt his legs tensing up, as if being shot through with dark, eldritch electricity. Instead of leaping, he fell forward, barely catching himself on his hands as the electrical sensation wriggled along his spinal cord and spread through his body. Whatever wicked ability the deviant had, it didn't require the victim to inhale.

Malikai tried to drag himself forward, but the paralysis sank deep into his bones. He fell face-first against the concrete. He could move his eyes and nothing more.

Growling satisfactorily, the seven picked the vigilante up and slung him casually over one broad shoulder, holding the cold Tang dao in one hand. He stepped through the doorway and entered a long gray tunnel lit sparsely by caged bulbs in the ceiling. Malikai tried valiantly to move, but went unrewarded.

He focused next on his surroundings. Since he still possessed his senses, he tried to figure out where they were and where they might be going. So far, all he had to go on was concrete and the faint aroma of excrement. Heading into the sewers, then. Yet the walls and floor of this corridor were surprisingly dry.

The seven carried him down the long hallway and thrust open a thick iron door. They entered another square room, but with only three sides; the fourth opened to the T-intersection of a broad corridor, three times again as wide as the narrow tunnel they'd emerged from. The room had once been painted the industrial green common to utilities, but now showed chips and bald areas where the paint had flaked off.

The pigman dropped Malikai onto his back. Malikai heard low murmuring in that same familiar-yet-unknown language. In his periphery, he saw a party of armed thugs head for the narrow tunnel, presumably to gather up their slain and wounded comrades.

A moment later, another man, dressed in a white button-down shirt and black trousers, stood over him. The seven, his left eye burned shut, came to stand nearby, glowering down at Malikai with evident hatred. He still held the dao by the lifeless blade.

"*Nee how*," the man said, or something like it.

But of course even if he'd been of a mind to speak, Malikai could not respond. The man smiled knowingly, clearly enjoying the vigilante's plight.

"I am Kien," he said. While his first words had been accented, his

English was not. "And you are an intruder. But you are no policeman. The LAPD and NPD do not hire sixes, or at least, not publicly. You are unable to speak. That is unfortunate, but Ching's attack will wear off eventually."

The giant pigman grunted. Malikai doubted he could talk through the colossal tusks jutting from his mouth.

"He may also require your left eye as payment for his lost one," Kien went on, still smiling.

Malikai recognized the expression on the man's face and knew Kien had to die.

This was a man so far removed from humanity, whether he was a deviant or not, that he could not be permitted to live. If this man indeed had Julia Lawson in his possession, there was no end to what sorts of brutalities he may have already visited upon her. Malikai had encountered one or two others like Kien—men who lacked a soul in any conventional or metaphysical sense whatsoever. Men for whom the world existed as a plaything. Men such as these could not be allowed to mingle with humanity. They required not justice, but punishment, swift and permanent.

Of course, such punishment would have to wait until he could *move*.

"We will talk more soon." Kien snapped an order to some thug outside of Malikai's line of vision.

Ching—the seven—picked him back up and carried him to the intersection. Malikai focused his attention on turns and landmarks in preparation for an escape. Ching turned left; right; then left again, taking them into another long tunnel. They passed other thugs, all armed. Just as they passed through a large open area in the tunnel, Malikai saw two men guiding a young boy between them.

The child could not have been into his teens yet, or else had been so abused that his appearance suffered. He didn't seem to notice Ching or the silver-haired, red-eyed deviant over his shoulder. Malikai watched him as best he could as they passed, but succeeded only in feeding his rage as he saw the hollow depths of the boy's eyes.

Malikai realized then that, for certain, he was in the right place.

Ching passed through the open space and into another tunnel. A short flight of iron stairs took them another level down, where he turned right. Here he stopped and tossed Malikai into an empty concrete room that appeared to have once been a storage area. The room had been refitted with a barred gate like a prison cell. Thick chains depended from a ring in the ceiling and Ching made short work of affixing Malikai to them so that he hung from his wrists, his toes dragging on the floor.

Ching lifted his prisoner's head up by the hair. Malikai stared straight into Ching's remaining eye defiantly, promising himself that Ching, too, would pay for whatever heinous sins were being committed here.

The seven grinned as if reading his thoughts. He raised Malikai's sword, glanced at it, then back at the vigilante. He tossed the sword away, out into the hall beyond the cell, and plunged his giant thumb into Malikai's left eye.

Pain like a slow motion sledge hammer pressed into him. Malikai would have screamed, but the paralysis prevented it; even though he did not need to breathe, certain reflexes were still in place. Inhaling for the sheer purpose of screaming as a release was one of them, yet he could not draw breath. The pain multiplied as Ching tried to gouge out the eye.

It wouldn't happen. Frustrated, and not appreciating just how much pain he had nevertheless caused, Ching relented and settled for a resounding blow to Malikai's abdomen. The punch squeezed every organ inside of him, leaving the vigilante feeling as though he'd been rolled over by a trailer truck. Level Six Deviant or not, he could and did still feel pain.

Ching marched out of the small room, slamming the iron gate closed behind him. He plucked the sword from the ground and shoved it through his belt like a pirate. Malikai swung gently from the chain, his body still reverberating from Ching's punch.

This was definitely not how he'd imagined things going.

*

"Whoa," Manic whispered, and immediately felt like a fool. Cripes, he wasn't some kid, he should be able to hang on to his appreciation a little better.

Still—the woman was worth the comment. She had Latina blood, Manic was sure, with sharp features, piercing brown eyes, and a tight physique just shy of a competitive female bodybuilder. She moved with the easy confidence of a soldier. Manic wondered if she had some kind of formal training, and if so, from where. Her dark hair curled naturally down over her shoulders, which were covered by a blue and gray fitted nylon top. She folded her hands on the table, her nails trimmed short and unpainted. Callouses marked her knuckles.

"Officer Cruce," she said, her voice soft and feminine and thoroughly self-possessed.

"Um—yeah," Manic said, then shook himself back into character. "No. Manic's fine. I'm not NPD anymore."

"Very well. How can I help you?"

"How about a name?" He flirted with adding a pejorative like "Sweetheart," but opted against it. No—*thought the better of it* was more accurate. For more than one reason, he did not want this woman angry with him.

The woman hesitated briefly. "Perdida Velasquez."

"Perdida Velasquez. Nice to meet you."

"Charmed. Now what can I do for you?"

Manic leaned forward, mimicking the way her fingers were laced together. "I need to know about a deev named Izanagi."

"Call him or any of my friends a 'deev' again, I'll take out one of your eyes. He was an omnihuman. Better yet, a person."

Manic smirked, admiring her fearlessness. "Right. I need to know about a *dude* named Izanagi."

"He's passed away."

"Yeah, I heard. What was he into?"

"*Into?*"

"I have it on good authority he dropped a few members of the Ice Dragons. Know anything about that?"

"I do."

When she offered nothing more, Manic raised his eyebrows and smiled mirthlessly. "Care to elaborate?"

Perdida Velasquez smiled just as falsely back at him. "Why are you here, officer?"

"Manic. Just poking around."

"*Manic*, we both know you're not just poking around. The sooner you're honest with me, the sooner I can tell you if I can help."

He bored his gaze into hers. She was cool, that was certain. He doubted that he could intimidate her into getting the information he wanted. Maybe she was a six, or at least a five. Or, maybe she wasn't, but she sure was surrounded by them on a regular basis. No wonder he didn't impress her. That truth bugged him, but Manic forced the irritation away.

"I heard he was fightin' against some human trafficking. That true? That's what I want to know."

"It is true."

"Great. Thanks. But come on, what else was he doin', huh? He had to have been into some heinous shit."

"Because he was a deviant?"

"You gonna poke out an eye if I say yes?"

Perdida studied him in much the same manner as he'd done to her. She was trying to get a bead him on him. Figure out what his endgame was, how far he could be trusted.

She unlaced her hands and leaned forward on her elbows. "I don't know why you're really here, Manic. What it is you're really after. But I find it highly suspicious that a friend of mine was killed, and now here you are, a little more than twelve hours later, asking all sorts of questions about him. What do you think might happen if I started asking *you* questions about his death?"

Manic gave her a theatrical shrug. "Try it and find out."

"How much do you know about the Ice Dragons?"

"Not much. They're crafty little bastards, they don't get sent to prison much. The other gangs tolerate 'em for some reason. That's about it."

"And you say you're not NPD."

"Not any more."

"Mind if I ask you what you do for work?"

"Look, lady. What I do for work ain't the topic right now. If Izanagi had dirt on the Ice Dragons, then I wanna know about it and check it out. You obviously know I ain't no fan of deevs, and—"

Perdida Velasquez moved at the speed of light, or so it seemed to Manic. The last consonant out of his mouth still hung from his lips as he found himself pinned against the bench, one of Perdida's hands clamped around his throat. Before he even realized he couldn't breathe anymore, one of her thumbs was pressed beneath his left eye, the eyeball bulging painfully from his socket. Not *out* of it— but not really *in* anymore, either. One more quarter-pound of force would pop his eye out like a bouncy ball from a gumball machine.

"Seeing as how I don't want to make a mess in my uncle's place, this is your one get-out-of-jail card," Perdida said. She was standing, leaning over the table.

Manic's hands flew automatically to her wrist and tried to pry her off his throat. She released him, but then with some kind of sleight-of-hand maneuvering he could only marvel at, she tangled up his fingers in hers until both of his hands were a twisted mess pressed against his left shoulder, immobile.

"Ah, *shit*," he wheezed.

"Have I made myself clear, Manic?"

Her thumb dug deeper beneath his eye. Any more pressure would squirt the thing out of its socket.

"*Yep!* Uh-huh! Crystal clear."

She released him, and ended up standing outside of the booth.

Manic bent forward, squeezing his eye shut, making sure it was still where it belonged and that she hadn't done any permanent damage to his hands. The mirror cuts on his knuckles ached beneath their new bandages, but otherwise the fingers seemed intact.

Damn she was good.

"There's a car out front," Perdida said. "I'm going to get into it and drive away. If you really want more information on Izanagi and the Ice Dragons, I suggest you find yourself in the back seat before I get there."

She pivoted and stalked out of the café, black Israeli-style combat boots soundless against the tile. Cursing, Manic lurched out of the bench and stumbled after her, keeping a palm over his left eye just to make sure it was secure.

Outside, idling illegally by the curb, a black town car sat waiting. Perdida slid into the back seat, and Manic had to leap to follow her in. The toe of his workboot dragged on the blacktop for a moment before he was able to pull himself in.

"I should shoot you," he grumbled, arranging himself on the bench seat.

Perdida, already seated with legs elegantly crossed, laughed. "Oh, I urge you to try!"

Manic shut up.

He kind of liked her.

The windows of the town car were tinted to a degree where it was nearly impossible to see outside. As a result, Manic had only a vague idea where they ended up. The window between the front and back seats was likewise shaded so heavily he couldn't tell whether one or two people sat up front.

"I suppose this is the part where I ask you where we're going," Manic said, unsuccessfully trying to roll down his window.

"Probably," Perdida said.

"Where are we going."

"To see my uncle."

"Yeah? He gonna give us candy?"

"He's more of a cigar man."

Manic sighed, sounding even to his own ears like a little kid. He certainly felt like one, with his inability to defend himself against Perdida Velasquez. On the other hand, he had to admire her skill. And legs.

"So what was that back there? What'd you do to my hands to tie them up like that? That was pretty cool."

He would have sworn she fought a genuine smile. "An ancient predecessor of aikido. I'm somewhat adept at it."

"Yeah?" Manic said. "You a deev? *Ian*?"

Her trace of a smile vanished. "Yes. Should I be killed for it?"

"You look normal."

"I suppose that's a compliment coming from you."

Manic shrugged. "You're kinda pretty. *That's* a compliment."

"And you're kind of odoriferous. That is not a compliment."

Manic studied her closely, making no attempt to hide that he was doing so. He saw absolutely nothing to indicate she was anything other than human.

"So what can you do, then?"

Perdida turned her sparkling eyes onto him. They were knockout, that was for sure, but not inhuman. "I thought you weren't NPD anymore. What do you care?"

"Just wanna know what I'm getting into."

He felt the car go down a steep dip, and the pressure in the car seemed to change, as if they'd gone underground.

"Mister Cruce," Perdida said, "you have no *idea* what you're getting into."

The car rolled to a gentle stop. Perdida opened her door. Beyond, Manic saw cars lined up in parking spaces. A standard concrete parking garage. They could be in any of a hundred different locations in the city that had such parking areas.

"I'm going to give you an opportunity now to end this

discussion," Perdida said. "I can have the car take you wherever you want to go. But if and when our paths cross again, or I hear your name associated in any way with a friend of mine who happens to get hurt or worse, then I'm going to have you killed. I assure you that's not an idle threat."

Manic nodded his appreciation. "Good to know. And what if I don't stay in the car?"

"Then you'll come with me to meet my uncle, who will tell you everything you want to know. He will take you into his confidence. If you betray that confidence—"

"He'll have me killed, yeah yeah. Gotta tell ya, lady, you guys need to work on your script."

Perdida eyed him. "No," she said carefully. "He won't have *you* killed. But he will make you watch."

For the first time that morning, Manic's heart rate sped up. "Watch *what*."

"Are you coming or going?"

Again, he wanted to shoot her. *Maybe* kiss her first, long and hard, but still shoot her. He booted his door open. "Cool. Let's do this, then."

They climbed out. The car had stopped at a bank of two elevators. Manic walked around the back of the car to meet her. The town car slid away, turning a corner and disappearing, leaving them with a half-full lot of newly washed vehicles, all makes and models, sparkling under fluorescent lights.

One of the elevator doors opened and they stepped in. She thumbed what looked like a fingerprint scanner, similar to those used at the NPD branch offices. Impressive technology for the owner of a small Los Angeles café.

"The two of us alone in an elevator," Manic said as they whisked upward. "Imagine the possibilities."

"Please stop," Perdida said. "I haven't had lunch yet."

That response pleased him enough to back off.

The doors opened after going up five floors. Perdida led the way down a hall where doors dotted the walls down the length of the building. The hall had no other distinguishing features; tan paint, pale gray carpet, and not a single decoration to be found. The effect was almost dizzying.

A few doors down, Perdida paused. The door was made of oak, and seemed to Manic to be much wider than was really necessary in an office building. The doorway could almost accommodate two people shoulder to shoulder.

Perdida turned to him. "He'll take your shit, but only for so long. Respect is the better part of valor, all right?"

Manic shrugged again, the shoulders of his jacket rustling. "You're the boss."

"No. He's the boss. I just recommend you remember that for the next few minutes."

Manic grinned. "I'll do my best."

Perdida narrowed her eyes for a moment, then opened the door. Manic walked in.

Then began to laugh.

THIRTEEN

"God damn," Manic said, pacing into the office. "Salvatore Malone himself. How's it going, Sally?"

The broad-shouldered man seated behind a dark wood desk gave Manic something like a smile, but it was a smile broken by years of stress. He lit a fresh cigar and gestured for Manic to sit in one of the leather chairs across from him. A hidden fan whisked the cigar smoke away before it could fill the room.

"Freddie," Sal said. "Gotta say, didn't guess where you'd end up."

"No?" Manic said, plopping down and casually flinging his right ankle over his left knee and bobbling his foot up and down. "Where'd I end up?"

The door closed behind him. Manic glanced. They were alone now.

"LAPD," Sal said, rocking gently in his sumptuous leather chair. Two lamps in the corners behind him made strands of gray in his hair wink. "NPD. And nowadays . . . well, that's what I want to talk to you about."

"Last time I heard your name," Manic said as if he wasn't listening, "you were working for old Vic back home. Where *you* been, huh? I mean, I saw the café, very nice, but come on, what's the real story? You ain't no six. I can't believe it's really *you*, man."

His joking tone had no beneficial effect on Sal's demeanor as the older man answered, "Tony."

Manic almost asked *Which Tony?* because in the old neighborhood, a double dozen *Tonys* ran around. But from the look on Sal's face, he guessed which one Sal meant.

His son.

"That don't sound good," Manic said carefully.

"He's dead. Died before his eleventh birthday."

Manic's foot stopped bouncing. "Accident?"

"Oh, no. He was a six, Freddie. A five, actually, not that anybody bothered to ask before they killed him."

"Hey. I'm sorry, Sal."

"That he's dead or that he was a deviant?"

Manic couldn't answer. People has been asking him that question a lot lately.

Sal waved the question off with his cigar hand. "Doesn't matter. You have anything to do with killing Izanagi?"

"Naw. Why?"

"Why're you lying?"

"Because Sal Malone has a reputation of whackin' people when he has a mind to."

Sal said nothing, only stared hard at Manic, who met his gaze without blinking or turning away. Manic wondered if Sal was armed, then worried that he didn't need to be. He had a sudden instinct that Sal wasn't exactly the type to rent an office. More likely, he owned the whole damn building. Hell . . . maybe the *block*. Or more. How much was old Sally worth these days? Enough to have some pretty high tech security, that was for sure.

"I own Dockman's," Sal said at last, which seemed to confirm Manic's theory that he owned a lot more than a half-assed deviant café. "Indirectly, of course, but it's mine. Izanagi was using it. He was doing me a favor."

"What kinda favor?"

Sal kept up his scrutiny of Manic's face. Manic fought to remain impassive. Sal took a few puffs on his cigar before saying, "You understand the rules here, Freddie?"

Manic dropped his foot from his knee and leaned forward, trying not to wince as his back ached beneath him. "Why don't you spell it out for me, I'm a little slow on the uptake. Somethin' tells me you ain't the old Sally from the neighborhood I used to know."

"That's right," Sal said. "That's real right. Okay. Here's the rules. I'm gonna tell you everything. And you're gonna tell *me* everything. And when we're done with all the telling, we're gonna come to an agreement. I'll aim for that to be mutually beneficial. Or I'll strap you to a table and stitch your eyelids open and make you watch a couple of my boys do unspeakable things to Lilly."

Manic froze as solid as a statue of ice. So that's what Perdida had meant when she said Sal would make him watch. From Perdida, it had sounded a bit like posturing. From Sal, it sounded like certainty.

"If you touch her—"

"Shut up, Freddie."

Despite himself, Manic did. For all the deviants he'd fought, all the blood he'd shed, this graying middle-aged man with the indeterminate East Coast accent scared him.

Salvatore Malone had been a first-rate enforcer for Vic back in the old neighborhood. It started at a young age, Manic remembered. While Manic was busy trying to figure out times tables, sixteen-year-old Sally was rumored to have spent two hours torturing a guy with his dad's toolkit because the guy had tried to sucker Vic out of some money. By eighteen, Sal had more notches on his .45 than many of Vic's oldest bagmen. He made good money for the family, and didn't work his way up so much as get kicked upstairs by Vic. Sal had shown remarkable skill at all aspects of the family business, including being a good manager of human resources. Manic doubted he ever graduated high school, but old Sally knew *people*—and that was a skill that couldn't be taught.

"You're right, I'm *not* the man I was," Sal went on. "But I keep that man handy because he has a way of getting things done when the need arises."

"All right," Manic said, his face stony.

"And I don't like going around threatening people's kids. I really don't. But you got to understand how serious I am, here."

"It's understood."

"Relax, Freddie. I mean that. Relax, right now. We get nowhere if your trigger finger gets itchy."

"I'll be honest with ya, Sally. There ain't a whole lot keeping me from giving you a double tap right here and now, bam bam, center mass. I don't give a fuck who you are these days, know what I'm sayin'? You said her name. That was a mistake."

"Actually," Sal said, unfazed, "there *is* something keeping you from shooting me, or you would've tried it by now. You ready to listen?"

Manic chewed on Sal's words for several moments. Goddamn if he didn't still have his old gift of working people. At last he sat back in his chair again and held out a hand. "Go for it."

Sal nodded once, tightly, and began rocking in his chair again. Manic, unable to shake his rage at the threat his old neighborhood acquaintance had made against Lilly, let his emotions take over—one of the many aspects to his sterling personality that earned him his nickname.

Nobody threatened Lilly. Nobody.

So this, in order of occurrence, is what happened next. It would take Manic two full hours to piece it together in his head, and it all happened in under three seconds:

Sal ducked beneath his desk.

Manic quick-drew his pistol, training it in the empty space Sal had just occupied.

The door opened and two enormous men rushed in, men with impossibly broad shoulders, like football players with full pads.

Manic pulled trigger. The bullet pinged off the window behind Sal and buried into one of the walls elsewhere in the room.

The two brutes felled Manic to the floor and expertly took his gun away, disassembling it into its component parts while pinning him to the ground.

He could not breathe.

Sal appeared from behind his desk again, straightening his tie. "I suppose I deserved that. Let him up, fellas."

The brutes let Manic get up and choke in a breath. "What the *fuck!*"

"It's my particular talent," Sal said, perfectly at ease. "As best as my people can determine, I live approximately one point three seconds into your future. It comes in handy, as you can see. Took me a long time to learn not to cut people off when I spoke to them though. Used to drive my mom crazy."

Sal gestured to the two men, who wore impeccable black suits, even higher quality than Weber's. They may have been twin ogres. "We're fine, boys. Wait outside."

The brutes walked out without giving Manic a second look. They shut the door softly behind them. Smoke from Manic's shot still lingered in the air as Manic struggled to grasp what had just happened.

"Now," Sal said. "If you got that out of your system, you want to talk?"

Manic scooped the remnants of his pistol into his coat pocket, then sat back down. "Yeah," he said. "Sure. Okay."

"And just so we're clear, if you try anything like that again, I'll let the brute squad rip your limbs off. All right?"

"Yeah . . ."

"You know I'm being literal there, right, Freddie?"

Manic nodded, still trying to regain his breath. What fresh hell had he gotten himself into now? Perdida was right: he had no idea.

Sal nodded back to him, then steepled his fingers. "Izanagi was a client. I helped him out once, and then I had him do a favor for me. That's how it works now."

"What is this, the day of your daughter's wedding? You the godfather now?"

"Something like that. I do favors for people. They owe me a favor back. It's that simple. Might not be easy, but it's simple. Maybe I give you a place to stay for a few weeks or years where the NPD can't find you. Maybe then I ask you to break into a bank vault with your particular set of skills. Maybe you need the guy bothering your daughter to take a walk. Maybe then I have you drive a package out to Jersey for me. Favor for favor. No proportion or fairness, just a one-for-one exchange."

"What did Izanagi need?"

"Protection."

Manic laughed loudly. "Guy had KA-BARs for fingers. I don't buy that for a second."

And with that, he'd just confirmed he did know who Izanagi was. Stupid error, but Sal didn't react to it.

"That's because you didn't know him. Izanagi was a peaceful man, a Zen Buddhist for Christ's sake. But the world wouldn't let him *have* peace. He had a crew looking to take him out because of some old grudge with his teacher back in Japan. I took care of that little issue for him, then asked him to do some recon for me on the Ice Dragons."

Manic raised an eyebrow, intrigued despite himself. "They keep popping up, what's the deal?"

Sal's expression darkened. "I know they're into some shady shit. Coming from a guy like me, that's saying something. Someone's got them on a hefty new payroll, that's for sure. I've been trying to find out who and why for awhile now. Another fella came to my attention not long ago who was looking for a girl who'd been kidnapped in Phoenix. Told me he traced her here to L.A. I gave him what information I could and haven't heard from him since."

"But it was the Dragons who took her, you sure?"

"Pretty sure, yeah. They're doing a brisk business in slavery. Sweat shops, prostitution, torture porn, domestic service. *Kids.* You name it."

Manic gritted his teeth. Sal pointed at him with the cigar.

"You starting to see why maybe deviants shouldn't be your biggest worry, pal?"

Manic said nothing. While with LAPD, he hadn't crossed paths much with the sex crimes guys. He'd been a beat cop. It didn't matter—he picked up plenty from the street and from locker room crosstalk. Not being a detective, he hadn't ever spent much time dealing specifically with such formalized syndicates, he only knew they existed in town. Hearing them spelled out by Sal, the reality of it hit home.

He knew he fit the jaded cop archetype. Most officers did. You didn't do the job without taking it home. Some guys drank, some beat their women, some just flat-out quit. Suicide wasn't as common as it was in the armed services, but the emotional scars ran just as deep as in combat vets. Differently, maybe, but deep. Manic, like most of the cops he knew, tried to focus on the job and keep people safe. That was it. Few people had the time or energy to go on a crusade against one type of crime.

Unless, Manic mused for the first time in his life, you counted going after deviants.

"You own this building?" he asked Sal.

"I do."

"And the shipping company."

"And a couple casinos, some private airports, things like that."

"Plus the café, don't forget. You got a café in the middle of Los

Angeles that no cop or NPD will touch. I don't know how the hell you pulled that off—"

"It wasn't easy."

"—but now I'm supposed to buy that you ain't got the resources to go after the Ice Dragons yourself? Bullshit, Sal. You're pussing out."

"This other guy said the same thing. So maybe I haven't been clear. I'm not a superhero. I'm a guy who gives and collects favors, Freddie. And believe me, I got my hands plenty full helping a whole lot of people. I'm trying to keep folks alive, the same people you and your NPD have been chasing down and making disappear. *And* their families, most times. I don't like the Ice Dragons or the repugnant shit they do, but my specialty lies elsewhere. I'm not a cop, and I'm not a general."

Sal snubbed out his cigar in a glass ashtray.

"You know why I had Perdida bring you here, Freddie? It's because I know you're connected to Izanagi getting killed. Now I'm pretty pissed about losing him, because he was a good man doing a good thing. But he wasn't on my payroll, or one of my favorite kids, so I won't raise a beef with you over it. It's not good for business. But I don't think it was an NPD job, and I don't think you're acting on your own, either. I'd really, really like to know what you're up to."

Manic lifted his shoulders. "Gotta new job."

"For who."

"Don't know exactly. But it pays pretty good. It's gonna put Lilly through college. Provided you don't, you know, kill her in front of me or something."

"Dammit, Freddie—"

"No, hey, look!" Manic snapped. "You threatened my kid, Sally. I didn't just *forget* that! I don't give a dead fuck if you were only makin' a point or not, you don't do that shit, you crossed the line. I don't doubt for a second that you could make my ass disappear, and that's fine. But seein' as how you lost your son, you of all people gotta know how far *I'll* go to make sure my kid's safe. I don't owe you shit, and you don't fuckin' scare me. You want something from me, you ask. Don't pull Lilly into it, you fuckin' liquor-store thug. I will make it my mission in life to make you watch everything you love burn."

He had Sal's attention. The older man glared at him, palms resting lightly on the blotter in front of him.

"Who's paying you, Freddie," Sal asked softly.

"Naw. Naw. You had your shot. You coulda asked me nicely. Hell, I woulda told you just outta respect for Vic. But you blew it." Manic stood and jerked a thumb toward the door. "Now I'm either walkin' outta here, or I'm shootin' outta here, which do you want?"

Sal listened to this without a single shift of expression. Only his eyes moved to track Manic standing. The two of them stared at each other for a long moment.

At last Sal's lips twitched. Then he chewed on them as if working on a gristly piece of meat.

"All right," he said. "You have a point. I'm sorry, Freddie. I got a little overzealous. It's the company I keep. Side effect of the job."

"*What's* the job?"

"Will you quid pro quo? Me and you, right now?"

Manic considered. He felt a hell of a lot more loyalty to Sal than to Weber, no matter who was paying the bills.

"Done," Manic said, but didn't sit.

"They killed Tony," Sal said. "A mob of norms, they killed him. Judy was killed trying to protect him. No one ever paid for it. Long as I live, I'll never get the bastards who did it. Just one big faceless mob of humanity."

Now Manic sat. He'd never seen anyone from the old neighborhood look like Sal looked right then: useless. Impotent. Back home you got tough fast or you died young. Sal *had* changed, all right. And this wasn't the old neighborhood.

"As luck would have it," Sal went on, "I met a guy who sorta turned my life around. Showed me another way. So I took it. Got Vic's blessing, and moved down here. Built a sanctuary."

"Wait a sec. You found *religion?*"

"Sanctuary in the classical sense. A place of refuge. Safety. Whatever it takes, whatever it costs, I help people now."

"You mean deevs."

"Yeah. *Deevs.* Watch your fucking mouth. So that's what I do. Now it's my turn. Who's paying you and to do what, and what'd it have to do with Izanagi?"

Manic shrugged and folded his hands over his stomach. "Honest to God, I don't know much about Izanagi. I heard he was some kinda crazy maniac six, that's it."

"He wasn't. Izanagi was a man who people wouldn't leave alone. He was a warrior in the true sense of the word, and he was awfully close to finding out more about what the Ice Dragons are up to around here. Now that he's dead, I'll have to start all over again because I told someone I'd look into it."

"Fulfill your promise, huh?"

"Exactly."

"Well, Sally, I tell ya. I don't know what happened to this Izanagi guy. You ever find out different, you let me know."

Manic stood up. Sal wrote on a small white pad of paper, tore the sheet off, and held it out to Manic over his desk like a prescription.

"This is where one of the gangs sharpens their knives," Sal said. "Check it out for me."

"Whoa!" Manic said, laughing. "I don't owe you nothin'!"

"Sure you do." Sal's eyes narrowed. "Because I *already* know different about you and Izanagi. I just wanted to give you the chance to be square with me. You weren't. Now you *do* owe me. What you did last night is bad for my business. So you owe me. You can say no, but there's a price. No one says no to me, Freddie. Not for long, they don't. You really stepped into it here."

Manic met his eyes, summoning every bit of logic, reason, and pure gut instinct he could to figure out if Sal was bluffing. It didn't take long to realize he wasn't.

He took the sheet with a snap. "We never were the best of friends, were we."

Sal sat back in his chair. "I don't got any friends."

"Naw, I suppose you wouldn't."

"But I'll do you a favor."

"What's that."

Sal shrugged. "Whatever. Whenever. Check into these guys, see if you can find an omnihuman named Malikai. Real vampire-looking guy, silver hair, red eyes, you can't miss him. You bring me back something actionable on him or the Ice Dragons, and I'll owe you one. Trust me, Freddie, I'm someone you want to owe you one. Maybe someday those new friends of yours you're working for don't play fair with you. Maybe on that day, I'm here to help. Who knows."

"You're a real bastard, you know that?"

Sal, for the first time since Manic had come into the office, smiled. It disfigured him. "I guess some things *don't* ever change. You need a car, cash, anything? I'm happy to help. It doesn't count against the favor."

Manic thought about that. A car was more than Weber had offered, although the arsenal back at his apartment surely hadn't been cheap.

"Sure, okay. Car'd be nice. Whaddya got?"

"Take a look around the garage. Anything parked between the yellow lines. Whatever strikes your fancy, just let the guard know."

"What if I wreck it?"

"That's my risk to take. Cost of doing business. Also a nice tax write-off."

"You pay taxes on all this?"

"I got one or two accountants in my employ."

Manic folded the note and shoved it into his coat pocket without reading it. "You got a deadline for this little adventure of mine?"

"A few days."

"What if I can't find anything?"

"Then we're even."

"I could lie."

"You could try."

Manic smirked. "Fair enough. Good to see you, Sal. I mean, in a roundabout kind of way."

"Feeling's mutual, Freddie. See you in a few."

Manic went to the door, but paused.

"So . . . Velasquez."

"She's family," Sal said, shortly. "Let it go."

Manic gave him a grin and a nod, and let himself out. The hallway was empty. He was tempted to walk up and down the length of it opening doors, just to see what else old Sally had going on here. Then he figured he might find something he didn't want to, and went to the elevators instead. He hopped in and thumbed the G button, half expecting the doors to close and the car to fill with poison gas. Who knew what Sal was capable of these days.

Instead the elevator dropped him off unharmed in the parking garage. He wandered around the lot, noting that there were in fact two colors of parking spot lines painted on the concrete, white and yellow. He scanned the yellow area for a few moments and grinned.

He went over to a guard booth planted between the entrance and exit lanes. Manic wondered why there only appeared to be flimsy black-and-white striped arm-style gates blocking the entrance, then guessed discretion was the better part of security. Making the place look normal and innocuous might well be Sal's first line of defense. Manic thought probably there were security measures in place he would never detect until it was too late.

Still grinning, he went up to the booth and knocked on the window. He'd never owned car, but he knew a good one when he saw it.

"Sal sent me. Told me to pick out a car."

The guard came out of his booth. "Which one?"

Manic pointed. "I think I'll take that black Equus Boss 770. Unless . . . does it come in red?"

*

Malikai did not know for how long he hung by the chains before he was able to move again. His paralysis ended slowly, as if whatever chemical Ching had put into him rose to the pores on his skin and oozed out. Eventually, he could move his extremities, and everything seemed to be in its right place. He tilted his head back to examine the chains; they looked industrial, designed for towing heavy loads, and his wrists disappeared into a mass of them. If he was going to break free, the iron ring in the ceiling might be a better bet; a plate of steel had been bolted into the concrete, and he thought that might be the weakest point to attack.

Of course, there wasn't much attacking he could do from here. He clenched his still-sore stomach muscles, and swung his legs out toward the gate. His feet didn't quite reach it, but at least he had some freedom of motion there. Perhaps he could attack with his legs, get a guard in a choke hold . . . ?

He wished he could sleep.

Without the sun or a clock, time lost all meaning, although the mute ticking of timelessness didn't bother Malikai too much; he was used to motionless hours at the farmhouse or even nights spent in Phoenix when his services somehow went unneeded.

So it might have been hours or days before footsteps alerted him to an approach, and within moments, Kien appeared on the other side of the barred door, flanked by two Ice Dragon guards with their AK-47s. Kien was dressed the same as before but with an added black suitcoat, which did not prove one way or another if more than a day had passed.

"You can move again," Kien said, smiling. "See? Did I not tell you? Now that you can move, you can talk. Tell me what brings you here, swinging your sword and killing my loyal men?"

Malikai didn't bother to explain Ching had done the killing. Kien knew. The boss always knew.

"Maybe you think you are the demon *buxiu?*" Kien went on. "Your costume is not terribly authentic. You're dressed like a bum. Your sword, however . . . beautiful."

Demon? Malikai didn't let the impact of the word show on his face; once Kien said it, his mind began to burn. A memory—unformed, yet sharp and curved like a talon—tore into his psyche. He suddenly and inexplicably longed for Betsy's gentle touch on his shoulder again, to feel her caring warmth.

Kien tapped a finger on one steel bar of the gate. "You chose your icon poorly, my friend. You should study more. The *buxiu* is a rapist and killer of women and children. Or, maybe you are here to apply for a job, eh? Eh?"

The henchmen laughed dutifully. Malikai said nothing as a deep vibration quaked somewhere in his chest, faint and inscrutable.

Something else Kien said triggered it, he thought. But what? And *why?*

"Why are you here?" Kien asked softly.

Malikai surrendered only silence.

"Mmm." Kien frowned and took an automatic pistol from under his flawless suit coat. The pistol's large bore aimed at Malikai's forehead. Malikai made no move; if the gate had been open and Kien just a few inches closer, he could have disarmed Kien with his skillful feet, maybe even gotten control of the criminal's neck with his legs, snapped his spine in two. But Kien proved too smart to commit such an error.

"Why are you here?" Kien asked again. His brown eyes narrowed, as if peering into whatever passed for Malikai's soul.

One of the two henchman said something in the staccato language Malikai still couldn't quite grasp; yet somehow, he now understood it clearly in his head: *Just shoot him, boss.*

"No," Kien replied in English, not moving. "See? He is not afraid. He does not fear me, or the gun."

Kien spoke in the foreign language, but quietly, so Malikai could not hear. The henchman scurried off.

"Smile, demon!" Kien said. "It is your lucky day. I have decided not to torture you to make you answer my questions. It would do no good, correct? You are endowed with demonic strength, so I could not break you. I wonder what will make you talk, though? I wonder if—"

The henchman returned with a boy. The same boy Malikai had passed in the hallway on the way into this cell, the broken boy.

"—it was someone else, would you talk then?"

Kien put the gun away and pulled an ornate dagger from a hidden scabbard beneath his opposite arm. He slipped the dagger beneath the child's earlobe and slowly began tugging it upward.

He did not draw so much as a bead of blood before Malikai spoke.

"I'm looking for a girl."

Kien laughed. "That is more like it, friend. Why? What girl?"

"I promised to find her."

The boss looked mildly shocked and amused. "You made a vow? *You?*"

To his cronies, he said in the other language, *He really does think he is the demon buxiu!* This brought chuckles from the other men, and sent another burst of vibrations off in Malikai's chest. He couldn't begin to understand how he could possibly now interpret their language as if it were his own. It was as if hearing it opened a door to his linguistic memory. He'd never heard the language while in Phoenix.

"What else?" Kien said.

"There is nothing else. I came for her. And I will leave with her."

Kien studied him, as if trying to sense a lie. At last, he shrugged and passed the boy back to the man who had brought him.

"Very well. It's no matter to me." He turned to the two thugs. "Kill him."

Someone asked, *How? He's a six, like Ching.*

Kien glanced at Malikai over his shoulder with disinterest, and sighed.

"Try fire."

Kien turned down the hall and walked away, shiny black shoes clacking.

One guard remained outside the gate. The other left with the boy. Criminal and vigilante stared at one another through the bars for several minutes before the second thug returned.

He carried a red gallon jug of gasoline.

If the vigilante's heart still beat, it would have begun to thrum and pound. Malikai grasped their intent.

They opened the gate, but did not enter; it was as if, like Kien, they understood not to get any closer than necessary. One of the thugs took the cap off the jug of gasoline, hefted it, and splashed the fuel onto Malikai. Instinctively, he shut his eyes against the liquid and turned his head away. The bittersweet smell cloyed, despite the fact that he did not need to breathe; perhaps whatever sort of deviant respiration his body still required was the same mechanism by which Ching's breath attack had affected him. Maybe membranes in his nose still functioned, or else the delicate tissue of his eyes still sensed chemicals.

The thug doused the entire gallon onto Malikai, much of the gas splashing on the concrete floor, but most saturating his shirt, pants, and hair. Grunting in their foreign tongue to one another, the two thugs stepped clear from the cell, well away from any stray puddles of gasoline. One of them produced a matchbook. Malikai assumed they would grin, smile, chide—give some sense that they were enjoying their work. But they didn't. Rather, they looked vaguely pained, as if they did not relish the job but were honor-bound to finish it.

The thug stuck a match, and without hesitating, tossed it to the floor.

Malikai experienced two seconds of hope, because that's how long it took the pain to register. With a dim whoosh, the gas caught fire and swirled up his body in a tornado of flame.

The vigilante screamed. His body automatically drew breath to accomplish it, for there was no other response available. He writhed as his clothes roared and his hair twisted with reeking black smoke, curling from his scalp. He could not measure the pain as the fire shredded his clothing and shoes beneath its angry, hot teeth.

Malikai squirmed and bucked, desperately and pointlessly trying to put out the flames by flailing. Fire leapt into his mouth and down his throat, scorching him from the inside out while his skin blistered, popped, and fell away in red-black flakes. He squeezed his eyelids tight, absurdly begging in his mind for his eyes to be spared. He felt it when his skin ruptured on top of his head and fell away, his silver-metallic hair destroyed.

The outer layers of his skin sloughed and fell as the fire slowly died. Malikai spun slowly from the chain, the odor of singed hair and freshly crisped skin invading what remained of his nostrils. As the fire petered out, his exposed muscle sang with fresh pain as air hit it and tried to cool him, but instead only burned with a different fiery sting altogether.

His head dropped, chin on his chest.

He did not move.

The two thugs waited a moment and talked in low tones. His death hadn't been merciful, but at least it had been quick. Quicker than Kien was capable of, anyway.

They shuffled off down the hall, leaving the seared corpse of Malikai behind.

FOURTEEN

Manic made it to his apartment from Sal's office in ten minutes at full throttle. It was as if his old buddies in LAPD had emptied the streets for him.

Manic, to his own thrilled, private embarrassment, literally shouted "*Yahoo!*" as he tore through both green and yellow lights, swerving in and out of lanes as if the car had some kind of automotive wing-chun black belt. If there was an opening, the car seemed to find it of its own free will, and Manic just went along for the ride, outright laughing more than once behind the wheel of this exquisite vehicle.

Sal hadn't had a red one, so he'd settled for the black. A minor point.

For the first time ever, he pulled into his apartment's parking lot. Once he'd turned the engine off, Manic sat back in the driver's seat, eyes closed, hands still gripping the leather-wrapped steering wheel and feeling it pulse with life beneath his fingers.

"I could get used to this," he muttered happily. "I could very much get used to this."

Eventually he peeled himself out of the car and headed for the gate, casting admiring glances back as if the Boss was a beautiful woman. Manic laughed at the thought that it had been awhile since he'd driven one of those, either.

Speaking of which . . . Perdida Velasquez wasn't hard to look at.

"And a deev," Manic reminded himself as he walked into the complex. Or at least, that was most likely. Yeah, a little voice said to him, maybe a deev, but a *hot* deev. Maybe it could be overlooked just the once.

Or twice.

Manic laughed aloud again as he jogged up the steps to his apartment. Perdida said Sal was her uncle. Whether that was literal or figurative, he didn't know and it didn't matter. Either way, he didn't think old Sally would exactly be granting blessings on them to hook up. And that assumed she'd give him the time of day anyway.

In the apartment, Manic packed a thin, flat crate with gear from Weber's people. His eye happened across the manila envelope containing his next assignment. He hadn't opened it yet. Manic debated whether or not to take a look inside as he carefully packed various grenades into a separate case. Weber hadn't said anything about time limits. Getting each job done is what mattered. There might be a time frame in the paperwork, but it couldn't possibly be less than seven days, like Izanagi. The cat man had frankly surprised him. He hadn't expected it to be quite so easy to find the deev.

Manic shut and latched the case. Could there be any chance Sal had been lying about Izanagi, about the deviant trying to shut down some kind of slavery syndicate? But why would Sal lie about something like that?

"Goddamn deevs," Manic said out loud, to hear his own voice. He felt the great mood he'd had driving the Boss threatening to take flight like a flock of startled birds.

Hell with it. He tossed the unopened dossier envelope into one of the cases, telling himself this side gig for Sal wouldn't take more than a day. The deev inside the envelope could damn well live another twenty-four hours. The truth was, having a favor owed him from a man like Sal could be extremely beneficial someday. It might even mean he wouldn't have to pay for Lilly's school at all, maybe that was the kind of expense a man of Sal's means could handle all by himself.

Or maybe Manic could just keep the Boss.

Mood restored, Manic drove fast to the NPD satellite closest to the address Sal had written down on the notepaper. He felt almost surprised as he passed easily through security. Weber had been proven right again: he still had immediate access to NPD resources.

Who *was* that guy?

No—who was his *boss?*

Each NPD station was laid out in essentially the same fashion. Manic let himself into a large room near the comm area, housing what would have otherwise looked like nothing so much as study carrels in a school library. Each carrel came equipped with its own computer terminal, patched directly into all of the NPD resources available to everyone of officer rank. Manic knew there were other resources, top secret Fed type stuff, that captains and lieutenants had access to, but it wasn't the sort of intel needed by the footsoldiers. And Manic had no problem thinking of himself and his buddies in those terms—there was a war on, and they were on the front line. Fact.

Manic slid into an empty seat and tried logging in with his usual credentials. They were accepted, and he instantly had access to the full power of the NPD databases and web of intelligence.

He began with satellite maps. The address, toward the west end of town, seemed populated with short office buildings and independent shops; mom-and-pop type places designed for tourists. He ran records of ownership next, scanned tax documents, looked up driver licenses, and patched into a few nearby security cameras.

The effort spent his afternoon. By the time he decided he'd seen everything there was to see, the sixcop's eyes felt as dry as sandpaper.

"Come *on*," Manic groaned, checking his watch and then scowling at the two monitors on the desk in front of him.

As far as he could tell, the place where Sal wanted him to go, the place where a supposed den of human slavers trafficked was, in fact, a goddamn video arcade.

"Horseshit," Manic said.

Bottom line, Sal had this whole thing wrong. Everything about the business checked out. Frustrated, Manic logged off and headed for the door. None of the officers in comm paid any attention to him, though a couple of captains eyed him on his way. Manic was reminded of stories J.T. told him about soldiers overseas who wore no identifying patches shoving their way to the front of chow lines, and the grunts knowing not to complain. A guy in fatigues with no patches was a guy you did not want pissed at you. It was a good feeling, except that those patchless soldiers worked as a team, and Manic now flew utterly solo.

Manic went out to the parking lot, surprised despite the time on his watch that the sun was already down. Chilly autumn air nipped his eyes. Cripes, he'd spend the whole day researching a completely legitimate business. Woo-hoo. He climbed into the Boss and thumped his fingers on the wheel. Now what? To hell with Sal, start working on the next case? Or follow-through on the arcade just to be sure?

Well, hell. He'd said he'd do it. Manic cranked the engine and tore out of the NPD lot.

Driving the Boss didn't cheer him quite as much as he'd hoped as he sped toward the video arcade.

Manic parked in a restaurant parking lot, ignoring signs expressly forbidding parking for anyone not patronizing the establishment. Inwardly, Manic dared them to call a tow as he wandered down the street, checking out the shops that lined it. A comic book shop, a coffee shop, a bicycle-powered smoothie stand, a T-shirt shop, skate shop, more T-shirt shops, and no less than five fashion boutiques for women of varying styles.

Among them all, on one corner, sat the video arcade. Manic stopped in front of its open face. It had no fourth wall, instead relying on a wide gate that rolled shut from one side when closed. Inside the arcade, a number of cabinet-style video games from the 1980s stood side by side, along with a crane machine, some old pinballs—KISS, Indiana Jones, and Pawn Stars—and self-serve popcorn and soda machines.

"Yep," Manic mumbled, staring into the place. "Big hive of villainy here. Nice job, Sally."

He walked to the back of the shop, pulling his wallet out as he went. The arcade was mostly empty; two boys shouted at a combat game and an older couple giggled over Ms. Pac-Man. Cute.

The guy manning the change counter at the rear of the arcade appeared to be playing, not without some irony, a video game on his phone. Manic handed over a twenty. The guy passed over a couple rolls of quarters with barely a glance.

"Good gig?" Manic asked as he weighed the rolls in his hand.

The guy shrugged. Manic placed him at mid-twenties, of Chinese or mixed Asian decent, and in need of a powerful exercise regimen and possibly delousing.

"Lotta kids coming through here, huh," Manic went on, thinking that the noise of chirps and beeps must act like a beacon to grade schoolers. The arcade was kept dark, of course, lit only by infrequent overhead fluorescents and the screens of the games themselves.

The cashier shrugged again.

"Man, that would bug the shit outta me after awhile." Manic leaned back against the counter as if he had no intention of walking away any time soon. He knew it would irritate the cashier. "Little shits running around all day. Or probably after school, I guess, huh? They come in here and smoke up, spill their drinks all over everything . . ."

"Not really," the cashier said, eyes still glued to his phone.

"Tourists mostly."

"Yeah? What about that comic shop down the street? That must get a lot of kids."

"Kids don't have money for comics. It's older people."

"Ah, sure, sure."

"Officer, are you here to ask me something?" the cashier said, not lifting his eyes from his phone game.

Manic stood up straight. "Whoa, *officer?* Why'd you call me that?"

"'Cause you're a cop." The cashier winced and tilted his phone as if driving it. "You're trying to find something out. Why don't you just ask whatever you got to ask so I can keep playing my game."

Manic turned to face him head-on, dropping his shoulders and lifting his chin. "You kidnapping kids and selling them on the black market?"

The cashier raised his eyes away from the phone. They were slow, half-asleep eyes, perhaps recently stoned. After a pause, the cashier grunted a quick laugh and said, "Okay. Sure."

Manic raised an eyebrow. "You don't sound surprised. People ask you that a lot?"

"No, they don't. It's just the stupidest thing I ever heard."

"Look, pal—" Manic began.

"Call my boss," the cashier whined. "Okay, man? Do you want to know how much I make an hour? I'm just sitting here making change and mopping up. You want to look around this place, go ahead, I don't care. But I didn't do anything wrong, and if my boss is into some shady shit, take it up with him, all right?"

Manic laughed. He appreciated a good line of bullshit. "Just might do that. Thanks for the tip."

He tapped the rolls of quarters on the counter and sauntered out of the arcade, letting his eyes sweep over as much of the place as he could, waiting for some actionable piece of criminal labor to catch his eye.

Nothing did. The cashier was no law abiding citizen, that much he knew in his gut. Maybe he dealt a little untaxed pot on the side, which would make sense for his tourist and youthful clientele, or he might fence a little property from time to time. No civilian would have pegged Manic as a cop the way the cashier did.

But was the kid a cog in an organized machine to traffic in human beings? Manic was not convinced.

He stepped onto the sidewalk and lifted his face to the sky. He felt sure he could actually taste less smog in the air these days. Whatever else L.A. might be, it was a lot nicer than the old neighborhood. He sweated under his coat but made no move to take it off. The coat was part of his identity now.

He debated going straight back to Sal's Café, leaving a message for the old man, and calling it a night, but rejected the idea. Enough had been *off* about the cashier to warrant a little more poking around, just to satisfy himself. If he could do that, then he could convincingly satisfy Sal that there was nothing to be found.

Plus he didn't have the "office" job anymore, and sitting around watching soaps at the apartment didn't sound appealing. Taking the Boss up the 101, now *that* had some appeal, and Manic decided he'd do that after exhausting his investigation for the night.

Something bumped into him. Manic's hand instantly sprang toward his shoulder holster, but dropped and relaxed before the person who'd knocked into him could have even noticed. His "assailant" couldn't have been more than fifteen, sixteen tops: a short girl of Chinese descent wearing a baseball jersey-style shirt in gray and black. A cartoon drawing of a monster leaped from the center. A werewolf, maybe, and the picture reminded Manic of Izanagi.

"Sorry!" she said right away.

Manic smiled, or what passed for a smile anyway. She'd been reading and walking. A comic book, though, not a phone as he would have expected.

The girl moved to go around him, already starting to glance down into her comic again as if she'd learned nothing from the crunch into Manic on the sidewalk.

"You like comics?" Manic said.

She stopped and looked back. "Yeah?"

"How about video games?"

Manic appreciated what happened next: the girl shifted her weight to one side and relaxed her right shoulder. That was all. But it was the instinctive movement of a fighter, maybe a martial artist. From that stance, she had her right arm and leg chambered, ready to strike, while presenting the smallest possible target. She'd stay to chat, maybe because it was polite or maybe because he'd touched on something she cared about, but she wasn't going to provide this grizzled guy in the brown leather jacket an easy assault if he made a wrong move. All of this flashed through Manic's lens of experience in less than a heartbeat.

"Video games?" she said cautiously. "Sometimes."

She met his eyes unerringly, unafraid. Manic almost nodded in appreciation. The girl would not only detect any attack and have plenty of time to react, she was quite possibly memorizing his face for later description.

Nice.

Manic kept his hands in his pockets as usual and didn't move his feet. He nodded toward the arcade. "Ever go in there? Play some of those old games? I'm thinking of buying the place out, but it's kinda empty right now. Do a lot of people go in there?"

"Some."

"Well, how many is that? If you don't mind."

"It gets busy. Weekend nights, usually."

"Really. They stay open all night?"

"I guess so."

Manic pulled his hands out and held them up at shoulder height. "Okay, okay. I'll shut up. Thanks for the insight."

The girl gave him one slow nod and took a step backward, lengthening the distance he'd need to leap if he was a creeper. But to his surprise, she stopped.

"They'll never let you have it," she said.

"Who's that?"

"The Dragons. They'll never let you buy it."

Manic pivoted to face her fully. "Dragons, huh? You mean Ice Dragons? Those weenies?"

The girl smirked. "Don't say that too loud around here."

"How come? This their turf?"

"That's what my uncle says."

"You know all about 'em, huh?"

"Not a lot. Just to stay away from them."

"That's a good idea," Manic agreed. "So they run this place?"

"I think so. My uncle told me never to go inside, so I don't. We're not supposed to talk about it."

"Talk about what?"

The girl pressed her lips together and shook her head. Manic recognized the expression as one Lilly had perfected at about the same age and knew he wouldn't get anything else out of her.

He switched gears. "Looks like the comic book store's okay though, huh?"

"Totally. Andy's cool."

"That the owner?"

"Yeah. I mean, he's a total nerd, but. So am I."

Manic nodded. "Gotcha. All right. I'll keep all that in mind. Thanks a bunch."

"You're welcome." The girl walked on her way, eyes pointed into her comic less than a second later.

Well, well, well. So Sal's intel had been right after all. Busier on weekend nights, huh? Manic made up his mind. He'd come back later tonight.

In the meantime, he cruised in the Boss. He took the 101 out of town, treated himself to dinner at a renown Mexican place in Pasadena, and generally didn't give one shit about the rest of the world.

For a man whose business was life and death, he didn't wallow in deep thoughts. Or, perhaps he didn't wallow in deep thoughts because his business was life and death. When he was a kid—*where* he was kid—you were either a guy like Sal or you were a guy who kept a guy like Sal happy. Little Freddie Cruce learned that lesson the easy way, by watching others make mistakes and pay for them in cash and blood.

He knew early in life what his choices were. Go deep with the neighborhood family, keep working for Vic, or else become a cop and end up working for Vic anyway. He'd respected guys like Vic and Sal, admired them even. They did what they wanted, when they wanted, and they provided for the neighborhood. Nothing wrong with that. The problem was, every so often, one of them would go missing and never come back. Every so often, one or two of them would end up sitting in prison. There was no honor among thieves, he'd learned that, too. Little Freddie Cruce wanted to know where he stood with people. Vic's crew couldn't be counted on if the heat really turned up. Some young punk almost always took the fall.

Little Freddie Cruce wasn't about to be that young punk.

So he'd left. He didn't want anything more to do with his mother by then anyway. Some people had drinking problems, she had a drinking catastrophe. Manic wasn't even sure, to this day, if she ever noticed that he'd left after graduating high school. As for his dad . . . he'd asked his mom once about him. One fast backhand across the face later, he decided knowing about his absentee father was something he no longer needed to worry about.

Sal had left town by then. Manic wondered as he drove back into L.A. later that night why he hadn't heard more about Sal's story around the neighborhood, more about the circumstances surrounding Tony's death. Gossip was currency, and he knew people talked. Or at least, they talked about things it was safe to talk about. If Sal, or Vic, had put out a gag order, no doubt the neighborhood followed it.

The clock in the Boss's dashboard showed midnight straight up when Manic pulled into the same restaurant parking lot where he'd parked earlier. He took up a position on a green wrought-iron bench about fifty yards from the arcade. The other shops were closed for the night, though a bar another block north admitted and disgorged patrons every so often. Some stumbled into the arcade since the gate was open. Most walked the other direction toward street parking and got into cars. Nothing fancy, Manic noted as he swung his legs up onto the bench and opened a newspaper. New model year Toyotas were about as lavish as they got. Sooner or later a cop would drive past and possibly try to hustle him on his way, and he'd have to go, because if he flashed his NPD creds, they'd leave him alone, and anyone paying attention would know this apparently homeless guy wasn't all he seemed to be.

Manic sniffed at the thought that he could pass for homeless right now. His cargo pants were a few days unwashed now. He hadn't shaved in at least a week. His old brown leather jacket fit him comfortably as always, but to anyone besides its owner, he saw where it could be taken as a symbol of destitution rather than a beloved, worn-in coat.

In the end he didn't have to worry about it. Things happened sooner than he'd dared to hope.

A silver BMW roared down the street and squealed to a halt outside the arcade, double-parked. A white middle-aged male got out of the car and jauntily quick-stepped toward the arcade. It was one a.m.

"Going a few rounds with Ms. Pac-Man?" Manic muttered as he flipped a page in the newspaper, not reading but peeking over the paper's top edge. "Now why do I doubt that."

Rich Guy—Manic's instant name for the man, who wore tailored slacks and a white silk button-up—didn't even pass the threshold of the shop before the cashier Manic had met earlier came out, waving his hands. They were too far to hear, but their pantomime read loud and clear: the kid wanted Rich Guy to move his car. Rich Guy wasn't having it. The kid pointed emphatically into the arcade, then raised a warning finger under Rich Guy's nose. Rich Guy got the message. He climbed back into the BMW and tore on down the street, skidding around the corner where Manic had taken up his position. He grabbed a partial license plate number as Rich Guy turned. Out-of-state-plate, BFR- something.

The kid watched him go, then shook his head and went back into the arcade. A minute later, Rich Guy reappeared, all but jogging down the sidewalk. Manic slipped his night-vision monocular out of his coat and watched the guy through it. Rich Guy went into the arcade. Manic could see he went straight to the rear of the building, most likely to the cashier counter. He lost sight of Rich Guy at that point, due to his position up the street.

Now what? Follow, or wait?

He opted for the wait. It would be a tad embarrassing if he went charging in guns blazing right now only to find the prick playing Donkey Kong.

But when twenty minutes passed with no sign of Rich Guy, Manic let his impatience take over. He folded the paper under his arm and swung himself off the bench, keeping his eyes trained on the entrance to the arcade. He stayed on the far side of the street, hustling down the sidewalk and glancing in many directions so as not to give away that his focus was on the arcade. It was too dark and too far for him to see clearly inside, but he got the impression it was empty.

Swearing, Manic darted across the street and stood in front of the comic book shop's picture windows, pretending to browse new issues propped up in display cases. The proprietor glanced at him, then away—he had no value if he didn't come inside.

The shop—The Comic Zone—sat ninety yards or so upstreet of the arcade. Manic kept his position, keeping an eye on the arcade, but no one went in or out. Rich Guy had been gone for a half hour by then.

"Hell with it," Manic grumbled, and walked toward the arcade, hands in his jacket pockets. He didn't hesitate as he reached the arcade, choosing instead to charge right in and find Rich Guy, maybe bump into him, beg his pardon, try to start a conversation.

Except that, other than the cashier, the arcade was empty.

Manic stopped in the middle of one row of video games, scanning the small building. Its square footage was no more than the average corner convenience store. No place to hide. Just the cashier counter. No bathrooms, either, unless the door behind the cashier's counter led to one, and if so, it wasn't for the public.

The cashier looked up from his phone with a bored expression.

And Manic instantly saw through it. Without a word, the kid was already lying.

Manic stepped slowly toward the counter, keeping his hands in his pockets. "Evening."

The kid nodded once.

"Lookin' for a guy who popped in here," Manic said, pretending to be casual, and doing a bad enough job that the kid would know he was anything but that. "You mighta seen him. Rich lookin' prick, nice clothes, white button-up?"

The kid shrugged.

Manic unzipped his coat fully as he closed the distance to the counter. Only ten feet away now. Whistles and bloops and bleeps of unplayed games followed in his wake.

"You couldn't have missed him. Matter of fact, you came out and told him to move his car. So I know that you know who I'm talking about."

The kid shrugged again. Manic moved closer.

"So whaddya say? Give me a heads-up, and you can go home tonight without losing so much as a drop of blood. Where's he at?"

Manic reached the counter. The kid met his eyes evenly, and Manic saw his stoned gaze was an act.

"We already been through this," the kid said. "What do you want?"

"Just what I said. Where's the rich guy?"

"I don't know what you're talking about."

"'Kay, see, now I'm pissed," Manic said, smiling. "Thing is, kid, if you think I'm a cop? I'm not. But I am a guy who can make things very sad for you. Okay? Last call. Where is he?"

The kid put his hands on the countertop and leaned forward. "*The thing is*," he said sarcastically, "I'm a lot more afraid of the people I work for than I am of you. So."

He gave Manic the same shrug.

Manic laughed. "Fair enough, man."

Holding a roll of the quarters, he fired a straight jab into the kid's sternum. The blow pushed the kid backward into the wall, where he slid to the ground with a splat.

Manic vaulted the counter and grabbed the kid by the throat. "What's behind door number one?"

"Rich guy," said the kid through a wheeze.

"Who else? Who do you work for?"

"Gentleman . . ."

"Oh, I find that hard to believe. What gentlemen?"

"Gentleman's . . . club . . ."

"All right," Manic said. "I'll just take a look for myself."

He yanked a loop of plastic zip tie concealed behind his back and deftly snapped the kid's wrists together. The kid coughed for air as Manic used a second strip of zip tie to lash him to a load-bearing pole behind the counter.

Satisfied with his work, Manic rushed to slide shut the gate over the arcade's entrance. He walked back to the kid and hunkered down, feeling along the bottom edge of the counter for an alarm button.

"Now when I open that door, what am I gonna find?" he said, satisfied there was no panic button.

"Stairs," the kid groaned.

Manic pulled out his weapon. "And where do those stairs lead?"

"Down."

Manic gave him a couple of taps on the head with the barrel of his nine-millimeter. "Ah, wise guy, eh? C'mon, don't start mouthing off now. What's down there, kid?"

The kid grinned painfully and met Manic's eyes. "Okay. You need to think about this, man. Why would who ever is down *there* have an asshole like me up *here* to keep an eye on things, huh? Do I look like a security guard to you? Maybe it's because anyone getting past me ain't gonna come back up. Ever."

"Huh," Manic said, and pulled his old badge out. "And, what if I'm NPD? What if I call a couple dozen wagons over here to back me up?"

The kid forced a laugh. "Good luck with that."

Manic's excitement dimmed as the fun he'd been having messing with the kid ended abruptly. The cashier wasn't bluffing. Manic made him nervous, maybe even afraid for his own safety, but the kid had absolute zero fear of anything Manic could bring to bear against whatever lay beyond that door.

What the hell had he stumbled into now? Only one way to find out.

"I'll just take a quick look," Manic said, standing. "You keep nice and quiet, now, or I'll bust you up. Got it?"

"Nice knowing you," the kid said.

Manic resisted an urge to boot the kid in the face. He went to the door and listened. Hearing nothing, he tried the knob. It turned readily.

"And . . . here we go," Manic whispered to himself.

Smiling, he opened the door.

*

Malikai awoke to pain he could not readily possess, pain so overwhelming that it seemed to belong to someone else entirely. His eyes peeled open and he gazed down at the blackened, crimson hunk of meat his body had become, naked and raw.

Still alive, he thought. *I am still alive.*

He listened closely, since listening was about the extent of what he was capable of.

Mostly what he heard was silence.

It unnerved him. Every so often, he would hear the clang of a gate or door being opened or closed. He once heard a shout, as of a name being called, and distant brutish laughter. But that was all. No water dripped in his cell, no movement in the corridors signaled so much as a guard doing routine patrols, and no plaintive wails of captured children wafted in from beyond the cell gate. This last detail concerned him, for there were only a few possibilities: the children were in sound-proofed prisons, they were gagged or otherwise unable to make noise . . .

Or they were not here at all.

But he reminded himself about the boy they'd passed in the hall, the one Kien had threatened—was it an hour ago, or a day? Longer? That boy had not been some merry wanderer. He'd been a captive, and he'd been broken. Malikai knew well the expression, or lack thereof, on the boy's face. He'd encountered it many times on the streets of Phoenix. It spoke of hopelessness and a dim desire for death. Malikai knew even if he succeeded in finding that boy along with Julia Lawson, and got them both to the light of day, neither child would be readily healed. Julia might have a better chance, since she hadn't been gone for too long and clearly had a wealthy family awaiting her, a family who could and would afford her the best possible psychological care.

The boy? Who knew.

He blinked as a short, thin figure rushed past the gate, glancing only once at him as it went.

Malikai grunted at it; it wasn't a guard, he was sure.

"Wait!"

Slowly, the smallish figure slipped back into view, and Malikai saw it was a boy, perhaps a middle teenager, his eyes wide and staring, mouth closed. He clutched a brown paper sack in both hands, and was dressed in ancient jeans and what had once been a white T-shirt. Wild brown hair stood up on his head and shambled down his shoulders.

Beyond that, he was descended from a wolf.

The boy's face, on closer examination, was covered in a fine down of white and gray hairs sweeping back from a slightly protruding mouth and nose. His brow furrowed forward like a Husky's, beneath which sat eyes of little human origin. Even the curve of his arms struck Malikai as canine, carried at his sides at severe angles like wounded paws. Somewhere deep in his golden eyes, the vigilante sensed pride, loyalty, and perhaps a savage hunger for prey.

But these feelings and instincts had long been suppressed, and likely beaten out of the child. Malikai instantly assessed the boy's place in this hellhole: a messenger. Probably too old or too damaged somehow to be of any use to the type of person looking to buy a child.

"What's your name?" he asked the boy.

At first the boy did nothing but stare, eyes gleaming gold beneath the sickly white fluorescents.

"Farrill," the boy said, the word muted through his swollen, jutting mouth. His voice seemed far too deep for his thin frame.

Malikai nodded encouragingly. "Farrill. I am Malikai. Can you help me?"

A long pause . . . then Farrill slowly shook his head, keeping his eyes fixed on the vigilante. Malikai knew it wouldn't help to push the boy; Farrill, despite whatever strength hid inside him, looked as though one loud noise would send him scampering for a bed to hide beneath.

Keeping his voice soft, Malikai asked, "You live here?"

The boy nodded, again after a pause, as if it took an extra second or two for the words to penetrate his ears.

"Do you know a girl named Julia? Is she here?"

Pause . . . then a nod. Malikai felt a small and brief surge of energy. He was close. Chained in a concrete cell under the earth, yes; but close.

"Can you help me find her?"

Pause . . . and Farrill shook his head. Malikai was not surprised, knowing the child must live in a constant state of low-grade terror here among bad men and beasts like Kien—never mind Ching, who Malikai thought might be too mindless to be truly evil. Cold comfort, that thought.

"All right," Malikai, trying for a soothing tone. "If I was to stand where you are, which way would I go to see her?"

Pause . . . and the boy slid his eyes to the left. Malikai could not tell if the slight gesture had been automatic or if the boy was trying to help. Either way, while it wasn't much, it was a start.

"That's good," Malikai said. "Thank you. . . . Would you like to go home?"

This time, the boy's brushy, wolfish eyebrows merely furrowed, as if he did not understand the question.

Malikai, on the other hand, perfectly understood his non-verbal response: what home? This was his only home. Whether by choice, which Malikai doubted, or by terror, which Malikai suspected, this child had no concept of life beyond this concrete labyrinth. Perhaps he'd never seen the sun. The irony of the thought struck painfully: where Malikai chose to avoid the sun for simplicity's sake, this child may not have been allowed to see it. To breathe fresh air, even if that air was the hot, fetid stench of Phoenix or the warm, clear air of Los Angeles.

Malikai promised himself, almost subconsciously, that when he got out of here with Julia, and maybe even Farrill, he would never forsake the sun again.

Then his conscious mind teased back, pointing out that getting out of this cell was currently a rather presumptuous plan.

Before he could phrase another question, the boy darted away down the corridor. Malikai barely heard his footsteps; he wore no shoes. Malikai wondered for how long that had been the case.

He looked up again at the iron ring from which he swung. His sword would make short work of it, he knew; but bare-handed? He didn't quite have the strength to pull chains like this apart. The Tang dao could probably melt through the links given enough uninterrupted time, but that fact helped him not at all.

The bolts holding the metal plate to the concrete ceiling, on the other hand . . . if there were some way he could get the leverage to pull them down out of the concrete—

Footsteps.

Malikai relaxed his scorched muscles, playing dead.

Waiting.

FIFTEEN

Manic detected no threats in the long concrete tunnel that lay beyond the arcade door. As the cashier had said, an iron staircase led down almost immediately beyond the door. Keeping his pistol tucked close to his chest in the manner of all NPD sixcops, he crept downstairs, his soft-soled boots nearly silent against the steps.

After a twenty-yard decent, the stairwell ended at another door, this one covered with a sheet of rusting iron. He tried the handle, which did not move. Locked. The knob had a single keyhole, and no space for a deadbolt.

"Easy pickin's," Manic said to himself, and laughed at his own pun. With the pistol in his right hand, he pulled a lockpicking gun from one pocket of his cargo pants, and in less than a minute, the door clicked open.

Manic paused, breathing slow and deep and silent, listening for any indication his presence had been detected. One minute. Two minutes. He stood motionless, pistol ready. Three minutes. Four minutes.

Nothing. Using the toe of his boot, he nudged the door open a crack and began slicing the pie, cutting the room into invisible wedges as he scanned for threats.

Empty. The door opened into a bare concrete room with industrial lights hanging from the ceiling. Though hard to say for sure without a crime scene kit, Manic was positive that blood stained the walls and floor. It had been scrubbed off for the most part, but blood had a way of really settling into surfaces.

Across from him loomed another iron door. Manic slid over to it and tried the handle. This one turned easily.

He listened again, heard nothing, then opened the door. Another long, concrete corridor, also empty. Manic quick-stepped down the length of it, pistol trained on the door at the end. He pried it open and found a square room with hallways leading off to the right and left at the far end. Nothing more.

"Ain't anybody home?" he muttered and slipped into the room. Maybe old Sal was off his nut. So far the biggest problem he'd encountered was an overweight video arcade cashier. Not exactly the kind of life-threatening villain he was used to. Still, the kid admitted something bad was down here, and Manic believed him.

He then noticed two sensory details, both on the very edge of his perception. The first slipped beneath his nostrils like a silk scarf being waved, but the scent itself caught on his tongue and made him gag. It came and went like a whiff of rancid perfume from a passing zombie.

At the same moment, he heard something underneath the dead silence. It was a sound he hadn't heard in years. At least fifteen, maybe more, but it rang deep inside him just as it had when Lilly was a kid.

For as dim and distant as the sound had been, it was unmistakably the cry of a child.

Manic grit his teeth as his heart rate sped up. If there was one thing a person did not do so long as he drew breath, it was hurt a kid. Every cop took that vow. Even career criminals avoided it. For as much as deviants ought to be wiped off the face of the earth, folks who didn't mind hurting kids were another kind of disease entirely.

Manic listened hard for the sound again, disregarding the foul odor he'd sensed to better hone in on the noise. Which direction, dammit? Where had the cry come from?

He chose the right-hand corridor, moving more quickly than his training demanded, and did not care. A kid needed help.

The hallway split into another T-intersection. Manic paused and peeked around each corner. Down the left, caged lights in the ceiling illuminated several metallic doors in the walls, and the hall ended in another split to the left and right. Down the right-hand corridor, however, the lights had either been broken or removed, leaving the hall in darkness. But down that darkened hallway, Manic spotted one thin line of sickly yellow light creeping from beneath the bottom of a door. Another plaintive but muted cry slipped from behind that door.

Manic snarled. Memories of Lilly helplessly bleeding and crying from her first bike accident zipped through his calloused mind. He'd agonized over that sound, so many years ago, and he agonized now as he heard a sound almost like it. Almost, but worse.

Much, much worse.

Growling softly, paternally, Manic fished for his suppressor. He quickly screwed the cylinder onto his weapon before slipping down the dark hall.

As he neared the door, another smell wafted past him. Cologne. Just a whiff of it tickled the hairs in his nose. While not a user of scents himself, he recognized it as not being the cheap shit some guys bought at Walgreens. This was the good stuff. Rich Guy stuff, maybe.

Manic got to the door and quickly double-checked his surroundings. Other than the noises behind the closed door, he heard nothing.

But the noises behind the closed door were more than enough.

He knew already, no matter what happened in the next few seconds, he'd never get those sounds out of his head.

Manic laid a hand on the doorknob, but it didn't turn. No factor: he scanned the perimeter of the door, seeing that it opened inward and wasn't the same sturdy quality as the other doors he'd passed through so far. This had once been a janitor's closet or something similar, not the type of room that needed heavy protection.

No, this door was for privacy, not security.

As another pained, muffled cry crept from beneath the door, Manic took a step back. He raised his right foot, took a breath—and kicked the door in.

It took his cop's brain half of one second to assess the scene, and his father's brain another half second to act. Rich Guy's clothes lay over a metal chair, immaculately folded. A pile of clothes beside them clearly belonged to the young boy now at Rich Guy's mercy. Manic knew he'd never scour the image from his memory of what Rich Guy was doing to the boy.

Rich Guy had only enough time to grunt and begin to turn to see who was interrupting him. Manic squeezed the trigger before Rich Guy could fully face him.

Rich Guy's brains smashed out of the left side of his skull with a pop. The man sank to the cold concrete floor in a heap where he belonged.

The boy sprang away and spun around to face Manic, keeping his back to the wall, his eyes wide, outraged, and terrified. Manic pointed the barrel toward the ceiling and raised his other hand, empty, to show him.

"I'm a cop. It's okay."

Actually, Manic thought, things were pretty fucking far from okay for this kid, but it was one of those nonsense comfort phrases that sometimes popped out of people before they could stop it. Manic stretched out his empty hand.

"I'm gonna get you outta here, okay? Come on. Come with me."

The boy didn't move, only breathed hard and stared.

"Hey." Manic sank to the ground, balanced on his toes, ignoring the great glut of thick blood beginning to pool on the floor as Rich Guy's body pumped it out of him at a prodigious rate. "You know what happens if you stay here. If I was gonna hurt you, I'd do it right now. So come on. Trust me, man. I'm getting you outta here."

The truth of the words seemed to work. The boy tiptoed toward him, clearly making an effort to not look at the remnants of brain matter on the wall. He swiped his clothes into his arms, then took Manic's hand. Manic pulled him into the hall.

"What's your name?" Manic asked, and noted that his voice had automatically taken on the same higher pitch and gentle glide he'd used with Lilly as a little girl. So long ago. Lilly. If anyone ever dared to do to her what he'd seen here—

"Liam Gray." The boy hurried to shove his clothes up and down his body.

"Okay Liam Gray, you know your way around this place?"

"You killed that man."

"Stay with me, Liam, okay? Focus with me. Do you know your way around this place?"

The boy nodded.

"Are there any other kids around?"

Liam nodded again. Manic swore to himself. That complicated things. What he wanted to do was drag little Liam around the entire compound, free every kid he found, and aerate every bad guy along the way. The cashier upstairs would be lucky to escape with a crippling wound as it was once Manic got back up there. But going on a one-man rescue mission was not the tactically sound move, and he knew it.

"Okay, okay," Manic chanted to himself, and pulled out his phone. He could hunker down here with the boy in one of the other private rooms. From there, given the arsenal he carried on his body, he could probably hold off quite an assault until the NPD wagons showed up and tore the place apart.

No signal. Not for the web, not for his phone.

"Goddammit!" He tapped furiously on various icons, trying to source the problem, and pieced it together a moment later: the underground compound was suppressing all possible signals. Electronically, the place was invisible. Whether it was the result of how deep under ground they were, or some kind of countermeasure, Manic couldn't tell and didn't care. He had to decide whether to skip out now or find the others.

What if it was Lilly down here?

He barely completed the thought before hunkering down beside the boy again. "Listen to me. You stay right behind me, and don't make any noise. Nothing, okay? Stay low, stay quiet. Can you do that, L.G.?"

Like any boy, being deemed worthy enough for a cool nickname had an immediate impact on Liam Gray, whose chest puffed out and chin lifted. Manic admired his strength. Kids could recover from unreal shit sometimes. He was proud Lilly had never had to.

"Yes," Liam said.

Manic gripped his shoulder and gave it a shake. "Good man. Where's the others?"

"That way."

Manic got his gun ready and led them the way he'd come, tactically checking corners along the way. In moments, they'd reached the room where the first T-intersection was located.

From here, he could either run for the stairs back up to the arcade, or take the left-hand corridor instead.

"That way?" Manic whispered, nodding toward the left corridor. Liam nodded.

Manic grit his teeth, swearing internally. Goddammit, they could get out *right now*. Go upstairs, deal with the cashier in a most unpleasant manner, and call in the cavalry. That was the smartest, safest move, especially towing a kid around like this.

But some bad guy down here would discover Rich Guy sooner

or later. Alarms would be raised. The compound might flood with thugs armed with who-knew-what. Maybe even a deev or two, hired muscle like Fracture. When that happened, more kids like Liam, or like the little girl Lilly'd once been, might be carried off site and taken someplace else. Or simply killed to prevent witnesses.

No. No, he had to find the kids. That was the priority. The cavalry would come eventually.

His next thought was to send Liam up to the arcade on his own. The cashier was lashed to the pole still—most likely—so all Liam would have to do was find a way out of the building and to a cop. Except if there was any chance at all the cashier had gotten free, or anything else went wrong, Liam would be all alone.

Shit. For the time being, the boy had to stay.

"All right, on me," Manic whispered. Together, they crossed the room and entered the left corridor.

They came to a corner. Manic peeked around it.

And found his first deviant of the day.

The deev might've gotten a bullet between the eyes if he'd stood any taller. But this six wasn't much taller than Liam Gray, barely reaching the height of Manic's shoulder. The deev also would have appeared as shocked and frightened as Liam had, except his canine face prevented normal human expression.

The kid was unarmed, and Manic couldn't help assessing him as just that: a kid, but a kid whose dad might have been an Alaskan timber wolf. His mouth and nose jutted forward slightly like a muzzle, and a thin coat of fine gray and white hairs covered them. The kid's brow furrowed severely, his eyes as yellow-blue as a sunrise. He carried his hands next to his flank, wrists bent and fingers cupped, his elbows cocked back at sharp angles, reminding Manic of a dog's hind legs. The deev—the kid—was otherwise human, and clearly scared half to death.

"Don't move," Manic said, leveling his pistol at the kid.

The deev blinked and froze in place. He may have been panting.

"Where are the kids?"

A canine whine came from deep in the kid's throat. Manic grimaced. Deevs.

"Can you speak?"

The kid nodded quickly.

"Then answer the question before things get ugly for you. Where are the kids?"

The wolf-boy stepped aside and gestured down the hall in the direction Manic and Liam had been traveling. Wonderful. No big help there.

"Got a name?" Manic said.

The kid huffed out a word that inflated his cheeks; two syllables. To Manic, it sounded like *Farrill*.

"All right, Farrill, turn around," Manic ordered.

Farrill obeyed. In fact, Manic noted, he obeyed like someone used to doing so. Farrill wore ragged jeans and a filthy white T-shirt. From beneath the collar of the shirt, Manic saw a still-healing scar, the shape of which reminded him of a belt or a lash of some kind.

Yes—this deev was used to following orders no matter who they came from. If he'd been a little more human, Manic might have even felt bad for him.

Or . . . felt *worse* for him, rather, than he did at that moment.

"You don't make a sound, and you take me right to where they are, you get me?"

Farrill nodded and started walking. Though his bare feet seemed human enough, they were covered in the same downy hair as his face. His gait struck Manic as being dog-like . . . although at that point, he may have been walking like any upright human, and his deviation made Manic only think he moved any differently.

"Recognize this guy?" Manic said over his shoulder to Liam Gray.

"No," Liam said. "What's wrong with his face?"

"Just a deev. Don't worry, I got him cov—what the *hell?*"

Farrill had led them around another corner. When they turned, the faint odor Manic had detected when he first entered the compound came at him full force. He recognized it and recoiled: burnt flesh. Not the pleasant aroma of a sunny summer barbecue, but the hideous, greasy stench of seared hair and roasted human skin.

He grabbed Farrill's shoulder. "Wait a sec, what's that smell? What's down there?"

Farrill whined again. Manic jammed the gun between his shoulder blades. "You take me to it. Go."

Farrill continued walking, but not as willingly as before. He led them down the hallway, then gestured meekly toward a break in the wall several yards down. Manic gripped the kid's shirt collar, keeping the gun trained on his back as they approached.

The smell became laced with the unmistakable acrid odor of gasoline. Manic subconsciously held his breath as they reached the turn. A barred gate, like a prison cell door, had been installed across a doorway to what might have once been a storage closet. Fresh metallic hardware had been installed in the walls, with concrete dust still piled up beneath the installations—thick steel rings that looked to Manic might have been normally used in construction for some kind of anchoring purposes. Chains snaked from the rings, and wrapped around the legs, arms, and chest of a figure suspended off the floor.

"Jesus," Manic gasped as his lungs gave out on him.

It was a slaughtered animal pretending to have once been human. While his limbs were intact, pulled taut between the heavy chains, his skin had been charred off his naked body. Raw patches of red muscle glared up from between areas of black burn marks.

The man didn't breathe, and for that, Manic gave thanks. No one deserved that kind of agony. No one but the kind who would enslave and trade in children.

He nudged the gun into Farrill's back. "You'd better pray I don't find any kids lookin' like that, buddy. You better just fuckin' pray."

Farrill shook his head. Manic decided to interpret the gesture as meaning no, he would not find any children in that condition.

The burnt man's eyes opened then.

Manic twitched back in shock. No one could survive wounds like that, not for long, anyway. But this man's eyes were red with silver irises, and Manic realized then he was looking at a deviant. A deviant who could survive catastrophic trauma the likes of which he'd never encountered in his time at NPD. Maybe a Level Seven.

He thought the deviant might say "Help me." Then he thought the deviant might say "Kill me." Instead, the deviant stared into Manic's eyes and said:

"Children."

His voice sounded as scorched as his flesh looked.

Instinctively, Manic thought he understood: this deev—this guy—had been trying to do the same thing he himself was attempting, and failed.

Sal's guy. Red eyes, that's what Sal had said. This had to be him. Or what remained of him.

Manic took a step back as the first shakes of panic invaded his limbs. In the best-case scenario, this deviant was strong enough to survive being burned alive, yet had still been unable to avoid capture and grievous torture. That didn't bode well for an ex-NPD cop toting an abused pre-teen in an underground compound about which he had zero intelligence or insight.

Bad call, Manic, he thought. *You stupid, useless jackhole, this was a bad idea from the get-go. Time to motor.*

"You know this guy?" Manic whispered harshly to Liam. Liam shook his head, his face pale as if trying to avoid vomiting at the sight of the skinless man.

"Okay, that's it," Manic decided. "We're outta here." He pushed Farrill back the way they'd come. "You. Move. Anyone comes after us, guess what? You get shot first."

Leaving the devastated six behind, Manic turned his crew back up the hallway, double-timing it now to get to the stairwell that led to the arcade.

That's when his luck ran out.

*

Malikai fought to speak again, but could not make his burnt vocal cords work as the grizzled human ran off the way he'd come. Then again, what could the man have possibly done? He'd clearly not belonged here, was not an Ice Dragon for certain. In fact it had appeared he'd been trying to save one of the many children Malikai was now convinced were trapped here in the labyrinth.

Whoever he was, it mattered little now. Malikai was on his own.

A new set of footsteps echoed in the hallway, coming from the opposite direction of where the man had gone. Footsteps, and muttering. Malikai played dead once more.

He listened intently as someone—who sounded as if they were alone—rustled something noisily outside the cell gate. A moment later, he felt the dull prod of something against this body, sending it swaying lightly by the chains.

The person shouted at him. Malikai kept up his ruse.

He heard grumbling again over the noise of the person rattling keys and pulling the gate open. The thug cursed in his native tongue as something clattered to the concrete floor.

Malikai struck.

The vigilante hoisted himself upward on the chains around his wrists, wrapping his legs around the young man's shorn and scarred head. With one quick, unmerciful twist of his body that sent shards of pain cascading through his scorched limbs, Malikai snapped the young man's spinal cord from the base of his skull. The thug dropped lifelessly to the floor, eyes open as if in shock that he was really dead. *They don't pay me enough for this*, his dead gaze seemed to say.

Malikai curled his back, biting an urge to scream in agony as his burnt flesh stretched and split. He swung his feet up to the ceiling and hung upside down like a bat, knees bent, the iron ring in the ceiling now between his feet. He was reminded, distantly, of one of the posters in the comic book shop he'd passed on the way to the arcade—he must look like one of those heroes right now. Spider-Man, he thought. Maybe that man was allowed to be a hero because he'd been human before he became a deviant.

Straining, Malikai flexed his knees, trying to straighten his legs and push as hard as he could against the concrete ceiling. The bolts securing the plate and ring trembled and rained fine gray dust on him. He pushed again, digging his heels into the ceiling while pulling the chain.

At last it gave way. He fell unceremoniously to the floor, the thug breaking most of the fall but not enough to prevent a fresh hell of pain shooting through his body. For the first time in his un-life, Malikai wanted to truly die; the pain was so exquisite, so refined, that it made him weep from the hopelessness and helplessness of it.

But he did not make a sound. He couldn't, not now; couldn't risk it. He was free—free from the bonds of the ceiling anyway, but still bound in chains, naked, and seared. The pain made it hard to think.

Malikai crept off the young man's body. He'd never killed on his patrols, only maimed and wounded the criminals he dealt with. If any of his wounds later led to death, then so be it, but he had no personal knowledge of it. Death held no great joy for him, except, perhaps, the death he was anxious to visit upon Kien.

Giving himself a bare moment to recover, Malikai noted a roll of plastic sheeting and a mop in the cell. The Dragon had used the tip of the mop handle to prod his body from the safety of the gate. The plastic, no doubt, was meant to wrap the dead six before disposal.

Moving through excruciating agony, he searched the young man's body. The thug carried a handgun, but it meant nothing to the vigilante. Then he found the weapon he hoped for: a knife, a balisong blade, what Westerners frequently mis-named a butterfly knife; the type with two handles that could fold to protect to blade, or else fold the other way and form the handle. It wasn't his Tang dao, but it was a blade, and a blade he could use.

Now, for the important test. It wasn't one he'd ever thought to do back at the farmhouse, and he cursed himself for it now. Malikai held the knife in both hands, staring at the blade, grateful his eyes had indeed been spared in his conflagration. He willed the blade to take on a laser-like sheen of blue flame.

The blade did not obey him.

So that answered the question: his sword's incredible abilities were intrinsic to the weapon, not to him, or else they were somehow paired together. Unfortunate, but not alarming. He had a sharp edge now. It would be enough. He would *make* it be enough.

Malikai climbed to his feet, grinding his teeth to fortify himself against his raw flesh cracking open and bleeding pus and other fluid. Consciously, he wanted to seek out Kien, make him pay for this agony, but he talked himself out of it. What would Xavian have him do?

Find the girl. Free her. Free them all. But find her.

He knew he didn't have much time. Wherever the young thug had intended to take his supposed corpse, he would be missed eventually.

Malikai, with every nerve fiber exposed to the air and screeching for relief, crept to the open cell door. He heard nothing, and risked peeking out. If he went right, he'd end up in the long corridor Ching had carried him down; but the boy, Farrill, who had stopped here earlier indicated Julia was somewhere to the left, at least in theory. Malikai went that direction, skinless feet shrieking anew at each step.

This end of the hall ended with a door in the wall, and beyond, a right turn. He tentatively tried the door, his exposed palms condemning him to hell for daring to touch a surface. The door felt securely locked. He listened, and heard nothing, so took the right turn. The corridor continued for another twenty yards before offering either a right turn branching away from the hallway, or continuing straight ahead.

Malikai listened again. Down the right hall, he heard voices, but they echoed, making it impossible to tell how far away they were. He longed for the outdoors of Phoenix, where he was used to operating and being able to judge how far away a voice, a scream, a pair of footsteps, or a gunshot might have originated.

He risked a glance around the corner. The right-hand corridor extended another fifty yards or so, and at the end of it, he could see several men smoking from small pipes. A tablet computer set up on a card table played a show, something Malikai couldn't identify from this distance. It seemed as though these men were on some kind of break.

He chose to go forward, edging past the turn in the hall, and simply hoping no one would note his passage. No one shouted, and the men's level of conversation did not change, so he assumed they had not seen him.

Two more corners loomed ahead, both to the right. The first appeared to open into a dark hallway; the second simply curved this hall that direction. Malikai paused at the first turn and peeked around.

Darkness.

Only darkness.

Light spilling from the caged bulb overhead did not extend far enough to reach the end of this black hall, but it did not need to; Malikai saw what he needed to see and heard what he needed to hear.

Several barred gates, like the one on his own cell, lined each side of this unlit corridor. From behind the gates, he heard occasional rustling, occasional sniffling. And then . . . the barely perceptible sound of the muffled cry of a child.

Malikai slid around the corner, knife gripped tight despite the pain it caused in his hand. He stopped just short of the first gate, back against the wall.

"Julia."

No response. He peeked into the dark cell, and saw only a bundled form on top of a blanket in one corner. It took several moments of staring to determine if the being inside the bundle was breathing.

"Where is Julia Lawson?" he whispered.

Nothing.

He went to the next gate—and found her.

SIXTEEN

Two men turned a corner up ahead of Manic and the two boys. Clearly the Ice Dragons hadn't discovered the brains or body of Rich Guy yet, because they appeared comically surprised at the sight of Manic, Farrill, and Liam clogging the hallway in front of them. One of the men shouted something in a foreign tongue as Manic took aim and dropped one of them with a double-tap to the chest. The other he clipped in the shoulder as the man tried to unsling an old-school AK-47 from his shoulder.

Game time, Manic thought, and the hallway erupted in gunfire.

The dead man fell across the hallway, soundless beneath the sputtering gunfire of the AK-47. The wounded man, either from pain or skill, curled into a small ball, clutching the rifle close and releasing short, trained bursts at Manic, Liam, and Farrill.

Farrill howled and spun from Manic's grasp as a bullet caught him somewhere Manic couldn't see. The young deviant twisted twice in a row, then sprinted down the hallway, away from the fight, red blood spraying behind him.

Manic spent no effort to stop the fleeing deviant. The ex-cop flattened himself, sandwiching Liam between his body and the wall to form a protective human shield. He popped off two rounds toward the wounded man, and scored a hit in the gunman's neck. The gunman gobbled and dropped the AK, clutching at the gory wound in his throat.

More guards would come now, Manic knew. Bad guys tended to notice things like automatic rifle fire.

Not bothering to issue instructions to Liam, trusting the boy would have enough sense to follow, Manic crouch-walked down the hall, pistol raised. Manic cleared the hallway around the corner before turning it, keeping the gun cradled expertly in his scarred and bandaged hands. His bomber jacket scraped softly against the concrete wall as they went.

Liam Gray was crying. Manic paused at the next turn in the hall, cleared it, then faced Liam. "Hey buddy. Shhh. I need you to keep it down, all right? I'm scared too, but we're gettin' outta here. Promise. Okay?"

Liam snuffled and nodded, wiping his nose along the length of one forearm and trying to pull on a brave face.

Manic loved the kid right then—he would have done well in the old neighborhood. Toughen up fast, or die even faster. Liam was toughening. He might have to drop a few grand on therapy when he got older, but by God and sonny Jesus, Manic would make sure he *got* old enough to do it.

"Hang in there, L.G.," Manic said, then spun around the corner.

He could hear the shouts of guards echoing down the hall, likely gathering in the large room where he'd first had to choose the left or right hallway. Not much cover in there. They'd most likely be jammed into the opposite hall and maybe in the doorway where he and Liam needed to escape.

Manic stopped at the next corner and peeked quickly around it. As he'd feared, rifle fire greeted him in response, spraying concrete dust into his eyes as he pulled back. The hallway around the corner extended twenty or thirty yards, then opened on the right into the large room. Past that lay the opposing hallway. The gunfire had come from there.

So most likely, Manic reasoned as the thrill of battle expanded in his lungs, they'd try to keep him pinned down here while other guys took up a position in the large room where they could wait until he popped into it to try and escape. He'd be caught in a withering crossfire that would be impossible to shoot his way out of. Most likely there was also a way to get to his back, and guys with guns would be headed that direction right now. In a minute or two, he'd be hemmed in on both sides.

All right then. He'd just have to clear a path forward. Getting to the staircase and out of the compound was his best bet to protect Liam. He'd come back for the others. He'd come back, and bring hell along for the ride.

The rifle fire stopped. Manic's ears rang terribly. He peeked quickly again, and saw three guards in the opposite hallway, weapons trained. They opened fire, and Manic pulled back.

"Listen up, Liam," Manic said, holstering his pistol and reaching into another pocket of his cargo pants. He pulled out a white cylindrical grenade and a small, clear box with what looked like two orange tablets inside. He handed the box to Liam. "Put these in your ears. Thing's are about to get real loud."

Remarkably, Liam raised his eyebrows sarcastically as if to say, *Louder than* this?

"When I grab your hand, we're gonna run for the door in that big room down the hall, okay? That'll take us to some stairs that'll lead us outside. But you gotta run, dude. Run fast. And if anything happens to me, you just keep going, got it?"

Liam nodded and opened the clear box. He shoved the spongy

orange earplugs into his ears, and Manic saw him wince as they expanded to fill his ear canals.

Manic nodded at him, then pulled the pin on his white canister. He grinned wryly, recalling his NPD training. The next few minutes were going to suck mightily.

He released the trigger and chucked the can down the hall. It bounced into the large room and issued a small pop, nothing more.

Then the ultrasonic waves began.

Instantly, Manic grimaced and cried out, clutching his head. Ultrasonics pounded through the compound, rattling his brain and internal organs. He pulled his pistol back out and grabbed Liam's hand.

"Go," he urged himself, and spun around the corner.

The three men in the opposite hallway were already retreating against the ultrasonics. They were feeling the same things Manic felt—crippling dizziness, instant nausea, and piercing pain through their skulls. The sonic grenade had been designed for use against deviants, because even the most mutated of them had to have a central nervous system. Sonics often worked better than any other NPD weapon.

The drawback to the grenades was that they were not directional like focused-beam weapons were, making NPD officers just as susceptible to its effects as the targets were. Ear protection helped to a limited degree, but then reduced communication between officers and curtailed tactical input from the field. They were by necessity weapons of last resort for NPD.

Manic slid his body along the hallway wall as it became the only way he could keep his feet under him. He fired shots toward the fleeing thugs, but couldn't tell if he scored or not. The pain drilled into his head like iron nails, while his intestines threatened to erupt out of his mouth.

Maybe this hadn't been the best idea.

He spun around the corner that emptied into the large room.

As he'd expected, a group of guards waited for him there, but rather than ambushing him, they now lay writhing on the ground, trying to claw their way to the far hallway or else to the door. Manic ran past them, stumbled once, got up, and stumbled again. He shoved Liam Gray past him in approximately the direction of the stairwell door, or so he hoped. His eyes vibrated in their sockets, adding to the sickness in his belly as he crawled on hands and knees after the boy.

Through the shaky haze in his vision, Manic saw Liam reach the door and bolt into the long, bare corridor leading to the stairwell. Good. At least *something* was going right. He pushed himself along the floor while the guards fought to get past him in the other direction, none of them bothering to try and shoot Manic along the way, and he not trying to shoot at them. Sonics had no allies.

Manic felt as if his muscles were being detached from his skeletal system as he at last reached the door and threw up bile on the floor beside it. Goddamn sonics, they worked like hell, that was for sure.

Groaning, he pulled himself into the corridor and shut the door behind him. It reduced but did not end the pain in his head. Up ahead, at the far door, he saw Liam waiting, hands clasped over his ears. Good.

Manic waved and hoped he shouted the word "Go!" but couldn't tell for sure if he was successful. In any case, Liam Gray opened the door and hiked up the stairs.

The ultrasonic waves stopped. That meant only twenty seconds had passed since the grenade exploded. Any longer could have been fatal, Manic knew. It would take about one minute for any of the guards to get their wits about them. That's how long he had to get Liam the hell out of this place.

Of course, it was taking him at least that long to gather his own wits, too. Spitting a sour taste from his mouth, Manic used the wall to brace himself as he shuffled down the corridor behind Liam. His pistol hung limp in his hand, and he hoped he wouldn't have to open fire in the next few minutes. Or maybe months.

He had no sense of how long it took to reach the far door to the stairwell, but it couldn't have been too long—Liam was only at the top of the staircase, struggling to open the door leading to the arcade. Shit, maybe the cashier was free and had locked or barricaded it?

No. The handle had stuck. Manic was halfway up the stairs when Liam pushed through and stumbled into the darkness and electronic noise of the arcade.

Manic followed behind, and found the cashier right where he'd left him. The plastic zip tie had bite marks on it, but the cashier was secure. Manic half knelt, half-fell beside the cashier.

"You knew." He pressed the barrel of the pistol against the cashier's right knee.

The cashier opened his mouth to reply, but the explosion of his kneecap prevented anything other than a keening wail of pain. Manic picked himself up and caught up to Liam, who stood in one aisle, scanning all around, looking for escape.

"Here," Manic said, gesturing weakly to the hand-crank mechanism that would open the security gate.

Liam followed the gesture to the crank and started winding it as Manic sank against one of the cabinet games. Ms. Pac-Man. He came perilously close to shooting the screen just for spite, but didn't want to waste the energy or the round.

A glow from the overhead streetlights outside slowly spilled into the arcade. Manic winced against it and tried to order his stomach not to revolt again. After the sonic assault, the glare may as well have been a supernova. When Liam had the gate open enough to walk through, Manic called to him.

"That's it, let's go."

Liam needed no more prompting. He darted out of the business and into the Los Angeles night, with Manic lurching behind him and the cashier screaming in agony behind the counter.

Outdoor air had never smelled so good to the old cop. Simply being away from the underground compound had miraculous healing properties on his rattled innards. Liam waited for him on the sidewalk, breathing hard and looking all around as if unsure of his real freedom.

"Told ya I'd get you out," Manic said, grinning sickly.

Liam smiled back, then burst into tears. Manic could see they were tears of relief, and he put an arm around the boy.

"C'mon. I got a car up this way, let's get you to—"

An NPD wagon pulled up alongside the curb, lights and siren both off. Manic laughed aloud. A better sight he'd never seen.

"Well, thank fuck!" he shouted, and pointed to the arcade with his pistol. "At the back, there's a door. They're downstairs. Load up and—"

A second car pulled up behind the wagon and idled as the NPD team carefully climbed out of their armored vehicle. They were not double-timing it. In fact, they looked to be in no hurry at all. Manic instinctively waved the black town car away from the curb, assuming it was a civilian wanting to be a citizen journalist with a cell phone.

Manic stopped waving as Weber climbed out of the back.

"Officer Cruce," he said, standing beside the open door. "Come have a seat."

*

Malikai recognized her hair immediately. Her captors had kept it long and well cared-for, and the thought penetrated the haze of pain in his skinless body and made him sick—she was to fetch a high price, after all, and must be *maintained*. Her blonde hair glistened stubbornly in the dim gray light, as if refusing to concede defeat.

Malikai took that as a good sign. He pulled back so the wall concealed him.

"Julia."

She gasped. "Who's there?"

"I'm here from your father."

"Daddy—!"

"*Shhhhh*. Listen to me. I am here to get you out, to take you home. Your father has been looking for you. He has tried everything in his power to find you. And now I am here to take you back to him."

Malikai heard her standing up and approaching the gate. He tensed; he did not want his appearance to scare her. Previously, such as the fuel station on the way into L.A., his looks gave humans pause. How he must look now, after the flames, he could only suppose.

"Who are you? Let me see you."

Julia's little voice sounded strong. Obstinate. Malikai thought she might well make a good recovery, if he could get them out of here. He responded, each word a sandpaper abrasion inside his throat.

"Shh. Listen. When you see me, you must not scream. My appearance will frighten you. But you must listen to me very closely, and you must do exactly as I say if we are to escape this place. Do you understand?"

". . . Yes."

"Good. I'm going to show myself now. Cover your mouth. Do not make a sound. All right?"

"Okay, I promise."

Malikai slowly extended one hand past the bars, so she could get an idea of what else was coming. He heard her gasp again, then muffle it quickly. Slowly he leaned over so he was fully visible.

The poor girl's eyes widened as she took in his horrific state. He was a nightmarish creature, and it was clear that Julia Lawson wasn't sure she should trust the thing before her.

"Do you know the way out?" he said, trying to get her attention fixed elsewhere.

She shook her head, keeping her mouth covered. She had not yet blinked.

"I know one way," Malikai said, doing his best to keep his voice level, but the flames had seared his tongue and throat as well as his outer skin, and the voice coming out of him was altogether different now—low and rough. He could still taste gasoline.

"But I have to get you first. Who has keys to this door?"

Julia slowly lowered her hands, but her nose wrinkled as his smell reached her. "I don't know. All of them, I guess. Can't you just break it down or something?"

Smart girl—she could tell he was six, and as such, maybe had the raw power to rip the door from its hinges. He'd been wondering about his strength as well, but felt sure of two things—first, that he couldn't force the gate to open silently; he would attract attention, and five or ten armed guards coming to check out the noise wouldn't bode well for either of them.

Second . . . Malikai could feel his strength waning.

The exertion of pulling the iron ring free from the ceiling in his cell had almost sapped him entirely. He assumed and hoped that his weakness was related to how much damage the flames had done. Regardless, he didn't believe he could force the gate open with brute strength. On his best night out in the city, perhaps. Today, after everything he'd been through, no.

So he didn't reply directly. Instead he said, "I will be right back. Make no noise."

Julia nodded and stepped away from the gate.

Malikai crept back to the hallway and followed it until he could peer around the corner to where the guards lounged. They still smoked heavily, and laughed at whatever they were watching on the tablet computer. He judged he could get fairly close before they'd see him coming, particularly if what they were smoking wasn't tobacco— and by the smell, it wasn't. He counted five of them, with possibly more hidden around the corners on either side of the doorway. With his sword and feeling his best, they wouldn't present a problem. Considering the damage he had sustained and wielding only the small balisong knife, it would be a much closer battle.

Malikai turned the corner and sprinted down the hall, wincing his blistered eyelids at the sharp pain each time his feet landed. Somehow, though, he'd retained his silent tread, and he was upon the closest of the guards just as the man was beginning to turn around, and just as he heard gunfire echoing far away in the labyrinth.

Malikai leaped. He jabbed the balisong up beneath the first guard's chin, all the way to the handles, causing the guard's eyes to fly open and blood to spray instantly from his lips. Without turning, the vigilante executed a perfect back kick into the sternum of a second guard, who flew over a folding chair, landing on the ground with a crash.

Two of the remaining three guards scrambled for their weapons, while the third only looked up dumbly, blissful in his opiate high. Malikai pushed his stabbing victim forward toward the first two like a tackling dummy, knocking them off balance. He yanked the knife from his victim, who, in his death, took the other two to the floor in a tangle of limbs and pouring blood.

Malikai stabbed the fifth guard in the base of his skull, severing his spine and killing the thug instantly. He felt blissfully remorseless; Xavian would have agreed that these were men who made the innocence of children a private currency. For that, these quick deaths were merciful. As one of the guards he'd toppled over tried to reach for his gun, Malikai stomped down on his wrist, shattering it—the maneuver incapacitated the thug for the moment, but also tore fresh wounds on Malikai's own heel.

Grimacing against the pain, Malikai dropped to his knees and killed the fourth guard with one graceful stab to the heart. The man he'd kicked managed to climb to his feet; sensing him, Malikai flung the knife that direction. Despite not being designed for such a throw, the balisong caught the thug in the gut, and he fell right back down onto the broken chair again.

His vision turning iridescent with agony, Malikai grabbed the hair of the man whose wrist he had broken. The man lay pinned beneath his comrades, unable now to defend himself in any way. Malikai lifted the man's head off the ground, holding their faces close. Another round of gunfire sounded, distant and aggressive. Malikai assumed it was related to the man in the brown coat.

Perhaps authorities were on their way? Even if so, he wouldn't wait for them.

"Give me the keys to the cells," Malikai said in his flame-scorched voice.

Clearly terrified of the vigilante's grotesque wounds, the man nodded and jibbered something in his native tongue while gesturing wildly with his good hand. Malikai, unable to discern the man's words because of their rapidity and slurring, followed the guard's gesture and yanked a ring of keys from the waistband of one of the dead thugs.

With that, he lifted the man's head a fraction higher, then slammed it down once onto the concrete floor. It cracked awfully, and the man went still.

Malikai got to his feet. The thug with the knife in his belly still breathed, mutely trying to extricate the knife from his body. Malikai helped by dragging the blade up, disemboweling him, then yanking the knife free. He moved quickly back up the corridor, knife in one fleshless palm and keys in the other.

While he heard no audible alarm, he knew the gunfire would bring every thug in the place running. Moving almost carelessly now, Malikai reached Julia's cell and fumbled with the keys until finding one that worked. Julia did not burst from her cage; rather, she stepped out gingerly as if wary of a trap. Malikai admired her caution.

"Now we must go," he said, and turned for the hallway.

Julia grabbed his hand.

The little girl reached out and put her hand in his own ravaged fingers.

This human child touched him.

Malikai spun, staring. Raw flesh glistened from the back of his hand—from all over his body. He was naked. He had bloodred sclera and silver irises, clearly a Level Six deviant even when not having been recently consumed by flame.

But she touched him. And it hurt, too; all contact on his flesh made the pain worsen. Yet he did not move, did not pull away, did not even feel the urge to scream.

She touched him.

"No," Julia said. "The others."

Malikai looked down the short hall of cells. Seven all together, and now with his eyesight growing accustomed to the darkness, he could see young faces peering back, or fingers wrapping around the bars of their cell doors.

Six more children. How on earth could he guide seven children out of this place?

"Please," Julie said. "We have to—"

Malikai held the cell gate keys toward Julia.

"Gather them," he said. "Tell them about me, what they will see. They must not make noise. Not a sound, no matter how frightened they may be. Do you understand?"

Julia nodded quickly and took the keys. Malikai gripped the balisong knife tightly, wishing for the first time he'd bothered to learn how to use a gun; the five guards would have made for a good source of weaponry had he any experience. He knew from his nightly patrols that merely having a gun in hand did not equate with being able to use it effectively; only those who had trained frequently with or otherwise used firearms had any real chance of actually getting off a fatal shot, or even a stopping blow. If he could find his Tang dao again, that would be something. Until then, the knife would have to do.

A minute passed. He listened intently up and down the hall. He heard shouts in the distance, but nothing nearby. Perhaps it was assumed the five guards would come running, so none of their comrades came to get them. Nearer, he also heard whispering and shuffling as Julia brought the other children from their cells.

The group of kids turned the corner and several gasped. One started to shriek, but Julia put a hand over his mouth.

Malikai knew then their escape would never work.

But he also didn't think Kien's men would shoot the children; surely they were too valuable. Not that Kien's thugs would lay down their arms and clear a path, either. No, there would be a fight, and the children would be sacrificed before the thugs' own lives were. Still, they might not fire at them right away, and that hesitation might be the only other weapon Malikai had to work with.

He took a step in the direction of where he'd come from his own cell.

"Wait," a boy with red hair said. "This way is the sewers. It's where they take the bodies. We could get out that way."

Brief, bright rage coursed through Malikai at the child's words. The red-haired boy couldn't be more than thirteen, yet his expression did not change when using a phrase like *It's where they take the bodies*. He was already crushed. Malikai wondered exactly what kind of freedom he was trying to lead them to if this was the type of psychological damage that had already been done.

Another boy—there were only the two of them, the rest were girls—sank to the floor with his hands over his ears. "No!" he cried. "We *can't* go, they'll come *after* us . . ."

Julia tried to scoop him up. "Joey, come on. This man is here to save us."

"He's *scary* . . ."

Malikai couldn't fault Joey for the comment; Joey was clearly the youngest of the group, with stark black hair and tremendous green eyes that made Malikai wonder if he had deviant blood in his veins.

"We must go, now. More guards will come, that is certain. Help this boy walk." He turned to the red-haired boy. "Which way to the sewer?"

The boy pointed in the opposite direction from where Malikai had come. Swiftly, still feeling the acute pain of his burns but no longer heeding it, Malikai went on down the hall and peered around the corner. Empty, at the moment. Two doors were inset on the left wall, and the corridor ended in what must be another large room. He could not tell for certain if anyone occupied it.

Turning to the red-haired boy, Malikai motioned with his hand. The boy hesitated, but then came quickly over.

"What is your name?"

The boy swallowed and licked his lips, but tilted his chin up defiantly. "Brayan."

"Brayan, I will need your help if we are to escape."

"Okay."

"Are you certain there is access to the outside through the sewer?"

"I haven't seen it. I've only heard them talk about it. Anything they put in will get out to the ocean eventually."

Malikai wasn't uplifted by the description. That could mean anything. So—better to go back the way he'd come, where there was some degree of predictability? Or follow the advice of this imprisoned and abused boy, who hadn't himself even seen the clear light of day by taking this route?

He thought of Ching, and wondered if the children knew of him. He guessed they did; a deviant with his face could easily be put to use frightening the innocent into obeying. It would also help explain why these kids seemed somewhat inured to Malikai's own abraded visage. They probably had seen Ching, and he'd probably scared them.

Malikai decided. They'd take their chances the way Brayan suggested.

"All right," he said to Brayan. "Straight ahead?"

The boy nodded. "There's a big room at the end of this hall, with a bunch of pipes and like gauges and stuff? There's a door that'll go downstairs to the sewer."

"Very good. I need you to be in charge of these children. Can you do that?"

Brayan nodded again. Malikai turned his attention to the hallway.

Gripping the balisong, the vigilante slid to the left wall and paused outside the first door. He heard nothing, so he moved on to the second door. Machinery whirred behind it; air conditioning perhaps, or some kind of generator. He glanced backward to assess the children.

Good as his word, Brayan had the kids lined up as if for some demented fire drill, following the right-hand wall. Julia brought up the rear. Good tactics, Malikai thought, since she had shown more presence of mind than he would have otherwise assumed for a child her age. They would need her calmer attitude at their backs if anyone came upon them.

Julia also seemed to be in charge of little Joey, who kept mumbling and whining with every step. Not a lot of noise, but unmistakable in a place like this. The kid would give them away sooner or later. Julia did her best to cajole and wheedle him, but Joey's stubbornness only increased.

"*Noooo!*" he wailed. "They'll co—"

Julia picked him up in her arms and smothered his mouth, whispering fiercely in his ear. Malikai—and Brayan, he noticed—gave her cold glares. Julia nodded silently, indicating she had control of the situation. Malikai hoped it was true.

Then: A shout from the end of the hall.

Malikai whirled toward the sound. In the entryway to the room at the end of the hallway, a man wearing khaki workpants and a blue work shirt was calling out and pointing at Malikai, raising an alarm.

Joey screamed through Julia's fingers as Malikai bore down on the workman at top speed, brandishing the knife.

But just before reaching him, another figure joined the workman, his enormous body taking up most of the doorway. Malikai, already committed to his attack, had no time to adjust course or change tactics.

The balisong jabbed deep into the top of the workman's shoulder. The workman cried out and fell to the ground—

Just as Ching's mighty fist ploughed into Malikai's head.

The monstrous snout-faced half-man roared with what sounded like genuine pleasure at seeing his old adversary. Malikai's sword was stashed in a leather belt encircling the Level Seven's waist, and for one brief moment, Malikai felt true happiness at seeing it again.

Then reality set in. Malikai tumbled to one side and crashed against an iron pipe that had once been painted yellow. He barely put together in his head that Brayan's description of the room was correct, and that this must have at one time been some kind of central wastewater processing area, with pipes of various sizes lining the walls and raised over the floor.

Vivid, intense pain exploded in his face where Ching had hit him, and Malikai had no time to adjust his swimming vision before the deviant was upon him again. Ching grabbed him around the middle with both hands, and swung the vigilante bodily across the room where he smashed into a pipe descending from the ceiling.

Malikai heard the children crying out and starting to scatter. Not good—if he lost track of them now, he'd never get them back.

He climbed to his feet, unsteady for a moment . . . until he raised his sword and bellowed, "Face me!"

Ching's eyes widened for a moment, and he even looked down at his belt as if to confirm what he was seeing: Malikai had managed to seize the weapon when Ching grabbed him.

Malikai turned the blade a glowing blue. The handle seemed to pulse in his hands as if welcoming his return.

"*Children!*"

Several yards down the hall, he saw the kids sliding around and knocking into each other, unsure what to do or where to go. As soon as Malikai shouted, however, the chaos froze. Brayan saw him first, and his eyes, like Ching's, got bigger at the sight of the glowing sword. Malikai watched Julia run to gather the kids together in a huddle in the hallway.

Ching paid them no attention. He roared and rushed for Malikai.

The children seemed safe for the time being, so Malikai leaped to meet his opponent. Pipes stood on raised legs between them, and Malikai slid beneath one as Ching leaped over it. Tearing pain shot lightning through his flank as his open skin raked across the cement floor, but Malikai felt little of it; the odd joy of being in combat with his own sword again seemed to mitigate much of the agony.

He sliced the sword behind himself as he slid, and felt the glowing steel meet one of Ching's Achilles' heels. The seven screamed in rage and pain.

Malikai rolled forward, putting more distance between them before popping to his feet, sword held aloft. Ching turned and came for him, stumbling now. He reached for the vigilante, but his anger outweighed his combat sense, and Malikai easily spun to avoid the outstretched arms. Keeping his momentum, Malikai pivoted on one foot and slashed the deviant's back. A bloody gash opened, spilling blood much darker red than any Malikai had ever seen.

Ching roared again, but like Malikai, it seemed that combat had deadened any acknowledgment of pain. He swiped at Malikai with his fists—right, left, right. Malikai gingerly stepped out of the way, just beyond the deviant's reach, so close he could feel a faint breeze whistle past his nose as the fists went past.

As Ching reared back to deliver a haymaker, Malikai dodged forward, sword horizontal. The blade cut across Ching's midsection. The seven crumbled to the concrete on his knees, holding his guts in with both hands and moaning sickly.

Malikai took up position behind him, instinctively seeking to sever Ching's head. But as he raised the fiery dao, he realized the children stared at him.

He lowered the sword. They'd seen enough, and Ching wouldn't be chasing them anywhere. Malikai called to Julia and Brayan. "Get us out of here."

Brayan nodded quickly and bolted through the room to a door on the left wall. Julia gathered up the kids, and together, they raced to meet Brayan and Malikai.

This door was unlocked. Malikai pushed it open and trotted down the hall. The hall seemed vaguely damp as it sloped downward, though Malikai didn't see traces of any water; indeed, the entire complex thus far had seemed oddly dry for being part of a sewer system. Opening another door Brayan pointed to, he thought he knew why, now: this system had been abandoned for years, possibly decades. Somehow Kien had come into possession of it, and spent the time and money to fortify this concrete urban labyrinth for his own purposes, perhaps even building the arcade atop the ground-level entrance for exactly the purpose of concealing it.

Malikai knew sewers were city-operated, or in some way municipal. What sort of corruption must be taking place in government offices for Kien to control such resources with so much impunity? Or perhaps the larger question, the one Malikai had no time nor energy for, ought to be:

Who was Kien answering to?

"This way," Brayan said breathlessly. "I saw them go this way this one time."

"And you've never been here yourself?"

"Well, no, but like I saw them taking a body this way?"

Too late to turn back. Malikai heard no more gunfire echoing through the labyrinth; whether that was from the end of the firefight or they were too far away now, he couldn't guess. Either way, the clock was ticking.

"Stay close," Malikai said, and went on through the door.

This passage opened into a cavernous concrete room. The doorway spilled onto a sort of platform, with a rusted railing lining the far edge about thirty feet away. Beyond that, five large concrete tubes lay on the floor, with large cement boxes mounted on top of them, the function of which Malikai could only guess. These tubes disappeared in either direction into the walls.

Apart from an empty utility closet and a slightly stronger mildew smell, the room was empty. There were no other doors, no other exits. A dead end.

Malikai heard shouts behind them. How far away? The pipe room where he'd left Ching? The way sound bounced around down here, it was impossible to tell. Nor did it matter.

Kien's thugs were close, and getting closer.

"Now what?" Julia said, rubbing Joey's shoulder. The boy was only barely hanging on emotionally.

Malikai leaped over the railing to the nearest tube and examined the cement box. The top of it was barred by an iron grate. The tube itself appeared dry and empty. If the grate could be moved, they could escape this way. Or get out of the room, at any rate; where these tubes led was anyone's guess.

Sheathing the sword, Malikai slipped his torn fingers into the spaces between the grate and pulled. The grate didn't so much as tremble. He changed position and tried again. Nothing. His wounds and exhaustion had taken a toll.

The children started to whine wordlessly. Julia tried to calm them while shooting terrified glances at the vigilante.

Malikai stared back down at the grate. Either he got it open and they took their chances scrambling down the pipe, or else he made a last stand here against anyone and everyone who would be spilling from that door any second. He felt no more confident about succeeding in such a fight than he had earlier. He himself may or may not die, but the children most certainly would in the crossfire.

The grate, then.

Malikai drew his sword again with ceremonial reverence, a deliberate move that seemed programmed into his muscle memory. He climbed atop the box and knelt on its edge, raising the sword high with both hands, the tip pointed down as if to stab the grate.

"That won't work!" a girl cried. "We're gonna die!"

Malikai focused on the weapon, ignoring the child completely. The blade glowed red, then blue, then finally white. Waves of heat cascaded against his burnt face, but he resisted the impulse to turn away. Slowly, he pushed the tip of the Tang dao against the iron—

and the blade sank in like a welder's tool, creating drops of molten metal that fell to the floor of the pipe and hissed.

"Looks like it's working to me," Julia said; and despite their deadly circumstances, Malikai heard the girl muttering an immature *Shut up!* back at her.

Like a chainsaw against a particularly thick branch, the dao slowly but effectively made its way through the grate. Malikai slid the blade around it as if cutting the crust from a pizza until the grate fell with a jarring clang against the bottom of the pipe.

Malikai fell forward, catching himself on one hand. His exhaustion was now complete. Though he hadn't needed food or drink since he woke up in the desert, he still felt like he should want a drink of water. His intense concentration on the sword to create the needed heat had taken a toll on his ravaged body.

He waved at the children. Julia said, "Okay, come on, let's go you guys, this way."

The children scampered for the pipe. Malikai sent Brayan down first to lead the way, and the boy showed a quick flash of pride at the nomination. He jumped down and reported it dry but dark.

"Just go," Malikai ordered.

Brayan went. The others followed, with Julia at the back of the line.

She paused. "How do you know it's this way and not that?"

She had a valid point. The pipe, of course, only went in two directions.

"To the right," Malikai said. "It leads outside."

Julia nodded and disappeared into the darkness. Malikai felt momentary regret at the lie; going to the right was no more likely to lead out of this place than going left was. He'd simply blurted out the first thing that came to mind. Luck would have to be on their side, that was all.

Except luck had yet to arrive, because something else was wrong. Terribly wrong. At first Malikai couldn't place it, but then Julia called up from the pipe, "Where's Joey?"

Malikai said nothing, weighing his options.

"You can't leave him!" Julia cried. "Please! We have to get him back, he must have run and hid somewhere back there!"

Somewhere back there was suicide. Probably Julia was right, the boy had hid out somewhere during Malikai's fight with Ching, and sooner or later, Kien would find the boy if he hadn't already.

"Go," he said to Julia.

"But Joey!"

"I will find him. Go, now."

Julia pouted fiercely, but obeyed. She ducked down and shuffled into the pipe behind the other children. Malikai dropped behind her and brought up the rear.

The pipe was too small to walk, so he crept along on his hands and knees. Far ahead, he could make out the bobbling outlines of the children, and realized he could perceive this outline because of a faint light far ahead. He'd chosen the correct direction. Whether that was a small miracle or merely the odds landing on their particular half of a fifty-fifty shot, he did not know or care.

They pushed on. The pipe emptied into a damp tunnel, and based on the smell, they'd reached an actual sewer. The light source came from above, where another grate was set in the ceiling above a tall ladder bolted into the wall. The grate opened to the outside.

Malikai climbed the ladder and pushed on the grate. It was heavy, but moved, so he shoved it up and off, then peered out, keeping his body below ground level.

An alley. The backs of buildings surrounded him, terrain he felt familiar with no matter the city. Dumpsters dotted the potholed road, though very little trash floated around like he'd see in Phoenix. To his left, the alley went on for half a block before emptying onto a street; to his right, the alley went another fifty yards before ending at another road.

Malikai climbed out, sunshine air burning his roasted flesh. He waved at Julia, who had come to stand at the base of the ladder. She climbed up rapidly. One after another, the other children came up, some of them starting to cry anew at their freedom.

"Whoa!" someone said.

Malikai spun, hand falling to his sword hilt.

A teenaged girl of East Asian descent appeared at the nearest corner of the alley, clutching a roll of colorful paper in her hand. Malikai awaited a scream from her that would doubtless elicit help from first bystanders, then local law enforcement, then a cadre of sixcops. If NPD flew in, Malikai knew his time as a free deviant would conclusively, permanently end.

Except the girl did not scream.

She took a step closer.

"What's going on?" she said, cautious but unafraid. "What happened to *you?*"

Malikai risked trusting her. "Get these children to safety. They were captives. Take them somewhere and then call the police."

The girl nodded and ran to them. Malikai marveled at her fearlessness. Children, some of them anyway, had remarkable presence of mind. Or, he reconsidered, perhaps being given orders from a naked, scorched man with a sword was a powerful motivator. The thought nearly made him smile.

"The comic shop is right over here," the girl said, shoving her roll of colored paper into the back pocket of her jeans. Malikai saw then that they were comic books. "Andy will help us. Come on, you guys!"

Brayan gathered the children behind the girl and began following her up the alley. Julia stayed behind.

"Joey," she pleaded. "Please, you have to—"

"I will get him back. You go."

Julia's eyes welled with tears. "Thank you."

She touched his hand. The touch to his exposed muscle hurt—but only distantly.

Then she was gone, running hard for the group which was turning the corner. Malikai climbed down into the sewer, pulling the grate closed above him.

SEVENTEEN

Manic's eyelids froze open wide. He turned his head to look at each helmeted NPD sixcop in turn, who now stood in a semicircle around him, weapons drawn but pointed at the concrete, their faces stoic.

Manic, perhaps for the first time in his life, licked his lips. "What the . . . hey. I'm a *cop*. I'm one of you guys."

Weber gestured to the town car. "Please, Manic. Come on in."

Stunned, Manic took a step back. Liam stayed with him, close to his leg.

"No . . ."

"Manic, please. This is already a delicate situation. I can see you have questions, and that's to be expected. Let me answer them."

"You're in on this." Manic had never heard such disbelief in his own voice. "You rancid motherfucker, you're in on this whole thing."

He raised his gun.

So did the sixcops.

Weber didn't flinch. "If you want a shootout in the middle of a pleasant Los Angeles evening, we can do that. But it's not what I want, and it's not what you want. It won't *get* you what you want, it will only get you and the boy dead. Put the gun away, Manic. Get in the car. Let me explain."

The rich guy, Manic thought. It had to be about him killing Rich Guy. Maybe he was an informant or some kind of undercover cop, and they'd been keeping tabs on him and Manic had blown an operation . . .

No. There was no mistaking what he saw Rich Guy doing to Liam Gray. No matter who he had been, Manic felt no regret for executing him.

Manic did not lower his gun. Neither did the men and women he would have otherwise considered his teammates. Their faces remained impassive as the barrels of their weapons picked out mortal targets on his body. He could take Weber, he knew that. He might even get one or two of his NPD brethren with lucky shots between their armored plates, if he'd been feeling in his prime.

Ultimately, though, Weber was right. He'd die here on the sidewalk, and probably Liam Gray with him. Not only was he hopelessly outnumbered, but the sonics had scrambled his reflexes.

"What about the kid?" Manic said. Still he kept his gun trained on Weber.

"He'll be safe, I promise you. We'll find his family, and if there is no family, we'll get him in the system and he'll be well taken care of. California has the best foster care system in the world, you know."

Yeah, yeah, Manic knew that and couldn't have cared less at that moment. His concern was whether Weber would really keep the boy safe or not.

Finally he dropped his gun arm. The sixcops hesitated, then lowered theirs as well. Manic turned to Liam.

"I think I gotta go with this nancy little prick. You ever ride in a sixcop wagon?"

Liam Gray shook his head.

"Well, tonight you get to. They're gonna take care of you, okay?" He knelt down beside the boy and drew him close, whispering in his ear, making sure the others couldn't catch it. "If you need something, you go to Sal's Café and you ask to see Sal. Hear me? *Sal's Café*. Tell them Manic sent you. Got it?"

The boy nodded. Manic impulsively hugged him, then pushed him toward the sixcops. "I find out anything happened to him," he said to the group, "your families suffer for it. You know who I am? You know what I do?"

The sixcops ignored him, though one man did do a slight double-take. It was enough for Manic. They knew him, all right. Liam Gray would be safe, at least with the NPD crew. He'd track the boy down later, make sure everything was all right.

And after that, he'd gear up and take out that entire underground complex.

"Officer?" Weber called pleasantly. "We shouldn't keep your employer waiting."

Manic waited until Liam had been escorted gently into the back of the NPD wagon before walking to Weber. He caught a glimpse of himself reflected in the tinted window of the town car, and impulsively threw a fist into it. The blow shattered two of his knuckles instead of the window, and bounced his fist right back at him. The pain didn't show on his face. He'd felt worse.

"Does that help?" Weber asked.

"You'd be surprised. And by the way, you're next."

Weber smiled patiently and stepped away from the open door. Manic slid inside. Weber climbed in after him, and the car pulled away from the sidewalk.

Manic carefully unscrewed the suppressor from his pistol in full view of Weber, and noted that Weber wasn't fazed by the weapon still being out. "So where we headed, Webs, old buddy?"

"To meet Governor Savage."

Manic laughed. He slipped the suppressor into a pocket and folded his arms, keeping the pistol in his right hand, finger near the trigger, alongside the barrel. "Yeah, okay. He just happens to be here in L.A. on a fishing trip, yeah?"

"In fact, he happens to be in Los Angeles for a series of meetings with senators and governors from several states."

"Uh-huh. And he's your boss?"

"Yes. And yours. You wanted to know so badly, well, there it is. The secret's out."

The vestigial grin Manic had been wearing slipped off. "You're not kidding."

"No, Manic. I've not made a single joke since the night we first met. I would've thought you figured that much out."

Manic turned in the leather bench seat to face him more squarely. "You're not shitting me? This entire set-up has been Savage's idea? The *governor?*"

"Yes." The car took a gentle right turn.

Corby Savage was in his second term as the state's governor. A tall man of indeterminate ethnicity and Hollywood good looks, he'd juggled his platform expertly to appeal to conservatives and liberals alike. Voter turnout for his first election had broken all state records, as had the number of votes he received versus the incumbent. Since his election, Savage had kept a low profile publicly, but the changes throughout the state—and in places like Los Angeles in particular—had been swift, surprising, and welcomed. He was a hero.

Manic figured that from his lofty pedestal the only way to go was down.

"So he knows what's going on in that hellhole we just left," Manic said.

"That, I can't say with certainty. He'll tell you everything you need to know."

Manic sprang. He jammed the pistol into Weber's temple while grabbing the man's head with his left hand, further digging the barrel into Weber's flesh.

"Listen, you smug fuck," Manic growled into Weber's face. "I just pulled a goddamn child out from under some rich prick who I am willing to bet paid top dollar for the privilege of having that kid at his mercy for a couple hours. Tell me I'm wrong."

Weber said nothing.

"Next thing I know you and a wagon fulla sixcops rolls up, when I didn't tell no one where I'd be. Now, maybe I didn't make detective, but I got a good feeling that means you and Savage know what's going on in that place. I already killed a coupla guys tonight, I got no issue killing one more. You're gonna talk, motherfucker, and you're gonna talk now."

He twisted the gun, spiraling a swatch of Weber's skin beneath it. The car rolled to a stop.

"We're here," Weber said, nonplussed. "I don't wish to die tonight, but if you're going to kill me, please get it over with. I don't want to keep the governor waiting."

Manic considered it. It would have felt good to take Weber off the face of the Earth. But he didn't pull the trigger. He needed more information, more proof of his theory.

He pulled away and gave a Weber a solid punch on the shoulder. "Ah, just messin' with ya! We'll talk later. I really, really mean that. Keep an eye out for me."

Manic booted his door open and got out of the car. It had stopped in the circular driveway of a twenty-story high-rise paned with tinted blue glass. Thick foliage surrounded the building at its base, arrangements of flowering bushes and shrubs that gave an otherwise cold, featureless face some color and warmth. Manic wondered idly if the bushes were fake.

"Top floor," Weber called from inside the car as if his life had not just been legitimately threatened. "And Manic? Show some respect."

"Yeah, yeah, toddle off now," Manic said. "Say, tell me . . . what's to keep me from running off right now and calling some of my old buddies to drop some TNT on that little operation under the arcade?"

"Your curiosity. Good bye, Manic."

Manic kicked the door shut. Damn if Weber wasn't right again. He didn't know who else was down there. He needed more intel.

The town car drove quietly away, leaving Manic standing alone. The bad guys at the underground compound were probably evacuating right now, clearing out any kids left behind. He wanted terribly to go back, right now, do everything in his power to get them.

The problem was the web he found himself in had gotten thicker and much more sticky. Whether the governor of California really was sitting up on the top floor of this building or not, Weber arriving with sixcops willing to shoot one of their own meant something a lot bigger was going on under the streets of Los Angeles. If he went back now, he'd maybe free five, even ten kids from that compound, but then what else might be missed? How far did this thing go?

The best and currently only answers were going to be on the top floor of this building.

Just for hoots, Manic kept his pistol out as he walked up to the glass front doors of the lobby. The doors slid open automatically as Manic approached. He checked the edges of the doors as he walked in, appreciating that the glass appeared to be the same type as used for NPD wagon windshields. Bullet-proof, among other things. He wondered if maybe the entire building was faced with the same material.

Given the resources he'd seen in action so far, the idea didn't seem far-fetched.

The lobby was done up in shiny brown speckled marble walls and a white tile floor that reminded Manic of ice skating rinks, though he'd never been on one himself. The ceiling rose two stories. On his right, a café servicing the tenants had closed for the night, while straight ahead two uniformed guards sat behind a desk, eyeing him as he approached.

Manic got rid of the last of the bile taste in his mouth by spitting expertly against the floor. He ambled up to the guards, smiling, making no effort to hide his weapon.

"S'up, fellas. Here to see the big boss, he's upstairs, yeah?"

"Last elevator on the right," one of the guards said, pointing to a bank of elevators on Manic's left. "It'll take you straight to the top."

Manic leaned his forearms on top of the guard's counter and leaned close. The barrel of his pistol aimed itself almost casually at the guard's chest. "Listen. Tell me something. You ever meet the man in black himself?"

"You mean Governor Savage?" the guard said with an irked tone. "No."

"But you're ready to die for him, yeah? I mean, if some maniac came in and started shooting up the place."

The second guard, a mammoth of a man whose uniform shirt seemed close to bursting, stood up. "Sir, please take the last elevator on the right."

Manic glanced toward the hall, then back at the pair. "Wait a sec. You're not gonna search me or nothin'? Tell me to hand over my weapon?"

"We're following orders, sir," said the mammoth. He very much looked like he would enjoy taking Manic's weapon away with a crowbar and propane torch.

Manic nodded thoughtfully. So these weren't rent-a-cops; they were the real thing, maybe former NPD even, or at least special ops, playing the *part* of rent-a-cops. Corby Savage, or whoever was charged with his safety, knew what he was doing.

Manic tapped the counter-top. "Right on. Be seein' ya."

He swaggered to the elevators, counting three sets of doors on each side of the short hall, then a fourth set along the right-hand wall. He pushed the silver button beside it, and the doors whisked open immediately. Yes, they were waiting for him.

Manic hesitated briefly, trying his damnedest to outguess the next few moments. If Weber wanted him dead, they could have taken him down outside the arcade, or in the town car. If anyone really wanted to get rid of him tonight, there were a million and one ways to do it that didn't involve all this wandering around an L.A. high-rise in the middle of the night. Hell, a guy like Tony or Vic—or Sal for that matter—could have whacked him twenty minutes ago without breaking a sweat.

He stepped into the elevator. The doors shut and the car rose swiftly. Like the lobby, the elevator was well appointed with gold-tinted mirrors and brass handrails. The floor indicators showed there were twenty-five flights, but a twenty-sixth floor indicator topped them, its button lit from behind with a bright white glow. Manic remembered the set-up of the elevators in Sal's office, and wondered who in the hell was responsible for making elevators to service the rich and powerful. Somebody was making a mint off these guys.

The elevator stopped, and the doors opened. Manic found himself facing Governor Corby Savage.

But Savage had seen better days. He wore khakis and a light blue button-down, his brown hair styled but not fresh. Dark circles punctuated his eyes.

"This way, please," he said tonelessly.

Manic stepped out of the elevator, into a black marble walled hallway. "Uh, Governor?"

"This way," Savage repeated, and shuffled down the hall in mildly scuffed wingtips.

Manic cupped his pistol in both hands and took a slightly more sideways stance to the tall, tanned man he recognized from news sites and television. It was him, all right. But clearly something else was going on. This guy was acting like a butler.

Manic walked behind the governor, eyes narrowed. They passed several glass doors, but since the lights were off, Manic was unable to discern what lay beyond. At the end of the hallway, the men came to a pair of wide double doors constructed of—or decorated with—some kind of shiny aluminum material.

"Go on in," Governor Savage said, and began to turn away.

Manic stepped in front of him. "One second. What the holy hell is going on here? You're the governor, right?"

Savage's eyes dropped as he coughed a feeble laugh. "Sure thing, buddy."

He went on his way, walking to the nearest glass door and opening it. Lights popped on automatically as he stepped inside, leaving Manic alone in the hall.

"*Gee*-zus," Manic said. "The hell kind of . . ."

Frustrated, he pushed open one of the aluminum doors and raised his weapon to clear the room.

The door opened into a plush office that measured, by his quick reckoning, to be around forty by forty feet. Manic's trained eyes took in everything as he sliced the pie, sweeping his gun in an arc as he checked for threats.

An ornate bar took up much of the left-hand wall. Delicate chandeliers lit the office in a warm yellow glow. On the right, dark wood bookcases were filled with what appeared to be a mixture of leather bound classics . . . and children's chapter books. Set within the bookcases was an enormous flat screen monitor, which gazed darkly at an empty brown leather couch.

Straight ahead, at the furthest edge of the room, stood a desk the size of a small pool table. A fast-food order of a hamburger, fries, and possibly a strawberry milkshake sat on top of a blotter. Beside the desk, a short, middle-aged Chinese woman in dark blue jeans and a white blouse stood with her head bowed and hands folded in front of her, like a demure or penitent servant.

And behind that desk sat a kid of maybe twelve years old.

Good-looking, with only a smattering of adolescent acne, the boy had jet-black hair swept off his forehead into fashionable thin spikes. His clothes were casual but designer. Manic could read the labels even from the doorway.

"The *hell?*" Manic said.

The kid laughed. "Language, dude! Come on in. You want something to eat?"

Finished with his sweep, Manic entered the room fully, lowering the gun to a safer level in front of him. "No, seriously, what the hell is going on here? Who the hell are you?"

"Corby Savage. I'm the governor of California."

EIGHTEEN

Malikai swept quickly through the sewer tunnel and into the concrete pipe, back into the room where they'd entered it. He didn't hear shouts anymore, but that didn't mean the Ice Dragons thugs weren't close. He climbed up from the pipe through the concrete box and approached the hallway.

Empty.

Keeping his sword up but not lit, he moved swiftly to the pipe junction room where he'd fought Ching. At the doorway he paused, listening intently.

"Come in, demon."

Well, so much for a sneak attack. They'd been waiting for him. They'd known he'd come back for the boy.

Malikai nudged the door open and scanned the room. The voice had belonged to Kien himself, but Malikai couldn't see him. Thugs stood at various points, some on top of pipes, some on the floor, all of them armed. They could easily, if so ordered, cut him down as soon as he took one step into the room. The vigilante weighed his chances of surviving such a crossfire; perhaps if he were at full strength, yes. Now, in his present immolated condition? He did not believe so.

"I am here for the boy. Give him to me, and your men will live."

Kien laughed the hearty, careless laugh of a man who holds all the cards. "Just as I thought. A hero. No, no—a demon who *fancies* himself a hero. I knew you'd come back, demon. Come in. Please. See where I've got the boy."

Malikai weighed his options, but came up empty on any real course of action that could protect little Joey. He had no choice; he had to enter.

He stepped into the room.

The guards tensed and squirmed in place, but made no move against him. Sliding slowly, ignoring the pain in his blistered feet, Malikai continued weaving through the pipes until he could see Kien standing in the middle of the room, Joey at his side. Kien held a revolver to the boy's head. Malikai did not see Ching anywhere, only a greasy smear of his dark blood on the floor.

"Ah, there he is," Kien said sagely. "Welcome back. Let us talk business, eh?"

"Give me the boy and you will live. That is my only business."

Kien shook his head. "In my line of work, demon, one holds one's life gingerly. You are not the first to threaten me. You killed Ching, so you are very powerful. You survived immolation. And I am quite curious about the properties of your magical sword. But whatever else you may be, you cannot both kill me and escape with the boy alive and well. You know that, demon."

"Why do you call me that?"

Kien looked genuinely surprised. "You do not know the legend of the boys who so dishonored their family that their father sent them away to learn self-sacrifice?"

The vague, stinging pain he'd felt earlier swirling in his chest bloomed again in Malikai. It was like a year's worth of hunger suddenly returning full force, nearly driving him to his knees. He'd never heard such a story, but something in Kien's words drove an invisible spike into his gut.

Kien beamed. "So if I were a man disposed to fairy tales, I would say you fit the profile. Perhaps you and I can share stories from our youth together—as soon as you put down your sword."

The queasy feeling in Malikai's stomach faded. "Then what."

"Then I will release the boy, and you accept a nominal weekly fee for your services."

"Services . . ."

"Ching was a good enforcer, but no friend of mine. More brawn than brains. You appear to possess both. That is a valuable asset. I don't know what your interest in this one child is, but he is clearly important to you. You could likely kill many of these men, maybe even me, if you so chose. But we both know you wouldn't last forever, and that the child would die long before you could prevent it. So? Let's come to an agreement instead."

It had to be a lie. Men like Kien didn't go around making offers to other men who'd just absconded with so much living, breathing profit. But what was his plan? If he intended merely to kill the vigilante, he would have had his men open fire by now. Malikai tried to stall, to give himself time to guess Kien's plan. Dealing with crime bosses wasn't his usual forte. Handling street-level thugs was one thing—thinking men were another monster.

"I'm not certain I should trust a man living in a sewer," he said.

Kien laughed. "Oh, this is just my day job. I have a penthouse downtown, of course."

"Of course."

"One day, you could, too," Kien went on with a generous tone. "Gifted men such as you can often rise—"

Malikai struck. He knew his odds were better while Kien talked.

Dismissing the pain that wracked his exposed nerves, he sprang forward and slashed the sword blade across Kien's gun arm. The man was still talking even as his hand fell to the floor, the revolver still clutched in it. Spinning, Malikai grabbed little Joey by the shirt and flung him toward the door leading to their escape.

Kien screamed just as the first bullets tore through the air. Malikai dove under a pair of once-red pipes, slugs pinging off the concrete over the shouts of the thugs giving orders to one another.

Malikai rolled to one side and popped up, sprinting for the nearest thug. The man saw him coming and emptied a clip of his AK at the vigilante, but scored no hits. The barrel smoked as Malikai bisected his torso from shoulder to hip. The thug fell soundlessly to the floor.

More bullets ricocheted off pipes and walls. Malikai spun, ducked, leaped, and spun again, veering toward the doorway where Joey sat curled up and screaming. Malikai could only see the boy's mouth open and the tears glistening on his cheeks; gunfire from a dozen weapons drowned out the actual sound of his cries.

The next thug dropped when Malikai ran him through with the Tang dao. The thug fell, dropping the gun and clutching his gut. Malikai dove over his prone body, coming up behind a series of pipes rising into the ceiling.

Joey sat by the door, still screaming; Malikai could hear him now, he was that close. He almost tried to order the boy to stop, to listen, to get him to run through the door, but quickly discarded the idea. They had no time to debate.

During a short lull in the gunfire as several of the men reloaded, Malikai ran for the boy. He leaned low and scooped the child up under his left arm. He was rewarded for his efforts with several slugs to the body, which pierced what remained of his skin. Deviant, demon, or otherwise, the gunshot wounds took a toll. He was not bulletproof. Perhaps, given enough time and rest, he could recover from them.

He'd have to escape first.

Malikai raced down the corridor toward the pipe room where the others had escaped. The guns stopped firing, replaced by shouts as the surviving thugs tried to regroup for pursuit. Malikai's feet ached and burned with each step, but he forced the pain from his mind and ran full speed, sword in one hand and child in the other.

Three bullets pinged around him as he reached the door to the junction room. Malikai tore it open, flung Joey inside, then followed behind and shut the door. He dropped the dao and kicked the blade under the space between the door and floor until the weapon lodged there. Wedging the sword in this way wouldn't hold the door shut forever, but might buy them the minute he needed to get Joey into the large pipe.

"Hey!"

Someone behind him. Malikai instinctively stepped in front of Joey, who was only just then climbing to his feet after Malikai's graceless throw. He dropped into a defensive crouch, but eased when he saw the voice belonged to Julia Lawson.

Julia popped up from the concrete box on top of the pipe they'd used in their escape, her eyes wide. Malikai pushed Joey toward her.

"Get him out of here," the vigilante growled, for a growl was all his vocal cords could manage any more.

Julia nodded and hopped out of the concrete box, motioning for Joey to run. Joey did, bawling. Julia helped him into the box, then climbed in herself as Malikai stumbled toward them.

"Hurry!" she cried at him.

Malikai reached the box as the frenzied shouts of Kien's men grew louder in the corridor. He shook his head.

"Go," he said, still marveling that the girl had come back here under her own steam. "Get him out. Call the police."

"They're coming. The guy at the comic book shop called them."

He guessed she must be referring to the shop near the arcade. Their escape had taken them right back to where his odyssey started. Briefly, he wondered if more of Kien's men would come pouring out of the arcade to retrieve the children, but then dismissed it. They could not do so without attracting unwanted attention. The children should be safe.

"Then go," Malikai said to Julia. "Now!"

"What about you?"

The door flew open, and thugs came spilling out of the corridor. "*Go!*"

Julia went. Malikai heard her and Joey scuffling quickly along the concrete tube.

The dao skid along the concrete platform and clattered aside. The thugs opened fire immediately. Groaning inwardly, Malikai laid himself across the top of the box where the grate had been, grabbed the edges tightly to block their access to the pipe, and held on. The manner in which he had been forced to cut through the grate wouldn't allow for it to fit on again—nor was there time to try.

The room filled with the deafening thunder of a dozen automatic weapons firing. Bullets slammed into Malikai's feet and legs, then his torso. He released an inhuman scream as the men stepped closer and kept shooting, a mobile firing squad, while Malikai took the shots without relinquishing his hold. He had to give Julia and Joey time enough to get to the end of the pipe and out to the alley. The thugs wouldn't dare follow that far, but if he didn't keep them blocked here and now, they could easily catch up to the two kids.

The men surrounded him, still shooting. Malikai closed his eyes, existing now in a world far beyond pain as searing lead chipped off pieces of his charred flesh and splintered his bones.

Still he lived.

The men didn't seem to notice or care; they came closer, closer, until one of them even stood only a few feet away. The thug grumbled something unintelligible as Malikai opened his eyes and looked at him. Then the thug shot him point-blank in the face.

Whatever deviant force kept his body intact at last weakened. The bullets tore Malikai's face into crimson shrapnel—

And still he lived through the piercing agony.

Inwardly, Malikai counted off the seconds, trying to guess how far Julia and Joey had gotten. Far enough now? Now?

At last his strength failed. Malikai's grip on the box slipped. He dropped on top of the large pipe, smearing blood and viscera. He felt as though he were breathing hard, or perhaps he only wanted to.

The thugs surrounded his naked, decimated body, pointing their weapons at him. The smell of gun smoke itched in his nose and seemed to sting his open wounds all the more.

They didn't shoot, though. Malikai lay there, thinking he might die now, at last. If he'd been human, he would have died long ago, not even counting his immolation.

Whatever omnihuman force kept him stitched together, he did not know, and almost did not care. Death would have been welcome.

Kien appeared. He should have been pale, shaking in shock, bleeding into a towel or past a tourniquet. Instead, the man appeared malevolently jovial as he stood over Malikai.

His hands—both full, healthy hands—were folded in front of him.

Kien was a six. Nothing else could explain how his hand had suddenly returned, fully functional.

"You are indeed an impressive specimen," Kien said. "But you clearly feel pain. That is unfortunate. You've cost me millions of dollars today, and I'll now have to send out more requests. You've saved a few, demon, but more will come. I promise it."

He gestured to some of the men, who slung their weapons backward over their shoulders and hoisted the vigilante up. Kien met his eyes.

"The money is not at all the point, you know. There's the embarrassment, the loss of respect. Ah, it will take many weeks to regain the trust of our customers and the respect of our competitors— though we don't have quite so many of those as we used to, so that's nice. Since you do not strike me as the type of man or beast that has an overflowing bank account, I will have to find some other way to extract my repayment."

They marched up the corridor. Malikai's bare, shredded feet trailed streaks of blood. One of the other thugs grabbed his dao and held on to it, standing far away as the group moved past him; they'd learned from Ching's earlier error and would not let the vigilante near the weapon again.

They took Malikai to the hall of cells where the children had been kept. As if prepared for such an eventuality, two more guards stood inside, holding thick chains and manacles.

His captors threw Malikai to the floor, where the guards made quick work of bundling him in the chains.

"Now," Kien said as they worked, "since you cannot repay the debt you owe me, I will see exactly how much pain you can withstand. How much, and for how long. Hours? Days? Years? I don't know. But we are going to find out, demon. You're not the first experiment I've been able to conduct, but you are the first six. My congratulations and thanks."

Malikai tried to form words, but couldn't. Exhaustion and agony ripped his mind in half. But the children were safe. Julia was safe. He'd fulfilled his vow.

Perhaps that was enough.

Perhaps he could die now.

"The Chinese have many hells," Kien went on, oblivious to Malikai's wonderings. "This will be but one of them. Maybe you really are a demon, eh? Maybe you can never die. Perhaps you are some kind of immortal."

Kien gave the chains a shake with his restored hand.

"But we'll have plenty of time to talk about that."

He muttered a command. A guard came in carrying a gallon of gasoline in each hand.

Kien leered down at him.

"Well, now. Let's put your immortality to the test. I think, though, that you will be with us for a very, very long time. We'll just have to test a number of methods."

The thug unscrewed one of the canisters. The mere scent of gasoline made what remained of Malikai's muscles tense. Kien watched the guard pour the gasoline into an insecticide spray bottle and tighten the lid. Kien produced a silver Zippo lighter and faced Malikai.

"No time like the present, eh?"

Kien smiled.

"Let us begin."

*

Manic stood still for a moment before relaxing his rigid posture. "Oh, hell. All right. Fine. I'm here. What the hell is going on?"

"Have a seat." The kid gestured to the leather chairs in front of the desk. "Sure you don't want anything? Whatever you want, man. I can get it."

Manic holstered his weapon and sat down across from the kid, sending an invisible plume of furniture polish into the sixcop's nose. This close, he could see the kid's eyes sparkling with intelligence. For a guy who'd stared down and *gunned* down his fair share of deviants, those eyes unnerved him. "Nah, thanks, I'm good. So you're Savage."

The kid sat back and shoved fries into his mouth. Something about it tripped an alarm in Manic, but it was a silent alarm, nothing he could pin to a cause.

"Yep," the kid said, his mouth full.

"Who was the guy out there, then?"

"John Callahan. He's an actor. Good one too, huh? He plays the part for me."

"You're a *kid.*"

"Wow," Savage said. "No wonder you didn't get promoted to detective. Things just take awhile to sink in for you, huh?"

Manic shrugged. "You wanted me here, apparently. What now?"

The kid smiled. "I wanted to bring you up to speed. Let you know that the test was over. A little sooner than I'd planned, but you don't get to my position without knowing how to roll with a few punches, you know?"

"What test?"

Savage finished off his milkshake with a satisfied *Ah!* and again something vague blared at the back of Manic's mind. He simply could not seize on it.

"Cocoa!" the kid said to the Chinese woman. "Make it fast."

The woman bowed and scuttled out of the room. Savage watched her go with a sexual leer on his face that turned Manic's stomach.

"She's handy," Savage said. "You should get one. Cheap, too, if you know where to shop. I could hook you up, if you want."

"Start talking."

Savage's grin grew wider. "Sure thing, man."

He cleared his throat and leaned back soundlessly in his chair.

"See, it's like this. I'm smart. Like, *real* smart. Smarter than most of the planet, I think. And I wanted to make a difference in the world, because that's how my mom raised me. I figured best way to do that was to run the country."

"You don't run the country."

"Meh. Not yet. I will. And you could be in on the ground floor of that. Take a look around, dude! I have three quarters of the retail and food businesses in this town paying their employees double the minimum wage, *voluntarily*. They're getting huge benefits for choosing to do that. People stay in their jobs. They show up on time, they work hard. Then I tax the employees, who are happy enough to be making a living wage. Everyone wins. I put the money into education. Kids stay in school because they know they have a hot meal at home. They get jobs, and they stay living here when they realize how great it is. They buy houses next to their black, brown, white, and yellow neighbors, and everyone gets along fine because they're fat and rich and happy. I got a good thing going here. Or at least, I did, until the goddamn deviants spoke up."

"*You're* the goddamn deviant!" Manic shouted.

Because by then, it was the only thing that made sense. No kid, no matter how smart he thought he was, could pull off what Corby Savage had pulled off.

"I'm an exceptional human being," Savage said with false modestly.

"You're fuckin' twelve!"

"Thirteen in June."

Manic stood. "I'm gonna end this right now."

"What, by shooting me? Oh, I *dare* you. Please. Shoot me dead."

It was enough of a dare to make Manic pause.

"Look," Savage said, rocking in his chair. "In 1942, the federal government enlisted the aid of the mafia to protect our ports, because the mob had strangleholds on everything coming into the country. It worked, too. It was in everyone's best interest to work together. Do you see where I'm going with this, dude?"

"Pretend I don't."

Savage grinned again. "Sometimes you got to make a deal with the devil to make the world safer for everyone. See, a few years back, this guy showed up in my office with a .45 pistol, a little perturbed that I was ruining his cocaine industry. He said he was making more than a hundred million a year before I took office. So *I* said, 'Go fuck yourself, I brought in one *billion* in economic impact from when we hosted the Super Bowl. How about you take a piece of that action with me?' He said he already had a piece of it. I said, yeah, but I can cut you a much bigger slice with no risk."

The governor laughed. "We've been good friends ever since."

Manic, despite himself, thought about the story. "You keep the wheels greased. Put one guy in charge, and regulate everything."

"Exactly. Vice has existed since the dawn of man. Better to keep the sharks fed than release them to an unsuspecting public. You can walk down any street in this city in total safety. First time in recorded history, my friend. *I* did that. People like you, all you see is bad guys, there's always gotta be bad guys. That's not true. There always has to be *vice*, but that's not the same thing. I made this city safer. The poor are getting educated. They're getting jobs. Unemployment has bottomed out at, what, point-nine percent or something? There's no more homeless on the streets who don't want to be there, and the rest are mentally ill. Those mentally ill are getting care like never before. It's all one big beautiful cycle, and it all generates a whole shit-ton of money. Meanwhile, with one group handling the vices the way I instruct them, everyone gets their dope and hookers and dice, but no one gets hurt. We all get rich. See? Being rich isn't about having more than the next guy. It's not a zero-sum game. That's what these douchebags at the oil companies and all those arms dealers don't understand. When my neighbors got money, *I* got money. It's that simple. I did that."

Manic pieced the last few hours together as he listened. It began making sense, or as much sense as it could in a place where a pre-teen had amassed the power of a state governor, managing the fifth largest economy in the entire world, without anyone catching on.

He understood why and how Weber had shown up at the arcade. The Ice Dragons were working, ultimately, for the governor of the state of California. And he, in one way or another, was responsible for what Manic had witnessed in that underground concrete hellhole.

"They're kids," Manic said, almost in a whisper as the enormity of his situation became clear. It forced him back into his chair. "They're your age. Bet you wouldn't like bein' down there."

"Oh, *hell* no. But that's not where fate has cast me, I'm afraid."

Manic leaned forward, putting his hands on Savage's desk. "You're a monster. Plain and simple."

"Well, you're entitled to your opinion."

Manic jumped up, pulling his pistol. In less than a second, the barrel was trained on the boy's forehead.

"Now what, you cocky little prick?"

The governor smiled calmly and spread his hands. "Dude. I let you in here with poor me all alone, knowing you had a gun. Do you seriously think I'm scared? Seriously. Think about it. What do I know about me that you don't?"

Manic kept the gun on him, but took a step back. "So you are a deviant. That's what I thought."

"I prefer the term omnihuman, but, whatever. You're a *human*. Trust me, man, that makes me sick to my stomach, too."

"I thought you said you hated them."

"I said everything was fine until they showed up and started making noise. We're not all kindred spirits just 'cause we got wacky DNA."

"What happens if I pull the trigger?"

Savage shrugged. "You'll die. Or, maybe I'm bluffing. But seriously, man. I didn't so much as have you frisked. You could have a vest full of dynamite on you right now, and I totally could not even care. So shoot. Or, settle down and listen to what I'm offering."

Manic wanted to shoot.

But he didn't.

The problem with Savage's words was that Manic had seen enough crazy deviant shit out there over the years to know that there was a good chance Savage was telling the truth. Sure, he *could* be lying. The reality was, deviant or otherwise, if Savage was even a little nervous about having a sixcop in his office, he would have taken more precautions. Would have taken *any* precaution, yet he hadn't. That was a pretty big gamble to take on a cop with a history of being difficult to intimidate.

Plus that nagging feeling of something awry in the room wouldn't go away. It wasn't just Savage's age—something else was wrong under the surface, and it itched Manic's brain.

"Children are getting hurt," Manic said, not lowering the gun.

Savage showed the first chink in his armor: his expression darkened.

"Don't get all self-righteous with me, dude. Your dumb ass wasn't supposed to go poking around in Ice Dragon business anyway. You had a job to do. Which you did quite well, by the way. You should have just stuck with it."

The gun didn't waver from its target, but Manic's mind spun. It was not until that moment that his memory betrayed him, reminding him of a small fact that he'd happily suppressed or ignored when he took the job.

Izanagi's dossier had listed no crimes.

Even Fracture's doss—Fracture, a known criminal—hadn't listed actual crimes. Just a paragraph on his associations and likely behaviors. Izanagi had lacked even that.

The paperwork hadn't even made clear whether the targets had their D-cards or not. Probably they didn't, but the dossiers hadn't specified. NPD had that kind of information, surely an organization who could afford to hire a hitman—

The word burned hot in Manic's stomach.

Hitman.

That's what Savage had hired. Not a cop, not even an assassin. Just a regular old hitman, out whacking enemies for the boss. The same the job he'd grown up believing he'd have before leaving home for the police academy instead.

He'd become exactly the thing he'd wanted to leave behind in the old neighborhood.

"Manic," Savage said gently. "I'm coming clean here so that you'll know you can trust me. Very few people know my secret. You're sitting at the big-boy table now. You want to know why? Because I need you, man. You do good work. So what do you say, huh? Come on in."

"Come on into *what?*"

The governor gave him a proud expression. "Into making the world a better place! That's what this is all about, man. Your first hit. Fracture. A real scum bag, but not even a boss-level character. He and the 56 Tigers were causing problems, I needed him out of the way, and NPD was having a hard time sticking to him. He was a test balloon for you. Izanagi, on the other hand . . . well, he was a pain in my ass too and needed to go, but again, I couldn't go sending in NPD for a guy like him. You have to get up close and personal with an omni like that. He'd have known NPD was coming. But I send one guy? One quote-unquote 'stupid ex-cop?' That wouldn't raise his hackles. See what I'm saying? Izanagi was a bad-ass, but you took him out. You did a hell of a job there. But now imagine a guy like that being a Level Seven. Or Level Eight. *Nine*."

Something in Manic's guts unfurled. "Those levels don't exist."

"Not as far as the public knows. Not as far as NPD knows, for that matter. But I assure you, all world governments, including ours, know just how tough a deviant can really be. You haven't seen anything yet."

The governor rocked in his chair.

"You're a cop, right? I don't mean in title, I mean in your bones. In your identity. You know if I'm telling the truth or not. So now you tell me if I'm lying: *the scale goes to ten.* Ten, Manic. There are omnis here, here in Los Angeles, with power you can't even imagine. That's where you come in, that's what I need you for. See, I need another five or six human guys just like you. And when I get you all in one room, there's almost no limit to the amount of good we can do in this world."

"What am I supposed to—"

"A human took out a near-Level Seven deviant with his bare hands. No artillery, no nukes, no indie drones. *Mano y mano.* These omnis, they underestimate just how strong humans really are. And Izanagi's got friends, big friends, and if they come out of hiding, everything L.A. has become goes up in flames. You can keep that from happening."

"So this wasn't about taking those deevs out…"

"Sure it was, but that's not all. You really need to start thinking on more than one level at a time, bro. If I just needed them dead, I could have hired some other six to do the job. But that doesn't help me. Number one, it risks pinning my name to a deviant if something goes wrong, which it would, because deevs are essentially stupid, in my studied opinion. And two . . . since I'm laying it all out there, yeah, like I said, it was a test for something a lot bigger."

"Bigger than *this?*"

"I'm thinking of a new office. Big. White. Shaped like an oval." The boy smiled proudly. "You passed your tests, right up until you went guns blazing into the Ice Dragon's business. But I'm willing to overlook that."

At the mention of the gang, Manic's thoughts darted to Liam Gray. Liam was the price for Savage's so-called better world.

Manic at last lowered his gun. "I've met a lotta deviants in my day. But you're the first monster I ever come across."

"I'm a pragmatist. Pragmatists always get made out to be the villain. These guys who make missiles and guns and stuff, and then they get used to destroy a hospital in the Middle East, where is their jury, huh? Why is what I do so wicked all the sudden?"

"Nah, no, you can't use their guilt to mitigate your own, kid."

Savage laughed. "Sorry! I don't mean to be rude. I didn't realize you could pronounce words with more than two syllables."

"Yeah, I can pronounce a lotta shit, actually. What you're doing to those kids—"

"I've never touched a kid in all my life. Short as it's been so far, albeit."

"What you *let* happen—"

"I play the numbers, Manic. The men who prey on them would continue to prey on them. You know that. Now, they pay top dollar for it. And it stays contained. That's all. Haven't you ever been to the dark web in all your years as a cop? They're out there, and they're organized. Bad men. They'll take what they want one way or another. I regulate it. I keep it safe."

Manic thought of Liam Gray again. Fury coated his words with bitter hate. "You call that safe?"

"Safe for the majority. For every one kid that pays the price for doing business, a hundred, a *thousand* are left in peace."

Manic's stomach turned. "Well clearly it ain't ever been done to you."

A shadow crossed the governor's face. "Aw, now what on earth makes you assume *that?*"

Twelve-year-old omnihuman Governor Corby Savage suddenly made perfect sense to the veteran cop.

"You want to meet the guy who did it?" Savage went on. Something had shifted in the youngster's eyes. Something well beyond anger, past rage, and even past evil.

It may have been agony. Internal, silent agony and hate.

"I've been keeping him around," Savage said. "For, oh, let's see . . . two, three years now. Got a special room all decked out in one of my houses for him. Coupla my employees see to it he keeps his strength up. And let me tell you, he needs it. I figure, I'm twelve now, so I got a long life ahead of me. So does he. For as long as I want. I'll keep him alive. You bet."

"So then if you know what it's like, how the hell can you let the Ice Dragons do that shit?"

Savage stood and rested his hands on his desk, leaning toward the old cop in the same manner Manic had done minutes before.

"Funny," he said. "I asked my dad the exact same thing."

Savage had been right about at least one thing: Manic could tell when he was lying, and he hadn't lied about much. And he wasn't lying now. He was a kid who'd been betrayed by his dad, and that's why he hadn't been able to foresee Manic's reaction to the labyrinth. He just didn't have the years on him.

He ain't old enough to have ever been a good dad himself, Manic thought. *If he was, he would have guessed what I'd do when I caught on.*

They held each other's gaze for a moment. Savage broke it first, sitting down and clearing his throat, looking like a miniature banker.

He opened his mouth to speak, but the doors swung open. Manic turned, expecting bodyguards. Instead it was only the Asian woman with a tray of two white ceramic cups and an ornate Oriental styled pot. Steam rose from one of the cups.

"Ah, she made some for you," Savage said. "That's nice of her, isn't it?"

"Splendid." Manic sat down again, for lack of anything better to do. He had zero idea what his next move ought to be. He sure as hell wasn't going to be working for Savage, and he sure as hell wasn't going to abandon the children he was sure he'd left behind.

The woman set the tray on Savage's desk in front of Manic, and turned toward him with a cup and saucer in her hand. Suddenly the cup and saucer dropped, coating Manic's front with steaming hot chocolate.

The woman squealed and began stammering in what Manic assumed to be Chinese. She pulled a purple cloth from her back pocket and tried to sop up the mess as Manic reared back, his hands raised. Savage shouted profanities at her.

Manic met her eyes as she rattled on in her native language. He suddenly felt one of her hands fishing around in one of his hip pockets. He almost cried out in surprise, then snapped his mouth shut as she maintained eye contact with him. He realized then that what should have been a very hot beverage was instead mostly only warm. The other cup still steamed on the service try, though. It was as if she'd made two drinks with two different temperatures.

Her fingers sneaked away from his pocket, and Manic felt the unmistakable jab of folded paper in there now. She'd passed him a note, and used the old ruse of a spilled drink to get it done. Given the look in her eyes, Manic thought she'd probably just risked her life to do it.

He did not give her any indication he understood her intent. It was too risky that Savage might pick up on it.

"Stupid bitch!" Savage went on ranting. "Swear to God, should have her thrown out a window, you know?"

"It's fine," Manic said. "Shut up for a second."

Savage eyed him, then laughed, but there was no mirth in it. "See, I like you Manic. That's the thing, I really do. I think you bring a lot to the team."

The woman finished cleaning Manic up before serving Savage his hot chocolate, very carefully. She then stood mutely by the side of the desk where she had been when Manic first arrived.

"So?" Savage said, ignoring the cocoa. "What do you say, man? You got a good gig here, you don't want to blow it, do you?"

Manic considered—not the offer, but how best to get out of here alive. Savage was smart, he accepted that now. But tactical . . . that was something else entirely, and he didn't believe Savage possessed that particular subset of intelligence.

The more he thought, the more he believed he was right. The look on the faces of the guards downstairs, for example. *They* had known it was tactically stupid to let him come up here fully armed, no matter what Savage's deviant abilities were. They'd known it was hubris, and hubris got guys killed. Guys like them.

So Savage thought he knew what Manic could do, but maybe he didn't. And maybe Manic did not in fact have a vest full of dynamite on him, but he still had plenty of toys Weber's men had left him to do his job.

"No," Manic said at last as he slipped a hand into one of his cargo pockets. "I don't want to blow it."

"Great!" Savage said, slapping his hands on the desk. "So let's—"

"What I want to blow is that cocky look off your face, you arrogant little shit."

In the time it took Savage to process what Manic had said, Manic yanked his hand out of his pocket and threw a net bomb at the young deviant.

The grenade popped on top of the desk as Manic dove around the chair, aimed for the double doors. He heard laughter as he raced for the exit. As he flung the doors open, Manic risked one look backward.

Corby Savage sat at his desk, laughing, as the rubbery tendrils of the net bomb flailed useless around—and *through*—the governor.

"See ya 'round, Manic!" the governor called, still laughing as if the netting tickled him as it passed harmlessly through his body.

No wonder he'd been so fearless, Manic thought he as beelined for the elevator. Governor Savage had no goddamn *body* to be threatened. It was a neat trick, that was for sure, and not one Manic had encountered or even heard about. How was it even possible? How could a person make their body as intangible as a damn ghost, as an odor?

An odor.

A scent.

Shit, *that* was it! Manic would have laughed if some other cop was telling him the story. He knew now what had been nagging the back of his mind. Everyone knew the rich, beefy smell of fast-food french fries. Savage's meal hadn't had any such scent. It hadn't had any smell at all.

Quite possibly, it hadn't *existed*.

Well, hell. It didn't matter now. Manic pressed the button on the elevator, keeping a wary eye down the hall, waiting for a team of guards to come for him. None did, and the elevator doors opened readily for him. Manic jumped in and pressed the first floor button, his brain still putting pieces together as fast as it could.

Maybe, given his resources and intelligence, the little shit governor did have a tangible form somewhere and the thing behind his desk had been some kind of interactive hologram. Hell, it made as much sense as a kid who'd ascended to California's top governmental position.

And who might very well have the skills to become President of the United States.

. . . Or more?

Manic shook the thought away as the elevator dinged on the first floor. That was too frightening to consider right now. Right *now*, what needed to happen was getting out of this building alive.

He took up position beside the door, his back to the buttons. The doors opened. He peeked around the corner, expecting the two guards to be waiting for him—

And they were. Bullets tore into the elevator car the instant he showed his head. Marble dust exploded around him as the rounds penetrated the walls.

"God *damn*!" Manic shouted, wincing against the noise and dust in the air.

Another net bomb would have been nice, but might not successfully hit both of them. He guessed these two weren't deviants, as deevs didn't tend to use guns. Shunned them, in fact, in his experience. So his 9-milimeter would be just fine against human torsos, provided he could get the shots off.

But he couldn't risk capture. Running was the best option.

Manic reached behind his back and pressed the button for the second floor. If it was just the two guards, they'd probably split up to cover the exits. One would stay watching the elevator, the other would cover the stairs, or maybe come up to keep the elevator covered from the second floor. Either way, they'd have to out-guess him.

So he pushed the third floor button too. The doors opened on the second floor. He kept himself silently pressed into an opposite corner, waiting to see if anyone would try to clear the elevator. No one did. The doors shut, and on he went to floor three.

When the doors opened again, Manic swept his gun in an arc to clear the immediate area. All was dark, but he could make out the usual office space furniture—reception desk, cubicles, a few offices. The scent of toner hung in the air.

The office seemed clear. Manic reached into the elevator and tapped the first and second floor buttons again, then raced through the office to the nearest window, hoping Corby Savage hadn't armored the entire outside of the building the way the lobby doors had been strengthened.

At a window on the north side of the building, Manic fired one shot. He exhaled a quick gasp of gratitude as the glass shattered then broke apart, leaving a jagged hole.

Manic zipped up his leather coat, muttering, "Here we go." He went to the vacant window and kicked jagged glass clear from the edge, then grabbed that edge and lowered himself outside. He took two deep breaths, preparing himself, then let go.

He made his body go limp as he had during his fight with Izanagi. The injuries he'd sustained from that fall hadn't exactly healed yet, of course, and he knew he'd be in for a bad tumble when he hit now. As he'd hoped, the bushes surrounding the building broke much of his fall—but not all of it.

"Ah, shit!" Manic roared as he rolled out of the bushes. He'd lost the pistol. Damn. No time to search for it. He had to get off the X.

Manic struggled to his feet, then cried out in pain as his right ankle gave way. Dammit, he'd done some real damage this time.

Something sang past his head. The primal part of his mind warned him shots were being fired his direction before the rest of his brain even heard the crack of pistols behind him.

Crouching low and dragging his wounded leg, Manic aimed for the street, where a few cars were parked along the sidewalk. He risked one glance back to see if he could get a bead on his attackers.

A bullet crashed through Manic's face.

It entered the left side of his cheek and exited the right, taking ninety percent of his teeth with it and all but tearing his entire jaw from his skull. It felt at first like a punch from one very large and very angry gorilla. Then the pain was gone, buried beneath warm layers of shock.

The force spun him in a full circle, dizzying him. Manic sprawled to the blacktop, blood gushing from what remained of his mouth.

This is bad, that same primal part of his mind pointed out. Really, really bad.

But he wasn't dead, so that was something. Still a chance. What did J.T. always say? *Just don't quit.* Manic flung himself to his feet, cradling his jaw in his left hand to keep it from falling freely to the pavement. If he could make it to the cars, just make it to the cars . . .

Manic collapsed on the far side of a newer model sedan and took cover behind the engine block, trying to stay conscious and think as clearly as possible. Not an easy task. Blood cascaded down his arm now and splashed onto his cargo pants, blending into the dark fabric. He tried to swear, and found he could not speak because he lacked the structure in his face to do so anymore.

He tried the handle of the car. Locked, of course. Governor Savage had created a safe town, not a stupid one.

Another cluster of shots came at him, pounding into the body of the sedan. The body, and the windows. If not for his mortal wound, Manic would have laughed at his good fortune: one of the bullets blew out the driver's side window, spilling chunks of glass to the blacktop.

He'd have smiled if he still had lips and teeth.

Forcing himself to ignore the shots, Manic reached up, unlocked the door, and pulled it open. The guards would be advancing, he knew. Leapfrogging toward him, with the man in back firing and the man in front moving to new cover, alternating back and forth until they reached him. He had seconds to get the job done he needed to do.

Sirens sounded in the distance. Savage's little safety-first goal was now going to screw the little governor up, at least a little. LAPD had doubtless gotten a shots-fired alert and were on their way. They'd slow down the guards just a little, because it would take time for the cops to distinguish who the good guys were from the bad.

Unless, of course, the cops who were coming were part of Savage's payroll.

Shit.

Manic reached under the dash of the sedan and found the wires he needed to get the car started. Some things he'd learned at the police academy, some he'd learned from Vic and Tony. Getting a car to start without keys came from the Vic and Tony school. The car fired up beneath his expert hand, and he dragged himself into the driver's seat. Newer sedans had their own weaknesses over the older models.

Blue and red lights reflected off buildings down the street. Bullets continued pinging off of and in to the sedan. Manic threw the gear into drive and slammed a foot down on the gas. The sedan growled, roared, then lurched down the street.

Still working primarily on instinct, Manic twisted the wheel at the first corner he came to, and raced the car down the empty city street. L.A. didn't sleep any more than New York did, but in this business area, no nightlife existed to tempt people out of their homes.

One last bullet knocked out the rear window. Manic ducked. He turned another corner and was out of sight of his attackers. His stomach lurched as pain slowly re-awoke in his face and his lap filled with blood. His grip on the steering wheel loosened, and he forced himself to concentrate on it hanging tight.

It was just a few miles, if he could make it just a few miles, there might be a chance . . .

Manic choked on blood pouring down his throat. He puked it back up and wondered just how much of a mess he looked like. Pretty bad, that was for sure. He distantly noted that his arms and legs were starting to get cold. If the people he was going to see wouldn't help him—and they sure had no reason to—there was an extremely good chance he'd bleed out in the next few minutes. But going to an NPD station was no longer an option, not after what happened at the arcade. An ER was no good, because his location would be picked up by LAPD *and* NPD, and he had no doubt Savage could have him killed within the hour.

So his options were either dying here and now . . . or bite the bullet, ha ha, and swallow his pride.

Manic pulled up in front of Sal's Café, grateful—in a numbed sort of way—that there were no other cars parked along the sidewalk.

He stumbled out of the vehicle, leaving it running. He crashed into the café door, tried to open it, and failed. Instead, Manic collapsed to the ground, his mind spinning, asking a dozen different nonsense questions and answering them with even more absurd responses. Yes, he was in critical condition now. If no one opened the door, if the good folks at Sal's had had enough of the old cop, then this is where it ended, this is where he hung it up, and the last thing on his mind and the last thing that tumbled grotesquely from his misshapen, wrecked mouth was only one word.

"Lilly . . ."

Then nothing.

NINETEEN

For a being who never slept and, so far as he knew, never aged, the passage of time meant little to Malikai. The subterranean concrete cave he now dwelt in didn't permit the cognition of sunrise or sunset, and Kien's people hadn't seen fit to provide him with a handy clock by which he could count the hours.

And days.

Malikai counted time now only in extremes of pain. No scale existed to quantify it. There existed for him only sharp, mind-bending pain, the kind that fell upon him when Kien's men used gasoline and lighters to char his already seared flesh, or the piercing, focused agony of when they laughingly shot nail guns toward him from behind the iron gate, rewarding one another with cigarettes or drugs. Once, Kien himself returned with a cart loaded with household chemicals and announced, "I have no idea what all these will do to you, but since you're here, I thought I'd find out. Research, you know."

On his flayed, exposed body, the chemicals had twisted Malikai's charred muscle into knots of burning nerve endings.

"Kill me . . ."

Malikai slurred this during one of Kien's experiments. Kien seemed pleased by the request. "Ah, now we're getting somewhere. Even the mighty hero has his limit."

"Kill me," Malikai said, "or when I am free, your suffering will be endless."

Kien laughed. "I'm not the immortal one, my friend. You should have died a double dozen times over, yet you remain. I know the risks of my profession. I accept them. It will indeed one day kill me, almost certainly. But you? You made the mistake of troubling yourself where you shouldn't have. As you can see, the price is dear."

He leaned down and pulled on an industrial black rubber glove, then scooped some white powder out of a bucket.

"Speaking of what you can and can't see," Kien said, and threw the chemical into Malikai's face.

The sounds popping from his eyes was nearly as hideous as the sensation of his eyeballs bubbling beneath the acid.

And yet, as time went on—dragged on—his vision did return.

When it did, as his vision began to clear, he realized he was not alone. A young man stood outside the barred gate, looking in at him with a curious expression. He wore a white medical brace on his leg and carried an aluminum cane.

It took the vigilante several moments to recall why the man looked familiar: He was the cashier from the arcade upstairs.

"You're alive?" the cashier asked. He wore almost the same thing as when Malikai had first approached him all those days or weeks or months ago: a distressed T-shirt advertising Squirt soda and denim shorts too big for him.

How long has it been? Malikai wondered. *How long down here?*

Malikai lifted his recently regenerated eyes enough to make them meet the cashier's, nothing more.

"My name's Ji," the cashier said. He wasn't whispering, but nor did he raise his voice. For no good reason, Malikai felt that it was night time out in the world; very late at night, perhaps just before dawn. Ji spoke as if he were the first person awake in a full house of people and didn't want to disturb anyone.

"You look like shit," Ji said. "You reek, too."

Malikai's broken mind couldn't even dream a response, much less offer one.

"Look, I shouldn't even be down here, but my grandpa used to tell all these fucked-up stories about China and shit, and I had to see for myself . . . Are you what they say you are? The *buxiu?*"

The word tickled something deep in Malikai's mind; *buh-zyou*. It meant . . . it meant . . .

And yet why should it mean anything to him? It may as well have been a nonsense word, a slip of the tongue. But it vibrated something inside him, some chord he hadn't known was strung from his heart to his head.

Immortal. It meant immortal.

Ji took a cautious step closer on the other side of the gate. "Everyone's talking about you. How you can't die 'n shit. Man, that shit's crazy. My grandfather would tell us stories, he was a crazy old man. But one of them stories was about these wicked *buxiu*. These brothers who were all wild and spoiled, and punished by their dad."

Malikai let his eyes drop. Exhausted and unable to rest, Malikai figured the break in the pain and monotony would be pleasant.

He said, "Tell your story, boy."

Ji gripped one of the bars. "During the Tang dynasty, a man became one of the literati. You heard of them?"

"No."

"They were guys who served the empire. Like, all literate and shit. Smart guys. Yeah, the Tang was ahead of its time. If you had skills, you could get to be kind of middle class, you know? Have some money and influence. So this one guy did a real good job and got pretty rich. All the peasants and farmers liked him and the . . . what do you call it . . . magistrates of his district, they all said good things about him. Had a good rep, I guess. Him and his wife had two sons. And because they had money, they gave the kids everything. They got spoiled, you know?"

Malikai lifted his eyes again as that same deep, inner chord was struck once more. He had heard this story elsewhere, it sounded so familiar. But where? Where in Phoenix could he possibly have encountered this legend? It was nothing Xavian had ever said.

So where?

"But they didn't realize how much they were screwing their kids up," Ji said, squinting at the vigilante as if trying to recognize him. "The two brothers grew up to be monsters, man. They figured everything in the world belonged to them. Even people. They raped men and women, stole their shit. They did whatever they wanted in the surrounding villages. So then people started to hate the literati's family. He tried everything to teach the kids honor, but nothing worked. Even the knights of the area couldn't keep a lid on them. They were *wild*, man. Outta control."

No, Malikai thought, but could not draw in the forced breath needed to say the word.

No, he had not heard this legend in Phoenix.

He had not heard it at all. Ever.

But he remembered it.

Ji paused, scrutinizing the deviant as if sensing his thoughts. "You heard any of this before?"

Malikai shook his head. Even that small gesture sent shocks of pain down his body. "Go on."

"Well, according to my grandpa, the dad invited his sons to a feast," Ji said. "When they showed up, he tried to talk them into giving up their crazy ways, but they wouldn't listen. Then their mom flew into like this rage, spitting at them and cursing them. So the brothers killed her. They killed their own mom, right over the food still on the table."

Malikai trembled.

"The father was too old by then to try to stop them, so he did the last thing he could. Because he was literati, he knew magic. Old magic, way before we knew about deevs. He used it to punish his kids and to protect the villages from their rampages. Didn't have much choice, I guess."

Ji stepped back from the gate. "I always figured it was a story Grandpa made up to get out of giving us shit at Christmas. He was pretty stingy, you know? But then I looked it up. The Chinese have been telling this story since the Tang dynasty."

Malikai's words came out in jagged rasps. "How . . . were they . . . punished."

"Sent away," Ji said, narrowing his eyes. "Far away. Far, as in, like, not just away from the villages or even to another country. Far as in, like . . . to another time, maybe."

Malikai's eyes slammed shut. No, no, *no* . . .

"They were supposed to learn what it meant to suffer. They were supposed to learn how to help people. They were supposed to pay for everything they'd ever done."

". . . And given swords."

"Yeah, that's right. They were given swords made outta fire and ice, Grandpa said. So does that sound like anyone you know, man?"

Malikai could not stop how his body, his soul, quaked beneath Ji's words.

"When does their torment end? Please. Tell me."

"Dunno. The legends don't say when. Or, you know . . . *if*. Just that a kid was supposed to tell them when it was over. Maybe when they learned their lesson, I guess, I dunno. Man, I sound like my grandpa, that's crazy."

Ji gazed steadily at the flayed vigilante.

"So is that you, man? Are one of the brothers? 'Cause I seen some crazy shit workin' for these guys, but nothing like *that*. You know, the government, man . . . TV and shit . . . they all keep sayin' you guys are science. Like they can explain what you do with test tubes n' shit. But I don't know about that, man. If you *ain't* magic, then . . . shit."

Malikai dove deep into his meditation practice. Even hanging here, scorched and naked, he could access that reservoir of silence and peace. It was difficult—Kien's infliction of pain had been brilliant in its execution, driving the vigilante nearly insane. But now he focused, ignored the pain, crawled more deeply into his own being than he'd even managed before, even in the quiet of the old farmhouse.

He perceived Ji speaking again, but the sounds were muted and insensible. Deeper and deeper into his mind Malikai dove, like a diver seeking pearls.

When he thought he could go no more inside himself, he discovered yet another layer. A dark place that seemed to have been concealed from him until now. He peeled back the darkness to study what lay beneath.

And remembered.

Yes.

Both Ji and Kien's words were true. Malikai understood that at last. While he was no metaphysical demon, he surely was a man accursed.

Certainly during nightly excursions in Phoenix, he'd witnessed many strange and marvelous things that deviants could do. His own peculiar and particular ability to turn a sword white-hot was only one such example. Yet never in his wanderings had the word *magic* ever occurred to him.

Did he even believe in magic? It mattered little. Whatever eldritch force of the universe existed as yet undiscovered or else unannounced by science, his own father had been able to call upon it.

His father's name eluded him but as Malikai sank deep into his memory, he felt sure the name would come. Perhaps he would discover his own, as well. Perhaps the name of his lost brother.

Perhaps even the name of his slain mother.

It occurred to Malikai as he swam among these fragmentary realizations that maybe these memories were not true; it was possible Ji was a six, capable of psionically influencing the minds of others. Malikai knew such deviants were especially rare but also most feared, and for good reason. Yet somehow, he did not believe this to be the case. Somehow, he knew Ji and Kien's words stood on their own as fact.

Indeed, tinkering with his mind might have been preferable to the images that began to flash in his head. His mother, a tall and elegant woman, being slaughtered by the blades of her own sons who had lost all sense of right or wrong. The face of his father, a ruined mask of loss, as he chanted incantations and lit the air with blue fire and crimson snow. Nearby, he imagined the face of a man similar to his own, but lacking the silvery skin and hair Malikai had prior to his imprisonment. With odd certainty, he knew it was the face of his brother.

In these nebulous moments, Malikai understood at last all that Xavian had taught him: the soul of his own father guided him now. Perhaps his "mistake" in the alley with Nicholas Lawson had been no accident at all; perhaps his father's ghost had led him to the error intentionally, knowing where it would inevitably lead. Whether Kien's torture was part of that plan or not, Malikai couldn't guess. Saving the children who were victims of The Gentlemen's Club, though; getting Julia Lawson home, freeing the boy Kien had threatened, rescuing anyone else trapped within this concrete labyrinth . . .

These were things of personal yet somehow cosmic importance.

Malikai next saw, as if from an incorporeal floating eye, the sins he and this brother had visited upon innocents. Ji was right: they were rapists and thieves. They acted without thought of consequence. They were barbaric.

Ji's words swam into his consciousness and Malikai screamed internally. What he saw, what he'd done . . . he deserved nothing less than Kien's tortures.

But now, perhaps, he could accept them. While he longed to continue fighting, to save innocents, to return to Phoenix and go on with his crusade, he could also stay here. Take whatever Kien had to hurt him, for as long as was necessary.

He had done right these past many months.

He had saved Julia. And more.

Nothing Kien did could change that. If death were possible, then Malikai was prepared to embrace it. His debt was paid.

Nearby, still standing outside the cell door, Ji's words came filtering into Malikai's battered consciousness.

"Ah, shit, they're coming back," Ji was saying. "Not really supposed to be talking to you, you know?"

Ji glanced down the hall, and took a step to one side. "Shit, I really gotta go. Here they come."

He'd found what he'd been searching for. Malikai bowed his head, and let peace fill his broken body. He may, in fact, have smiled.

"Let them."

TWENTY

Soft beeps trickled into Manic's consciousness. He opened his eyes after an eternity of attempting to do so. Pressure swelled in his face and neck, but he was breathing, and that was something. He was also hungry, but that could wait.

First things first: assessment.

Without trying to sit up, Manic let his senses rove around. He was stretched out on a bed in a nondescript room. Hospital? Tubes and wires attached to him in various places, he could feel that much, and the beeping came from what he took to be a heart monitor. But the bed wasn't hospital issue. Matter of fact . . . the coloring of the walls and the drop ceiling made him think of a middle manager's office.

Manic started laughing but stopped quickly as pain flared in his jaw. He lifted his hands to his face and found bandages, thick and dry. An IV needle poked out of his hand, and he followed the tube to a pair of bags hanging behind his headrest.

Gingerly, Manic moved his tongue around in his mouth. Well, he still *had* a tongue, so that was a good start, but it was dead thing, like he'd just had a dose of Novocain. Still, some sensation remained, and with it, Manic discovered he now had teeth again.

But they didn't seem like normal teeth. Between whatever pain meds were being pumped into him and the numbness in his mouth, he could only guess at what kind of reconstruction had been done on him.

Ten feet from the foot of his bed, the room's only door opened, letting in cold fluorescent light. Manic, even in his precarious and uncertain position, couldn't help raising an appreciative eyebrow as Perdida Velasquez peered in at him. She started to close the door, but re-opened it, as if doing a double-take.

"Hey," she said softly, and her voice felt better to him than all the painkillers in his body. Perdida let herself in and gently shut the door behind her. She came to the side of his bed and looked down at him. "You look like hell."

Manic thought maybe he smiled beneath the bandages.

"Well, the good news is, you can't talk right now," Perdida said, smirking. "I like you like that."

Perdida turned to grab a metal folding chair from the corner. Manic enjoyed the view as she leaned over to pick the chair up. She moved like a dancer, or a gymnast, tall and self-possessed.

She brought the chair to the side of the bed and sat, leaning forward with her elbows on her knees. "You probably have a lot of questions, so I'm going to guess them and tell you what I can. Okay?"

Manic tried to nod, but wasn't sure he was successful.

"You're not going to like all of it," Perdida said. "But you need to stay still. Hear me? No flipping out. Don't go 'manic,' Manic."

He tried to nod again. *God* he wanted to talk. He'd never realized how mouthy he was until the ability to speak was taken from him.

"So here's your situation, *cop*," Perdida said. Manic winced at the scorn in her voice. "You're *persona non grata* in the state of California.

We cleared everything out of your apartment before anyone else could get to it. You're welcome. Looks like you'll be staying with us for awhile."

Manic grunted.

"Yeah, it breaks my heart too," Perdida said. "Meanwhile, you're still alive. Again, you're welcome. When you can move, we've got a suite set up in the room next door for you. All your stuff is in there."

Perdida paused, searching his eyes. Manic turned away slightly, to indicate *What are you looking at me like that for?*

"Then there's the issue of your beautiful human face," Perdida said. "The docs had two choices. Either let you sip your meals through a straw the rest of your life, or try to give you some semblance of mastication. That's means 'chewing' if you didn't know. So they opted for the latter. But you need to understand, we're not a trauma ward, and we're not plastic surgeons. Maybe someday if you got enough money you can change what they did, but for the moment, you'll just have to accept what the docs had to do."

Manic said, "Uh." Meaning, *What?*

"When the bandages come off, which I believe will be later today, you're gonna have one hell of a huge jaw. I mean, huge. They had to stitch together some additional muscle to make it all work. Your teeth were generously donated by an omnihuman who regenerates his own, kind of like a shark. You might have to learn to speak again, but you'll be able to enjoy a nice steak. That's the trade-off."

Manic heard the monitor beep more rapidly as his heart rate picked up. Perdida interpreted the change and leaned even closer.

"That's right," she said, her voice soft again—half callous, half sympathetic. "You're one of us now, buddy. Good thing you can't show your face in the bright light of day in the great state of California, huh? People might think you're a dangerous deviant."

Manic closed his eyes.

"Speaking of which, you want to know something really interesting? Because I am dying to tell you."

He opened his eyes.

"The doctors had to do a lot of tests, of course, while they were saving your life. Now, I'm going to guess you've spent your whole life thinking you were red-blooded American four, right?"

"Ugh . . ."

"Well, the funny thing is, according to the Global Normative Standards scale, you're a five-point-nine, buddy. And depending on better instrumentation and some subjective evidence, you might even be a . . . well. You know."

The heart monitor beeped twice as fast. Perdida glanced at it.

"What's really curious about that, of course," she said, keeping her eyes on the monitor as if she were a physician, "is that NPD had to have known. So either somebody way high up covered for you, or something very, very interesting is happening at the Normative Policy Division."

Manic felt new pain through the drugs coursing in his system. What he did not know was if it was physical.

He almost leaped out of the bed when Perdida placed a hand on his shoulder.

"Ready for more, or you want me to take a break?"

Manic forced himself to breathe slowly, using the heart monitor as a guide to reduce his heart rate. Eventually it did, and he gingerly circled one hand, gesturing for Perdida to continue. Cripes, why not?

"You are plumb out of money," Perdida said. "We checked. Everything's gone, you've been wiped out."

Lacking any other way to communicate, Manic rolled his eyes. It wasn't surprising. Why would Savage let sixty grand or so sit around in an account for him? If he could put it in there, he could sure as hell take it back out. Not a huge deal. He'd been broke his whole life.

But Lilly's school . . .

Lilly! What if Savage had gotten to her while he recovered?

"Sal checked up on your kid, by the way," Perdida said, making Manic wonder if she was a Class M and had read his mind. "She's safe, but we have a detail on her. Anything looks fishy, they'll snap her up and get her to safety."

Manic gave a two-syllable sound.

"You're welcome," Perdida said, with less snark this time. "Sal takes care of his people."

He felt her hand squeeze his shoulder, and Manic turned his eyes to hers. Perdida's were nearly violet.

"That's what you are now, Manic. You're either with us, or you're against us. Sal hopes you're *with*. I personally don't have a preference. Just remember he saved your life. He's keeping you and your daughter safe. And you have nowhere else to go. So, you know—choose wisely and all that."

He nodded, and realized he had the strength to do so. He tried to focus on that as a good sign, but it didn't last. The information Perdida had given him swam in his head, confusing everything else.

"I'll go tell the doc you're awake," Perdida said, standing. "He'll take care of the bandages. You might be able to have some soup or something later, if you want, but wait till he says so. Do you want me to contact Lillian?"

He shook his head, slowly.

"Okay. Be seeing you."

"Ugh!"

She paused. Manic pantomimed a pencil. Perdida brought him a pen and a pad of sticky notes. Carefully, Manic printed out the name Liam Gray.

"Friend of yours?" Perdida said.

Manic tapped the pad hard. Perdida searched his eyes.

"You want me to find him?"

Manic nodded and wrote the word "kid." Perdida shrugged and tore the note from the top of the pad.

"I'll see what I can do. Get some rest."

Perdida let herself out of the room, and this time, Manic didn't watch her backside as she went. Instead he counted slowly in his head, giving himself a solid five minutes before trying to swing his legs over the edge of the mattress. He noticed then he was completely nude under the bedsheet.

Whatever. It didn't matter. He managed to maneuver his feet to the floor without toppling over. Carefully, knowing he might be dizzy when he stood up—if he *could* stand up—Manic removed the IV from the port on his hand. He took deep breaths for a moment, then hiked uneasily to his feet. When he did not fall over, he shuffled an inch at a time to the door and opened it, noticing only then that his ankle was in a cast.

The hallway was empty, and Manic heard nothing, no other signs of life. Using the wall to brace himself, he went to the nearest door on this side and tried the knob. It twisted easily, and Manic let himself in.

The room had once been an executive office, he thought. Though empty of furniture, the boxes he'd first received from Weber were stacked along the left wall, as well as bags and suitcases he did not recognize. When he opened one of them, he found his clothes and other items from the apartment. Manic was surprised to see that his possessions took up no more than two suitcases and a duffel bag. Laying atop the duffel, he found the clothes he'd been wearing the night he was shot.

How long ago was that? A week? A month? Manic glanced around, but saw no calendars or clocks. He'd have to ask first chance he got.

As the memory of that night replayed in his head, Manic knelt down beside the folded clothes. He put a hand in one hip pocket, and found the folded paper the Asian woman in Savage's office had stuck in there. *She* had been real, anyway, even if the little prick deev wasn't.

Manic swore silently. The scrap had become soft and fragile in the wash. Sal's people hadn't found it when they emptied his weapons and gear from his pockets. He pulled the paper apart as gently as he could and squinted down at the washed-out pen marks.

The message contained four numbers, he could tell that much.

Beyond that, the handwriting looked like Chinese script. Manic thought maybe Sal's people could decipher it, because *he* sure as hell couldn't. But he desperately wanted to know what the message said.

Climbing to his feet, Manic noticed now the room had its own private bathroom. He stood there, barefoot and naked, with only several inches of white bandages swathing his head, the carpet thin and harsh under his toes.

He told himself not to do it. He argued with himself to follow orders for once, go back to the bed, and lie the hell down.

Instead he inched toward the bathroom. The trip took forever, and by the time he reached the doorframe, his heart thrummed at a steady hundred miles per hour.

Manic felt along the inside wall for a switch, and turned on a strip of decorative bulbs over the mirror and sink. Slowly, he forced himself to the sink and gripped its edge, getting his first look at the bandages.

His head appeared to be the size of a basketball. Most of that, he hoped, was the bandages and gauze.

Don't do this, Manic thought. He tried to intimidate the image in the mirror. *Turn around and go back to bed, jackhole.*

Yet his hands moved as if on their own. He found the place where the bandages terminated and began to unwrap himself.

The procedure took several minutes. Clean wraps soon turned to dried purple wraps and gauze, which Manic dumped into the sink as he went. When the job was finished, he stopped breathing.

His chin was as big as two fists held together. Some of it he knew was post-surgical swelling, but all the ice in the Arctic wouldn't change the depth and width of his new jaw. The skin color wasn't his either. Some of it was bruising, but it was plain that whatever deev magic the docs had performed, it hadn't included using swatches of his own skin. The skin on his massive jaw was darker than his own, and possibly deeply spotted—whether that was just bruises or not, he couldn't tell.

Manic pried his mouth open, and pain shot through the joints in his face. He ignored it, and pulled his lips apart.

He looked like an animal. Perdida had not been exaggerating when she said some six had donated teeth. Manic's new teeth were as tall as quarters, triangular and jagged.

You look like a fuckin' land shark, pal.

Manic's right hand curled into a fist as he stared into the mirror. Then his left curled tightly as well. Were there enough mirrors in the world to let him release the rage building inside? The familiar punching muscles in his arm, shoulder, and back tensed in preparation for release.

He kept on staring at his new, horrific visage. Perdida was right: the world would see him as a six now. Even if the corrupt, deviant governor of California *wasn't* hunting him down, he couldn't be seen in public anymore. Someone would take a shot at him just for how he looked.

Because . . .

That's what people do to sixes, he thought. *And you might just be a real one anyway, remember?*

If he tried to buy a pack of gum at Circle-K, he'd find himself surrounded by a cadre of sixcops thanks to some helpful citizen's phone call. They'd take him, and test him, and after only God knew how long, they might determine he was not a threat and let him go.

Except he knew that letting people go wasn't a high priority on the NPD list of shit to do.

He knew exactly what life held in store for a Level Six deviant.

"Sh . . . sh . . . shix," Manic said through his sharp teeth, his entire head starting to ache. "You . . . are . . . a . . . shix."

Corby Savage would pay. No, not for this disfigurement and condemnation to a life of prejudice. He could handle all that. But the kids within the concrete labyrinth—he had to go back, find them. Savage would pay for endenturing the Chinese woman, who Manic was sure now must be being held against her will.

He'd pay for what happened to Izanagi. For what Manic had *done* to Izanagi.

Manic kept his own gaze in the mirror. Whenever his full strength returned, he'd load up and empty out the underground compound, then scorch the whole thing from the inside out. He'd find Savage's slave and get her out of there. And then, one way or another, he'd take out little Corby Savage himself.

On the edge of the sink, Manic's left hand relaxed. Then his right. Manic reached out and touched his reflected image for a long time.

Then he turned, shut off the light, and walked gingerly back to his room and climbed into bed. The sooner he healed up, the sooner he could get back on the street.

He lay relatively motionless for a very long time. How long, exactly, he couldn't say for sure. Eventually his door opened and a slim man came over to the bed.

"I'm Dr. Lange," he said. "You weren't supposed to take your bandages off."

Manic turned his head and met the physician's eyes. The doc took a quarter-step backward in response.

Slowly and carefully, Manic spoke.

"Get me Sal."

"Well, all right, but first I need to—"

"Now."

The doctor weighed his options only briefly before giving Manic a curt nod and letting himself out of the room. Manic lay back, controlling his breathing, letting his tongue wash back and forth over his teeth. Holy hell, what a balls-up this was.

He hadn't thought to bring his watch in with him, so he wasn't sure how long it took for his next guest to arrive. Only it wasn't Sal; it was Perdida Velasquez.

She came to the foot of the bed, arms crossed. Manic noticed she was wearing different clothes than an hour ago, which then led to the startling realization that it probably hadn't been an hour at all. He must've slipped unconscious again, and for a good long time, too.

"I need to see the sun," he slurred.

Something flashed in her eyes. "Frankly, it's overrated. What can I do for you?"

"Where's Sal?"

"Busy. Last chance. What can I do for you."

Manic sighed. "Lilly."

"Safe and sound. Although it sounds like she's having some financial troubles."

"I'm not gonna ask how you know that."

"That's probably for the best. We could take care of that if you want."

"I would appreciate it."

"Done. But there is the matter of her security."

Manic narrowed his eyes. Perdida raised an eyebrow.

"As I said, she's safe right now. But we can't keep her covered twenty-four seven. Security's not cheap."

He let a dismal laugh cough from between his wide lips. "I am dead ass broke, remember?"

"Yes. But you have talent. Sal is always in need of talent. He is prepared to give you a favor. Standard rates apply, of course."

Manic laughed, painfully. Standard rates? He'd be indebted to Sal for the rest of his life.

"Guess I don't got a choice."

Perdida scowled and let her arms fall to her sides. "*Don't* say that. Don't ever say that, it's a bullshit cop-out. You can say no, that's your choice."

"Sal knows I can't say no."

"You could grab Lilly and flee the state. The country. There's an option. You could kill yourself—Savage won't have any reason to come after you or your family then, there's another option. You could rob a bank, hijack a plane, get a job at McDonald's. Those are all choices. Whether you like the consequences of those choices is up to you."

Manic gazed up at her. Goddamn, the fire in those eyes . . .

"Fair enough," he muttered. "Favor accepted."

Perdida's shoulders relaxed. "Good. When you've healed up, we'll talk about your new job description. There are a lot of people out there who need help, so, you know . . . hurry it up, *officer.*"

"What about the boy?"

Perdida pulled a printed color photo from her pocket. "This him?"

"Yeah. Liam. You found him?"

"Safe and sound with his parents. Sounds like someone saved his life from some godawful place." She slipped the photo back into her pocket. "For an asshole, you somehow manage to get a few things right."

"Must be my deviant power."

Perdida's lips twitched. She stepped toward the door.

"I got played," Manic said.

Perdida paused, looking back at him. She seemed to weigh a number of responses before leaning her shoulder casually against the wall.

"Yeah. You did. Pretty good, too. But you also did more in a day than most people do in a lifetime."

"So I'm the hero now?"

"Oh, I didn't say that." She smirked at him—but somewhat kindly. "But as starts go, yours wasn't bad."

Manic said nothing. Perdida didn't move, as if intuiting that he had more to say.

He did. "I'm gonna need a couple things."

"I'm listening."

"I need to talk to Lilly."

"That's not a good—"

"We both know it'll be the last time for a long time. Maybe

forever. Before I disappear, I gotta talk to my kid. You know I'll find a way regardless."

Perdida nodded once. "I'll have a secure line brought in. What else?"

Manic thought he might be grinning when he spoke next, but the pain meds made it hard to tell for sure. "The, uh . . . the black Boss I was driving awhile back, is that still available?"

"It is. Nice choice."

"Thanks. I was wonderin' . . . is there any way you could, like, trick it out a little? Make it kind of like a . . . like a Manic-mobile?"

Perdida grinned. "We got a guy. I'll look into it. Anything else?"

"Dinner and a movie?"

"Don't push it. I'll have the phone sent right up."

Perdida left. Manic forced himself to keep his eyes open, not wanting to fall back to sleep again. The thought of talking to Lilly for what might be the last time made his eyes hurt.

A woman with purple, scaled skin came in and set a flip phone on his lap without a word or a look. Manic didn't mind. Word was probably out about him throughout Sal's organization, and the sixes around here weren't apt to throw him a welcoming potluck.

He opened the phone and dialed Lilly's number, the only one he had memorized. She answered.

"Hi, this is Lilly?"

"Lil. It's your dad."

"Dad? Where are you calling from, I don't recognize the number."

"Uh . . . don't worry about it."

"Whoa, you sound terrible."

"Yeah, I . . . I'm comin' down with something maybe. Listen. I gotta head out for awhile. For work. So I might be outta touch for some time."

Her bright voice hurt his eyes again. "Oh. Okay. Where are you going?"

"Not far. But it's . . . I won't be able to call. I'm not sure when

I'll see you next."

"Dad? Are you okay? You're kind of freaking me out."

He shut his eyes. "I'm fine. And you'll be fine too, okay? I got school covered. And a car, I want you to get that car we talked about."

"Oh, don't worry about it. I got a job."

"A job?"

"Well, paid internship. At Makura Biolabs, the guys who were funding my grant."

"I thought they went belly-up."

"Yeah, well, I guess not. Whatever the lawsuit was about got settled, I guess. So, I'll be interning there starting next month."

"That's great, kid. I'm proud of you."

"Thanks. So, when can I see you again? Are we talking days, weeks?"

"Longer than that, I think, Lil."

"Um . . ."

"Listen. Just listen for a sec. Take the money. If you don't need it, put it in the bank. Or invest it some stocks and shit, whatever. Just take it. Get a reliable car, something that won't leave you stranded on the highway."

"Okay, but—"

"And Lil?"

"Yeah?"

The pain in Manic's eyes reached an intolerable level. Something warm seeped from them.

"I love you so goddamn much, kid. So goddamn much. And I need you to know that I will never, ever let anything happen to you, you hear me? Not now, not ever. I got your back."

Lilly's voice was soft. ". . . I know."

"Okay. Good. I gotta go. I love you, Lil."

"Dad—"

"See ya."

He hung up and threw the phone across the room. It smashed against the far wall.

"All right," he whispered through his aching mouth. "All right, goddammit."

He'd done everything he'd set out to do. Lilly would be safe under the watchful eye of Sal's people, whoever they were. She'd have enough money to get her life started. He'd told her he loved her. And, Manic reasoned, she knew it was true. Was there anything more important than that?

Maybe if things worked out well, he'd be able to see her again sooner than he feared. Maybe it would only be a year. Maybe two. That wasn't so long. Soldiers went on deployment for longer stints. He'd see her, though. Oh hell yes he would. One way or another.

Just not today.

He shoved his hands under the pillows and shrugged his shoulders until comfortable.

"All right," he said aloud once more. "Let's go to work."

Vigilance.

Diligence.

Humanity.

Tom Leveen is an award-winning author and Bram Stoker Award finalist who has also written for the comic book series *Spawn*. He brings more than twenty years of live theatre experience to his classes, keynotes, and panels at conventions and conferences around the country.

For more information, visit:

linktr.ee/tomleveen

Human trafficking is a very real and very serious problem in our nation and around the world. It is particularly focused in the author's home state of Arizona.

Please take just a few minutes to visit this site and learn more, and help in any way you can:

www.erasechildtrafficking.org

CPSIA information can be obtained
at www.ICGtesting.com
Printed in the USA
LVHW091634270420
654539LV00009B/112/J